BLOOD
NEVER LIES

Books by Penelope Haines

The Lost One
Helen Had a Sister
(previously published as Princess of Sparta)
Blood Never Lies

The Claire Hardcastle Series:
Death on D'Urville
Straight and Level
Stall Turns

BLOOD
NEVER LIES

Forged by History, Bound by Time

PENELOPE HAINES

For information contact

www.penelopehaines.com

Published by Ithaca Publications, Wellington, New Zealand

Blood Never Lies / Penelope Haines. -- 1st ed.

ISBN 978-0-473-55139-1

For Victoria,

my granddaughter,

with a world of

love

and loss

and longing.

PROLOGUE

Ninth Century, Ireland

ALL IN ALL, SISTER ROWENA thought, it was just as well she had permission to leave the abbey and gather fresh herbs early that morning.

The previous evening, her nemesis, Sister Brigid, had taken issue with her diagnosis of a patient. As Sister Rowena knew she was correct, it had been a galling experience to be reprimanded by a woman who was less able and knowledgeable than her. Even worse, she couldn't defend herself against the injustice because Sister Brigid was her superior.

Every stride that took her further afield, every scent carried on the clear morning air, served to settle Sister Rowena's resentment and improve her state of mind. By the time she'd filled her basket with wild mint and watercress, she was several miles from the abbey, and in a much better mood.

When she stopped to cut new spring growth from the willow trees, she was humming under her breath. The morning filled her with joy. Why did God seem so much closer out here than in the stuffy confines of the abbey? This is my chapel, she thought, as she looked across the meadow to where it dropped to the water's edge.

Out across the sea, the light in the sky still held the pearl colours of early morning. A ship was sailing some distance from shore. She watched it idly for a few minutes before her eyes narrowed. Nothing about it was familiar: the large, square sail; the long, low line of the hull; and the carved serpent head of the prow—this was no local boat.

She was almost too frightened to give credence to her suspicions.

Vikings? Surely not. Not here, not heading for the abbey!

She dropped her basket and began to run. She was still a mile or more away from the abbey when the cloister bell, which had been tolling, setting the rhythm for her strides, stopped ringing.

The sudden silence unnerved her. She couldn't believe it was a good sign, and her pace slowed and then stopped as she stood to listen.

It took a few minutes, as her breathing eased and her heartbeat quietened, before she heard the dull roar which had been subsumed beneath the noise of the bell. The sound surged and receded in waves, terrifying in its implications of what must be happening at the abbey. She needed to see for herself, although the nightmare visions of what she might find petrified her.

She started to walk.

Close to the abbey, open meadows gave way to a wood of oak and ash, interwoven with rowan and holly. Sister Rowena's path wound through the trees, so the abbey was hidden from her sight. From there, the way passed small meadows and garths before dropping in a straight line down the little hill towards the village.

She had already caught the scent of smoke. Now she saw the abbey and church were burning. Dark figures ran between the small turf-roofed bothies, setting fire to them as well.

Too terrified to move closer, she tried to make out the details of what she was seeing. Were those bodies lying on the ground? She was too far away to tell, although she feared so. Had the raiders killed everyone?

She was on the verge of panic, ready to bolt, when a man stepped from the woods behind her. His eyes widened on seeing her, and he lunged and grabbed her by the wrist before she could flee.

She fought like a wildcat but in vain. She was tall and robust, but that was nothing to this man, whose own height and build so much exceeded hers.

There was little apparent effort spent in throwing Sister Rowena over his shoulder and carrying her down the track. She struggled and cursed, but he held her firmly as they passed the burning buildings and went onto the beach.

From her inverted position, it was difficult to make out all the details of the destruction. The heat from the blazing buildings pressed painfully on her face and arms. Her abdomen was crushed against her assailant's shoulder, effectively winding her. She made out the crumpled body of the Mother Abbess by the crucifix that a warrior was busy ripping from around her neck. Other dark heaps must be her sisters, patients and priests.

She closed her eyes in horror. Only to open them again as the man rolled her off his shoulders and tipped her onto the pebbly beach beside the longship, where a pile of loot from the abbey lay tumbled. She recognised the jewelled chalice, so familiar from its place on the chapel altar. She identified other goods as well—the carved altarpiece, a tangle of crucifixes, candlesticks and lengths of rich brocade which had hung in the church, separating the nave from the chancel.

Her captor bound her wrists and ankles while she swore at him helplessly. When he finished, she wriggled herself into a sitting position as he stood and watched. When she'd managed it, he gave a slow grin of apparent approval and reached out to grab her braid. She flinched, uselessly, as her bonds held her tight.

He studied the rich chestnut of her hair, nodded, and said something to her.

She didn't understand and shook her head.

He dropped her braid. "Orm," he repeated, pointing to his chest. "Orm."

Was that his name? Rowena didn't know. She closed her eyes and turned her head away.

CHAPTER ONE

Erin

Present Day, New Zealand

FIRE. SHE WAS SO CLOSE TO IT. *The flames towered over her head, blocking the clear sky above as they twisted and writhed, borne on the wild currents of air from the inferno. The wind-tossed sparks showered down, clinging as they landed on her cloak and skin.*

Later, she would find entire lengths of hair missing from the left of her head, scorched away, frizzled to nothing in the fiery heat. Her skin blistered, her eyes dried waterless, and the air in her lungs burned. She fought to reach the pyre, although the post they tied her to held firm against her struggles.

⁙

Erin tossed restlessly on the bed, her head flinging from side to side as she tried to avoid the bite of ashes falling against her skin.

A woman screamed, and Erin cried out in sympathy.

The sound woke her, and she opened her eyes. The abrupt transition to silence was disorientating. The fiery roar lingered in her hearing; she could feel her flesh blistering beneath the searing bonds on her wrists, and her body still heaved and shook in terror.

The nightmare had been so real. The fire, heat, pain and grief resonated through her mind and flesh. Her heart pounded, and she caught her breath in short, frantic pants. She rubbed her wrists, surprised to find no peeling blisters. It took many moments before she recognised her surroundings and relaxed.

Just a dream, she reassured herself as she snuggled back into her pillow. As she shifted, she realised with distaste that her light cotton PJs were damp with sweat.

Jesus! From what part of her subconscious had all that sprung?

Cautiously, she ran a hand over her abdomen. There was nothing to feel yet, but she was sure, and the supermarket test had been positive.

She hadn't told Luke. That could wait until she came back from the doctor today, she promised herself. If he confirmed it, she'd share the news.

Four months ago, she'd been confident and told Luke she was pregnant. Their mutual disappointment to find she'd been wrong had been wrenching. This time she would wait until she was sure.

Dawn was breaking; she could see the lighter colour rimming the top of the curtain rail, a sure sign it was morning. She glanced at the clock: 6.45 am.

She reached for the familiar shape of Luke's arm beneath the sheets and ran her hand down until her fingers entwined with his.

He gave a sleepy grunt as she pillowed her head on his shoulder. "What're you doing?" he asked.

She settled her back into the familiar angles of his body and relaxed against him. "A terrible dream. It woke me."

He gave an inelegant snort. "I warned you you'd regret eating so much of that Indian takeaway last night."

She jabbed an elbow into his ribcage to show what she thought of that remark.

"Ow! What was that for?"

"You shouldn't be rude to your wife."

That elicited an evil chuckle. "But I can be rude *with* my wife?" he asked as he freed himself from her grasp and ran his hand over her body.

"We haven't got time," she protested. "It's a workday!"

He showed her what he thought of *that* excuse.

"I told you you'd make us late," Erin complained half an hour later as she watched her husband get dressed.

"Yes, but it was worth it," he grinned. "Where did I leave the bloody car keys?"

"On the windowsill. Please don't be late this evening, will you? Remember, we've got the barbecue tonight."

"Yeah, yeah." Luke rolled his eyes. "I know. You told me. Don't nag. And Fergal's coming with his new girlfriend. That's why you're antsy."

"I'm not jumpy. But we haven't met her, and Fergal says she's young. I just hope she fits in."

Luke gave her a knowing look. "It'll be fine. Stop fretting over Fergal. He's damn near forty and old enough to make his own choices. If he likes this girl, then that's OK by us, isn't it?"

"I suppose." Erin was still dubious, but Luke was Fergal's best friend and unlikely to be critical of anything he did.

"Anyway, at least it shows he's over Maddie," said Luke. "Frankly, I was glad to see the back of her, sour-faced, ungenerous cow that she was. I knew she wasn't right for him. It's good to see him dating again." He gave Erin a quick kiss. "You'll be late for work yourself if you don't get moving. I'll see you this evening. Have a good day."

Once he'd left, the house was quiet. It was as if the air itself thickened and stopped moving. Light sparkled on motes of dust slowly falling beside the open window. Even the scent of daphne from the bush outside became more intense in the stillness.

Erin liked the sense of silence surrounding her—although it wasn't complete. Birds were trilling in the garden, and a low rumble of traffic the street.

She pottered about, tidying up the kitchen and getting ready for work.

Beneath her surface calm, her excitement was building. Let today be the day! It would be hard to keep her mind on the job in the hours before her appointment.

Fortunately, the morning was busy. Erin's role as business manager at the local bank was demanding and dealing with clients suited her outgoing personality. She enjoyed the variety of the work, whether she was counselling clients about investments, helping them get mortgages, or simply working as a case manager to ensure customers felt good about their bank. It was a mixture of face-to-face contact with people and backroom paperwork—a balanced role that pleased Erin.

It was morning teatime before she remembered the dream. The details had faded but not her disturbing response. She frowned. It was the second time that week she'd dreamed of fire. She must have seen something on the news that triggered those powerful images. She gave a small shiver as she stirred her coffee. Maybe it *had* been the Indian food working on her subconscious mind.

The visit to the surgery wiped other concerns or considerations from her mind. Yes, she was pregnant, although only by about three weeks. The GP offered his congratulations and gave her a list of midwives.

His prosaic attitude amused her. It was such a contrast to her excitement. She wanted to share her joy with everyone—well, mostly, she wanted to tell Luke, but she also wanted the moment to be right. She didn't want to break the news over the phone. She'd have to wait until tonight.

Unfortunately, the barbecue was also tonight. Erin hoped Luke would be home early so she could tell him before their friends arrived. It would, she thought, *kill* her to spend the whole evening in silence waiting for everyone to leave before she could. It was far too early to share their secret with anyone else.

She phoned him anyway. Ostensibly to remind him again to be home early, but primarily because she wanted to hear his voice.

"I'm working on it," he said. "I'll get away as soon as I can, I promise, but we've got a situation developing which could make me late. The world markets fell last night and show no sign of stabilising yet, so we've got all the fallout here to deal with."

Erin sighed. She was savvy enough about investments and how the financial system worked. Still, she'd never been able to muster the passionate fascination with the stock market's behaviour that gripped Luke and his colleagues. Stockbrokers were a very odd breed.

"*Try* to get home on time," she pleaded. She wondered whether to give Luke a hint—suggest she had something to tell him—as a lure. Luke was so damn smart, though, he'd guess the news immediately. She preferred to see his face when she told him.

Her mood was temporarily alleviated when she reached home and emptied the letter box, discovering two envelopes bearing the logo of the national geographic genographic project.

"Woohoo," she said to herself. She and Luke had been waiting for the results since they sent their swabs off for analysis two months earlier.

This curiosity about their genetic origins began as a natural extension of their plans for parenthood. The more they fantasised about their future offspring, the greater the interest they'd shared in what qualities a child of theirs might inherit. They'd exchanged DNA testing kits with each other as a shared Christmas present. That information now resided in two sealed envelopes lying side by side on the kitchen bench.

She peeled the potatoes with vicious efficiency, digging out the eyes with spiteful thoroughness before chopping onions, dicing bacon and whipping mayonnaise. By the time she tipped the completed potato salad into a large serving bowl, she'd worked off a good deal of her resentment. It was unlike her to be so moody and childish. Perhaps this was the first sign of the emotional and hormonal upheavals of expectant motherhood.

This additional confirmation of her pregnancy cheered her up. She watched the minutes tick by with resigned equanimity.

CHAPTER
TWO

IT WAS INEVITABLE, GIVEN LUKE'S ABSENCE, that their guests arrived right on time. Even Fergal, known for his usual tardiness, was only ten minutes late.

"Luke not home yet?" Doug asked as Erin opened the door to let him and his partner Petra in. "I didn't see his car outside."

Erin shook her head. "Hopefully he won't be too late. Something big is happening in the world of international finance, and they need Luke to sort it out. Come on in."

Doug chuckled. "Can't tear himself away is more likely. Thank God for my quiet world. I don't think I'd cope with the highs and lows of Luke's line of work."

Erin smiled. "I'm certain it wouldn't suit me. It's much too demanding. Mind you, I imagine Fergal's is just as stressful, only in a different way."

"No, I wouldn't make a good helicopter pilot either," Doug agreed. "Let alone when you consider the conditions in which those guys do some of their rescue work. High winds, big seas, low cloud. You can keep it."

Erin liked her best friend's husband. When Petra had first introduced them, Erin was curious about the kind of man who had captured the interest of pretty, blonde Petra. She was so lively and quixotic, it seemed impossible she would ever settle down with one man. Yet, in Doug, she had found her soulmate.

Of average height, thin and already balding, Doug had a quiet, dry sense of humour that sat lightly over the deeply principled character at his core. It hadn't taken Erin long to appreciate how his steadiness complemented Petra's vivaciousness. Together they made a great team.

"I've brought marinated chicken and a salad," said Petra. "I'll put it in the kitchen."

Doug busied himself opening a beer. "Do you want one, Petra? No? What about you, Erin?"

"No, thanks," said Erin as the front doorbell rang. "That'll be Fergal. I'll let them in. Make yourselves at home."

"I can't wait to meet her," said Petra. "I'm dying with curiosity. We'll all have to be on our best behaviour so as not to scare her off."

"I'm always on my best behaviour," protested Doug.

Erin raised her eyebrows at him as she went to the door, opening it just as Fergal lifted his hand to ring the bell again.

"There you are," he said. "I thought you might all be outside and wouldn't hear me ring."

"Hi, Fergal." He leaned forward and gave her a quick kiss on the cheek.

"Good evening," he said, stepping back to introduce the woman standing slightly behind him. "Erin, this is Brianna."

"Hi, Brianna." Erin smiled, although she could feel her eyes widening in shock. It took all her manners not to stare. "Please come in," she said, standing aside to let them pass.

Brianna was tiny and finely built. A little china doll, with long, shiny black hair, enormous blue eyes and the fairest skin Erin had ever seen. She barely came up to Erin's shoulders. And so young. Very young. Even though Fergal had prepared her, Erin was startled.

Snow White. For an awful moment, Erin thought she'd said the words aloud. Even if she hadn't, there was a wry look on the girl's face that suggested she was perfectly aware of Erin's reaction. "Luke's running late. He's not here yet," Erin babbled to cover her embarrassment. "Something to do with international financial markets."

"We can wait for him. Are the others down the back?"

Fergal led Brianna down the hall. Erin paused at the mirror. As she fiddled with straightening her collar, trying to regain her composure, she watched the couple in the reflection behind her. Fergal took up almost the whole door frame. It was fortunate, mused Erin, that although his personality was larger than life, he was such an amiable and good-tempered man. His size and physique meant he automatically commanded any situation.

Erin had always rather enjoyed feeling small and petite beside him. It wasn't a common experience for her, with her tall athletic frame, and she was considerably larger than Brianna. How Brianna coped with the size difference between herself and Fergal was anyone's guess. Then there was the age difference. Erin wondered just how old the girl was. Putting the kindest construction on it, Fergal was cradle-snatching.

When Erin joined the others in the kitchen, Fergal had already introduced Brianna, and Doug was pouring drinks.

"Shall we go outside?" asked Erin. "It's a lovely evening, for all its early spring. Seems a pity to be inside. If Luke's going to be late, we might as well start without him."

"I'll fire up the barbecue," offered Fergal. "It'll take a while to heat."

"I'll start bringing the food out," said Erin.

The small responsibilities of being a hostess occupied her for a while. By the time Erin could sit down beside Petra and help herself to chips and dip, they had broken the ice between the members of the group.

Doug was chatting to Brianna. Bless him. It was typical of him that he would try to make her feel welcome.

Petra, who had a job in the music industry, was busy telling Fergal about the latest band touring New Zealand. She arranged accommodation and organised any other requirements and requests the group made. "Honestly, what a bunch of tossers," she exclaimed. "I don't mind getting them crates of champagne, or a vat of vodka, if that's what they want, but this lot are never satisfied. They're constantly complaining about the food, the temperature, the venues. And they've all got different dietary requirements. Gluten free, lactose intolerant, vegan, vegetarian, keto diet—you name it."

"Are they any good?" asked Fergal.

"Maybe. I don't think they're very talented, but the young kids like them and think they're OK. I'm over self-absorbed, demanding people. I talked to the drummer, and he assured me they were all conscientious about their health—I might even believe it if it wasn't for the alcohol they pour down their throats morning, noon and night."

"It comes with the territory," said Doug. "At least this lot haven't trashed a hotel room yet or asked you to organise strippers for them."

"The barbecue's just about hot enough," interrupted Fergal. "Do you want me to cook the meat?"

"I guess so," said Erin. She heard a door in the house opening.

"Finally! That sounds like Luke now," she said.

"Hi guys. Sorry, I'm late."

Erin watched her husband step through the door. He grinned at his friends and Erin watched the stress drop off him.

"Someone pour me a drink," he begged. "A large red wine would be great. It's been a very long day." He pulled a chair up to the table.

"Can I introduce you to Brianna?" Fergal said. "Brianna, this is Luke."

"Hi, good to meet you."

Erin went to pour Luke his drink. When she returned, he was chatting to Brianna.

Erin had to admit that Brianna was well mannered, confident and composed.

Luke seemed taken with her. "How did you meet Fergal?" he was asking.

"I was on placement in the psych ward when an attempted suicide was brought in by the rescue helicopter. Fergal was the pilot, and we got talking."

"You work at the hospital?" Petra asked.

Brianna shook her head. "No, I'm studying psychology. But I do some volunteer work as a counsellor. It gives me some real-life experience to supplement the theory."

"Dealing with attempted suicide sounds gruelling," remarked Erin.

"It can be tough," agreed Brianna, "particularly when the patient is very young. It seems so sad they've reached that point."

"Meat's ready," Fergal announced, "What do you want me to put it on?" he asked Erin.

"Damn, I forgot to bring the platter out," she said.

"I'll get it," said Luke. "I want to get changed anyway. Be back in a second."

When he returned, besides the platter, he was carrying the National Geographic envelopes. "Hey, did these just arrive?"

Erin nodded. "I haven't opened mine yet."

"Are they the DNA test results you told us about?" Fergal asked, seeing the symbol on the envelope.

"Yeah. Come on, Erin, let's open them now," urged Luke.

"There might be something in there that's confidential," Erin protested.

"Nothing we can't share with our friends," Luke said. He looked around for support. "Right, guys?"

The others nodded, so Erin shrugged. "OK, I guess so. Pass me a knife for the envelope."

Luke had already ripped his open and was spreading out the paper.

"So, what does it say?" asked Petra.

Luke shook his head. "It's not what I was expecting, that's for sure." He looked at Erin. "You go first."

"Mine's boring," Erin warned. "OK. Here goes: 1.3% of my DNA is Neanderthal, while the average is 2.1%. I guess that makes me a little less Neanderthal than the rest of you."

"What else?" asked Luke.

"The non-Neanderthal stuff is 100% Irish. That's it. No other racial markers. No exciting, exotic pedigree in my bloodline. I come from generations of potato-munching Irish peasants."

"That sounds fairly exotic to me," Brianna remarked in her

musical voice. "All those ancient kings of Tara, Deirdre of the Sorrows, Druids and minstrels. Not to mention all the songs. And the Irish were famous for drinking and fighting. It's a place I've always wanted to visit."

"Fair enough," said Erin. "What does yours say, Luke?"

Luke was staring at the report. "Well, that's the thing," he said in surprise. "I thought my heritage would be like yours, but it's much more muddled. It tells me I'm 58% Scandinavian, 27% British, and 14% Southern European."

"Wow," said Erin. "That's a definite jumble and much more interesting than mine."

"It doesn't sound right, though," said Luke. "I understood my parents were English to the core. Are you sure the results aren't muddled up? Could you have received my ancestry by mistake?"

"Not unless you're female," Erin laughed. "Go on. You're just jealous of my Irishness because you like Irish pubs and having a singalong."

"Probably," said Luke, looking sheepish. "I never expected to be quite such a mongrel."

"There'll be a story there, that's for sure," said Fergal.

CHAPTER THREE

"LET'S EAT," SAID ERIN.

They passed plates around and helped themselves to the array of salads and barbecued meats.

"Wine, Erin?" asked Doug, holding the bottle over her glass.

"Oh, no. No thank you," she said, slightly flustered. She was going to have to get used to the new regime that having a baby would impose.

Petra's head snapped around.

"What's that about?" asked Fergal in surprise.

"I'm not that much of a lush," Erin tried protesting. "I can choose to go without a drink occasionally."

There was a moment's silence as her friends stared at her.

Typically, it was Petra who reacted first. "Oh, my God. You're pregnant, aren't you?"

Erin could feel her cheeks turning scarlet and looked up to see Luke staring at her.

"Are you?" he asked after a long pause. "Are you pregnant?"

She bit her lip and looked at him. "I'm sorry, I didn't mean to break it to you in public like this. I wanted to tell you when you came home from work this afternoon, but then you were late. Yes, I'm pregnant. The doctor confirmed it today."

With a wild war-whoop, Luke gathered her up into his arms and hugged her. "That's wonderful news." He gave her a long, slow kiss. "You clever girl." He turned to his friends. "Hey, I'm going to be a dad. Can you believe it?"

"Congratulations, mate."

"This calls for a celebratory drink," said Luke. "Apart from Erin, of course. Can I get you a fruit juice or something, darling?"

There was a happy hum of conversation around the table.

"Let's raise a glass to the baby! And Erin and Luke," proposed Fergal.

"Just as well you had your DNA tests done," said Doug. "At least you know what you two are passing on to the baby."

"My contribution seems to be a bit of a mongrel," Luke reminded them. "He'll be a citizen of the world."

"Well, the baby will be a mix of both your DNA—Erin will provide genetic stability and you'll provide variety," said Fergal.

Doug was looking thoughtful. "I read a paper last week that showed DNA isn't as static as we were all taught at school. Certain experiences—trauma, for instance—can alter it. We believe now it also affects how some people are vulnerable to certain diseases. You'll want to provide a stress-free environment for your baby."

"I didn't know DNA could be modified," said Erin. "I thought you were stuck with what you inherited."

"You are," replied Doug. "Trauma doesn't change the *sequence* of your DNA, but it does mean certain factors can cause biochemical alterations that silence key genes. The term for it is epigenesis, and nowadays it's considered probable that the changes that occur from our own experiences get passed to our children."

"Jeez, no wonder the human race is so fucked up," said Petra. "Every person alive today must have had something terrible happen to at least one of their ancestors over the term of human history. Think about it. Wars, rape, persecution, famine—all the fun stuff that goes on generation after generation. No wonder we're a mess if we're wandering around with screwed-up genes."

"I think that might be a bit far-reaching as a concept," laughed

Doug, "but it's a fascinating area of science."

There was a brief silence.

"Do you know if the baby is a boy or a girl yet?" asked Petra.

"No, it's too early ..." Erin started to say.

Brianna, who had been staring into her wine glass, unexpectedly looked up and said, "It's a boy."

Erin looked at her sharply. "What makes you say that?" She tried to keep any note of hostility out of her voice, but really, what an odd thing to say. It felt inappropriate and intrusive.

Brianna blinked. She suddenly looked young and confused, and a wave of colour swept up her face. "I'm sorry. I shouldn't have said that," she muttered.

"Well, no harm done," said Luke. "After all, there's a 50 per cent chance you're right, isn't there?"

Fergal reached up and covered Brianna's hand with his own. He gave it a gentle squeeze. "Sometimes Brianna knows things," he said quietly. "I don't know how she does it, it's uncanny, but I've never known her to be wrong. She's an old soul. I wouldn't discount her prediction."

"What, you mean like a psychic?" asked Petra, who was now staring at Brianna. "Can you tell fortunes?"

Brianna looked even more miserable as she shook her head. "No. Information comes to me sometimes. I can't control it. It just happens."

"So, you're saying Erin's baby is going to be a boy?" asked Doug.

"I'm sorry." Brianna was addressing Erin. "I shouldn't have said anything. It just sort of popped out before I stopped to think."

"That's OK." Erin was prepared to be generous. "Boy or girl, we'll love whatever we get. All I ask for is a healthy child."

"Ditto," said Luke. "I'm just thrilled I'm going to be a father."

The conversation moved on. Had they considered names? Would Erin continue working after the birth? Eventually, the immediate excitement faded slightly, and other topics took its place.

None of their guests stayed late, for which Erin was grateful.

She wanted some much-overdue private time with her husband. When Petra and Doug got up to leave, she was pleased Fergal and Brianna said their goodbyes as well.

CHAPTER FOUR

❝WHAT DID YOU MAKE OF BRIANNA?" Erin asked as they were getting ready for bed.

"She's a pretty little thing. I can understand what Fergal sees in her," he replied.

"Oh, for pity's sake, I didn't ask whether she was pretty," she said. "Get your mind above the waistline. I meant, what did you think about her otherwise?"

"She's fine." Luke wasn't much interested, being far more concerned about his new status as a prospective parent.

"What do you think of Brianna's bizarre statement that the baby's a boy?" asked Erin.

"Maybe it is," Luke said. Nothing was going to dampen his spirits tonight.

"Hmm …" She put no store in Brianna's odd statement and assumed it had been a somewhat awkward attempt at self-importance on the girl's part.

"What do you think Fergal meant when he said she was an 'old soul'?"

"Probably trying to justify the fact that he's cradle-snatching," said Luke. "Let's face it, if her soul's old, it's the only bit of her that is."

"It just sounded a strangely fey thing for someone like Fergal to say. He's usually so sceptical and scientific about things. How old do you think she is?"

"Nineteen? Twenty? She's nearly finished her third year studying at uni. How old would that make her? Perhaps Fergal just wanted to give her some support. She looked pretty embarrassed. Don't make a big deal out of it."

"I wasn't," said Erin, indignant. "I just thought the whole thing was a bit odd."

"Forget about her," Luke urged. "We've got more interesting things to talk about."

Erin smiled. "Like?"

"Like us, and how you're feeling, whether you're going to get morning sickness, and what we'll call the baby and that kind of stuff."

"I'm feeling great. No morning sickness yet. The doctor said I was a very healthy woman. He didn't even comment on my age, which I thought he might have."

"Thirty-five isn't old. Lots of women have babies in their thirties these days," said Luke.

"They do indeed," said Erin as she cuddled up beside him on the bed. "It wasn't quite the way I planned to tell you the news," she chuckled. "And I hadn't planned to let anyone else know— well not until I was at least twelve weeks gone, when we'd be certain."

"Ah, well, it's probably for the best," said Luke. "I'm so excited I'm not sure I could have kept it to myself, anyway. This way, everyone gets to share our joy. Also, if Brianna is to be believed, it *is* all certain."

Erin gave a scornful snort. "She's just a silly girl," she said, dismissing the subject.

She slept well that night. Worn out by excitement, she fell into a deep, dreamless slumber and didn't wake until the alarm went in the morning.

CHAPTER
FIVE

Ciarnat

Ninth Century, Ireland

IT WAS LATE AUTUMN, AND THE rain was so heavy Ciarnat could hardly see her father, a grey shadow, barely a horse's length ahead of her on the ancient trading track. The rain had persisted all day, and the road they followed turned to a sludgy morass where the horses slipped and slid. Her pony had at last given up tossing his head in complaint and now plodded, head down, through the deluge, misery manifest in every step. Mud kicked up by Filan's horse covered the legs of her pony and spattered her skirt.

The heavy woollen cloak kept her warm but dragged on her shoulders with its saturated weight. She shifted experimentally to ease the ache across her back, succeeding in broaching a puddle of rainwater, sending a cold trickle down the gap between the garment and her throat.

Her father could not possibly have heard her soft moan of protest, but some awareness made him slow his horse down until he rode beside her. "Is it good with you, sweeting? We're very close now."

Ciarnat straightened her back and set her shoulders squarely. "Aye, I am well," she assured him. She would have died before admitting weariness and misery to her father.

It wasn't just pride, although she had her share of that. *Filan na Cláirseach*, Filan of the Harp, her father, was bard to the High King. He was an important man who'd taught her to show respect for his position. She would never allow herself to be an encumbrance to him.

She forced her cold lips into a smile. "Although I am looking forward to getting there."

Filan snorted. "I'm looking forward to some hot food."

"And dry clothing," answered Ciarnat.

"And a mug of ale," added Filan.

"And a warm fire."

"And a soft bed with fine linen sheets."

The banter passed the time, and the list of their requirements grew longer and more outrageous.

"You cannot wish for a cloak that makes you invisible," Ciarnat protested at last. "That's impossible. All right, if you have that, then I want a gown of the finest silk, woven by the hands of the faerie queen herself."

"I'd settle for the faerie gold, myself," answered Filan.

The road turned a bend and ahead they saw their destination—a squat, bracken-thatched hall with a huddle of turf bothies around it. A dark plume of smoke rose from its roof, promising warmth and dryness.

"We've arrived."

Ciarnat breathed a weary sigh of relief as her pony was led away to the stables and she turned to follow Filan into the hall. A woman took their sodden cloaks and handed them a bowl of water to wash, and cloths to dry their hands and faces.

"Filan, you old rogue! What sort of weather is this you've brought with you?" Daragh, Chief of the hall, greeted them and pulled Filan into a bear hug. "It is good to see you, man."

"It is good to be here if only to get out of the pissant rain,"

Filan replied, returning the hug with enthusiasm. "I'm getting too old for all this. I'd fain find a nice spot by a great chief's fire where I can write songs and invent stories. Not go roaming the country in foul weather."

"You'd be dead of boredom within a week," laughed Daragh. "Not that the High King would ever waste you like that. You're much too useful, and we know full well he relies on you to be his eyes and ears. Besides, he is much too shrewd and ambitious to waste a talent like yours."

"You talk too much," complained Filan, but he was smiling as he freed himself from his friend's embrace.

"Ciarnat!" Daragh engulfed her in a gentler hug than he'd given her father. "Lovely to see you as always." He scrutinised her face. "Filan, your daughter grows prettier each time I see her."

Filan studied Ciarnat. "She looks like a drowned rat to me," he said.

Ciarnat pulled a face.

"Well, of course, the poor wee maid is soaked," said Daragh. "It's a terrible day for you to be travelling." He gestured a plump middle-aged woman forward. "Maire will help you with your bags and show you to your lodging place where you can wash and get dry. She will find you some food as well. Do you want to go with them, Filan? Or come with me, and I'll pour you a drink first."

"A drink, of course."

"I shall want the news from the court in exchange."

Filan laughed and followed his friend. "I suppose you want to hear the gossip now and not wait until I perform tonight?" he teased.

Daragh snorted. "I want real information, not polished poems that can hide half the meaning of what you say."

Filan feigned offence. "Are you saying I am a bad poet?"

"You know full well that I am not. Your words flow as smoothly as warm honey. But I am mindful your master is an ambitious man with an eye to being the next High King."

Filan nodded. "Aye, he's ambitious and effectively High King already. But he's also a strong man and a good leader, which is what we need. Let's face it, his predecessor's authority had been failing for years. Now he's gone, every petty king and warlord is stirring, trying to stake a claim to the High Kingship. Without strong leadership, there will be chaos."

"Sa, sa." Daragh nodded his head. "Your advice is that a prudent man should ally himself to Áed?"

"Aye," Filan answered. "I would, if I were a man looking to the future. Besides, there is other news. You knew, years past, that Reachlainn Island was invaded and the monastery at Rechru sacked?"

"Aye. I remember hearing tell of it."

"The raiders left, and we heard nought of them for years. But now, it seems, they are back. There have been new reports of these Norsemen moving southwards along the coast and raiding as they go. If they find a church or monastery, they sack it and take what treasures they can. Mostly, though, they take our people as slaves. It's another reason we need to unite behind a strong king and warrior."

Daragh whistled softly. "We live in troubled times."

"We do indeed, my friend."

The men sat by the hearth, mulling over the news. Filan stretched his feet out towards the fire.

"I can see the steam rising," he remarked, looking at his wet boots. "It will take a while to get everything dried out."

"You will stay a few days?" asked Daragh. "It's a bad time of year to be on the road. How do you keep your harp dry in this weather?"

Filan smiled. "Ciarnat looks after it. She'll have wrapped it in layers of waxed cloth and bundled it up like a wee baby. She is a responsible lass. I can trust her to care for it."

Daragh pursed his lips. "I meant what I said, you know; that girl is going to be a rare beauty."

"Don't tell her that, whatever you do," grumbled Filan. "You'll encourage vanity, and our village priest wouldn't approve. Father Niall doesn't approve of her travelling about with me anyway, although he doesn't dare say so directly."

"Well, it is an unusual arrangement after all—a twelve-year-old girl travelling the land with a harper," said Daragh. "Most young maids her age are home learning domestic skills to prepare for their eventual marriage. Have you thought about her future?"

Filan shrugged. "When her mother died five years ago, it seemed best to keep her with me. Now she's as much my apprentice as my daughter. You'll hear her sing with me tonight."

His mind ran back to the night he had made his decision. Filan would never have considered such an option had he not discovered his only child had an ear for music. He had listened to her singing as she scattered seed for the chickens.

"When I realised she could sing and hold a tune, I knew she had the gift," he told Daragh. "I don't believe we can refuse when the gods so freely bestow such skills on us. I am a bard; sharing my art and developing her young talent is my responsibility."

He smiled at the memory. Raw with grief at the loss of his wife, he'd yielded easily to his small daughter's entreaties to go with him, even though his mother Betha had protested at the irregularity. 'She's a girl and needs to learn how to become a woman.' Her voice had risen. 'What place is there for her as she grows older if you drag her all over the country? You serve your vanity, not her needs.'

Filan remembered the rage that had filled him. The thought of being separated from his child had suddenly become intolerable. 'How dare you claim I serve myself in this. She is my daughter; she comes with me!' he'd shouted. Then he'd seen the grief in his mother's face and had softened his voice. 'I swear, I will return her to you when the time comes or if there is a need. In the meantime, she comes with me.'

It seemed Daragh was even more persistent than his Ciarnat's gran. "But what happens when she's full grown? You don't expect her to be a travelling harper, surely?" he asked.

"She can do and be whatever she chooses," Filan replied with a touch of arrogance. "If she chooses to settle one day and marry, she can surely learn what she needs then."

Daragh chuckled. "My wife tells me it takes years to learn those skills. I've watched her with my daughters, and I rejoice I was born a man."

Filan shrugged. "Áed has gifted me land and cattle. I'm a wealthy man, and workers are easy enough to find. It's by her own choice that my mother still lives simply. If she wanted, she could have as much help as she needed. It will be the same for Ciarnat."

"You don't worry about her future?"

"No. Ciarnat has more than enough talent to do whatever she wants."

"I didn't mean her music. I refer to men. She will be a desirable marriage proposition simply because she's your daughter, and that's leaving aside her beauty. You will have your work cut out minding her in the coming years."

"She's much too young for that to be an issue," Filan reassured him. "Besides, she is not an empty-headed sort of lass. She'd not do anything silly."

Daragh recognised defeat when it faced him. "Aye, no doubt you know your own business best," he agreed comfortably. "I look forward to hearing her sing tonight."

CHAPTER SIX

CIARNAT SMILED GOODNIGHT AS SHE TOOK leave of the hall. They had performed a couple of duets and then she accompanied Filan on the drum as he sang some of his jaunty, humorous songs to amuse the crowd. The hour was late, and the drinking was getting heavier. Women pulled children to their feet, ignoring protests as they hustled them off to bed. It was time for Filan to entertain the men with poetry and heroic stories of warriors and battles. The serious end of the evening was about to begin. Filan's poetry and songs weren't pure entertainment but were a way of sharing court news, tribal matters and other national concerns. Ciarnat knew the inevitable questions and discussions that followed would go on for hours.

She'd sung well and knew Filan was pleased with her. The audience had applauded, of course, but her father was more critical. He'd hear a scooped or flat note instantly, but she'd committed neither of those sins, and he smiled when she finished.

Now she was free to go to bed. She stepped through the door and bumped hard into a man returning to the hall.

"Watch where you're going!"

It took the breath from her, and she reeled sideways, knocked off balance by the impact. The man roughly shoved her away as she teetered, on the edge of falling.

"Sorry, I didn't see you," she gasped.

"Move, you silly brat." His reply included a of foul invective as he brushed her aside, which unbalanced her even more as she flinched from him.

Strong hands grabbed her upper arms and held her before she fell. "Steady there!"

Ciarnat looked up as she succeeded in righting herself. Whoever the newcomer was, he held her safely.

She smiled. "Thank you. I thought I was going to hit the ground."

She saw he was young. The hair on his face still had a boy's sparseness.

"You're the bard's daughter."

She nodded. "Aye."

There was a moment's silence as they studied each other.

"Who was that horrible man?" she asked at last.

"Him? His name's Ultán. Did he hurt you?"

"No. But he was foully uncouth."

"He's a bully, and heavy drinking doesn't improve him, but I don't think he recognised you or he'd have been more mannerly to a guest. I apologise on his behalf."

She glanced down to where his hands were still on her arms.

"Oh, sorry," he said, letting her go. She was amused to see he was embarrassed. A flush crept up his cheek. "I didn't mean to...!" He had a friendly face.

She shook her head and smiled again. "It's fine. I have to go to bed."

"How long do you stay in Daragh's hall? Will I see you tomorrow?"

"A few days, I suppose. We got very wet today, and some of our baggage was soaked, so we need to dry out before we move on."

"Then I will see you tomorrow. And my name is Rian." He grinned as he moved aside. "Goodnight."

"Goodnight, Rian," she echoed as she passed him.

Unseen by either, Daragh had watched the whole exchange

from across the hall. He turned away, a faint frown on his forehead. Filan was shrewd, a great poet, musician and the High King's valued *ollamh*, but Daragh, father of three girls himself, thought Filan dangerously unprepared for steering his daughter through the tumultuous years ahead.

His tablemates were staring at him, and their gaze drew him back to his surroundings.

There was a break in proceedings while the young children and the women who cared for them left the hall. Then it was usual for the chief to stand, welcome all comers and hail the High King's chief poet.

Daragh respected tradition and duty. He rose to his feet, mug in hand, to make the toast.

·⫶·

The following morning Ciarnat used every fence, railing and bush available to hang out their wet clothing. There seemed no end to the sodden lengths of material she spread out to dry in the morning sun.

Once dried, she had to brush them free of the mud that had spattered and stained them.

Her work was regularly interrupted as people stopped to talk, wishing her good morning, or complimenting her on her music.

"I see you're hard at it already." Maire paused beside her, watching as the young girl picked a clump of free with her fingernails.

Ciarnat smiled. "I will be glad to have this done. Your roads have a particularly sticky sort of mud. See how it is glued on to this cloak."

"It must be a hard life, moving from place to place all the time," Maire remarked.

"Not really. It is not often we get caught out like we did yesterday. Usually Da rides only when the weather is good."

"But does the constant travelling not become tiring for you? You would never get a chance to settle down, have friends, stay in one place?"

Ciarnat straightened her back and gave a slight shrug. "I have done it for so many years I would not know what it was like not to move around. It means I have friends all over the country. And we usually spend winter at the High King's hall, although last year we were with my gran. She's getting older, and Da worries about her."

Another woman hailed her from across the courtyard. Ciarnat waved to her. "You see? Everyone loves a harper, or in this case, the harper and his brat."

"I suppose they do," Maire chuckled. "When you've finished, brat, come and find me and I'll introduce you to some more friends."

By the time she'd finished brushing the mud from the clothes, the rest of the linen was dry and she was alone as she folded up the garments.

"I've been looking for you everywhere," a voice grumbled, and she looked up to see Rian.

"I've been here all morning," she said.

"Well then, I didn't look here."

It was such a silly statement that Ciarnat laughed, which was just as well.

She wasn't shy talking to strangers or performing in front of them. But although she'd spoken freely last night in the darkness, it was different by daylight.

She glanced sideways at him. He was much older than her. Maybe sixteen or seventeen. An adult, or nearly so. She was both flattered by his attention and embarrassed, uncertain of what to say or do.

"As you see, I am still here, but I was about to leave. Most of our clothes are dry, and I am taking them inside." She sounded awkward, even to herself. And why, when Da had taught her to sing whole phrases without needing a break, was she suddenly so breathless?

"I brought you an apple," offered Rian, opening his hand to display a couple of small, rosy apples.

Ciarnat hesitated.

"Go on, they're good," he urged, as he took a bite of his own.

"Thank you," she mumbled as she bit into one. She expected the fruit to be tart, despite its beautiful red skin, but Rian was right. The crisp, white flesh was intensely fresh and sweet, filling her mouth with its late summer flavour. "Oh, that's lovely," she exclaimed.

"Told you you would like it." There was smug satisfaction in Rian's voice.

"It is early in the year for apples. I thought it might be sour," Ciarnat confessed.

He shook his head. "Not fruit from our trees. We grow the best apples in the land."

Ciarnat grinned. "Really? I suppose this is the best hall in the land as well?"

"Of course. With the bravest warriors, the most beautiful maidens, and the noblest cattle herd as well."

"I am surprised you aren't a bard with your talent for storytelling" Teasing Rian was fun.

"Will you sing again tonight?"

"That's Da's decision. Probably not. It would never do to use all our songs too soon or wear out our welcome." She smiled mischievously. "I do need to get these clothes inside, though, and then practice. Some of us have chores"

"So do I, he said. "I took the time out from my busy day to bring you refreshment. It's a duty to be courteous to a guest."

"What were you busy at?"

"Cattle herding. I had to come back to fetch more liniment for the cows, which is why I had time to find you."

"Oi, Rian, you lazy bastard. What do you think you're doing? Colm needs you up in the pastures, not down here chatting with girls when you're supposed to be working."

Ciarnat looked at the man walking towards them. She thought she recognised him, even before Rian named him.

Rian pulled a face and whispered, "Ultán. He is always trying to be self-important, throwing his weight about where he's not wanted. Colm hates him. He would never have sent that idiot to find me, but I suppose I had better be going anyway. I don't want to waste my time getting into a quarrel with him."

He stood up abruptly, and Ciarnat saw Ultán had stopped.

"I'll see you this evening then," Rian said.

Ciarnat watched him as he ran, jumped the fence and headed for the pastures. She felt pleasantly exhilarated by his infectious energy as she turned to gather up the pile of clothing.

"You'd better watch yourself, lassie. Flirting with boys in secret and putting them off their work. You will earn yourself a bad reputation."

Ciarnat started and turned to see Ultán standing right behind her. She hadn't realised he had approached. "What?" she asked, more startled than offended.

"I said, girls who entice young men to dally when they should be working are likely to lose their reputation as well as their virtue."

Ciarnat was stunned. "How dare you?" she gasped. No one had ever spoken to her so coarsely. Worse, Ultán was looking at her with an unpleasant smirk. His eyes wandered offensively over her body before returning to her face with a knowing leer.

"How dare you?" Ciarnat repeated. "Is this the way men treat guests in Daragh's hall? You were rude to me last night. Today, instead of apologising, you choose to insult me directly. Get out of my way, you worm of a man."

Sudden doubt wiped the smirk from Ultán's face. His eyes narrowed as he re-evaluated the girl in front of him. She wasn't reacting the way he'd expected.

Ciarnat's anger was so intense she lacked words to express her outrage. She glared at him as she bundled the clothing in front of her like a shield. She stepped around him and strode towards her chamber.

Cold fury swept through her, and her hands shook as she dumped the pile of washing on the pallet. Ultán's boorish rudeness was terrible enough, but the insinuation she was some silly, loose girl astounded her and offended against her honour. Nothing, nothing she had said or done with Rian could have earned such an accusation, she assured herself.

Her first impulse was to complain to her da. He'd be furious at the insult, and there would be severe repercussions for Ultán.

But by the time she'd folded the clothes and packed them away, she'd reconsidered. Filan would certainly avenge the insult to her, but in doing so, it might also cause trouble for Rian.

Rian had casually dismissed Ultán as a known bully, so perchance hers was an overreaction. Ultán had not realised who she was, and his unpleasantness was so innate he probably treated everyone with the same contempt.

It would be best, she decided at last, to say nothing about the incident and make sure she kept well clear of Ultán for the rest of their stay with Daragh.

CHAPTER SEVEN

"HOW LONG DO WE BIDE WITH Daragh?" Ciarnat asked. She kept her tone casual.

"Why, do you not like it here?" Filan was surprised. Ciarnat usually had the happy knack of making herself at home wherever they stayed.

"Nay. I mean, I am happy here. I wondered, nothing more."

"Less than a week. I've lingered longer than I need, but Daragh's an old friend, and it has been good to spend time with him. Summer is waning, and I want to see how your gran is before we travel back to Áed's hall for the winter."

So soon, thought Ciarnat in dismay. Usually, she was happy to journey on, but Rian had become a friend. More than a friend, she thought. He was like the big brother she'd never had, teasing her and making her laugh. Then again, there was something else. He made her feel special.

He would arrive as she was working at some task, casually sit beside her and chat. She hadn't realised talking to a boy was so easy. There was no stiffness or awkwardness now between them.

The first time Filan became aware of the lad hanging around Ciarnat, she had watched his eyebrows lift in surprise, but to her relief, he'd made no comment. If anything, he seemed mildly amused by Rian's persistence and would nod to him in a friendly manner whenever he met him.

For his part, Rian was utterly relaxed. He would ask Ciarnat about her nomadic life, or tell her about his tasks guarding and herding the cattle. Daragh was a good chief and his people prospered, but Rian already knew their security relied on the vigilance of the warriors and their readiness for battle.

"From what your da says, war is coming soon," he said cheerfully that afternoon. Ciarnat had been tuning the harp, and Rian squatted beside her on the ground. "This time, I'll be going along with my father. Maybe I'll be a hero." There was no missing the excitement in his voice.

Ciarnat, familiar with endless ballads about ancient battles, was less impressed. "They sound like boys' games to me. Lots of shouting and sword waving, and at the end, one person is called a hero, and everyone else is dead. What's the point of it?"

She saw she'd shocked Rian.

"The point? Well, for glory, of course, and love of the battle. But also for land and cattle; power, too, I suppose. How else do you decide who's going to be king?"

Ciarnat was silent. Áed had been king for as long as she remembered. As he won every battle he fought, there didn't seem any point in arguing about it.

"Da says we leave tomorrow," she said at last.

Rian turned. "So soon? I'd hoped you'd stay longer," he said slowly.

Ciarnat gave a wry smile. "As did I, but Da wants to visit Gran before we go back to Áed's hall for the winter. He has only stayed this long because he and Daragh are old friends."

"I would as lief you stayed here. Could you, if you wanted to?"

Ciarnat looked at him and shook her head. "Nay. My place is with Da." She gave a slight smile. "Who would look after him if I was not there to do it?"

Rian drew his legs up to his chest and rested his chin against his knees. "I have liked having you here." His voice was muffled in his leggings.

"I have liked being with you as well, but we both knew I would have to move on. It's what bards do."

She cast around for something consoling to say. "Sometime next year we will return. I'll see you again, and we'll remain friends."

They were both quiet for a while, lost in their thoughts. Finally, Rian gave a slight sigh. "Will you sing in the hall tonight?"

"Probably; maybe; if Da says so. He won't want to be up late tonight if we travel tomorrow. But aye, probably."

"Sing that thing you sang the first night. It was pretty."

"I'll ask him."

She wanted to reach out and touch his hand, to say she would miss him. She hesitated, but wasn't brave enough to stretch across the distance between them. Eventually, she stood up and gave him a sad smile. "I will see you tonight."

⁘

The big hall was full of people that night. Even those whose duties meant they were usually too busy to attend had made a point of coming to watch the last performance.

Although the autumn had been mild, everyone knew winter was only a handful of weeks away. Once the snow set in, there'd be few travellers on the roads and even fewer chances for entertainment. Besides, Filan was the most celebrated bard in Ireland and this one of the rare opportunities for them all to hear him.

Faithful to his duties as host, Daragh and his hunters had ensured there was plenty of venison, wild boar, river fish, berries and greens to go around. There was water, milk, ale and mead to drink. Besides, Daragh had elected to celebrate the occasion by serving dark red wine, imported, so he informed Filan, from Poitou, in exchange for exported Irish cattle hides. By the time Filan stood up to entertain the crowd, they were a cheerful and raucous group.

Filan had more than enough skill and experience to control an unruly audience, and he judged shrewdly the moment they had relaxed under the spell he was weaving. He stamped his authority on them with the powerful invocation of Amhairghin; he led them, laughing, through the choruses of popular songs, and then he seduced them with a love story. He smiled when he saw a burly warrior surreptitiously wipe away a tear. They were his!

He felt the energy flowing between the crowd and himself, that magical mingling of artist and audience that was the reward for his craft—the moment when his listeners would do anything for him. He stepped back and nodded to Ciarnat to take his place.

The crowd's mood had softened, and Ciarnat's pretty youthfulness and pure voice had a receptive audience. Her simple innocence made her listeners sentimental and malleable, a light relief from his own more sophisticated skills.

Filan was cynical enough to know his daughter enhanced the whole performance, and acknowledged her developing talent. *Apples always fall close to the tree*, he thought smugly.

For her part, Ciarnat had as keen a perception of her role as her da. She already understood the art of working an audience. Her youth limited the skills she had available, but she knew already a cheeky smile, a wink, or a suggestion of a tear would draw her listeners to her.

"Be careful to limit the use of such 'artifice'," Filan had warned. "They are good tools, but no substitute for craft and talent. Learn the material you will use. Nurture your voice, your breathing, and above all, practise with your instrument until you *cannot* make a mistake. Then, and only then, can you hope to become a bard."

Tonight was good. Ciarnat felt the growing power in her voice, and the audience roared its appreciation at the end of her performance. When she left Filan on the podium to perform the balance of their show, Ciarnat stepped lightly, carried high on her elation.

She saw Rian who beckoned to her to join him on the bench. She nodded, then indicated she was going outside for a minute but would return. She threw him a smile as she left the hall with Maire.

"I've needed a piss since your da started the performance," Maire shared. "I held on so I could hear you sing, but now I'm desperate."

"If only you had told me," Ciarnat laughed, "I'd have taken a verse or two out of my songs to make it easier for you."

"Nay, lass. It was worth the wait, but now I'm in a hurry."

"You go first then."

It was a chill but pleasant night. The dew lay heavy on the grass, promising a frost by morning. The night they had arrived, the moon had been a fine crescent; now it was three-quarters full. Ciarnat, leaning against the wall of the wooden building while she waited, thought how fast their time in Daragh's hall had flown.

Tomorrow she would say goodbye to Rian. He'd become a friend, so swiftly and naturally, although she'd never felt the need for one before.

There was a big difference between sharing her thoughts with her father, however close and loved he was, and talking to someone nearer her own age.

She heard a door bang somewhere behind her. Caught up in her thoughts, she never turned. A hand grabbed her by the shoulder, cruel fingers dug into her skin and, looking up, panicked by the sudden assault, she found herself face to face with Ultán.

"You've been avoiding me, haven't you, girlie? Playing hard to get, just like all the others, have you? And when that didn't work, you came and loitered out here, waiting for me."

He was drunk. Very drunk. His breath, rank with alcohol, filled her nostrils.

She glared at him. "Let me go. Get your filthy hands off me, you foul oaf," she shrieked in anger as she squirmed in his grip. She looked around frantically. Maire still hadn't reappeared, and there was no one else around to help her.

He laughed. "You're still playing silly games with me, aren't you? Don't think that little-girl act is going to save you. You think you're better than everyone else, don't you? Tonight I'll show you what you've been missing. I know what little maids like you need."

He shifted the grip on her shoulder. For a moment she thought she'd win free and twisted wildly to break his hold, only to be slammed back against the wall when he tightened his grip again.

She realised the change in his grasp had allowed him to free up a hand while the other kept her pinned to the wall. He struggled one-handed to tug her tunic up her legs. She lifted her knee hard into his groin, but he turned sideways and evaded her. Then she tried to kick him hard but made no impression. Worse, a thumb invaded her most intimate space as his fingers scrabbled at her sex.

She screamed her outrage, twisting and squirming desperately in his hold, but her strength was no match for a full-grown man.

And then she was released. Unexpectedly, her cry had been heard.

Direct as a spear thrown from the open doors of the hall, a man flew towards them. "Leave her alone! Put her down, you brute. What do you think you are doing?"

Ultán dropped Ciarnat and spun to face his challenger. She slumped, breathless, against the wall, watching as Rian closed the distance between them.

"Get away from her, Ultán; you'll answer to Daragh for this."

There was a moment in which Ultán crouched as Rian ran at him, then he raised his arm in a quick, vicious gesture. Rian stopped.

It happened so fast that Ciarnat had time to wonder why Rian was standing there uselessly before she saw the knife hilt protruding from his chest as he slowly crumpled to the ground.

Someone else was screaming, and their cries brought warriors running from the hall. Other hands gently wrapped a cloak around her; people gathered around Rian's body while others held Ultán as Daragh approached.

Ciarnat saw and heard none of it. She knelt beside Rian, shaking and gasping for breath as the shock hit her system. She clutched his hand and tried to pray as the priest had taught her, but random thoughts pounded with the rhythm of her blood. Rian hadn't had to go to war; he already was a hero; he had died defending her. He was her friend, and she'd caused his death.

If she hadn't screamed, he would be alive. They hadn't said goodbye.

"Rian, my son. Oh, no!" A woman came running from the hall and threw herself to her knees beside his body. "Sweet Virgin, how could this happen?" she cried as she kissed Rian's forehead and stroked his cheek.

Ciarnat released his hand and sat back but made no other move.

Filan tried talking to her. He knelt and put his arm around her. When all else failed, he gathered her in his arms and lifted her to her feet.

He took one look at her vacant eyes as he pulled her up, then held her in the circle of his arm with her face hidden against his shoulder, achingly unable to heal her pain and incapable of watching as she suffered.

That glance had shown him there was more life in the rapidly cooling body of the boy on the ground than in his daughter's frozen face. He cradled her against him, trying to give her his warmth, willing her to be strong, to come through the shock and horror she'd faced.

Daragh came to stand beside him and put a hand on his shoulder in comfort. Filan closed his eyes briefly, grateful for the fellowship implicit in the touch.

CHAPTER
EIGHT

CLAN JUSTICE WAS DARAGH'S RESPONSIBILITY, and his warriors and a few onlookers assembled in the hall the next morning for his judgement. Daragh was seated in his chair as they brought the culprit before him.

Ultán had sobered overnight and was patently terrified. Unfortunately, this made him more belligerent than ever as he struggled and cursed the men holding him.

Maire gave her evidence, her fury palpable as she gave her testimony. She'd walked out in time to see the last few minutes of the drama: Ciarnat had been held against her will and was fighting to prevent her attacker from raping her. Rian had come to her rescue when he heard her scream. Ultán had drawn a knife and murdered the boy. There was no question of a duel, fair fight or any mitigating circumstance.

When asked if this was a truthful and fair presentation of the facts, Ciarnat nodded. Filan, standing behind her, grasped her shoulders in support.

"So," said Daragh, "rape has been prevented, and a promising young man died defending the girl. His kin has lost their son, and our clan has lost a future warrior. Rian was of noble birth and high status, and Ailbe, his father, is pre-eminent among the warriors gathered here today."

There was a murmur of agreement from the audience.

"Ultán, do you have anything to say?"

"I didn't mean to kill the boy." Many a man would have apologised. Ultán's voice was aggressive and arrogant. "He came at me. I drew my knife by reflex. Any man would have done the same."

The scorn in Daragh's voice was withering. "He came at you because you were assaulting a young lass—a woman guest with us, whose father is the High King's bard. Rian was bound to defend her. Any decent man would have done the same. You disgust me."

Daragh stood up and faced the assembled group. "Brehon law dictates the penalty for this crime. It tells us a murderer owes two kinds of compensation to the kin of their victim. The wergild, and an 'honour price' appropriate to the status of the murdered man."

Daragh paused. "Are those of you here in agreement with this?"

Again, there came a rumbling assent.

Daragh faced Ultán. "I stand here, as your chief, in the presence of the High King's *ollamh* and the warriors of our tribe, to pass sentence on you for your crime. My judgement upon you is this. You are sentenced to a fine of twenty-one milk cows as wergild and a further twenty-one as the honour price to be paid to Rian's family."

Filan nodded his head slowly. "I agree," he said.

Daragh looked at the others. "Ailbe?"

The man stood. "No fine, no penalty you can inflict, will bring back my boy," he said wearily.

"Ultán?" Daragh's voice was harsh. "You have received my judgement, agreed by those here today. Forty-two cattle will be the sum of your fines. Do you have anything to say?"

"You know full well I cannot pay it. I am a poor man. I do not own forty-two cattle, nor am I ever likely to," protested Ultán. "Why should I have to pay anyway? The boy launched himself at me. It was his own fault he died."

Ailbe's fist smashed into Ultán's face with brutal force, and Ultán collapsed to the ground.

Filan flinched. It was a killer blow, delivered with all the anger Ailbe could muster. He was surprised Ultán was still alive.

Ultán clutched a hand to his bleeding face and slowly crawled to his knees at Ailbe's feet. "You've broken my nose," he accused Ailbe between wheezing and moaning.

"You got your just deserts, nothing more," said Daragh angrily. "You've been found guilty. Now be quiet."

None of the others moved or spoke as they watched the man trying vainly to staunch his bleeding nose with shaking hands.

"It is usual in such an instance for a man's kin to help meet the blood debt," said Filan at last. "It is their responsibility to pay whatever you cannot."

Ultán pulled his hand from his face. "I have no family. Not since my mother died two winters ago. I cannot pay," he wailed, then flinched as Ailbe moved sharply beside him.

"None?" Filan was openly startled. It was a thing unheard of, for a man to be without an extended family.

"It is the truth," Ailbe confirmed. "His father came as an itinerant pedlar many years ago, travelling with his wife and young baby. The man was sick when he arrived and died a few days later. His wife chose to stay here with her child."

"Then these are the options," Daragh told Ailbe. "You have the choice of waiting for payment until Ultán *can* pay you, or of selling him into slavery for whatever you can get for him. The choice is yours."

"There is a third option," said Ailbe slowly. "There is a blood feud. I have the right to kill him for the loss of my son."

"Ahhhh." Daragh exhaled heavily. He glanced at Filan. "Let us discuss that."

He returned to his chair and sat for several minutes, rubbing his chin, evidently deep in thought. He glanced briefly at Ultán, who was now cowering on the floor.

"What think you, Filan?" Daragh asked at last. "Give us your counsel."

"Brehon law does not generally support capital punishment,"

answered Filan. "Old bardic tales and learning tell us in the old days our customs were different. Then the Christian priests arrived on our shores, and they argued for forgiveness and reparation for a crime. It is rare now for any court to invoke the death penalty."

Daragh nodded agreement. "And in this case?"

"What purpose does taking his life serve? Nothing will bring Ailbe's boy back, and executing this wretch won't give Ailbe or his kin much satisfaction. It's a swift punishment for the murderer, but Ailbe and his wife will bear the loss of their son for the rest of their lives."

"I want vengeance!" Ailbe cried.

"Let Filan finish," Daragh ordered.

"If you desire real vengeance, then sell the man," urged Filan. "Take him to Dublin and auction him at the slave market there. Let him live out his miserable life with an iron thrall collar around his neck, chafing and reminding him of his slave state. Let him be subject to the whims of a master. It's a harsher punishment than a quick knife in the ribs. He will pay his blood debt in the profit you make from the sale of him. You can use the money to some purpose for your family."

Daragh leaned back in his seat. "Filan speaks wisely. Does any man here also wish to speak?" he asked.

Most of the warriors shook their heads.

Ciarnat looked at Ultán. His earlier truculence had entirely gone. His attempts to wipe his face had left thick smears of blood. The only clear areas of skin were two white tracks down his cheeks where his tears ran through the mess. The bully, the rapist and the murderer was a snivelling, shivering mess on the floor.

For a moment, Ciarnat almost felt pity for him before she remembered his crimes.

"Ailbe, will you accept Filan's words as judgement?" Daragh's voice was quiet.

The only sound in the hall was Ultán sobbing.

"You believe he will suffer more this way?" Ailbe asked.

"Aye, I do." Filan's voice was confident.

"It is in my mind that he will, too," Daragh agreed.

"It will not bring back my boy." Ailbe's face wrenched in grief, and he closed his eyes for a moment. Ciarnat's own eyes filled in sympathy with the warrior's pain.

Ailbe opened his eyes and took a deep breath. "I agree," he said slowly. "He goes to Dublin for sale. May God curse the rest of his existence with pain and misery."

Ailbe looked at Daragh and then cast a sweeping glance over the warriors watching him. "Let it be done," he said, before turning abruptly and leaving the hall.

CHAPTER NINE

B Y THE TIME FILAN AND CIARNAT took their leave
of Daragh, Ailbe had already left, with Ultán tied to his
horse, for their journey to Dublin.

"Good riddance to bad rubbish," Filan muttered under his
breath.

There was little pleasure taken in the beauty of the day as
Filan and his daughter rode south. Usually, Ciarnat would have
delighted in how the bright light turned dewdrops into strings of
diamonds clinging to spiders' webs trailing over the bushes. She
would have commented when they passed a fairy ring or sniffed
the scent of gorse or pennyroyal carried on the clean air.

They had buried Rian the day before, a few hours after the
trial of Ultán, and Ciarnat rode in silence, grieving. Rian had
been like sunshine dancing on water, but now he'd sunk beneath
the surface, leaving only widening ripples to mark his passing.

The burden she bore was overwhelming. It was her fault, she
thought. Had she told Filan about Ultán's crude remarks the
first time he'd accosted her, Daragh would have dealt with the
situation. Had she been more careful, had she not left the hall at
that time, had she not annoyed Ultán... Her sense of culpability
curdled her thinking until, if asked, she'd have claimed entire

responsibility for Rian's death. Nothing would bring him back; nothing would heal his family's hurt; nothing could ever assuage her guilt.

Filan felt his daughter's silence settle about him like a weight which grew more burdensome as the long miles passed behind them. He glanced at her a couple of times—she was pale but outwardly composed. A lovely, empty-eyed copy of his usually animated daughter.

His inability to ease her pain depressed him, as did the conversation he'd had the night before with Daragh.

"I'm sorry for your girl," his friend had said sympathetically. "Ultán always was a surly wretch and unpopular with many, but I never thought he'd try and force himself on a woman."

"Barely a woman," Filan corrected dryly. "She's only twelve."

"And a guest in my house. I apologise for my lack of oversight."

Filan sighed. "It's not just *your* oversight, though, Daragh. A greater portion of the blame must fall to me. I'm her father. Before this tragedy occurred, you criticised the way I was rearing my child."

"Not criticised," protested Daragh. "I just said it was unusual."

"You asked if I was concerned about her future. You meant this sort of thing, didn't you?"

"Not specifically, but aye, as a general concern." Daragh looked uncomfortable. "She's a lovely wee maid and full credit to you. But with her looks, she's going to receive unwanted attention. You can't be there to protect her all the time."

"But you think she'd be safer at home with my mother than out on the highways with me?" Guilt made his tone rougher than it should have been.

Daragh shrugged. "Only you can know that. It is the decision most men would make."

Today, after a mostly sleepless night, the conversation replayed in Filan's head. He loved Ciarnat but was honest enough to know how he valued her talent—how fostering it, watching it grow and develop—was an all-consuming joy for him. All those years ago, Gran had warned him his choice reflected his comfort more than his daughter's well-being. Now guilt exposed that decision as an arrogance that had nearly resulted in his daughter's rape.

He was determined not to continue in his error. He would speak to his mother, and when he left on his travels again, he would be alone.

The two travelled in silence, neither prepared to discuss with the other the burden each carried.

CHAPTER
TEN

Erin

Present Day, New Zealand

"WE NEED TO PLAN THE LAYETTE," Erin said.

"The what?"

"The things the baby will need—you know, clothes, nappies, all the gear. Then I suppose we'll need a bassinette, a cot and ..."

"Enough," groaned Luke. "We're having a baby, not mounting a bloody expedition to climb Mt Everest." He saw Erin's disappointment and softened his tone. "Oh, sweets, get whatever you think we'll need. You know better than me."

"I thought you'd want to come with me to help choose it," said Erin.

Luke gave a short laugh. "I wouldn't have a clue what I was looking at."

"Neither would I, but I thought we could learn together." Erin's tone reflected her frustration. "This isn't just my baby, you know."

"I know that. I'm the clever guy who's going to be a daddy."

Erin rolled her eyes. "Then it'd be nice if you joined in the planning."

"OK, I will." Luke's smile was ingratiating. "It's just there's been a real rush on at work, and I've got a lot on my mind."

Erin turned her attention back to the baby magazine on her lap. "Fuck your work," she muttered under her breath. "There's always a rush on."

"I heard that. You won't be so dismissive when you're a stay-at-home mum and we're living on just my salary."

It wasn't that she didn't get his point, it was the smugness behind his statements that infuriated her. She'd thought having this baby would be a shared affair.

Erin was still angry with Luke two days later when she met Petra for lunch at the café on the Pipitea campus, a venue handy for both of them. The building also housed the Wellington Law School, and the brasserie was packed with students peering earnestly at their MacBooks and arguing legal torts.

"Or whatever it is law students do," said Erin airily, having for the last ten minutes sat beside a table of four young people deep in discussion on legal procedure.

"Don't they look incredibly young," Petra grumbled. "We used to be like that."

Erin gave a wistful smile. "Seems like centuries ago, doesn't it? I loved being a student. That self-important mindset that we could go out and save the world as soon as our parents let us—although I'm not sure why I thought that. I was studying accounting."

Petra snorted. "I can see the headline: 'Planet saved by a battle-weary accountant'. Not *that* likely. Anyway, how's the baby doing?"

"The baby's fine. And that's why I wanted to meet you for lunch so I could tell you. I had the gender scan yesterday. It's going to be a boy!"

"Wow! That's great. Are you pleased? Luke must be beside himself with excitement. Don't all guys want boys?"

"I don't know about all guys."

Petra frowned. Erin's head was down as she played with the

napkin, successfully avoiding eye contact.

"Hey, Erin. Look at me," she said. "I'm your friend, remember? Are you saying Luke wanted a daughter? Is he upset it's a boy?"

Eventually, Erin sighed and raised her eyes. "I don't know," she mumbled. "I haven't told him."

"Haven't told him?" Petra's voice rose an octave in disbelief. "Wasn't he there with you? What the hell's going on?"

"He wasn't there with me," Erin confirmed. "That's the problem," she said, her voice heavy with indignation. "He was happy enough to get me pregnant. And he's keen on getting the kudos and congratulations from his mates for fathering a baby, but every time I try to get him to participate in the process of pregnancy, he tells me he's too busy at work."

Petra sat back, staring at her friend. "Shit," she said at last.

"Quite." Despite trying to sound upbeat, Erin could hear despondency flattening her voice.

"Oh shit," Petra repeated. They both sipped their flat whites in silence for a few moments.

"Um, not wanting to cross the line or anything, but are you still having, you know," —Petra's voice dropped to a whisper— "sex? I mean, the baby isn't causing an issue in that department, is it?"

"Fuck, no." Erin's face was grim. "There's no problem there— at least not on Luke's part. I'm the problem. I'm so frustrated by his attitude, I'm starting to fake it."

"Jeez!" Petra said, shocked. "I never thought I'd hear you say that."

Erin's expression was wry. "I never thought I'd have to say it." She shook her head. "Maybe it's me. I'm pregnant, so I'm hypersensitive and probably getting it all wrong. Of course, it's right that Luke wants to be a responsible income earner when there's a baby on the way. I just feel kind of ..." She took another gulp of coffee, incapable of expressing herself.

It took a few minutes before she could continue. "I sort of feel abandoned, if you know what I mean—I'd planned we'd share our lives, and now I'm wondering whether I made a ghastly mistake."

"Did Luke want you to have a baby?" Petra asked. "He seemed very happy the night of the barbecue when you told us all."

"Yeah, we discussed it, and he agreed. Now, of course, I wonder whether I pushed it." Erin rubbed her forehead. "I'm so damn tired all the time. I'm probably not thinking rationally." She smiled bleakly at Petra. "I'm not trying to diss Luke. You must know that. I love him. I guess we're both adjusting, that's all."

"Why are you so tired?" Petra asked. "Is this normal; have you discussed it with your doctor?"

Erin shook her head. "Nah. I'm getting nightmares, so I try to stay awake. I don't get them every night, but when I do, they aren't much fun."

"You aren't dreaming about giving birth, are you?" Petra said cautiously. "I've seen a programme about it. That would be enough to give any woman nightmares, but I gather it usually all ends happily."

Erin gave a short laugh. "Hell, no. That would be bad enough, so I'm not dwelling on it. No," her forehead furrowed as she tried to explain. "It feels like I'm a spectator at some horrific event. There is a massive fire and noise, and a woman screaming her head off." She shook her head to shake off the residue of memory. "It's got to the point where I'm almost identifying with the wretched woman. It's like I can feel her fear, her pain, her grieving. Something terrible is going on, and I don't know what it is, let alone what to do."

"Fuck." Petra was staring at her. "Are you on medication?"

"No." For the first time, Erin gave a genuine chuckle. "If I were, I'd have stopped taking it weeks ago to escape the night-time stuff."

"Have you discussed it with your doctor?"

"What? That I'm stuck in the middle of some bizarre fantasy? Hell no! They'd cart me off to the psych ward, and I'd probably never be allowed to see my baby." Her humour had evaporated.

"You're not insane," Petra ventured, unsure what the correct response was.

"Not more than most people." Erin's smile was reassuring.

"But I'm getting some crazy stuff in my dreams. I've told Luke, who just thinks I overeat cheese close to bedtime, or some stupid excuse." She sighed. "Perhaps he's right, well, not about the cheese, because I'm a responsible mum-to-be and not eating it. Truly, Petra, it's better to believe I've had too many calories for dinner than the alternative."

"What alternative?" Petra felt she had lost the gist of the conversation.

"Supposing I'm channelling—is that the word? —something that happened in real life. Is it possible I'm supposed to know what's going on? It feels so real, and it's like I'm there."

"You're kidding, right?" Petra stared at her; concern written all over her face.

"I don't know, but bless you for the total normality of your response." Erin gave a smile. "You remind me what the real world is about. Now, what did you think about Fergal's latest? Brianna."

"I was going to say, didn't she tell you that bub would be a boy?"

"Yes, she did." Erin's eyes drifted away from Petra's face.

"Well, it was a 50–50 chance, wasn't it? No particular skill at prediction required?" asked Petra, concerned that Erin, usually the most focused, cynical person she knew, seemed to be losing the plot.

Erin appeared to snap to. "Sorry," she apologised. "Reality no longer seems to be the immutable thing I thought it was." She shook her head at Petra. "Probably just 'pregnant mum' brain is going on. Ignore me."

"We were discussing Brianna."

"Luke fancied her, I could see that," Erin said.

She saw by Petra's face that she'd shocked her friend. "I didn't mean it that way. He thought she was lovely and young, that's all. We laughed because Fergal said she had an 'old soul'! Luke said, if so, it was the only part of her that was old." She smiled at the memory.

"Well, she *is* very young ..." Petra advanced cautiously.

"With an old soul? Fergal seemed to think she knew what she

was talking about and worth listening to. Perhaps she knows stuff."

"Like what? Don't tell me you're buying into some spiritualist mumbo jumbo?"

"She was right about the gender of our baby," said Erin firmly. "I'd like to find out what else she knows."

"Are you sure pregnancy hasn't gone to your brain?"

Petra looked rattled, so Erin gave a slight smile and let the matter drop.

"How're rehearsals going?" she asked.

Petra gave a rueful smile. "Like all rehearsals in amateur theatre! Heaven and hell, although mostly hell at the moment. There are evenings when I don't want to go out, and then, when I get to the theatre, I get into the buzz of it all and enjoy it. I'm nervous about my part as well. I haven't had a starring role before. I can sing OK, but there's dancing as well. I've got two left feet. I'm terrified I'll stuff it all up."

"You'll be wonderful," Erin assured her. She wasn't lying either. Petra was disingenuous. She'd been in numerous productions, and if she hadn't starred, she'd had some very meaty support roles and had shone in them. Some amalgam of natural prettiness, confidence and showmanship meant she had an eye-catching presence on stage that made for compelling viewing. The audience was drawn to her every time she appeared.

"We'll come to opening night," Erin assured her friend.

CHAPTER ELEVEN

Thorkell

Ninth Century, Norway

THORKELL WAS SEVENTEEN THAT AUTUMN, AND his mother dead barely a year when Orm brought his new wife home.

Thorkell waited on the beach with Hagen and the other warriors as the boat pulled in to shore. Asger, his uncle, stood at his shoulder amongst the rest of them, watching as Orm carried his bride to dry land.

"She's very young," came a disapproving mutter from behind him. "Barely half his age, at a guess."

Thorkell recognised the voice. Rowena was a thrall who'd served as his nurse in his infancy. She'd loved him, cared for him and taught him, as a boy, to speak her native tongue. It became a secret language between them. Despite her captivity, she'd been loyal to Thorkell's late mother and had grieved terribly when her mistress died in childbirth.

Orm set his wife on her feet. There was a smile on his face as they turned to greet the people waiting for them.

"By Thor's hammer, she's beautiful," Asger gasped as he saw her face.

Thorkell scowled. It was true, although recognising it seemed like a disloyalty to his late mother. He was furious with his father for remarrying so quickly anyway, but he could, he told himself, have accepted it if the new bride were plain and older. All rulers have responsibilities, and astute marriages made for strong allegiances between the clans.

Yes, thought Thorkell. An alliance based on duty would have been acceptable.

But it was obvious, looking at the woman, that Orm's choice of a wife had little to do with duty and a good deal to do with lust.

Orm was Thorkell's father. To take such a young bride was disgusting. Orm was old.

Thorkell turned away as Asger pushed past him to be first to greet the couple.

Hagen's hand on his shoulder served to steady him, although his friend said nothing.

Thorkell gulped. He would have to face this.

Eventually, Thorkell gained control and forced himself to congratulate his father and welcome Odell. He knew, of course, as his father's son, he should have been the very first to offer her the kiss of kinship. His father's face made it clear that he'd noted this omission, although he said nothing.

Thorkell tossed his head and told himself he didn't care. He'd recently felt there was nothing he could do to please his father, however hard he tried. His father could just add this incident to all the other times he'd been disappointed in his son.

Odell was lovely. Despite his resentment, Thorkell couldn't fail but be charmed by her. "I hope we'll be friends," she was saying. "I'm not here to replace your mother. You must miss her terribly. I hope you'll give me a chance to learn to be as good a wife as she was."

Thorkell reluctantly warmed to her. "Er, *já*." His voice, which had recently dropped into a man's register, gave an unfortunate squeak. "You're very welcome here."

Odell's smile didn't change, but Thorkell caught a malicious grin on his father's face which brought a bright blush to his own. Cursing his youth, gaucheness and his father, who was undoubtedly at the heart of his misery, Thorkell withdrew.

Later, at the feast, he kept his distance from the married couple and contented himself with drinking ale until he vomited his grief and rage out into the waves that lapped the beach.

CHAPTER
TWELVE

IT WAS IMPOSSIBLE TO DISLIKE ODELL. It was equally impossible not to see she was winning over Orm's usually monosyllabic warriors. Where they used to nod briefly in the direction of Orm's first wife, before continuing their discussion of ships and plunder, it was noticeable they now made a point of being early to meals and jostled to sit closest to her at table. Asger frequently claimed kin's right as her brother-in-law to be beside her.

Even Thorkell, determined to fault her, found nothing to complain of in her manner or her behaviour, and Orm was all too obviously happy.

Lost in the misery and self-absorption that plague a boy transitioning to a man, Thorkell found it easy to blame his frustrations on his father and accuse him of disloyalty to his dead wife and neglect of his only son.

Thorkell was uneasily conscious the young bride was having another effect on him, eased only by certain surreptitious acts beneath his blankets as he waited for sleep at night. His disloyalty to his father, implicit in those thoughts he couldn't resist, served to make him ever more confused and resentful.

It was a long, hard winter for them all. There was always

work to do, of course. The women wove and spun, repairing the *Sea Serpent*'s worn sail and mending tents. Men worked metal in the forge, or scraped and cleaned its hull—but cleaning and oiling leather, sharpening weapons, fashioning new bindings and stitching fresh rimming around the edge of a shield can only occupy a fighting man for so long.

Drinking was heavy and fist fights frequent. It took all of Orm's considerable authority to maintain discipline. Far worse than any physical penalty was the power Orm held of removing a culprit from the crew of the *Sea Serpent* for the coming season, and this was the automatic punishment for any fight or disagreement that incited a blood feud. The men chafed and muttered amongst themselves about his control but complied.

Thorkell and Hagen kept themselves clear of trouble by avoiding the hall whenever possible.

Hagen had discovered a young thrall girl willing to explore what their bodies could do together and spent as much time as he could in her company.

Thorkell, missing his friend and his mother, and resentful of his father's happiness, spent some miserable weeks wondering whether he wanted to become a warrior after all.

There was a skald staying in his father's hall this winter, and from him and his music, the children were learning about great men, their deeds and courage; they also learned about beautiful women and the gods and goddesses.

Thorkell listened to the sagas, poems and songs the skald brought to the hall, and wondered whether he'd found his calling. He spent evenings composing gloomy verses that mirrored his misery. He wanted to ask for the skald's opinion about these attempts, but shyness imprisoned him, and enough common sense remained to remember the man would have spent years learning his craft. Still, there were enough sad stories from Asgard for him to use. If he fleshed out their stories with his own confused emotions, then so be it.

∴

One morning he awoke, and the world was reborn. The wind had changed and blew from the south. When he walked from the hall, half the village was out already, enjoying the clear skies and soft, warm air.

Icicles clinging to the edge of buildings dripped, drilling deep holes in the snow that lay below. There was a rustling as hard-packed snow fell from eaves, and Thorkell fancied he could hear the first sounds of trickling water beneath the ice surface of the stream on the beach.

Hagen, having recovered from the malaise that had kept him bed-bound all winter with his young thrall, met him on the shoreline. They walked the length of the bay together in companionable silence.

When they turned and were on their way back, Thorkell looked sideways at his friend. "Was it as good as they say it is?"

"*Já*," Hagen said thoughtfully. "A man could lose himself there for a while. But, *nei*. In the end, I missed you; I needed more than she could offer. She's a nice girl, but I was getting bored." He grinned at Thorkell. "I'm glad it's spring."

"Race you to the boat and back," challenged Thorkell, ripping off his clothes and plunging into the icy water.

Hagen shrieked as he followed him in.

After the weeks of idleness, the burning cold cleansed the mind and scoured the skin. Happiness flooded through Thorkell as he turned for shore.

A few men watching cheered when Thorkell reached the beach. Hagen was close behind. Their teeth chattered as they pulled their tunics over their heads.

Thorkell hugged his friend in an impulse of affection and relief. "I won. See where fooling with a girl all winter long gets you."

Hagen's laugh was warm and his clasp close before he stepped back and lightly cuffed Thorkell. "You wait until it's your turn."

There was a crunch of gravel behind them. "Well done, lad. You, too, young Hagen." Orm patted his son on his back. "It's good to see we still breed them tough," he told the other men, "not like you lot."

"I've grown some brain now as well as some balls," Asger laughed. "You *boys* had better get yourselves back to a fire and get warmed up."

Had he imagined it? For an instant, when Asger spoke to Thorkell, his smile had seemed less friendly, and his emphasis on the word boys intentionally belittling.

Thorkell puzzled over that fleeting impression as he and Hagen jogged up the path, then forgot the episode when they caught the scent of rye bread coming from the hall.

"Honey and fresh bread." Hagen moaned as he bit into the rich slice.

"Take your time, lads. This feast is going to celebrate spring, not just fill the bottomless bellies of you two."

"We know, and we won't," Hagen mumbled, biting into his second slice.

Rowena scowled at them, and Thorkell blew her a kiss.

"You're the best cook." He smiled as he, too, grabbed another slice.

Rowena flapped a wet clout at him. "Be off with you," she chided. "Flattery gets you nowhere."

They were laughing as they left the hall.

Later that evening Thorkell learned he and Hagen were allowed to join the crew of the *Sea Serpent* for the first time.

His father announced the crew after the warriors had eaten in the hall. Thorkell was so delighted and excited he forgot the ill treatment he'd been so sure he suffered, forgot his father's execrable behaviour in marrying a young woman, and the various adolescent miseries he had suffered over the past few months.

He laughed and cheered with Hagen and the men for the first time in months. Happiness lifted his face into a grin, his eyes sparkled with cheeky joy and his enthusiasm was unbounded.

He couldn't have known how relieved Orm was, nor of Odell's gratitude for a respite from his surly moodiness. He would have been mortified if he'd realised she had identified him early as the most significant risk to her marriage.

Asger was assigned to mentor Thorkell through his first

season. He was experienced, having been a warrior on the *Sea Serpent* for the last six years. He was known as a bold sailor and fierce in battle. He looked at the enthusiasm on the stripling's face and grinned. A few years earlier, he would have looked the same, he thought. Soppy, wet behind the ears and in dire need of hardening up into a man.

The relationship between the two was unusual. A fifteen-year age difference separated Asger and Orm, with only a nine-year gap between Asger and Thorkell. Consequently, Orm had been more a father to Asger than a brother.

It was probable, thought Asger, that Orm himself had come to regard both him and Thorkell as children, with Thorkell cast as the younger sibling.

It suited Asger very well to have the boy for tutoring. He had plans of his own for the future of Orm's lands and title when the older man died, and they didn't include Orm's only son.

CHAPTER
THIRTEEN

THE DAYS LENGTHENED IN THE WEEKS before spring, and the work was endless. The *Sea Serpent* had to be recaulked for the coming season. Every seam of her hull needed to be packed watertight with a smelly mess of wool and animal hair mixed with softened tallow and tar.

Orm might have made use of the thralls, but this work was too important for mere slaves, and he insisted his warriors knew their ship intimately. "If you want to be a warrior on my ship, you'll know how to fix every part of her," he told the crew. "You'll know her ways better than you know your women." This last always got the laugh Orm expected, but his purpose was serious. The lives of the men depended on their ship being seaworthy, so warriors worked beside shipbuilders, fixing ropes and rigging, replacing broken oars, checking the big square sail ran freely as the men hauled it up the mast.

Thorkell had no idea his muscles could ache so much. He laboured on the ship in the morning, then trained with weapons in the afternoon.

He knew how to use a sword and axe, of course, but now the men sparred and fought with renewed purpose. The moves they practised were no longer steps in a drill but the difference between life and death. A fierce intensity marked each exchange and, short of death or maiming, they didn't spare each other in the training bouts.

Asger was a relentless taskmaster and made him drill and fight long after Thorkell was exhausted. "You think an enemy is going to wait until you've had enough sleep?" he jeered. "Do you think your brothers can wait while you break your fast or have a shit?"

Thorkell would shake his head miserably, lift his sword, now impossibly heavy at the end of his arm, and return to the fight. He felt he was wading through the pitch used to caulk the *Sea Serpent*'s seams. None of his swipes ever connected with Asger who was able to get his hits past Thorkell's guard every time.

There was nothing gentle about Asger's blows either, and Thorkell's body bore the marks of a thorough beating.

Hagen happened to see it. "Thor's bollocks," he exclaimed. "What happened to you?"

"What's probably happened to you as well," Thorkell answered. "Training isn't easy, and we bear the bruises."

"Bruises, yes," said Hagen brutally. "I've got them as well, but those are bruises upon deeper bruises. Asger's a bully doing that to you. The way he's going, he'll render you a cripple before you ever get on the *Sea Serpent*."

"It's not deliberate," Thorkell protested, "and nothing's going to stop me getting on that ship."

"Asger might," Hagen replied. "I have watched him look at you sometimes and wondered whether he is what he seems."

"What do you mean?"

"Well, he's beating you up as if he enjoys it," said Hagen. "Gunnar's training me, but I don't look like you do. Also, I know Asger's your brother and all that …"

"He's *not* my brother." Thorkell startled himself with force the words burst from him. From where had that intensity come? "He's my father's youngest brother, that's all. He owes everything he has to Orm's generosity. It's silly to suggest he is deliberately trying to hurt me. If he offends Orm by maiming me, he could be banished or killed."

"Unless he claims it was an accident."

Thorkell sighed. "Which it would be. I am not fast enough or strong enough, that's all."

Hagen snorted. "You're not that slow. You are faster and stronger than I am. Have you thought of talking to your father about it?"

"What, complain to Orm? About his brother? Who is doing the task he was ordered to do —training me ready for the *Sea Serpent*?" Thorkell was appalled. "He'd consider me a tell-tale and a baby, and rightly so. He would pull me out of the crew and never allow me another chance. That's the last thing I would do."

Thorkell had no difficulty imagining an enemy would equal or exceed Asger's viciousness when they were under attack. He had become so used to being thrashed it was now a foregone conclusion, and Asger had probably come to feel the same. Even so, in a small way, Hagen's words bolstered Thorkell's resilience.

They didn't discuss the matter again, but Hagen had planted a seed. What if Asger's brutality was personal?

Had Thorkell known it, Orm was well aware of what Asger was doing to him. He'd watched the training bouts with increasing frustration and, behind an impervious mask, had winced as he saw the punishment the boy took.

"Turn around and fight properly," he wanted to shout at his son. "Don't let him dominate you so easily."

Even Odell had commented on Thorkell's stiffness and black eyes. "Can you not do something?" she asked. "Give Thorkell to someone else to train with?"

Orm shook his head. "I'd shame the boy forever if I did, and I won't do that to him. He's my heir, and one day he'll need to control warriors. A reputation for weakness would be fatal for his future."

Odell understood that men were different in their attitudes to these things, but she hated the bullying she saw.

"No." Orm was firm. "This is Thorkell's fight. We are a people to whom fighting is the very stuff of life. He will win no respect if he yields every time. He needs to learn to harness his skills. If he can't, then let him fail. He'll be no son of mine."

CHAPTER
FOURTEEN

THE DAYS WERE DRAWING IMPERCEPTIBLY longer. Work on the *Sea Serpent* was complete, and the crew launched her in the fjord to test her seaworthiness.

It took Thorkell time to fall into the rhythm of rowing with thirty-nine other oarsmen. He'd fall behind the beat or, as he struggled to keep pace, his blade would enter the water unevenly, breaking the surface with a messy splash. Hagen was making the same basic errors.

Most of the warriors were wryly amused. They'd all made the same mistakes, so their teasing was kind and inclusive.

Not so Asger. "You've got yourself a right training session coming this afternoon, you useless boy," he shouted at Thorkell. "I'll make a man of you yet, even if I have to skin every bit of flesh from you to do it."

There was an uncomfortable silence from the crew. It wasn't their place to intervene, but most thought Asger had gone too far in shaming the lad in front of his shipmates.

Thorkell's face flamed, but he said nothing. He kept his head down and concentrated on keeping the rhythm as they turned the ship back to shore.

They'd barely hauled her up onto the beach than Asger yelled at Thorkell to get his weapons and meet him for his punishment. "I'll show him some new tricks today," he said, grinning at his shipmates. "He won't be walking comfortably for a day or two after this."

A couple of men shook their heads as they walked away. They stepped aside to make way as Thorkell returned to the beach armed with his axe and sword, and by silent consent the crew turned to watch the pair on the beach.

"This is a bad business," Gunnar muttered to Hagen. "Thor knows what Asger thinks his spitefulness will serve to teach Thorkell."

Although they were too far away to hear, it was clear Asger was berating Thorkell. Maybe he was mocking him as well, because Thorkell suddenly lifted his head and stared at his abuser.

Asger moved forward, his sword raised as a signal the bout would begin, but faster than any eye could follow, a knife flew from Thorkell's hand and pierced Asger in the shoulder. Asger gave a startled cry of surprise and turned instinctively to examine his injured arm. Before he could make another move, Thorkell had stepped forward beside his opponent. A massive blow to the back of Asger's knees with the flat of his sword brought the man floundering to the ground. A well-considered kick from Thorkell's foot into his solar plexus curled him into a ball, and Thorkell's blade pointed at his bare throat.

No words were spoken between them. Asger's chest rose and fell as he fought to catch his breath. His hands scrabbled at the pebbles he'd fallen on as if he still believed he could rise and regain control.

Thorkell, his sword unwavering, kept his eyes on Asger's face. His mouth had set in a grim line, and he breathed, too quickly, through his nose. Nothing was giving or boyish in his face. Whether he would have or could have killed his uncle was, for a frozen moment, unclear to either of them, and Asger seemed incapable of the simple phrase 'I yield', which would have ended the stalemate.

In the end, it was the warriors cheering and whooping on the high ground above the beach that ended it.

Hagen came running down the dunes towards his friend. "You did it. You were magnificent!" He flung his arm around Thorkell's shoulders. "You've also won us a small fortune. I bet on you winning. I'll share it with you, seeing as you did all the work."

Thorkell surfaced slowly from the cold, dark waters of the fjord he'd been navigating. Hagen's arms were around him and Thorkell understood the words he said, although he still seemed so very far away.

On instinct, he'd thrown the knife at Asger and allowed himself to drop into those waters. It had been a dangerously dark place. Now he was riding upwards on the ripples it had formed as they became more expansive and shallower, and he returned to himself.

The others surrounded him. Many thumped him on the back in congratulation.

"I lost good money on you," Gunnar grumbled, "but you did well. I won't make that mistake again."

Thorkell's attention returned to the still-silent man at his feet. "Do you yield?" he asked at last and watched a spasm cross the man's face.

Asger's eyelids flickered as he looked at his crewmates above him. He had no choice, and every man there knew it. "*Já*, I yield," he said.

Thorkell withdrew the sword and stepped back as he sheathed it, allowing the man to rise before turning his back and striding off with Hagen towards the hall.

⁙

Thorkell shook his head.

"It just happened," he replied. He wasn't anxious to remember the wave of fury that had engulfed him and sucked him down.

Hagen wasn't stupid. "Did he insult you?" he asked. "Only it looked like he said something, and then you were suddenly concentrating. After that, the fight was all over in a minute. What made the difference?"

"Nothing." Not for anything would Thorkell repeat Asger's taunt—an accusation he'd been sexually submissive with Hagen—the implication being clear: a man who behaved so would do the same in other areas, being of necessity a follower rather than a leader. For a jarl's son and heir, it would be hard to find a more serious insult.

Orm, who'd watched the whole fight unfold, stepped back, unseen, into the shadows of the doorway.

"In the end, he won easily," he told Odell later. "He was fast, clever and cunning. If he fights like that when we make landfall on this voyage, he'll be one of the best."

"What do you think made the difference?" Odell asked.

Orm shrugged, less concerned with the why of the affair than of its results. "If you tease and poke a bear cub, one day it will turn and rend you," he said.

CHAPTER
FIFTEEN

Erin

Present Day, New Zealand

ERIN STOOD IN FRONT OF THE long mirror in their bedroom. Her hands stroked her belly. "Wouldn't you think something would show by now?" she asked Luke. "Do you think I'm getting fatter?"

Luke shook his head as he studied his wife. He liked to see her naked. "Nothing is showing yet." His eyes narrowed. "If anything, you look as if you've lost weight. You are eating properly, aren't you? Remember you're supposed to be eating for two."

"That's pretty much a myth," Erin scoffed. "The doctor told me not to believe it. I don't want to end up fat after I've had the baby, and I've heard that if you're fat during pregnancy, it sticks on like a limpet afterwards."

"Yeah, but you don't want to get too thin. It's not the time to go on a diet." Luke frowned. "What have you eaten today?"

"I'm fine." Erin was impatient. "Truly, I'm not dieting or

anything silly."

"Have you lost weight?"

"A bit," she admitted. "But it's not significant. The doctor said that could happen, what with morning sickness and so on. It's still early days, remember."

"But you haven't had morning sickness." Luke's tone was flat.

"No, thank heavens, and I should be past the time it kicks in. At least I've been spared that. Maybe I'm a bit pickier with my food? After all, I'm not supposed to eat a whole lot of yummy things—no prawns, ham, cheese. Wouldn't anyone lose weight?"

Luke shrugged. "All I'm saying is look after yourself. I'm just concerned."

Erin gave a taut smile. "For me, or the baby?"

"What? For you, of course." He pulled her into his arms. "You are OK, aren't you? Only you've been pretty wound up recently."

She relaxed against him. Maybe he was right, and she'd been taking everything too seriously. If only she could get enough sleep, she'd be right. "I'm fine," she reassured him, "and we'll be late if I don't get dressed."

⁂

"How's the mum-to-be?" Fergal hugged Erin.

"Well, thank you. Hi, Brianna. You guys picked a great day for a picnic."

"Not bad, eh? It's been an incredible summer."

Luke dumped the bags, and Erin busied herself spreading their rugs out.

"Has anyone been in yet?" Luke asked, looking at the river.

"Nah, I dipped my toe in, but it was freezing," said Brianna.

"Maybe when the sun gets a bit higher," replied Fergal. "We can't come to a picnic and not swim."

Erin pushed a folded towel under her head for a pillow and stretched out across the rugs with a sigh of contentment. "That'll do for me. I'm happy just to soak up the sun," she said.

"Me, too," Brianna agreed.

"Pack of sissies," said Luke. "Are you on for a swim, Fergal?"

"If you two can watch the fire for me while I'm gone?" asked Fergal.

Brianna nodded. "I'll keep an eye on it. Is that billy hot enough for coffee yet?"

"Should be," he said as he pulled off his shirt. "Give it a try."

The women watched Luke and Fergal pick their way over the stones. Two enormous splashes broke the surface of the deep pool as they dive-bombed into the water.

Luke roared as he surfaced. "Christ, but it's fucking freezing."

"Why can't guys ever just walk quietly into the water?" Erin asked. "You don't catch women chucking themselves about like that."

Brianna laughed. "Dunno. It's a bloke thing, I guess." She lifted the lid off the billy. "Do you want a hot drink? The water's boiling."

"Thanks, coffee would be great."

"So, how's the pregnancy going?"

"Great. You know, you were right about the gender. It is a boy."

"Ah," Brianna wrinkled her nose. "Well, I guess there was a 50 per cent chance either way. Nice to know I got it right."

Erin propped herself up on an elbow and frowned as Brianna handed her the coffee. "I thought you said sometimes you just knew things? That sounded like something more than just a lucky guess."

Brianna looked wary. "I shouldn't have said anything. I felt bad after that evening. I thought I'd upset you."

"But you did say it Did you mean it?"

"I shouldn't have said anything," Brianna repeated. "It made you uncomfortable, and it was none of my business anyway."

"Fergal seemed to believe you." Erin refused to be deflected.

Brianna smiled. "He's a good man." She looked across to where Luke and Fergal were now diving into the pool from a boulder. "Look at them, like a pair of kids splashing about."

"I just wondered if there was anything else you knew."

Briana sighed. "Like what? What do you want to know? I'm

not a fortune teller."

"Yeah, I understand that. You told us as much." Erin dipped her head in embarrassment. "It's just, I've had bad dreams, and I've come to wonder whether they're related to me being pregnant."

Brianna's gaze sharpened. "What sort of dreams?"

"Nasty ones. It's like a movie, and always the same thing. There's fire, a lot of it, and a woman screaming. The worst thing is that I'm not just seeing it, I feel as if I'm there and part of it, and in my dream I'm terrified of what's happening. I wake up soaked in sweat with my heart pounding. It's horrible."

"That doesn't sound good," Brianna said cautiously.

"So now, of course, I'm permanently tired, and yet I'm scared to shut my eyes and go to sleep."

"You said you thought it was because you're pregnant?"

"It sounds silly if you say it out loud," Erin admitted. "It was just a guess. I've never had nightmares before—at least nothing like this."

"And you wondered whether I knew anything that could explain it?"

"Something like that. Don't get me wrong, I'm a dyed-in-the-wool sceptic. No ghosts or ghoulies for me. But I couldn't help wondering whether there was a connection, and if so, what it meant." She bit her lip. "I suppose that means I'm more credulous than I've ever admitted to myself."

Brianna gave a soft chuckle. "So are most people. Just watch the atheists pray when their plane looks as if it might crash."

"No," she said after a pause, "I haven't 'seen' anything that could help you, but …" She sat back on her heels, staring at Erin.

"But what?"

"When I first met you, I knew you were one of the special people. No," she cut Erin off as she tried to interrupt, "I don't mean that as a compliment. It's just that sometimes, with a very few people, I feel a sort of resonance."

Erin felt herself slump. Even though she knew she was silly, she'd pinned her hopes on Brianna's feyness to help with the dreams.

"You know how you can run a finger around the rim of a glass and get a tone out of it?" Brianna continued. "It's not an accurate description, but it's the closest I can get to describing what happens. It's how I knew you were carrying a boy." She combed her fingers through her hair in frustration. "You understand I can't control, channel or monitor what comes, but you're someone who can project information to me. I haven't got an answer to explain your dreams, but something may trigger that connection. If it does, I'll tell you."

"Oh well, it was worth a try." Erin climbed to her feet, already trying to distance herself. It wasn't often she allowed herself to be vulnerable. The whole conversation had been a mistake. "Thanks for letting me witter on about it, anyway. Let's forget it. Why don't we go for a swim?"

The shock of cold water soon washed away Erin's embarrassment, and by the time the four of them had swum and returned to the bank, the moment had receded far enough away for her to put it behind her.

They nibbled on cherry tomatoes, stuffed olives and chips while Fergal took charge of the cooking. Brianna and the men had a beer, while Erin sipped on soda water.

She lay back and allowed herself to drift. Somewhere in the background, Fergal and Luke were talking. Across the rug, Brianna was also lying quietly. Erin could hear fantails and other birds in the trees around them. Close by, a shining cuckoo called out. Bliss, she thought, as she let her eyelids fall, and relaxed for what felt like the first time in weeks.

All too soon, Fergal called out, "Lunch is ready!" and woke her.

She stood up and went over to help.

The men had been busy. Luke was unwrapping small loaves of garlic bread while Fergal forked succulent steaks and pieces of chicken onto a large platter.

Erin sniffed appreciatively. "Mmm, yum," she began.

It was like being hit in the stomach. No sooner had she properly registered the fragrant smell of barbecued meat than her stomach lurched uncontrollably with a wave of nausea. She clapped a hand to her mouth in dismay. "Oh God, I'm going to be sick," she exclaimed in horror as her stomach convulsed. She dashed away to a secluded spot behind some bushes.

By the time Luke joined her, she had vomited up everything she'd eaten that day, and probably the day before.

"Jesus, Erin, are you OK?"

Erin was wobbling; her legs felt weak. "Probably, maybe. I don't know," she said. "It just hit me."

"Is this some sort of morning sickness thing, or should we go to the hospital?" Luke asked.

"Dunno. I don't think it's morning sickness." Erin straightened up. "Shit, that was horrible."

"What caused it? Have you eaten something you shouldn't?"

She shook her head. "It was the smell. That awful smell of burning, cooking flesh. It was unbearable."

Luke stared at her. "Cooking f-? Oh. Do you mean the barbecue? That's not like you. You're usually up for a good barbie."

Erin shook her head, unable to share the horror the smell had evoked.

"Come on, let's get you back to the others. They'll be worried." He held out his hand and she took it wordlessly.

With the other, she gestured towards the pool of vomit splattered on the ground. "I should clean…"

Luke shook his head. "It's OK. I'll tip some water over it. Come on, you need to sit down. I'll get you a glass of water to rinse your mouth." He led her back to the clearing and settled her down on the rug. "Do you think you should go to the doctor?"

Erin shook her head, too weary to discuss it. She wouldn't be sick again, but nausea hung, a lead weight in her stomach, even though much of the barbecue smell had faded. Even with her eyes shut, she could feel the others staring at her like a freak.

"Sorry, Fergal," she said at last, opening her eyes and seeing his worried face. "You did such a great job on the cooking, and I completely wasted it. It looks as if I might have to be vegetarian for the rest of the pregnancy."

"No worries," Fergal said. "We're just concerned that you're

OK. Is this sort of thing normal?"

Erin had recovered enough to be amused by the male panic in his voice. Surely his job ferrying injured passengers to hospital after accidents had toughened him up? Apparently, even hard men were disconcerted by women's biological mysteries.

"I think anything's normal when you're preggers." Erin gave a faint smile. "Sorry to have been a pain." She shut her eyes again.

Luke and Fergal were quietly discussing whether she should go to the hospital. She felt the rug move beside her as Brianna sat down, but apparently, she felt no need to talk.

Erin felt herself falling. For a moment she was terrified, sensing the endless pit opening beneath her. Then she felt gentle fingers grasp her wrist and hold her, tethering her to safety and reality. She gave a soft, whimpering sigh and slept.

CHAPTER SIXTEEN

Ciarnat

Ninth Century, Ireland

"HE'S ALREADY GONE," GRAN TOLD HER when Ciarnat climbed down the ladder from the loft where she slept.

"Gone? He's left? Da's gone? Without me?" Ciarnat's voice rose in disbelief. Filan wouldn't have left her. Not without discussing it, seeking her opinion, considering her point of view. That was the way things were between them.

Gran shook her head. "I told him he should have stayed and talked to you, but he'd not be moved. Told me it was time you had a more secure home. Then he left at first light. I think he was afraid to face you."

Ciarnat stared at the woman in front of her. Gran was tall, Ciarnat's height, and slender, if you were complimentary. Others would describe her as wiry—just as everyone agreed she was tough. If age had limited her physically, it wasn't apparent, and nothing in her demeanour indicated anything but fierce independence, intelligence and resilience.

Although Ciarnat was blind to it, there was a strong resemblance between Gran, her son and granddaughter. Not in looks, but in their fierce realism and refusal to compromise. Sarcasm and a profound disinclination to tolerate fools were the more obvious of their shared traits.

"I don't believe it," Ciarnat exclaimed. "He'd never have willingly gone without me." She'd been betrayed. She cast around for a reason, and it was easy to pin the blame on the woman in front of her. "It was you, wasn't it? You made him leave me here. What did you say? That you needed a companion in your old age?"

A flicker of anger crossed the older woman's face. "Don't be insolent, even if you are upset." She drew up a stool beside the table and sat down. "When your mother died, I urged your da to leave you with me, that's true enough. You were a little girl, and I thought it would be best for you. Your da decided otherwise. But I had nothing to do with his decision this time."

"You must have. Why else would Da have done it? I'll go after him. I won't stay here. You can't make me." Ciarnat was almost panting the words out in her distress. She paced around the floor.

Gran shook her head. "I can't stop you, that's for certain." She calmly watched Ciarnat stride from one side of the room to the other. "But think before you rush after him. What made him suddenly choose to leave you here? Did something happen that changed his mind about keeping you with him?"

Ciarnat paused in her pacing and stared at Gran. "No," she answered automatically. Then she corrected herself. "Well, aye, something did happen, but I can't see why that would change things between us."

"So?" Gran required an answer. "What went wrong?"

Ciarnat looked away, reluctant at first to disclose so much to a woman in so many ways unknown to her, but Gran was persistent.

"I was attacked," she began. Haltingly she described her short friendship with Rian, Ultán's assault on her and Rian's tragic death as he defended her. Although she didn't specifically mention it, the sense she was responsible was apparent throughout. Her voice caught at the end, Rian's death still too close and raw for her to discuss easily. Her eyes filled with tears, and she looked away as she struggled to compose herself.

Gran sat in silence for some moments, apparently deep in thought. To her relief, Ciarnat's report confirmed what Filan had already told her. She'd needed to hear the girl's version and check nothing worse had happened to her granddaughter—a point she'd been uncertain of from Filan's description of events.

"So," she said at last, "it would seem your da was sufficiently worried about what happened to decide you would be safer here. I am not saying he's right, mark you, but I can understand him."

"He had no right to make such a decision without talking to me." Ciarnat was angry and adamant.

"Ah, 'rights'." Gran breathed out heavily and looked at the stormy face of the girl across from her. "Your da has every right to decide your life—from where you live, to whom you marry. He's your father. It's the law, and I think you know that full well. Filan may have led you to believe the rules were different for you, but they are not."

"You can't make me stay," Ciarnat stated.

"I have no intention of trying. When you get over feeling sorry for yourself, I rely on your good sense to decide for you. You are my much-loved granddaughter and always welcome in my home." She gave a wry smile. "This won't be an easy transition for us, but we will make it work." Gran stood up. "Now, if you stay, you need to understand you work for your keep each day, as I do. This house and the lands are your da's, and it's our job to keep it in fine fettle for him. I will expect you to do your fair share."

It took Ciarnat time, and she would never acknowledge Gran was right, but there *was* no realistic alternative for her. Da had left her with Gran, so here she would have to stay. But the concession was bitter.

She'd been betrayed. There was no other more comfortable word for what her father had done. After years of believing herself essential, she'd been abandoned, like a set of old clothes. The more she probed the wound of his leaving, the clearer it was he'd judged her responsible for Rian's death and punished her accordingly. As if she wasn't bearing a heavy enough burden of guilt herself. She was devastated. For years, Da had been her lodestone. Now, faced with clear evidence of his bleak judgement on her conduct, she was bereft.

He'd walked, free and whole, back to the life they'd shared for six years, leaving her in the care of a woman she hardly knew.

What about her music? It had been central to her life, and now she had no harp, no teacher and no opportunity to train her voice or practise her instrument. She mourned for that nearly as much as she did for her father.

In the place of music were any number of petty rules she had to learn. There seemed no reason behind them, and they chafed her terribly.

Ciarnat was used to freedom—and with that, she'd clearly understood, came responsibilities she'd willingly accepted. Now she was forced into a life of few adult responsibilities and almost no freedom.

There were the daily chores: feeding chickens, milking the cow, cleaning out stalls, hanging out washing, baking, churning butter, setting curds for cheese, weaving, spinning, laundry— the list was endless—and Ciarnat had never been taught the skills needed so was frequently scolded for her efforts. Just this morning Gran had watched critically as she'd struggled to make her spindle twist a smooth skein of thread from the carded sheep's wool.

"Gentle with your hands, child!" Gran exclaimed. "Goodness me, I had it in mind you would find this task, at least, easy. Your fingers must be supple after all that harp playing. Instead, I swear Padraig and his sons could make a better fist of it than this cobbled mess of knots and lumps."

Ciarnat dropped her eyes so Gran wouldn't see the hurt anger in them. Impossible to retort that almost certainly the hard calluses on her fingertips caused by years of harp practice were catching on the fibres and contributing to her difficulties in spinning a smooth strand. Why could the old woman never give her credit for trying?

Equally frustrating, she found herself constrained by unexpected practices. Women, young women at least, were forbidden from several things Ciarnat had taken for granted. In Gran's world, modesty and submission were applauded. Being too independent and outspoken was unsuitable, taken for insolence and probably disobedience.

Ciarnat noted that few of these rules applied to Gran. Gran did what she wanted without fear of criticism from anyone—not from the poor parish priest she terrified, nor the elderly patient in love with her nor the young mother whose fears she soothed. None were allowed to dictate to Gran.

Gran, it seemed, was beyond the confines and rules she intended to impose on Ciarnat. When questioned, Gran told her to respect her elders. Reared to respect logic, Ciarnat couldn't help but roll her eyes at the flaws in Gran's argument.

The good manners her father had taught her, her guilt and mourning for Rian, Da's abandonment—all coupled with the realisation that she regularly failed at her tasks—kept Ciarnat silent, miserable and compliant for several weeks.

But trouble was brewing. Neither Ciarnat nor Gran had been prepared for the changes Filan's decision had forced on them. Thrust into an intimacy neither of them had wanted, the cracks in their courtesy quickly showed.

Ciarnat was twelve summers old, and not naïve. Even before Ultán, she'd understood what went on between a woman and a man, and there'd been plenty of times Filan shut himself away and forbade her to enter their room. She'd obeyed, of course. But that hadn't stopped her hanging around their chamber door to watch her father farewell yet another woman.

It took Ciarnat precisely two weeks to recognise that Gran's resistance to her presence had much to do with Padraig, the cattleman. She could have shrugged her shoulders and ignored them, but Gran had chosen that particular day to lecture her on modesty, submission to the Church, and the importance of virtue and virginity.

Ciarnat had had enough. She listened, head bowed to hide her anger, waiting until the older woman had finished, in apparent submission to Gran's lecture. "May I ask a question?"

Gran was surprised. Ciarnat had so far resisted any guidance. Most of Gran's orders and advice had gone unheeded. She nodded. "Of course."

Ciarnat drew a breath. "At what age do these rules no longer apply to women?" she asked. "I've observed they don't apply to men, and they don't seem to apply to you, either. So how old do you have to be to choose your path, take your lover—as you have with Padraig—and live on your own terms?"

She was both delighted and frightened to see Gran gasp and turn pale, shortly followed by an angry flush across her cheekbones. Suddenly Ciarnat was absurdly close to tears. She rarely felt like a child, but this conversation was taking all her courage and had her shaking with nerves, although she wasn't prepared to back down. She was willing enough to play a role, if that's what Gran wanted, when they walked weekly to the village church, but she wasn't prepared to listen to lies and evasions presented as a virtue.

Gran's eyes flickered sideways, trying to avoid her gaze as she sought to regain control. Her lips were pressed tightly together in a narrow line.

"I speak nothing that isn't the truth," Ciarnat asserted remorselessly.

"You insolent brat," Gran began, clearly beginning to build to a full diatribe about her granddaughter's imperfections.

"You can't deny it. It's true," Ciarnat said, sharply cutting off whatever angry remark Gran was about to make.

Gran opened her mouth, met her granddaughter's steely stare and relented. She sighed. "Aye, I forget how differently Filan raised you," she said at last, shaking her head. "I suppose it's useless to try and fight that. You understand things beyond your age, even though most five-year-olds would be more useful around the house."

Ciarnat gave a small nervous chuckle as her gran continued to study her.

"Sit down. We need to talk," she told Ciarnat. "Not about Padraig," she added hastily. "Yes, he's my lover and has been for some years. No, you may not ask me about him."

"It seems, after all, we're much alike," Gran told her granddaughter. "I wasn't certain about that. Your mother came to us as a stranger when Filan wed her. She was lovely, sweet, pretty and kind." Gran's lips quirked. "All the qualities I've tried to teach you these last weeks and failed."

An unwilling smile came from Ciarnat. Good, thought Gran, at least the girl's honest, aware and has a sense of humour.

"Filan loved your mother dearly. When she died, he was lost for a while. Then he saw your latent talent and fell in love with it and with you. The rest you know. You've spent the last few years with him. But you are not your mother and not, I think, very like her at all."

Gran stood up to fetch a folded paper. Ciarnat already knew about Gran's store of herbs she kept for treating the sick. "We never know how these things will run," she resumed. "A bitch will have a litter of pups and some favour the dam, some the sire. I've asked the priest why, but he has no answer for this. Says it is the will of his God."

"Is it?" Ciarnat was curious.

Gran gave a scornful sniff. "Maybe." She paused as she drew the kettle onto the flames. "Padraig says good stockmen have always known that when you want to breed quality, you look to the sire's dam. Male animals, although perhaps outstanding in themselves, will not reproduce that in the next generation. Instead, if they breed daughters, it is they who pass that greatness to their foals and calves. That progeny will have all the excellence of the dam's sire as well as her own strength and courage. Padraig swears he's proved it true many times in breeding cattle and horses. Perhaps people are like that."

The water began to bubble, and Gran tipped in a scoop of herbs.

"In our family—from grandfather to mother, to son to granddaughter—the bloodline runs straight and true through us, just as I inherited it from my granddam. All proud, all independent women and not easily constrained or bullied." Gran stirred the mess in the kettle. "You notice I didn't list virtue, sweetness, gentleness or kindness, although I don't despise them," she said. "Our priest and I disagree on this. He wants to win our souls to his God with virtue and godliness. He sees a heaven of kind, gentle people, all doing good things. I think that would be a nightmare. Boring, mediocre and very inefficient. Human beings need challenges. I don't like ineffectual people, particularly women. I claim strength and purpose will achieve God's heaven faster, and the gentle sheep in his congregation will always be prey to the wolves of this world unless those who are stronger protect them."

She poured a mug of infusion from the kettle. "Here," she handed it to Ciarnat. "I want you to drink it."

"Why?" asked Ciarnat.

"Because I want to see your future and what you will need to meet it."

The brew was too hot, so Ciarnat put it on the table. "So, what you're saying is that I will carry babies that inherit my da's music? Is that what I am? A carrier?" She frowned at the steaming liquid in the mug. "Is that all I am?"

"Partly," Gran replied. "In some measure, it's what we all are. We are born, we live, breed and die."

"That's it?" Ciarnat had never thought in such terms before. The bleak vision of her future appalled her.

"Of course not, you silly child." Gran was amused. "In between, we fill the spaces with love and laughter, music, poetry and all the magic and richness we infuse into our lives. The gift of learning is ours to use as wisely as we can. At least I believe our priest when he tells me that God gave us free will to make or mar our lives."

She sat down opposite Ciarnat. "Think for a moment. Your da, Filan, was an ordinary boy. His father, my husband, was a fisherman. We were ordinary folk. But *my* father had been a poet, although Filan soon outstripped him in skill and learning. It makes sense to me that my father passed his talent to his grandson. Even more so when you know my great-grandsire was a Druid." She leaned forward to press her point. "And if that holds true and women pass their sire's talents forward, think about the female line. Perhaps strong women pass their strength through to their granddaughters."

There was a wry twist to Gran's mouth. "Our priest, of course, would call me presumptuous for these thoughts and tell me that God decides our talents at birth. But when I deliver a baby, sometimes it's obvious that it takes after neither the mother nor the father. Blood never lies."

She smiled at her granddaughter. "Now drink up, and let's see what lies in store for you."

CHAPTER
SEVENTEEN

CIARNAT SCREWED HER FACE UP BUT drank the brew obediently. To her relief, it didn't taste too bad. She thought she detected a woody scent mixed with the green tang of fresh herbs. She tilted the mug back to drain it, only to feel leaves against her lips and teeth. "Ugh," she spluttered, pulling the mug away before she could swallow them.

"Don't drink the leaves," Gran said. "I need them."

"You could have warned me they were there," Ciarnat said, picking the last of them from her teeth.

"That will teach you to be more careful," Gran said unsympathetically. "Here, pass it to me."

Ciarnat handed it across and watched curiously while Gran slowly swirled the dregs around. It took a while before she realised Gran's gestures were deliberately slow and ritualistic, and she was reciting something under her breath.

Gran pulled the wooden chopping board over and tipped the contents of the mug onto it. Leaves fell in an untidy spread over the wood and liquid ran across the board and table, dripping to the floor below.

Ciarnat automatically rose to fetch a clout to mop it up.

"Sit down, girl," Gran snapped. "Don't interrupt while I'm

doing a reading."

Ciarnat threw herself back onto her seat and watched impatiently while Gran slowly turned the board, studying the leaves from every angle. At one point, her eyebrows rose sharply, and she glanced across at her granddaughter before returning to the leaves in front of her. At last, with a sigh, she pushed the board away and sat back.

"What does it say?"

Gran tilted her head. "The leaves don't *say* anything as such. They are a guide, no more, to your future. Whether it comes to pass is partially up to you and the decisions you make along the way."

"Well, what does it indicate then?"

"Are you sure you want to know?"

Ciarnat was nearly beside herself with frustration. "Aye, who wouldn't want to know?"

"Sensible folk," said Gran. She gave a slight smile as Ciarnat scowled. "All right. The leaves show me a girl who is strong and complex and will grow into an interesting woman. They fell into strongly defined patterns, which indicates both the strength of your personality and the probability of the shapes and patterns being true."

"But what do they promise?"

"Promise? There's nothing promised. You will need to be bold because your fate is also strong and complex. You will love and be loved. You will experience hardship." Gran gave a fatalistic shrug. "But all this is some years away. In the meantime, written more finely on the outer perimeter of the leaves, is that you are, by nature, a healer. As am I. You'll come out with me from now on when I see patients, and I'll teach you all I know."

Ciarnat stared at Gran. "Is that all the leaves tell you?"

What an anti-climax. Whatever the leaves foretold, she didn't feel at all like a healer—she was a minstrel.

Gran stood and turned away as she scraped the leaves into the compost bucket. She hid her face as she bent to her task. Not for the worlds would she have told her granddaughter just how ominous the reading had been.

CHAPTER EIGHTEEN

Thorkell

Ninth Century, Ireland

IT HAD BEEN TWO WEEKS SINCE they rowed away from Ormsfjord. Soon they'd reach land and the fighting would begin.

Thorkell wondered when, and who, would be his first kill. There had been that moment when it could well have been Asger, but his tormentor had since backed off and, although civil enough, spoke little to him now. They were crewmates forced to cooperate on board, Orm's discipline saw to that, but otherwise giving each other a wide berth.

Thorkell had come to understand Hagen had been correct. Asger disliked him, Thorkell could think of nothing he'd done to offend him, or why the friendly uncle of his boyhood should have changed. But there it was, and now that Asger had lost his power over him, it didn't bother Thorkell over much.

A few days later, Hagen perched beside him on Thorkell's sea chest to share their morning meal. If the older hands were right, they'd make landfall that evening and, all going well, their first raid would be in the dim pre-light of tomorrow's dawn. "I'll be glad to have dry land under my feet again," Hagen grumbled.

Thorkell smiled. He didn't share Hagen's feelings. He'd felt nothing but joy since they'd left their home fjord. Given the freedom of choice, he thought, he'd have kept the *Sea Serpent* heading westward forever. He loved the feel of the planks flexing beneath his feet, allowing his body to move with the longship. He exalted as she leaned into a breeze or when the wind shifted, could barely control his excitement when she ran fast and true like a wild horse with the wind behind her and the waves slapping at her sides.

They'd met with rain and rough weather on this journey, of course, but he hadn't been afraid. Tucked beneath the cover of the sail they'd lowered to shelter them, he'd felt as warm and protected as he had in his father's hall.

He knew the purpose of this voyage was to plunder as much treasure as they could find and bring it safely back home. The sailing and the fighting were fun, but winning trade goods was their purpose.

The first trader of the season had come into their fjord some days before the crew were ready to leave. Thorkell's new-found familiarity with the *Sea Serpent* made him appreciate the differences between her and the trading knörr.

Broader and heavier than a longship, the cargo ship was designed to carry freight. Orm and its captain haggled over the value of the furs, gold and slaves for two nights before reaching an agreement.

"Where's it going to?" Hagen asked the next day.

"The trader claims to be heading for the Far East. There's a big market for our slaves there apparently. If you mean where's he sailing next, he mentioned Hafrsfjord. From there he heads through the Skagerrak. He was talking to Orm about the possibility of pirates as he passes through the islands there."

Loading had begun, and Thorkell watched slaves from the previous year's raids, the girl Hagen had spent the winter with among them, being herded on board for the long journey to the markets of the East.

"It'll be us leaving here soon. Excited?" Hagen broke in on his thoughts.

Thorkell gave a wry grin. "I suppose so. It's hard to imagine what it will be like. The first time for something is always difficult, but I imagine we'll be fine. I'll just follow Orm."

In the event, when Orm set the orders for the first raid, Hagen and Thorkell were directed to go with Gunnar. A sea mist was clinging to the shore, and the *Sea Serpent* was low enough in the water that anyone watching from shore would be unlikely to see them.

Orm spoke softly as the men gathered round. "I'll take twenty men—you Asger, Harald, who else? Get yourselves sorted. We'll take their church. The rest of you go with Gunnar and search the settlement. You know what we're seeking. Gold, jewellery, money. Anything valuable. If you see a likely captive, take them. If anyone resists, kill them."

They stopped rowing and shipped oars some distance from the line of surf to avoid any splash from the blades giving them away. The *Sea Serpent* was positioned in the water so waves and tide carried her to shore. Rune stood on the stern, guiding the rudder to keep them on course. They beached and ran the ship onto the sand. There was a brief check to secure the ship, with Rune staying to guard her.

The small church stood on a rise above the beach, and Orm and his men headed straight for it, scrambling up the dunes. Gunnar led his party further left, rounding the spit of sand. From there they could see the small group of houses clustered in the shelter of the dunes. The church stood on the rise above them.

Thorkell heard Gunnar chuckle. "Here we go, lads," and he drew his sword and charged forward. Then they were all running, their feet pounding on the flat sandy beach as they raced towards the buildings.

Thorkell felt a surge of excitement. It was exhilarating to be part of that wild rush. He glanced briefly at the men around him and saw they were all grinning. Thorkell realised he was doing the same.

Shouts came from the hill above them. They'd been seen. Men were running up the crest of the hill towards the church. Thorkell heard the bell ring twice before it fell silent.

Ahead of him, a house loomed. It was still too dark to see much, and Thorkell paused. There was someone in the doorway and Thorkell swerved as they came rushing at him.

Something sharp snagged his side, scratching him and tearing his tunic as he twisted away. He turned and brought his axe down hard. His attacker died instantly.

There was no time to think. Other houses, other defenders had to be taken care of—time enough, when they were subdued, to take stock. If there was treasure to find, it was still too dark to see it.

Thorkell turned and ran on. At one point he found Hagen beside him.

Hagen shouted and pointed.

A small group of defenders had banded together. One had a torch. Thorkell shook his head. What a stupid mistake. It made it easier to see and identify them. They only had one sword and a few cudgels between them. The man with the sword stepped forward. His sword wobbled as he held it out, and Thorkell felled him with one blow before turning to the others. One more tried to hit him with a stave, but when Hagen killed him, the rest fled.

Suddenly it was over. Upon the hill the church was engulfed in fire, throwing light and twisting shadows across the village. The men regrouped around Gunnar and stood watching as flames climbed the steeple. A framework of black timber stood for some minutes, silhouetted against the fiery backdrop, before collapsing.

Gunnar grunted in satisfaction. "That's their God destroyed. What sort of people worship a dead man? No wonder they're so useless in a fight."

Down among the houses, it was quiet, the silence punctuated by their own heavy breathing, and an occasional sob or moan from the wounded and dying.

"Is everyone here?"

"Looks like it," one of the men replied.

As Thorkell recognised Feng, he realised dawn had broken. It was now light enough to make out his surroundings.

"Any injuries?" Gunnar asked. No injuries. "Well done," he said. "Let's look around and find out what we've earned this morning. You two, come with me. Look in there and show me what you find," Gunnar instructed Thorkell and Hagen.

The hut was dry and well maintained, but after checking along the shelves and sorting through the few old garments in the chest, it was evident they weren't going to find anything worth taking.

Gunnar snorted when they relayed the information. "*Nei*. It's a bigger place than the others. Probably belonged to the chieftain. Of course, there's going to be something. Let me show you how to search. Lift the hearthstone."

He pointed at a patch of coloured earth. "Dig there," he ordered. Sure enough, a small pouch with a few coins was hidden. "Sometimes," Gunnar explained, "if they plan long enough ahead, they'll bury their valuables then soak the whole area with water, so it all dries together. The earth then all looks the same, and there are no give away marks like this. Now we check the roof." He grinned with excitement. For Gunnar, this was nought more than a game. A quest with knotty problems to be solved. "Check the thatch. You would be surprised what can be hidden there." He continued showing them places where small items could be concealed—behind a loose knot in a timbered beam; beneath a loose stone in the foundation; under a flagstone. "Put yourselves in their shoes. Where would you hide your valuables? Try and think like them."

It wasn't much, but the house had yielded coins, a hidden dagger and a thin golden torc. Thorkell added it to the pile the men were making on the ground outside.

"Orm's back!" came a yell from one of the other houses.

Thorkell looked up to see his father striding down the slope towards them. Asger carried a sack which he swung off his shoulder when he reached their treasure pile.

"It's a piss poor village," Orm said disparagingly, "but the church had a few things of value. Look at this." He held up church plate, a fine gold goblet, a platter, metal statues and some crucifixes. "Add this to what you've taken and it's not too bad for the first morning's work," he said with pleasure. "Find some food and drink. We'll eat back at the ship."

Thorkell picked up one of the objects from the church and studied it. "Why is this man tied up? No, nailed up?" he asked curiously. "What does it mean? Do they worship this?"

"Who knows?" Gunnar answered. "If he's their God, he doesn't protect them very well. I've heard tell he's dead, and they eat his body and drink his blood."

"Thor!" Thorkell recoiled in disgust and dropped the crucifix. "What savages."

Orm strolled through the village, stopping to check the fallen. "Cut his throat," he said, indicating one man still clinging to life, although a sword thrust had pierced his belly. Asger made a neat slice across the man's neck.

Thorkell was grateful he hadn't been the one asked. It was one thing to kill when your blood was up, or your life depended on it. He wasn't confident he would be able to do it on such a casually made request.

Other warriors were doing the same to the fallen. The living had fled.

"Should we follow them?" Gunnar asked.

Orm shook his head. "It's early in the season, and they won't be worth it."

Thorkell turned aside at the hut where he'd made his first kill. To his surprise, his father followed him. They stood looking at the boy that lay crumpled on the ground.

"Your first?" asked Orm.

Thorkell nodded. "Aye." Someone had to be first, he thought, but he still felt a stab of pity for the lad, probably younger than himself and armed only with a pitchfork. He remembered the cut on his rib. It must have been a tine that caught him.

"You'll get used to it," Orm said, reading his thoughts. "But you always remember the first, and it's good that you honour his death." Orm bent, covered his fingers with the boy's blood and striped it on Thorkell's cheeks. He smiled at his son. "Now you're a blooded warrior. You're truly one of us."

When they reached the longship, Thorkell saw Hagen's cheeks were also marked. The crew, even Asger, made a point of congratulating them on their new status, and toasts were drunk to the new warriors in the band.

Hagen grinned across at Thorkell. They'd both done well, his grin said. Thorkell smiled back—only he knew the relief the grin hid because he felt the same.

CHAPTER NINETEEN

FOR THE REST OF THE SUMMER, the *Sea Serpent* worked her way along the western side of the island. Whenever they saw a likely target, they beached the ship and attacked it. Churches were a rich source of treasure; many situated close to the coastline and convenient for a roving band of warriors. Monasteries, smaller towns and hamlets were sacked whenever they found them.

Thorkell soon came to understand his first raid had been unusually mild and suspected Orm arranged it merely for the new crew to be blooded. Later engagements were bloodier and more brutal.

The villagers often outnumbered the band, but the Viking's reputation outran them in the small settlements along the coastline. Fear and panic usually defeated the inhabitants before Orm's crew even landed. Resistance was useless against forty battle-seasoned warriors, and putting up a fight encouraged the raiders to be more violent. Only that morning Thorkell had watched Asger as he stood over a plump, middle-aged man found cowering behind a large millstone.

"Where's your money?" Asger asked, his sword at the man's throat. "Show me where it's hidden."

The miller wept and shook his head. He might not have understood Asger's words, but he comprehended the intent and showed Asger the pouch at his belt, empty but for a crust of bread and a lump of cheese. He was shaking, his tunic soiled with his terror.

Asger snorted in impatience. "I'll swear you are hiding something," he said and turned to reach into the small fire burning by the door.

Thorkell, sure the man had nothing, looked away to where Hagen was searching through the thatch.

A scream brought him sharply around to see Asger had plunged a burning twig deep into the man's right eye. He writhed and shrieked out his agony, his hands clutching at his face.

Asger kicked him lightly in the ribs. "I ask again, where are you hiding your treasure?"

An incoherent babble burst from his victim. Asger looked at him in disgust and bent to pick up another stick from the fire. As he turned back, the burning twig in his grip, the miller yielded and pointed at the ground at the back of the hut. At first glance, nothing gave the cache away, but the man, now frantic to escape further punishment, dug into the soft earth with a sharp stick he grabbed from the pile by the fire. An inch below the surface, the consistency of the soil changed, and it was clear the earth had been disturbed. Eventually, after much digging and scraping, they could see material at the bottom of the hole.

Asger muttered, pushed the man aside and dragged the bundle from the earth. "What have we here?" he asked in satisfaction as he opened the sack and thrust his hand inside. "Finely wrought jewellery, chains, cloak pins. My, my, you have got some nice things here," Asger said, almost chattily, to the maimed man. "Here, Thorkell, take this and add it to our pile."

He passed the bag over, took his sword and slashed the miller's throat. "A pleasure to trade with you," he said, his voice dripping irony as blood flooded the ground.

He looked at Thorkell. "Well, what are you staring at? I said put that sack on the pile."

Thorkell nodded and turned, then stopped. "I really didn't

think he had anything of value," he confessed.

Asger gave a sharp laugh. "It depends on how you ask the question." He bent and wiped his blade on the man's clothing. "This one was a fool. He might have lived if he'd handed it over at the beginning. Watch and learn, boy. It pays to be a hard man."

He *was* learning, thought Thorkell, to whom violence still didn't come easily unless in the heat of battle, then he and his axe became one and killing was a necessity. It took a different sort of determination to cold-bloodedly force a man to obey your will with torture. Later in the season, as summer ripened the barley in the meadows and fruit formed on the trees, Orm began to collect captives. Young adults, male and female, who looked strong and healthy, were marshalled onto the *Sea Serpent* and bound with chains, one to the other.

On those nights, new screams would be heard as the men, fed and rested after a vigorous day fighting, drew lots for the prisoners and took their enjoyment from them.

Orm's orders were specific. The men were entitled to their recreation, but the captives were to be used, not damaged. They were valuable stock to be sold as thralls at the slave market in Dublin or taken across the sea for traders to buy for the markets in Byzantium and other exotic places.

Thorkell won a tall, fair woman some years older than himself and took her, at once gratified by the intense pleasure to be found in a woman's body, but disconcerted that she wept silent tears throughout her ordeal as he sought his release in her flesh. The next day he felt oddly dissatisfied by the experience.

"Is it different if the girl chooses you?" he asked Hagen.

Hagen gave a light shrug. "If they're a thrall, it doesn't matter, does it? Even if you aren't forcing them, they still have to please you. You're the master."

"Ah," Thorkell breathed out slowly. Hagen hadn't mentioned that when he talked of his conquest last winter. Then he'd boasted the girl couldn't resist him.

Hagen gave a sly grin. "A wife might be a different matter. Then she could choose, I suppose, and you might have to please her. But again, marriage is about alliances, so she still has to please her husband."

Thorkell nodded, recognising his friend's practical wisdom.

They turned north and followed the coastline around and down the eastern side to Dublin, where they unloaded the captives on the wooden quay that stretched out from the waterfront. Asger took charge of getting the slaves to the market.

It was the largest town Thorkell had ever seen, and he and Hagen had new coins in their pockets from their share of the spoils. Together they explored the streets and alleys, intrigued by the clusters of buildings—drinking houses, brothels, shops and markets.

They spent the first day sampling produce from the food stalls.

"I don't know about you, but I've had more than enough *tørrfisk*," Hagen said. "I'm beginning to look like one."

Thorkell laughed. Dried cod was a staple of Viking life, but after weeks on the *Sea Serpent*, fresh, hot food was to be relished. The two ate until Thorkell could hardly move.

The next day they were more discerning and went further afield. Orm had warned them to be careful in the rougher areas. 'Not all the natives are pleased we have a place on their land,' he had advised. 'Stay away from narrow lanes and dead ends unless you are with the rest of the crew. It's too easy to get trapped there.'

Thorkell was fascinated by it all. He hadn't realised his people had a base already in this land and it was reassuring to hear his own language spoken. He watched trade going on all around him—buyers and sellers reaching agreements and money changing hands. It was a new concept to him. Goods he'd never seen before were in plentiful supply and all for sale—leather shoes and bags, smoked fish, ambergris, fur, jewellery and slaves.

After a lot of thinking, he chose a finely fashioned knife and sheath from a metal worker. The cost was higher than he'd expected, but the artistry was beautiful and he had the money.

"Do you want me to engrave the blade for you?" the vendor offered. "I'll do it at no extra cost, just tell me what you want."

Thorkell thought. "Can you do Thor's hammer?" he asked at

last.

The vendor smiled. "Of course. Wait a few minutes, and it will be done."

That night Thorkell slid the knife from its sheath and studied the blade. True to promise, Thor's hammer marked the shiny metal forever as his.

They stayed in Dublin long enough for the slaves to be auctioned, the ship to be reprovisioned and the crew to enjoy their recreation.

CHAPTER
TWENTY

WHEN THEY REBOARDED THE SHIP, THORKELL noticed the days becoming shorter and the mornings were noticeably colder.

"We'll do one more sally along the coast," Orm said, "then turn for home before the winter storms sweep down from the north."

There was mumbled assent from the crew. They were refreshed and ready for a scrap. Some had gambled or drunk a large proportion of their earnings away in Dublin and were hopeful of an opportunity to win it back.

Several days later, as the light of a beautiful afternoon flattened towards dusk, they reached the mouth of a wide river. Orm and Rune checked their surroundings carefully. There were sandbanks to avoid, and a marshy area ran along the southern bank. On the northern edge, willows and alders grew down towards the water and hid the land beyond, but there was no sign of human habitation.

The river was wide enough for easy navigation and the *Sea Serpent*'s draught sufficiently shallow for them not to be concerned about her bellying out on a bank.

"We'll pull in here for the night," Orm ordered. "Hagen and

Thorkell, get yourselves ashore and find out what's on the other side of those trees. Go further upstream and see what you can find. Make sure you stay out of sight."

The two were glad enough to clamber up the bank. Getting through the thick wall of trees was tricky, but on the other side, the land gave way to rolling grasslands that stretched alongside the river for as far as they could see.

"We'll climb to the top and look at what's ahead," said Hagen.

"Just keep hidden below the ridgeline," cautioned Thorkell as Hagen jogged across the meadow.

They climbed the low hill and lay on their bellies gazing at the valley beyond. A large herd of cattle grazed peacefully in the basin below them.

The other side of the bowl was steeper, and although they couldn't see over its rim, plumes of smoke were visible, rising straight and true in the still evening air.

"Could be quite a large settlement," Thorkell said quietly. "We'll check it out?" he asked.

It was a foregone conclusion—the trick being to cross the basin before them safely and without being seen. This close to houses, the likelihood of someone being about increased enormously.

"We could go down to the water's edge. There's more shelter against the trees," muttered Hagen.

Thorkell nodded. They glanced to check that no one had come up behind, but the landscape was still empty, and the two worked their way across to the riverbank. At least they would be harder to see against the backdrop of the trees.

Cautiously they crossed the basin, then up its steeper slope on the far side. Here it was easier to crawl under overhanging branches until they reached the ridge.

Thorkell's eyes widened. Below them, and a mile further along, was a significant settlement, the largest he had seen on this trip. A hall stood surrounded by stables, forge, storage and other outbuildings. Smaller huts, bothies and buildings lay beyond the hall. The middle distance was defined by a wooden post-and-rail fence that surrounded the apple garth.

People, both men and women, were moving around, quietly performing their tasks—bringing in linen from the line, feeding chickens, gathering up children and splitting firewood. Several boys kicked a leather ball between them, running from one end of the yard to the other, their progress hampered by the dog playing with them.

The sound of hammering came from the forge. A small group of men waited sociably outside the door.

"Those look like warriors," Hagen hissed.

Thorkell nodded. It was impossible to miss the torcs around the men's necks or their well-muscled bodies. Some wore swords, but it was apparent none were expecting trouble, just relaxing on a pleasant late-summer evening with their friends.

"We have to get back," said Hagen. "We're losing the light."

"A minute more," said Thorkell, committing to memory what he could of the layout of the settlement.

To the right, a road ran down to the river. If there was a bank or pier, it was too far around for him to see. In the other direction, a well-formed road headed north out of the valley and wound through neatly kept fields of oats and barley. Further away, cropped land gave way to rolling wooded hills. "Care to guess how many warriors they've got?" he asked.

Hagen did a tally. "Could be twenty. Equally, twice as many could already be in the hall having a nice drink." He glanced at the light.

Thorkell grunted in satisfaction and wriggled back under the cover of the branches.

They made it back to the *Sea Serpent* as the last light was fading. Scrabbling around through the trees to the riverbank was in the dark, and Hagen swore as a branch slapped his cheek.

"That's all I need," he grumbled, rubbing the spots of blood off his face.

The ship was almost invisible, lying low in the dark water, and Thorkell was grateful they'd known exactly where to find her. With any luck, it meant no one else would chance on her that night.

Orm frowned slightly. "I'm surprised the warriors are here

and not on campaign with their chief, supporting the High King."
He shrugged. "Maybe they're back early for the harvest." Then
his eyes gleamed. "A worthy enemy at last," he said cheerfully.
"You hear that lads? Tomorrow will be a good day. Rest while
you can tonight because we'll be up early to be in position at
sunrise. No fires, of course." He laughed. "There'll be enough
fire tomorrow for us all!"

They agreed to divide the force: the *Sea Serpent*, with a half
crew of twenty, would go upstream to whatever beaching or
docking was available at the settlement; the rest of the crew,
under Asger's command, would retrace the boys' route and
attack from the hill above the hall when the *Sea Serpent* was in
position.

Orm was depending on the fear caused by a warship appearing
on the river distracting the villagers from the danger behind
them.

Thorkell lay down to rest but couldn't sleep. He was familiar
now with the tension before an attack and had seen it work its
way in other men. Some talked or laughed more loudly than
usual, as if celebrating each lovely moment of their precious
lives. Others folded into themselves, developing a quiet calm
and focus.

He thought of the warriors he'd seen lounging around the
smithy today. He'd counted them, and tomorrow some would
die. No one, he thought, dwelt on dying, although going to
Valhalla as a warrior was noble. He wondered what dying was
like for Christians with no such future destination ahead of them.

CHAPTER
TWENTY ONE

THE MORNING WAS OVERCAST. A LOW mist lay along the water. Orm smiled. "We'll be concealed until we reach the village. The gods have already decided in our favour," he declared.

The land-based party, Hagen and Thorkell among them, made their way in the dark across the meadows and climbed the hill behind the settlement.

Thorkell lay on the dew-drenched grass beside Hagen and looked down at the houses below. There was just enough light now to pick them out. He tensed as a door opened and a woman stepped out. She carried a bucket, and they watched as she walked across the courtyard to the cattle yards.

"Milking," muttered Hagen.

Thorkell nodded. His mouth was dry, and he could feel his heart beating. It was always the same. The hardest part of any raid was before the attack commenced. It was a time for fear, for nervousness that told you to run from the fight, to wish you weren't here. A man could become a coward if he listened to the voices in his head. He licked his lips. Soon, he told himself. Soon.

More people were stirring now. Threads of smoke rose above

the huts and hall. Water would be heating, and cooking would have started. A man and boy entered the forge. Another fire lit, judging by the smoke.

Thorkell drummed his fingers on his shield. When would the *Sea Serpent* arrive? What was keeping her? The purpose of the attack was to catch the settlement asleep and unprepared. He huffed under his breath. If they waited much longer, it would be broad daylight.

A dog's bark. Thorkell's head turned to find it. A large hound stood facing the river keeping up a volley of warning barks and growls.

People turned to stare down towards the water, and Thorkell, watching them, saw the moment they realised they were under attack. The quiet morning scene had turned into one of frantic activity. There were panicked shouts. Men rushed from their huts, buckling on swords and grabbing spears. Women gathered up children then stood around uncertainly, in the way, wondering where to go.

Other hounds had joined the first, adding to the commotion. As their owners came up, still adjusting their weapons and jostling to form a shield wall, the dogs went to stand beside their masters—war hounds, loyal, trained for battle, and a fierce enemy in their own right.

"Now!" Asger's command came urgently along the line.

Thorkell scrambled to his feet, tightened his grip on his spear, patted his belt to check his axe was still safe, and then they were off down the hill, the slope giving them speed as they raced towards the melee. He found himself shouting with the rest. "Thor! Thor!"

The fighting was already fierce. Orm's men had engaged with the leading warriors, and the morning rang with war cries, oaths and screams. There was a clash of bodies as Asger's warriors crashed into the fight. It took some time for the defenders to recognise the new threat, and for the first moments, Thorkell was able to wreak damage on men unaware he was behind them.

It was a necessary, indiscriminate slaughter.

Soon enough, men turned to deal with the new onslaught,

while their brethren continued to struggle with Orm.

These were seasoned warriors, not the simple villagers Thorkell was used to dealing with, and they fought fiercely, proudly and with discipline. When one man fell, another stepped forward to take his place. It felt like hewing and hacking at a solid wall.

Thorkell's breath was heavy, his lungs and legs weary and his axe arm ached, but there was no alternative except carry on swinging, warding off, twisting and hacking—again and again, and again.

Beside him, he heard Gunnar yell, but Thorkell was committed to his opponent and couldn't turn. Each stride forward was achieved with pain, and he didn't dare waver.

It felt like they had been fighting for hours when Thorkell suddenly broke through the wall and found himself facing Orm. They almost killed each other before Orm recognised his son and stepped back.

It took longer for Thorkell to realise they'd fought through the opposition, and his axe was perilously close to his father's neck before he withdrew it.

"Ach! It's you!" Orm exclaimed, as he slapped Thorkell on the back, then strode forward, sword raised, into the mess of bodies and dying warriors in front of him.

It was over, and they'd won.

Thorkell had never felt less victorious. He felt intolerably drained, and every bruise, scratch and strain shrieked for attention. If he could, he'd board the *Sea Serpent* and take her out to sea—away from the sounds and sights around him.

The clamour had been unbelievable. Even now, as the noise died, the echoes of it seemed to cling to the surrounding hills.

He followed his father through the ranks of the fallen. Orm had paused, and Thorkell joined him standing beside Gunnar who lay in a pool of blood. He was still alive, but a sword blade had pierced his abdomen.

Orm knelt. "This is not good," he said as he examined the wound.

Thorkell nearly gagged and turned his head away. Gunnar's

bowels were exposed, and the faecal stench was overwhelming.

Gunnar fixed his eyes on Orm. "Please," was all he said.

Thorkell looked up at that.

Orm said nothing, just remained beside his old friend with his head bowed.

"Please," Gunnar whispered again. His hand reached for Orm. "You know what to do," he said as he clasped Orm's hand.

For a long moment, Orm didn't move, then his fingers clenched and he gripped Gunnar's hand tightly for a long time. Slowly he raised his head. His eyes met Gunnar's, and he nodded.

Orm stood up, his movements slow and heavy, his features sad as he intoned the funeral prayer. "Go to your father. Go to your mother and your brothers. Join the line of your people back to the beginning. They are calling you to take your place among them in the hallowed halls of Valhalla, where the brave shall live forever."

Orm raised his sword. The blade fell fast, straight and true across Gunnar's neck, in a line above the torc that protected it. "You were one of the best," Orm whispered to his dead friend. Without another word or backward look, he walked away.

Thorkell stayed, staring at the body after his father had gone. Gunnar had always been kind to him, and now he was dead, killed by his father. He was shocked by the speed of the event. It had never occurred to Thorkell a chief might have to help a friend towards death in such a manner. It made sense, of course. If a horse or hound could be put down to end their suffering, why not a man?

Thorkell went in search of Hagen. They'd run side by side down the hill together, but he hadn't seen him since the battle. He scanned the field again without success. He retraced what he fancied had been his path during the fight, stepping around the bodies of the slain. He recognised one of the fallen men, but there were others of which he had no recollection. Had he killed them himself? He couldn't remember. One man is very like another when they come at you with a drawn sword or an axe.

He'd reached the far side of the battlefield without finding Hagen. Many of the crew had started work, walking among the wounded enemy and dispatching any that still lived. Others had gathered around Gunnar.

Thorkell watched as they lifted him and carried his body reverently to clear ground. Soon another corpse was laid beside him. Thorkell walked across and discovered Feng was also dead. A deep axe blow had left its imprint in his head. At least it wasn't Hagen. Thorkell shook his head sadly and continued his search.

"Are you all right?" Thorkell looked up at Asger and nodded.

"You?" he asked shortly.

"*Já*, thank Thor." The other man spat on the ground. "These bastards killed Gunnar. Did you know?"

Again, Thorkell nodded. Speech seemed to be coming to him very slowly. Actions were simpler. "I'm looking for Hagen," he said after a pause. "Have you seen him?"

Asger shook his head and frowned. "He was close to me at first. I don't remember seeing him since."

"I'll carry on looking."

"Go back to where we started and work from there," suggested Asger.

Thorkell nodded his thanks, too worried about Hagen to say anything else.

The *Sea Serpent*'s crew had won every scrap to date and prospered from each encounter. They would have a celebratory feast as soon as they could afterwards. It had come to seem the proper way of things.

Although he'd realised he could possibly die, he'd never considered his companions might be seriously wounded or killed. Gunnar's and Feng's death had shaken him badly. He couldn't rest until he'd found Hagen.

Bodies were two or three deep in one place on the field. Fighting must have been fierce there, and the corpses were twisted and entangled. They'd been felled in the very moment of trying to strike their opponent, so arms entwined with arms, legs straddled legs, and bodies fallen sideways had blocked retreat. It was there Thorkell found Hagen.

He'd missed him earlier because he'd passed to the north of the pile. Approaching this time on its southern side and scanning more closely, he recognised the metalwork on the belt.

Hagen had died from a spear wound, entering his heart from behind. Likely he'd never seen the man who took his life, thought Thorkell. He must have been too busy fighting the enemy in front of him. The two had died together, Hagen's falling weight having pushed his sword deep into his opponent.

CHAPTER
TWENTY TWO

THEY LABOURED ALL THAT AFTERNOON, scavenging wood and building a pyre for their shipmates. They levelled the wooden walls of the smithy to make an improvised platform. Around this, they piled logs ripped from the walls of the hall and huts. It was dark by the time they set it ablaze. Thorkell stared into the clear night sky, watching the smoke as it trailed up and over the hill. The light of this fire must have been visible for miles.

He wondered what the women and children who'd fled the settlement that morning would think when they saw it. Their men were left unburied where they'd fallen.

Orm had forbidden the crew to move them. "Take what you want from them, but otherwise leave them alone."

Someone had found time to butcher a cattle beast, and the scent of its roasting flesh mixed with the smell from the funeral pyre. Thorkell felt nauseated, but he was hungry. He hadn't eaten since the night before—and that had only been a small cold meal of dried meat and biscuit. When he received his portion, he ate it greedily enough and took more to eat later.

A store of beer had been found and was passed between the men. Thorkell took a mouthful, washed it around his mouth and spat it out. He had no desire to drink that night.

The enormity of Hagen's death oppressed him. They'd been friends since infancy. Schooled together, trained together, enjoyed the same activities. They'd hunted, been bird-nesting, swum, sailed and rowed together. They'd sworn to be blood brothers. Now that was over. His grief twined with the remembered pain of his mother's death. What was left? His loved ones were gone. Orm had a new wife. Odell was beautiful, but he felt nothing for her. Asger had distanced himself. Thorkell felt utterly alone.

In search of some privacy, he separated himself from the crew and sat down on the rise some distance away. Sentries were standing guard in case of an opportunistic attack on them that night, but Orm considered the chance negligible. Who was left to fight them? Women, children and the elderly. They'd have a hard-enough time surviving the coming winter without their menfolk.

Orm's men still wandered among the slain, searching for valuables. They wouldn't find much. The bodies had been picked over earlier. Thorkell watched the light of their torches as they moved among the dead. Otherwise, this side of the pyre he was alone to mourn Hagen.

He jumped when something moved close to him and reached for the knife in his belt. In the dark, he couldn't make out what it was and for a moment thought he might have imagined it.

Then he saw the flicker of movement again. It took time, but his eyes adjusted as the creature came closer. A hound. Or rather an overgrown puppy, not yet mature, was cautiously eyeing him up. Thorkell snorted in relief. This was no dangerous war hound; this was a pup. He put a hand out to the animal. It flinched back immediately. Tail between legs, it cowered away from him, head dropped submissively.

Thorkell lowered his arm. "Here, boy, come here," he said softly. The dog relaxed a little but didn't move. "Come on, boy. Are you frightened? What happened to your master?"

The dog tilted its head, evidently listening. It was torn between wanting to come closer and fear of the strange human being. Thorkell wondered what horrors the animal had seen that day. No wonder it was frightened. His master almost certainly lay among the dead on the field. The noise, blood and brutal violence would have been terrifying.

Thorkell remembered the meat in his pouch and drew it out. "Are you hungry? Would you like to share some food?" Ears pricked, the pup licked its lips. "You are hungry, aren't you? Here you are." Thorkell held out some meat.

The dog was still more than an arm's length away. Without moving its feet, the animal leaned forward, its nose quivering as the scent of meat reached it, but it refused to step forward.

"Come on." Thorkell tore off a chunk and tossed the meat onto the ground between them. The dog waited until Thorkell had leaned back again before cautiously stepping forward, wary eyes fixed on Thorkell the whole time, and taking the food.

It took a while, and Thorkell had nearly finished his store of meat before the pup stepped close enough for him to touch it. The animal cringed but didn't resist as Thorkell ran his hand over the rough coat. It shivered as Thorkell stroked it. "You realise we're both suffering from shock?" he asked.

He was talking to it all the time now—meaningless phrases intended to calm and reassure the hound. There was a band around the dog's neck, from which hung a short length of cord. He must have broken free and been roaming around on the perimeter of the battlefield.

"That was silly. Anything could have happened to you."

The dog sighed in agreement.

Thorkell smiled and fondled its ears. He took his hand away for a moment to scratch his nose, and the dog responded by shoving its muzzle under his arm and giving it a little lifting shove of encouragement. "You want me to carry on?" Thorkell gave a little laugh. "You're bold now, aren't you?"

The dog responded by sitting down beside him, leaning its weight against Thorkell who lifted his arm around it.

Beyond them the pyre continued to burn, sending sparks into the air. It was a mature fire now, settling into the serious business of consuming the large logs they'd stripped from the hall.

Somewhere in that conflagration, Hagen's body would be

turning to ash, mingling with Gunnar's and Feng's. Perhaps the three of them were now meeting in Valhalla and sharing stories of their courage and valour. It was cold comfort to those left behind.

As misery swept him, Thorkell buried his face into the dog's ruff and tried not to weep. As if sensing his distress, the animal whimpered softly, turned its head and licked his cheek.

"Thank you," Thorkell muttered, and tightened his arm around the dog's shoulders.

They spent the night huddled together on the hill, watching as the pyre slowly consumed itself. After hours of fierce heat, and shortly before dawn, the flames began to die down.

Thorkell's eyes were heavy. The vigil he had kept seemed necessary—an offering to Hagen's spirit and the life they'd shared. He watched now as men moved around the fire, raking logs towards the centre, pushing embers and burning twigs back into the flames. The blaze would burn for several more hours, but at a more sober and steady pace.

Thorkell wrapped his cloak around him and at last allowed himself to lie down. The dog curled against his back. Between the fire and the animal's heat, Thorkell was warm. He shut his eyes.

A low, grumbling growl woke him. Asger stood above him. He could hear the dog growling its displeasure at the man's proximity.

"I'd begun to think you were dead as well," Asger remarked. He didn't sound distressed by the thought. "What's this creature with you?"

Thorkell turned and ran his hand down the dog's coat, calming him. "This is Ulf. My hound."

"Your hound?" Asger laughed. "What use have you for a hound? You can't take that on *Sea Serpent*."

Thorkell pushed himself up from the ground, finding it almost impossible to straighten up. Every ache he'd acquired yesterday had stiffened, rendering him nearly as crippled as old Jotun, who spent his days dribbling by the fire back at home. "Thor, I'm stiff," he muttered as he tried to stretch the aches out of his back and arms.

"Get rid of the dog," Asger commanded as he turned away.

"No. He's coming. He's mine." And with that, he pushed past Asger and made his way towards the pyre.

Ulf growled a warning as Asger reached to stop Thorkell.

"Good dog," Thorkell whispered as he continued on to meet his father.

The fire had now died down, and white ashes covered the ground, interspersed with lumps of blackened wood. A few flames still flickered in the embers, but there was little left of the house-high bonfire that had burned the previous night.

"Thorkell," Orm exclaimed. "I wondered where you had got to."

"I spent the night on the hill," Thorkell said.

Orm looked tired. With a rush of sympathy, Thorkell suddenly appreciated some facts about his father. He was no longer young; the responsibilities of leadership were an endless burden, however willingly Orm carried them, and he, too, mourned his best friend.

"What's that?"

"He chose me. He's mine. He comes with me." Thorkell's voice was calm and firm.

Orm gave him a strange look but said nothing, just nodded. "We'll soon be able to gather up the ashes. Once at sea, we will scatter them. In the meantime, get some food. Then we ransack this place and see what it has to offer us."

They ripped the settlement apart searching for anything of value.

Orm gave a crow of pleasure when he found tanned cattle hides, already packed in bundles for travel, stored in one of the outhouses. "These will be trade goods," he said as he happily counted the packs. "Get them to the ship."

A few pieces of jewellery came from a box in the hall. "Whoever wore these won't be needing them again," Asger said as he took the lot. "No doubt her husband's rotting outside with the rest."

By the end of the day, they'd stripped the settlement of

everything they could find. Thorkell replaced his spear, lost early on in the battle, with a fine new one. From another body, he took a cloak and sword. Others sported new weapons gathered from the battlefield.

Asger also carried a new sword. "Fine workmanship," he commented as he drew the blade. "Pity we didn't find the smith; he'd have made a valuable thrall."

The *Sea Serpent* sat low in the water when they'd finished loading her. Along with the hides, they'd reprovisioned her with fresh food and a store of wine and ale they'd discovered.

Throughout the day, Ulf stayed close to his new master's heels. As they went to board, Asger stopped Thorkell, and Ulf began to growl. Asger stepped back cautiously and looked at the dog in disgust. "Get rid of that mongrel now. It's not coming aboard."

"Ulf is my hound. He is coming with me," Thorkell said firmly. He put his hand down to reassure the dog. "Quiet boy," he cautioned.

"Don't be stupid," said Asger. "Do I have to run it through before you see sense? You can't have a dog on board. It'll shit and piss everywhere."

"You lay a finger on this animal, ever, and I'll kill you." There was ice in Thorkell's voice.

"Leave him be," commanded Orm, who'd come up behind them. "The hound comes with Thorkell."

With a curse, Asger turned his back and climbed aboard.

Thorkell helped Ulf scramble over the gunwales then leapt in beside him. He could hear Asger muttering from his place at the oars ahead of him.

Ulf gave a soft, distressed whine as Thorkell led him to the trunk which served as his seat as well as storage for his clothes. He folded up his new cloak and put it down on the deck. "This is your place," he told the hound. "You stay here when we're aboard." He stroked Ulf's ears as the dog sniffed its improvised bed. Ulf must have approved because he eventually settled beside him on the pile.

They rowed downriver; the rhythm of the work—the steady

repetition of stretching, pulling and bending—served to free Thorkell's mind and release his taut muscles. As they crossed the bar at the river mouth and felt the sea air freshen as they headed north, he smiled. He was back at sea and in his rightful element.

After a while, Ulf leaned against him and rested his head on Thorkell's knee.

CHAPTER TWENTY THREE

Erin

Present Day, New Zealand

THE THEATRE AND ITS SMALL ADJOINING restaurant was already buzzing with people when Erin arrived.

Fergal stood up as she approached the table. "Erin," he exclaimed as he hugged her. "How're you feeling? Did you get over that nausea, or are you a committed vegan now?"

She smiled as she hugged him back. "I'm great, thank you. I'm sorry about all that. I just seem to be extra sensitive to everything, and that day the smell of the barbecue was too much. I've been fine ever since. And no, I haven't had to give up meat at all—anything casseroled, stir-fried or baked is fine. Even grilled steak isn't a problem." She shrugged. "Just one of those things, I suppose. Hi, Brianna." She smiled at the woman across the table.

Erin looked around the room. "Not a bad turnout for opening night. Mind you, everyone loves *Les Misérables*."

"Is Luke joining us?" asked Fergal, looking at the door.

Erin grimaced. "No, he's taking a rain check. There's yet another crisis in the world markets. Some country has imposed tariffs—or may have withdrawn them—and that's caused a meltdown in the market, and currency rates are volatile again." She smiled. "I wasn't paying a lot of attention, to be honest. I've heard it all before. Anyway, he's working late and can't make it."

"That's a shame," said Brianna.

"Well, maybe," said Erin. "To tell the truth, musicals aren't really his thing. He's more an opera sort of guy."

"Really?" Brianna looked surprised.

"Yup, my husband's full of surprises," Erin said. "He's even managed to get me liking opera, and I didn't expect that the first time we went together."

"Is he musical?" Brianna asked.

Erin laughed. "Well, he likes music, but he can't hold a note to save himself."

"He's always liked music," Fergal said. "What a pity he can't be here, though. Petra looked as if she needed all the support she could get when I saw her a few minutes ago."

"She's always like that before a performance," Erin said, "and she always shines once the curtains rise. Where's Doug?"

"Getting us a round of drinks. Can I get you something?"

"No, thanks. Water's just fine," said Erin reaching for the jug.

"I'll go and help Doug," said Fergal.

"I've got a small gift for you," Brianna said.

"For me?" Erin was surprised. She liked Brianna, and they'd met a few times now, but it wasn't a particularly close relationship.

"I hope you don't mind, but after you told me about your dreams, I thought you might like this." Brianna pushed a small box across the table to her. "It was my nan's, and I think it might help."

"Well, thank you," Erin said, accepting it. "Are you sure?"

"Very sure." Brianna smiled. "I think it might have been waiting for you."

Erin looked at her quizzically. A certain amount of spiritual nonsense she could handle, but not if Brianna was going to take all that New Age stuff too far.

Brianna returned her look as if she knew perfectly well what Erin was thinking. "Open it," she said quietly.

"Holy shit. I mean, wow." The antique silver ring setting surrounded a deep blue cabochon stone. "It's stunning. What is it?"

"The technical term is iolite. It's often referred to as the Viking's Compass because apparently they used it to find the direction of the sun when they were at sea on really overcast days. Something to do with the way it polarises light. I don't claim to understand that part. But for now, it has a reputation for clearing thought forms, opening intuition and helping you express your true self, free from the expectations of others. Iolite can help you become more discerning, act on your intuition and recognise your insights knowingly. If you believe the magic, it releases discord within relationships. I think you'll find it will help you with your dreams."

"What a lovely thought." Erin looked at the ring. "But I can't accept this. It's clearly antique and probably valuable. You can't give your nan's things away."

Brianna smiled. "My nan was a special person. She was a healer. She would have wanted you to have this. Nan didn't leave me stuff so I could hoard it. She knew that someone, sometime, would need this."

"Even so ..." Erin was at a loss. The ring was lovely—a pretty violet concoction. Iolite. The very name suited it. Unusual, classically elegant and subtle.

"Put it on," Brianna said.

If it doesn't fit, Erin thought, I won't take it.

It slid easily onto her finger, as if, as Brianna said, it had been waiting for her. Erin turned her hand a few times, admiring the play of light on the stone.

"I think it's yours," said Brianna. Erin saw she was amused. "Am I right?"

Erin shook her head. "I don't know. Are you sure?"

"It's meant for you. Keep it."

"Everything OK?" asked Fergal, picking up on the vibe as he returned to the table.

"All good. Is that my wine?"

Erin nodded. "Brianna gave me a present. I think it's one of the prettiest things anyone's ever given me." She showed Fergal the ring and watched his eyebrows lift.

"That's nice," he said. "It suits you, Erin." He sat down beside Brianna as Doug joined them.

Erin repressed a jealous twinge as she saw Fergal give Brianna's hand a brief, gentle squeeze. Damn Luke for not being there.

"No Luke? Where's the dad to be?" Doug carefully set down a couple of drinks on the table.

"Work," Erin explained.

Doug lifted his eyebrows but refrained from comment, for which Erin was grateful. Doug, she thought, had a very open face. It was easy to read his disapproval.

"How's Petra?" she asked.

"She hates me, she hates the show, she hates how she looks. She can't sing, act or dance." Doug grinned. "She'll be wonderful." He was teasing, but Erin caught the real affection in his voice.

"Par for the course," Erin commented.

"Here's to Petra," said Fergal, raising his glass.

"Here's to Petra," they echoed.

"May she break a leg," added Erin.

⋮

True to form, Petra shone in the production.

"I've always thought Éponine was the lead female role," Erin said as they left the theatre together. "Cosette is a bit insipid, and Fantine dies before the show gets going properly. Petra did bloody well," she said.

Doug was smiling. "She's excellent is our Petra."

Fergal was softly singing, *Do you hear the people sing."*

"I hadn't seen it before," said Brianna. "What a great musical."

"You haven't seen it?" Erin was startled. "Where've you been living?"

"She wasn't," Doug said quietly in Erin's ear. "She wasn't born when it came out."

"Oh, God!" Erin's face flamed with embarrassment. "Sorry, Brianna. I didn't think." She smiled apologetically as she tried to recover lost ground. "You're so on to it; I forgot how young you are. You make the rest of us look old."

Mercifully, Erin thought, Brianna looked amused rather than offended.

Fergal put his arm around her shoulders. "We're off home. You sure you don't need a lift, Erin?"

Erin gave a wry smile. "If ever there's a sober driver, it's a pregnant woman. I'm fine. You two drive safely." She turned to Doug and muttered, "I need to stop putting my foot in it."

"Doubt if Brianna or Fergal minded very much. She's a sensible sort of girl."

"I'd better be off, too. Give our love and congratulations to Petra," Erin said. "Please tell her lots of apologies from Luke as well."

"Luke can make his own apologies next times he sees her." Doug was unusually curt. "Tell him to look after his wife." He gave her a wave before he went back to the theatre.

Erin was staggered. Doug was such a nice person he didn't usually criticise anyone.

CHAPTER TWENTY FOUR

LUKE STILL WASN'T HOME WHEN SHE let herself in. There was an echoing emptiness in the house without his presence. Erin stood in the hall and considered Doug's comment. Were their friends becoming critical of Luke? It wasn't a thought that had previously occurred to her.

Luke might be a bit casual, and he wasn't participating as much as she'd hoped in the build-up to parenthood, but that wasn't a problem—was it? Probably the majority of men were like that.

Erin prided herself on being emancipated, independent and competent. She deliberately shut the door on the small voice that said Luke could indeed do more, could care more, support her more. Even, and she shut *that* thought away quickly, on the big one—that he could love her more.

She brushed her hair in front of the mirror. The stone in her new ring caught the light as her hand rose and fell in a soothing, gentle rhythm. She turned her hand to examine it. A pretty thing, she thought, although not something she would typically wear. For one thing, it was an antique, and Erin's wasn't the sort of family in which heirloom jewellery was the norm. Iolite. A gentle word for its subtle beauty. The light playing on the stone was soft and silvery with no suggestion of its earlier radiant violet hue.

Fit for Arwen, thought Erin, recalling her teenage heroines, or perhaps Galadriel—jewellery for fey elvish princesses, or maidens in ancient Druidic rituals. Not the kind of ring a career-focused, serious, 21st-century business banking manager would wear—but then again, why not?

Her eyes narrowed as she considered Brianna's generosity. Usually she searched for motive, assumed there was a profit margin attached and did her best to 'follow the money', as all the textbooks urged. When it came to Brianna, she was stumped. As far as she could see, the woman *had* no ulterior motive—nothing other than kindness and genuine care from one woman to another. She leaned forward to brush her teeth, conscious of the stone on her hand.

Bugger it. If she dwelt on the ring too long, she'd end up in some hippy, tree-hugging, spiritual belief matrix, and Erin had spent a lifetime avoiding such doctrines.

She lifted her chin. "See what you can do about my dreams," she challenged the stone.

Luke still wasn't home when she climbed into bed. She'd intended to wait up for him, but the warmth and comfort overtook her. Her eyes were heavy, and before long she found herself nodding off. It had been a long day, and she was so sleep-deprived, it wasn't funny.

The dream was waiting to claim her. Like dark tentacles, the strands of smoke twined around her, and the fire drew her forward into its warmth and light.

There were people around her, although she couldn't see them. Somewhere near, she heard the high piping voice of a young child and the laughter-filled voice of the answering woman.

Erin frowned in confusion. This was the landscape of her dream, she was sure, but no captive woman cried out her anguish, and there was low-voiced, happy chatter from those around her.

The fire was benign—no more than a large bonfire around which the crowd had gathered. It must be summer, for although the night air was fresh, the warmth of the fire was sufficient to ward off the chill.

The crowd seemed to be waiting, so Erin stood with them.

There was a collective sigh as the church bell began to toll. She counted as it spoke twelve times. As the last chime rang out, the crowd cheered. Friends, husbands, wives, neighbours greeted each other, and there was happy chatter as the crowd milled around the bonfire. People embraced, and children were kissed.

Someone thrust a warm drink into her hand. She sipped and nearly gagged on the unfamiliar taste but remembered to smile her thanks.

It was a celebration, and Erin appeared to be part of it. She felt communal happiness as if it was one she shared. What were they celebrating? Christmas, New Year? Her dream didn't come with explanations.

She looked across the fire and saw him watching her. An unambiguous jolt of pure joy surged through her. If she'd doubted her feelings before, she couldn't now, not when every part of her rejoiced so wholly. She couldn't lie to herself. He'd come back!

Luke was wearing a cloak and sword, but she'd know him anywhere. He began to walk around the fire to her, and she moved to meet him, her eagerness making her clumsy as she pushed past other revellers.

No more than a pace away from him, her hands already eagerly extended, she found she was wrong. It wasn't Luke.

Fergal had come to claim her.

He pulled her into his arms, and she went willingly, her body accepting him. For a long moment, they stood together in silence.

"You came back ..." she began.

"I promised."

She heard the rumble of low laughter in his voice as his arms tightened around her. As it always had, the timbre of his deep voice melted the path to her heart.

She lifted her head to look at him and smiled.

His lips met hers, and she closed her eyes, savouring the sensation. She cherished the familiarity of his scent, his touch, the texture of his lips against hers.

Beneath his cloak, his hand moved to her breast and caressed her gently.

Erin woke. Luke was propped up on one elbow beside her, his hand teasing her nipple. She stared at her husband like a stranger. "What are you doing? I was asleep," she said groggily.

"I know. I thought you'd never wake up," he said. "I tried kissing you. It might have worked on Sleeping Beauty, but not on you. You were miles away."

There was a strong smell of alcohol on his breath as he leaned forward to kiss her. Involuntarily Erin turned her head away.

Luke's hand traced a path down her body. He gave a satisfied grunt when he encountered moistness, and he pulled her into position.

Erin was too disoriented and confused to protest as he pushed into her. Her body had already been primed, and Luke could read the signs.

Sometime later, Luke rolled off her, and Erin, now wide awake, lay in the darkness trying to untangle her thoughts. Dreams aren't real, she told herself. Wherever they come from, howsoever they're generated, they don't mean anything. She liked Fergal, but he was Luke's friend, and there had never been anything suggestive between them. If she hadn't met Luke first? Then maybe she and Fergal might have been drawn to each other. She was honest enough to admit there was a latent spark there which in different circumstances might flare into life, but she was married to Luke and loved him. She wasn't the sort of a woman to be unfaithful, she reminded herself. She and Luke had made vows to each other, and she intended to keep them.

So why had it been Fergal in the dream? Why had it seemed so right?

Something else had been odd about the dream. It took a while to fathom it out. Then Erin realised that previously she'd been a passive, invisible spectator. In this last episode, she hadn't merely watched what was happening to the young woman—she *was* the young woman.

As it faded from her memory, there was one truth she couldn't put aside—the absolute, visceral sense of joy she'd felt when she'd seen him across the fire. That couldn't be disguised or ignored. She didn't know why she'd confused the two men. Dreams were like that, she supposed. But the joy was irrefutable. One of them had triggered that response in her. It had been too honest a reaction for her to doubt herself. Not when it remained so vivid in the morning light.

Why, who or when ...? Those were problems to be dealt with tomorrow.

Hours later, when she got up from another unsatisfactory night's sleep, she looked at the ring on her hand. Well, the dream started out great, she addressed it mentally, but boy, did it go haywire! Frankly, Brianna, I don't know whether to thank you or curse you.

CHAPTER
TWENTY FIVE

Ciarnat

Ninth Century, Ireland

THE PANTING CHILD STOOD IN THE DOORWAY. "Mam's time has come," she announced to Gran. "She sent me to fetch you."

Gran gave a tch of irritation. "Why now?" she grumbled under her breath as she thumped and kneaded the dough.

The child looked puzzled. "Because she's in labour," she replied seriously, which garnered a snort of amusement from Gran.

"So she is, Mara. And I'm making bread. If I leave it now, the dough will all go to waste."

"But you *must* come!" Mara wailed. "Mam needs you."

Ciarnat put her spindle down. "I can go," she offered.

Mara ignored that, her attention focused on Gran.

Gran's eyebrows rose as she turned her head to study her granddaughter. Slowly she nodded her head. "Aye. You could go," she agreed. "You're more than ready to work without me, and it should be a simple delivery."

Ciarnat gave her a wide smile. "I'll get the bag ready."

"Is *she* going to deliver the baby?" Mara asked, doubt written across her face.

"Aye. You'll not find a better healer. Ciarnat will do a fine job for your mam."

"But ..."

"But nothing," Gran said sternly. "Ciarnat has studied with me for five years. You treat her and her skills with respect."

Ciarnat took what she needed from Gran's kist. "Cord, knife, birthing stool, medicine ..." she murmured to herself as she packed the bag. "Let us go," she said to Mara.

·╬·

Ciarnat was both excited and nervous. She had helped Gran with many deliveries and was confident she knew what to do. Even so, being totally responsible for managing the birth on her own felt lonely and intimidating.

As they entered the village, Mara ran ahead to apprise her family of the change of midwife.

When Ciarnat entered the cottage, everyone stared at her, and not every face was friendly.

"God be in this house," she murmured politely as she squared her shoulders and put what she termed her 'healer mask' on as she walked across to the pregnant woman. "Is it well with you, Fiana?" she asked gently. The woman nodded. "Let me examine you," Cairnat said, helping the woman to her feet. "It's time for your menfolk to be outside."

There was some shuffling, but the men left.

"That's given us some more space," Ciarnat said in relief. Her audience had dropped by half. "We will need boiling water—a lot of it—and clean linen," she said to the remaining women.

Now that she was involved with her patient, Ciarnat's nervousness disappeared. Her experience and competence took over as she focused on the labouring woman and her needs. When the time came to use the birthing stool, the delivery was as straightforward as Gran had predicted.

"You have very gentle hands," Fiana said when she finally lay back on the bed with her new-born son in her arms.

"Thank you," Ciarnat smiled. "You are a very easy patient."

"This is my fifth wean," Fiana said. "My body is used to it." She gave a great yawn, and Ciarnat chuckled.

"You need to sleep," she said. "Let me give the little one to his granny."

Ciarnat was busy gathering up the soiled linen when Fiana's husband approached her. "I thank you for your care of my wife," he said.

"She did well, and you're the father of a fine wee son," Ciarnat replied.

"Aye." There was a pleasing bashfulness about the man that amused Ciarnat.

"I wanted to say that you did a fine job for Fiana. Mara said your gran told her you would be good. She was right. Your gran would be proud of you."

It was dark when Ciarnat returned home.

"How is Fiana?" Gran asked as she passed Ciarnat a bowl of stew and a plate of bread.

"She is well," Ciarnat answered. "She has a new son." She bit hungrily into the bread.

Gran searched her face and was evidently pleased with what she saw. "Good," was all she said.

CHAPTER TWENTY SIX

Thorkell

Ninth Century, Norway

THORKELL SAT IN THE EARLY SPRING sunshine, knife in hand, taking vicious swipes out of the small log he held. If all went well, his efforts would result in a little wooden dog, but Thorkell knew, as well as the woman who watched him warily, that he was carving to release his tensions.

Why couldn't he be out at sea? Life was so much simpler when all there was to worry about was the wind and the tide. It was people who caused all the trouble in the world.

Take his uncle, for example. Gunnar's death had promoted Asger's status amongst the crew. He was recognised as Orm's second in command, and even Thorkell admitted the man was competent and courageous, but the tension between them remained.

Thorkell was careful to treat him with respect in public, kept away from him in private and avoided antagonising him wherever possible. Ulf remained a source of friction between them. He'd matured into a fine hound and was Thorkell's constant companion. The undeniable bond between them was such that Orm had continued to allow Thorkell to keep the animal on the *Sea Serpent*.

Asger had to respect his jarl's command, but Thorkell sometimes caught him watching Ulf with malice in his eyes. Asger wouldn't be foolish enough to disobey his lord directly, and Ulf was well able to defend himself if he was attacked.

Thorkell had to rely on that as sufficient protection for the hound, and Ulf was always with him anyway. He shrugged the threat away as irrelevant but made sure to keep Ulf close. Just that morning he'd seen Asger, unaware Thorkell was behind him, take a kick at the dog. Ulf had easily dodged the blow, but it was a symptom of Asger's unwavering malice towards the animal.

Then there was the woman who watched him with cold, angry eyes. Aileen was a red-headed thrall Thorkell had taken in last year's raiding. She cared for his clothes and lodgings and shared his bed on cold nights when he sent for her. He wondered why he bothered. Aileen was obedient, he had to give her that. You could even describe her as competent. But she made no effort to disguise her bitterness and contempt. He'd considered beating her into a better frame of mind, but looking at the proud set of her jaw, he doubted it would achieve the desired effect. Thank Thor he'd be at sea soon.

Another winter had passed, and with the spring came the usual rush to restore the *Sea Serpent* to fighting condition. She wasn't a young ship, but the crew were proud of her, and their constant care kept her sound and seaworthy.

Each spring brought new boys into the crew—boys eager to prove themselves as men, as Thorkell and Hagen had done before them. And each winter saw older warriors retired from active campaigning. For a man who'd served well, being relegated to shore was a bitter blow.

Orm soothed hurt feelings and kept peace amongst the men of his holding, but he was ageing. Orm was still vigorous, fit and a well-respected leader, but his age meant the *Sea Serpent*'s crew were now more nearly aligned with Asger's generation than Orm's.

"You need to understand this is the normal progression of a fighting band," Orm instructed Thorkell. "One day, and by Thor's hammer may this be far in the future, you will step into my shoes. As my heir, this holding is yours—to protect, to fight for, to love."

Thorkell listened with half an ear, ignoring the urgency in Orm's voice. Orm was indestructible. It would be years before he'd be content to sit beside a fire and eat sops with the other old men.

Orm saw his disinterest and opted for patience. Like Thorkell, he thought he would have years to train his son to be a leader. Thorkell had promise—no doubt of that. Tall, handsome, courageous, he was popular in Orm's hall. But his interest was of the sea and exploration. He had to be brought to understand his responsibilities to his land and his people.

Asger posed a threat, and if Thorkell was too blind to see it for what it was, Orm understood it very well. A younger son with no rights of succession, if Asger wasn't contained, he would pose a risk to Thorkell.

Orm had no specific reason to distrust Asger, who always complied with his orders meticulously, but cautious suspicion is the mark of a good leader. Orm trusted no one.

That extended to his wife.

Orm had hoped Asger might look to the fertile lands in Ireland they plundered each season and choose to set up his holding there. Many Norsemen had already done so. Occasionally he'd mention it to Asger as an exciting possibility, but his brother hadn't taken the bait.

Towards the end of their raids last summer, Orm had taken the time to visit the titular High King of Ireland and seek permission to set up his own trading station in Dublin.

Áed had welcomed him and seemed willing to offer him a patent to trade. But Áed was engaged in one of the endless internal wars from which his nation suffered, and Orm had come away without a formal agreement.

Asger and Thorkell had gone with him, and he'd hoped to spark some interest for the venture in his brother and educate his son in the ways of diplomacy.

"Perhaps I'm growing old," Orm confided in his wife. "Once I was like Thorkell and couldn't see beyond each raiding season. Now I see sense in moving to a warmer, more fertile land where crops and cattle flourish. A savvy trader could do well if he was shrewd and set up a good train of supply from Dublin."

Odell nodded obligingly, and Orm immediately wondered what she was thinking. They'd been married six years, and the ways of her mind were still opaque to him. Would she be prepared to move to Dublin with him?

For all their combined efforts, Odell remained barren. Orm could have torn his hair out in frustration but was too decent a man to put his wife aside. He already had a fine heir. Even so, Orm was old enough to recognise a beautiful, bored, childless young wife was a menace in her own right. The court she held in the hall with his younger warriors was no longer just a compliment to her—it represented an obvious risk to his own rule. It hadn't missed his attention that Asger was the warrior most constantly at Odell's side.

Orm had begun to consider strategies whereby the threat from his dangerous younger brother could be minimised—and if all else failed, how to eliminate Asger forever.

CHAPTER
TWENTY SEVEN

THORKELL GAVE A SWIFT GLANCE AS the man came running towards him.

"You must come. There has been an accident." The thrall was panting from his exertions which made his heavily accented speech almost incomprehensible.

Thorkell frowned. This was Asger's man, captured in the same raid that had gained him Aileen. "What's happened?" he asked sharply. He liked Asger's thrall as little as he liked his master. Some quality in the man rasped Thorkell the wrong way, an instinct that Aileen had agreed with. 'He causes trouble with the women,' she had said when asked why she obviously despised the man.

"An accident on the slipway. Your father's injured."

"Orm?" Thorkell pushed to his feet.

The man nodded. "The framing gave way under the *Sea Serpent*, and Orm was underneath. He's hurt."

"Odin's beard!" Thorkell thrust past the man then paused. "Get Rowena to come down immediately. She's nursed many injuries."

He ran towards the bay, Ulf close behind. There were men, both warriors and thralls, gathered around the ship. He saw at a glance that it was leaning at a strange angle; the cradle that should have supported her had collapsed on one side. "How is he?" he asked, striding through the crowd.

Asger was there already, his face white with shock.

"A strut broke and brought the framing down. Orm was working underneath. We've managed to lift the weight off, but his leg is hurt."

Thorkell looked at the framework looming over them. "For Odin's sake, make sure it's wedged up safely. I've got to get under there with him. We'll have to pull him to safety before we can do anything."

Thorkell knelt beside his father. Orm's eyes were shut. His face was pale, and sweat beaded his forehead. "Odin's beard!" he said again, looking at the blood-soaked ground surrounding his father's thigh. "We're getting you out of here," he said to his father. "You and you," he gestured to two of the thralls, "give me a hand. Get a grip under his shoulder and pull."

Orm screamed obscenities as they began to move him and his leg dragged along the ground. Thorkell flinched. Orm was a tough man who usually shrugged away pain and discomfort. It would take extreme agony to break down that control.

Once they had pulled Orm clear of the ship, Thorkell, at least, breathed easier. Orm was silent, and Thorkell thought he might have fainted. "Make a stretcher," he ordered.

"Quickly men," Asger said. "Those two poles—*já*, those. Ultán, get the oilskin. We can make up a hammock to carry him."

A relay of men took turns to carry Orm to the hall.

Rowena, with Odell standing behind her, met them in the doorway. Rowena had brought her kist with its supply of medicines. "How bad is it?" she asked as the men laid Orm on his bed.

"I'm about to find out," Thorkell said and unsheathed his knife. "Move back," he growled as he knelt and began to cut away the leggings. "We need to see the damage."

He tried to be gentle, but despite his care and the sharpness of his blade, there were times the knife caught in the blood-soaked fabric and jerked the leg. Orm groaned in anguish each time. There was a collective gasp from those watching when the bloody material was finally pulled free from the leg.

"Thor!" Thorkell muttered, looking at the mess. Sharp daggers of bone protruded from the skin in two places, one of which bled profusely. The straight line of Orm's thigh was broken and crooked.

Behind him came the sound of retching. Thorkell turned to see Odell clasping her hand to her mouth. He couldn't blame her—he didn't feel much better himself.

There was a gentle touch on his arm. "Thorkell," Rowena said calmly, "I need short pieces of wood to straighten this. About so long." She demonstrated what she wanted with her hands. "I'll need cloth to use as bandages and warm water to wash him. I also want a large flask of wine. Get a thrall woman to fetch it."

Thorkell gave orders while Rowena examined the wound. "It's not pretty," she muttered to herself. "Thank the gods it didn't crush him any higher. We'd never have stopped the bleeding. Her eyes closed as her hands moved gently over the broken angles feeling for the damage hidden beneath the skin. She looked up when the supplies were delivered to see Odell slumped against the wall. "Asger, take Odell away. Give her into the care of her thrall woman. She's in shock. Then come back here. Thorkell, clear the others out, but stay if you would. I need you and Asger to help."

Thorkell watched as his old nurse poured wine into a cup and mixed it with a couple of drops from a small flask in her bag.

Rowena answered his unspoken question. "It's to dull the pain. But mostly it's to send him to sleep. What comes next will hurt him."

"Give him plenty then," Asger said.

Rowena gave a faint smile. "No. This is a dangerous medicine. The dose must be correct—too little, and it won't work; too much, and it could kill him."

"Where did you get it from?" asked Thorkell as Rowena held the cup to Orm's lips.

"Orm bought it from a trader who'd come back from Byzantium. It's potent, and the trader made sure I knew how to use it before he let me have it. He thought it originated from even further east than Byzantium," Rowena said. "It's rare, expensive and only to be used in dire circumstances."

"Well, this is a dire circumstance," Asger agreed.

Whatever potion Rowena used, it sent Orm to sleep, which was good enough for Thorkell, and the only relief he and Asger had over the next gruelling minutes.

Having staunched and padded the bleeding wound, Rowena picked out as many fragments as she could before she made them forcibly pull and straighten Orm's leg out so she could splint and bind it. Neither man had any idea how strong the muscles in a man's thigh could be.

After their first two abortive efforts at stretching it straight, Rowena lost patience. "Do I have to get the entire crew of the *Sea Serpent* in here to do the job? Surely you understand if it isn't stretched straight, it won't heal cleanly? Even then, if pieces of bone remain, it may rot. If you don't try, then Orm is lost."

For the first time in years, Thorkell and Asger shared a moment of sympathy. Warriors weren't spoken to like that by *any* woman—not even by Thorkell's nurse.

Thorkell glared at her, and the look Asger gave her was far from friendly.

After some discussion, they tied a rope above and below his knee, and with the two of them hauling on it with all their strength they managed to stretch the leg out far enough to satisfy Rowena.

"Hold it there," she commanded.

Thorkell watched her strong hands as they kneaded, pushed and pulled the bones of the thigh into a semblance of their original shape.

"Keep on holding it," Rowena growled, as she reached for the splints and bandages she'd ordered. She strapped, bandaged and tied the wood to the limb to hold it in position, then checked the bleeding was under control. When she'd finished, she closed her eyes for a long moment, hands resting on her knees, her head bowed.

She was old, Thorkell realised, and she'd carried the weight of the day on her shoulders. If his father recovered, he surely owed the woman her freedom.

"Let the leg go," she said at last. "You've done good work today, lads. If Orm lives and walks again, he will owe it to your work."

"Come and have a drink," Asger said as the men walked out.

Thorkell nodded. There was mead and ale, of course, but Thorkell elected to drink wine, so Asger joined him. Both men drank deeply but said little.

Thorkell allowed the rich, heavy drink to work its magic. It would take a long while for him to forget how vulnerable Orm had been today, and Thorkell wasn't comfortable with the thought of his father so fragile and damaged. It upset a law of nature—Orm was supposed to be the strongest and toughest, and more robust than any man in his holding. He'd always seemed invincible to his son, and Thorkell wasn't ready for that to change. What they'd shared had temporarily stilled the hostility between him and his uncle.

"What happens next?" Asger asked after a while.

"I don't know," Thorkell said honestly. "If Orm survives, he'll have to make provision for a season without him on the *Sea Serpent*."

Asger nodded slowly. He shot an unmistakably speculative glance at Thorkell but said nothing.

As he registered the changes in Asger's expressions, Thorkell realised how much his world had been changed by events that day.

CHAPTER
TWENTY EIGHT

ORM MIGHT BE INJURED, BUT THERE was nothing wrong with his mind, and his orders were clear and precise. "You will captain the *Sea Serpent* this season," he told Asger, "and Thorkell will be your second in command." He shifted irritably on his bed. "Asger, you're a man of experience. Let's see how you handle the responsibility. I know of the bad blood between you two, but I'm trusting you to work together for the good of the ship. Put your differences aside for the crew and the success of the voyage. There's no place for such folly on the ship."

Asger nodded. "We shall," he assured Orm.

"Now, with me out, we're a crew member short. Who do you suggest takes my oar?"

"Ultán," Asger replied immediately.

"Your thrall?" Orm was startled. "Why would you want to take him on such a voyage?"

"He may be a thrall, but he's a warrior, he's strong, and he can handle an oar. When he is not rowing or fighting, he will be my shield-bearer and keep my equipment clean and sharp."

Orm's eyebrows lifted. "You are raiding the land of his home. How would you trust him? Remember, too, he was a slave when we captured him. His own people condemned him and put that thrall collar on him. He'll be a criminal. Do you even know what crime he committed?"

"An unpaid blood debt," Asger said. "Ultán has already told me about it. He killed a boy by accident and couldn't pay the fine. He's been a thrall for five years and has no love for the land or the people that forced him into slavery."

Orm looked sceptical. "It's equally likely he's a difficult character who got his just deserts. He's told you his side of the story—doesn't mean it's true."

"I trust him," said Asger. "I have given him a better life than he had working for his old master and he's grateful for it." Orm winced at the self-congratulation in Asger's voice. "He was mistreated. I've seen the scars on his back."

Orm grunted. "That simply shows he is probably a villain and deserved everything he got. I would not trust a man of his surly mien." Orm shook his head. "No, you haven't persuaded me, but if you are to be leader, you will have to make your own decisions and your own mistakes. It is the only way you will learn. On your head be it. I hope you've made a wise choice."

"I have," Asger said.

"There's another thing," Orm said. "I want no trouble about that hound of Thorkell's. It goes with him on the *Sea Serpent* as usual, understood? You can have your thrall, and Thorkell can have his hound."

Asger's mouth tightened. "There is no place for the animal on board. You have been too soft with Thorkell these last few years, allowing it to happen."

Orm looked at him narrowly. "Let me make myself clear. If you want to command the *Sea Serpent*, you will accommodate the dog. Otherwise, I'll find another captain for the season."

There was real anger in the look Asger gave him, but Orm held his gaze, and eventually Asger yielded to the older man. "I agree," he said shortly.

With that assurance, Orm had to be content. He waved Asger away.

Orm's leg caused him constant pain which made him short-tempered and quickly tired. He didn't trust Asger's unwilling agreement, but Thorkell was going to have to deal with it himself if there was trouble on the voyage.

He cautioned Thorkell when his son came to say goodbye. "Asger has sworn an oath to work with you for the good of the voyage. You have to do the same. There's no room for friction. Mark my words, trouble aboard has ruined many a voyage. Men make stupid decisions when there is conflict, and that can lead to deaths and even shipwreck."

Thorkell nodded. "I have already decided to be as peaceable as possible."

"He's agreed to taking Ulf, although he hates it. Keep the dog close to you."

"I shall."

"How is that thrall of Asger's working out?"

Thorkell shrugged. "He is surly and aggressive, but competent. He can keep the beat with an oar, and he can fight. I don't like him, but he's Asger's man."

"What do the men think of him?"

"He's a thrall. I don't think they dwell on him at all." Thorkell registered the frustration that crossed Orm's face. "We will manage fine," he assured his father. "It will be a successful season, and we'll come back laden with trade goods. It will be different without you as captain, but if you listen to Rowena and let yourself heal, you'll be back with us this time next year."

"I am counting on it," said Orm. "It's no plan of mine to die in my bed."

CHAPTER TWENTY NINE

THE WEATHER SET FAIR, AND THE first days of the voyage were uneventful. It was a time for this season's crew to settle into the rhythms of seafaring life and learn each other's strengths and weaknesses. Some of the men had sailed together before, but there were three new youths yet to be blooded.

Then there was Ultán, who said little and focused on his work. Thorkell imagined his heavy accent made conversation difficult for him. He was a thrall. There was a clear division between him and the other crew members, who were all Orm's men and members of the same settlement. They'd known each other from childhood, and many were interrelated.

Had Asger brought Ultán precisely because he was the only man on board bound unequivocally to himself? Thorkell could see no other reason for the man's inclusion in an otherwise close-knit group.

For himself, he was content to enjoy his time out on the ocean, and keep Ulf clear of Asger. It seemed Asger, too, was set on honouring the promise he'd made to Orm.

They'd reached the northern point of land, passing a series of islands, when they received an unexpected challenge.

"Are they mad?" Asger asked, watching the ship that closed quickly on them. "Do they think they can best us at sea?"

"Pirates?" asked Thorkell, eyeing up the vessel. It was larger and heavier than the *Sea Serpent*.

"Must be. Thor knows what they think they're doing. Even if they win, we have no goods yet for them to claim. To arms, men!" he cried. "Have your spears and shields ready."

The crew hurried to obey, and waited on the deck, ready for battle.

The wind initially favoured the attacking ship, driving it powerfully towards them. It soon became apparent their purpose was to cleave the *Sea Serpent* in two with their more massive hull.

"To your oars!" Asger yelled.

The crew pulled mightily, but it was close, and Arne, steering the long, heavy rudder, was sweating and cursing profusely as they just managed to spin the *Sea Serpent* out of danger.

It was so close Thorkell could have reached out and touched the other ship as it slid past their hull.

"They have just blown their one chance," Asger said with satisfaction. "Now we hold the dice, and we'll board them."

The attacking ship had been carried some distance by its momentum. The result was the *Sea Serpent* was now behind it and in a commanding position. Helped by the wind filling its sail, the longship quickly overtook the vessel as it lost speed trying to gybe. She made short work of coming alongside and tying up to the heavier ship.

"Up!" cried Asger. "Up the ropes, men! Show no mercy. Kill the lot of them."

The defenders had spears and the advantage of height, their deck being higher in the water. They tried to ward the *Sea Serpent*'s crew off, and the first minutes were fiercely fought, as the *Sea Serpent*'s men had to stab upwards and work to wrest spears from the men above and drag them down and into the sea.

Thorkell soon found that his axe, applied to the legs of the men on the deck above him, cleared his way. He vaulted onto their deck and set about hewing and swinging at the enemy.

Around him, his crewmates were having equal success. Blood made the deck slippery, and there were dead men to step over as Thorkell made his way forward to join Asger. "We have taken control," he said.

Asger nodded. "They didn't have much fight in them," he grumbled. "They had one trick, and when that gamble failed, they had nothing left. They weren't even good fighting men."

Thorkell raised an eyebrow. "The new lads have been blooded, though, which is always a good thing."

Asger gave a grim smile. "I remember my first time like it was yesterday."

"Me, too. You always remember the first kill, Orm told me."

"These weren't real pirates." Asger poked his toe into the nearest body. "They look more like fisherfolk to me, not seasoned fighters. They must have stolen the ship, or lucked into it somehow, and thought they would have a go at making their fortunes."

The crew disposed of the bodies by tipping them into the sea. They searched the captured vessel for anything of value and came up empty-handed.

"Odin's eye, there is nothing here worth looting," Arne complained. "These idiots had nothing."

"What do you want to do with the ship?" Thorkell asked.

Asger looked around the deck. "She is a nice enough vessel but useless to us. We can't spare the men to sail her home, and her draught is too deep for our kind of work. It's a pity—none of us would destroy a ship lightly, but we have little choice. We'll set fire to her. Let's hope anyone watching from the shore will learn their lesson and not try the same fool's trick again."

It was easy enough to start a fire with kindling from the smashed decking. Thorkell was last to leave when the flames finally took hold. He watched as it began burning intensely into planks and beams. "She is well alight," he confirmed, leaping back onto the *Sea Serpent* and taking his place as they pushed away from the hull. The crew applied themselves to their oars, putting as much distance between them and the dying ship as possible.

Ulf rested his massive head on Thorkell's knee, and he spared a hand to caress the hound's ears. "There was no fighting for you today, was there?" Ulf gave a low growl of contentment. "You'll have to learn how to climb ropes."

"I told you that dog was a waste of space," Asger said.

Unwilling to get into an argument, Thorkell turned his head away and kept his eyes focused on the blazing hull. Hours later, when he could no longer see the ship itself, the plume of smoke that still hung in the sky marked its death throes.

CHAPTER
THIRTY

Thorkell

Ninth Century, Ireland

SOME DAYS LATER, LUCK DESERTED THEM. They were making their way along the western coastline of Ireland, looking for likely villages and settlements among the islands, peninsulas and headlands that characterised the rugged landscape.

The weather had been kind, and they'd enjoyed unusually smooth sailing since they left home. This day started fine and mild. By mid-morning a light, misty cloud covered the sky, but it remained warm with a gentle breeze.

It was Arne, standing by the rudder, who first saw the tell-tale signs of wind on the water and cried a warning. In minutes they were in choppy seas with frisky white caps playing and dancing on the waves as the wind strengthened. The clouds thickened rapidly and began racing, dark and heavy across the sky.

Thorkell shivered as the temperature dropped, and wrapped his cloak around him.

"We are in for a bit of a blow." Asger's voice was calm and relaxed. "All eyes on the coastline for a suitable place to beach."

The crew were seasoned sailors, familiar with the temper tantrums of the turbulent northern seas they called their home. But for all their experience and combined weather wisdom, none could have predicted the speed with which the storm hit.

A fine cobweb curtain of rain came first, sheeting in from the western ocean and shrouding the rocky shoreline ahead of them. Visibility shrank to two boat lengths ahead, at best, and in the poor light, it was hard to judge distances or their speed.

From one gust to the next, the sea, once so calm, had turned to angry, pounding waves that battered the ship and threatened to swamp her.

"Get the sail down fast!" Asger yelled, although Thorkell and Ultán had already begun wrestling with the heavy wet material.

Between them, they lowered the sail, which at least slowed their path through the waves and gave them more control.

Ulf crouched low beside Thorkell's trunk, whining softly as the ship lurched and bounded. His claws scrabbled vainly for stability on the wood, and he was soon sitting in a deep puddle of seawater.

"Row," urged Asger. "Row for your lives."

They rowed, and peered as best they could through the murk ahead of them. Every man knew the danger of the black-fanged rocks that rimmed this coast. Water collected around their feet, and every few oar strokes they had to bend and bale the seawater that threatened to engulf them.

The sea was groaning angrily, and below that, like a deep drum, Thorkell could hear the heavy waves smashing against rocks. The noise was so intense it drowned out any other and resonated through his blood. He gritted his teeth and tried to balance on his trunk as he forced his oar through the waves.

At the prow, Asger studied the sea in front of the *Sea Serpent*, although Thorkell doubted he could see much. Suddenly he shouted. "Hard over!" pointing left. "Turn her, Arne. Push her over hard. Men, keep her moving. Row, you *ergi*, put some muscle into it!"

They strained and pulled. The cloud thinned for a moment, and Thorkell saw rocks to the side of him. "Oh Thor, save us," he muttered.

"Row!" Asger screamed. Again and again, every oar length they gained going forward, they seemed to lose on the returning wave. "Pull!" he cried.

Suddenly, without warning, the *Sea Serpent* slipped into calmer water. A dark shadow loomed on their right, and a sudden clearance in the cloud that surrounded them enabled Thorkell to see they had come up in the lea of a headland. Here the wind and seas were lighter and the visibility better.

"Ease up, men. We've got to pick our way through here," Asger cried.

Ultán stood and went to help Arne with the steering oar.

Thorkell reached his hand down and caressed Ulf. "Good dog. It looks like we are going to make it after all." He grinned with relief as he rubbed the enormous head. Ulf licked his hand and gave a feeble wag of his tail.

They moved slowly as Asger guided them along the narrow channel. Then Asger gave a triumphant shout. "We've reached the beach! All hands to get her rolled up onto the shingle."

CHAPTER
THIRTY ONE

THE STORM RAGED ON AND OFF for days. The crew, initially elated and relieved to have survived, soon became bored and irritable in the cramped, confining conditions. They were comfortable, dry and warm enough in the rough lean-to shelter they'd rigged beneath the sail. There was sufficient dry driftwood hidden in the coombs and crevices of the narrow cove to keep a campfire going under a rocky overhang and provide them with hot food.

Even fresh water wasn't an issue. The rain, after all, was unrelenting and formed torrents of waterfalls that tumbled down the steep black crags above them. If the rain eased, it was immediately replaced by a clammy sea mist that destroyed visibility and clung to their cloaks and skin. It was hard to determine which state the crew detested more.

They couldn't move beyond the shingle beach that had been their salvation. High cliffs hemmed them in on all sides. Unless you approached, as they had, from the sea, the chances were no one had ever discovered this beach— "Nor," as Asger said sourly, "would any bastard want to."

There were some, like Thorkell, who'd spent their boyhoods raiding birds' nests on the cliffs at home, who tried to climb the cliffs. They came back from their attempts looking sheepish. There was no route out of this crevice, they reported. They downplayed that their hands were sliced and shredded on the sharp basalt.

Asger watched Gorm, one of the younger crew, fumble as he reached for food, and investigated. "By Tyr's hand," he roared, looking at the ripped hands, "how do you expect to fight with your hands torn to pieces? We'll be out of here in a few days. That damage could take weeks to heal."

After that, trial ascents were forbidden. They'd all failed, and their frustration with their imprisonment was palpable. They could see, even protected from the worst as they were, that the waves further out were ferocious. At night their sleep was punctuated with the dull boom of the tide breaking against the rocks beyond their haven. It gave them all nightmares.

The day brought a sense of relief—at least they could see their danger.

A highlight of the day was to watch the turbulent tide climb the beach, and mark the high point with a stick of driftwood. Many expected the *Sea Serpent* to be unexpectedly waterborne by such a wave. Money was placed on the chance. And yet their haven stayed dry and above the waterline.

The only crew member content and happy in their isolation was Ulf, who chased the seagulls around and around the small beach they counted on for their safety. Thorkell was uneasily aware his barking was another point of tension for the men marooned there.

The crew had to bear this inactivity with patience—but they were not by training, nor by disposition, patient men. A more experienced leader might have kept the crew busy. They could have inspected the ship and checked her keel after the journey through the rocky channel. Perhaps fishing rosters could have been organised. Regular drills and sparring may have worked. They might have gathered driftwood for the fire as one of the formalised duties. Songs, story competitions, or even physical competitions would have distracted them. Thorkell himself favoured wrestling bouts but would have been content with any activity that bonded the anxious, bored crew.

Asger did nothing.

It was as if the man had used up his store of energy in fighting the storm that had brought them here. Worse, given the innate tension between the two men, Thorkell didn't feel free to approach Asger and suggest strategies to assuage the boredom and breakdown in discipline among the crew.

Day followed day in that tight, claustrophobic cleft that represented their safety, and small irritations soon escalated to significant disputes. When one of the quarrels was between the younger crew, Thorkell felt confident intervening. There had been some snapping and ill feeling between Gorm and another lad. Thorkell finally had enough and told them to take themselves to the sea strand and wrestle each other until they had sorted out the problem. Both returned with black eyes and bruised cheeks, but neither spoke of the fight and from then on appeared to be good friends. If only he could do the same with the rest of the crew.

These were mostly men of Asger's age. Thorkell knew they still viewed him as a stripling, and besides, he had no desire to challenge Asger's authority. But these were grown men, and when they fought, it was with knives. If Asger refused to take control, someone was likely to be maimed or killed. It was a thought that kept Thorkell awake through many a cold, dismal hour.

Things came to a head when a quarrel sprung up over dice. Thorkell had been sitting close to the fire, idly pulling Ulf's ears, his back turned to the rest of the crew, when a fight broke out behind him. He turned to see two men had wrestled each other to the ground and were grappling with each other. He stood to find the cause. By the time he reached them, a circle of excited men had formed around them, cheering them on.

"What happened?" he asked and was told that Arne, a man Thorkell respected and had sailed with on previous voyages, accused Toke, a newcomer that season, of cheating.

Thorkell cursed beneath his breath. Such an accusation was a serious charge among a people where all men betted regularly, and dice was one of the only games whose outcome was supposed to be purely determined by luck. To cheat, or be labelled a cheat by your crewmates, was tantamount to a death sentence. He watched the men still fighting on the ground. Arne was more experienced and stronger, but the younger man was supple and swift.

There was a critical moment when their movements slowed, and it was clear the end was near. Arne's muscles bulged as he brought both his weight and strength into play and strove to crush Toke's spine. For a few seconds, there was a respectful silence among the spectators. Then a concerted groan, as the younger man twisted and contorted his body with almost unnatural skill, and escaped injury.

"Thor's hammer, he's a slippery little serpent," the man beside Thorkell swore.

"That looked impossible," Thorkell agreed, impressed despite himself as the lithe Toke slid out from beneath Arne's grip.

"What does he bathe in? Tallow?"

There was a roar of laughter and appreciation. The mood of the men had changed. Anger had turned into good humour. Toke's supple skill had defused an ugly situation. The original charge had dissipated as they enjoyed the show, and all could have been well. Thorkell took a relieved breath.

Then Toke pulled a knife from his boot.

It happened so quickly; few saw his hand move before Toke had buried the blade in Arne's shoulder. It was Arne's bellow of rage that alerted them. He flung Toke aside—his light weight little matter to a man who handled the steering oar on the *Sea Serpent*. Contemptuously he pulled the knife from his shoulder, then turned for revenge.

Toke was a dead man, thought Thorkell as he jumped between them. "No!" he bellowed at the enraged Arne. "This is a matter for our leader. It goes to Asger. Asger alone decides what happens here."

It was touch and go. Arne's anger was palpable. His eyes were unnaturally narrowed, his muscles bunched with frustrated strength and his usually pleasant face was a mask of vicious hate as he reached to grab Thorkell.

It said a lot for the man, Thorkell realised, that he managed to gain control, hold back and ultimately decide not to destroy the person standing between him and Toke.

For a long moment, Thorkell knew his life teetered in the balance. He kept his eyes firmly fixed on Arne's and waited as the man returned to himself, recognised Thorkell and eventually dropped his gaze in token submission.

Thorkell had quelled horses by the technique but never used it on a man.

There was a collective hush from the onlookers as they watched Arne, a man much admired among the crew, return to himself. Toke, perhaps realising he'd lost everything, had curled into a ball on the ground.

"This goes to Asger," Thorkell repeated. He felt relief in repeating the line. Their leader was the only one who could mediate now—and he had to take into consideration the future success of their voyage, the various culpabilities and penalties to be imposed on the protagonists, and make his judgement palatable to the men of the crew.

Thorkell was thanking his lucky stars being spared such a responsibility when he felt a heavy thump across his back. He turned in surprise, so the next blow landed squarely in his solar plexus. "What the ...?" he gasped as the air rushed from him.

"I'm the leader here, you little turd," hissed an enraged Asger.

"How dare you make judgements for me. How dare you try to undermine my authority. *You* are not the leader here. I am."

Thorkell forced enough wind back to whisper, "No one has stolen your authority. I made that clear ..." He was solidly slapped across the face for his efforts.

"You've created a massive problem for us all—how am I supposed to make a team out of the chaos you've created among the men?" There was a loud growl as Ulf came to stand between them.

At that moment, Thorkell loved his hound for all his entrenched loyalty, but Ulf's timing couldn't have been worse.

Asger's eyes narrowed. "Call your hound off. If I decide to

discipline you, I shall, and if that animal gets in the way, I will kill it. No oath to Orm blocks me from reasonable retribution."

"Asger, I am not your enemy," Thorkell gasped out. "You're our leader. I made that clear. The decisions are your own."

"And if I wanted the men to sort it out for themselves? If I thought it healthier for the crew? Now you've made the whole mess my responsibility, and it all could have been avoided." There was an overt, manic rage in Asger's face.

Thorkell fleetingly thought of Orm—had he ever behaved in such a way, whatever the provocation?

No.

That answer strengthened him. He stood up straighter, trying to ignore the breathlessness that cursed his speech. "The only thing I have told the crew is that you are our leader. You cannot fault me for that, Asger, and your blows are an unforgivable insult to my honour."

The crew were watching, of course, and both Thorkell and Asger knew it. Neither could afford to look weak.

They glared at each other, while each wondered what to do.

CHAPTER
THIRTY TWO

❝THE WIND HAS SHIFTED." EVEN THE lowliest, newest member of the crew would have listened to *that* news. It was automatic for Thorkell and Asger to swing towards Arne who had his head up, sniffing the wind like a great hound. "The wind has changed," he called again. "It is blowing from the land, and if we follow, it will take us safely to the sea." Arne squinted at the pale sun, barely visible through the mist. "The tide won't turn for an hour. If we are quick to launch, we'll be free of this cursed inlet. The seas are easing."

All eyes turned towards the sky. It was true. In the last hour or so the wind had shifted, the sea was gentler, and for the first time in days, the *Sea Serpent* had an excellent opportunity to escape from its prison.

"Launch the ship!" Asger shouted at his crew. "Let's get to sea."

His eyes were fixed on Thorkell's, his grin almost friendly as he spun on his heel towards the *Sea Serpent*.

Thorkell and Ulf followed some distance behind. For all Asger's sudden apparent friendliness, Thorkell felt a chill. He'd seen the rage in Asger's eyes and feared the worst.

The timetable of the tide dictated their speed, and the crew were, in any case, efficient. The sail was rolled, rigged and stored ready for the launch. The fire was doused, the makeshift kitchen stowed. The men climbed aboard to take their positions.

As was usual, Thorkell hung towards the rear, his responsibility to ensure all the men were aboard before he took his place.

Finally, confident they were all there, he walked forward, Ulf beside him, to climb over the side of the *Sea Serpent* and take their place.

As he strode towards the ship, his shoulder was gripped by Ultán.

"No further," the man said.

Thorkell was outraged. "Get your hands off me, you cursed thrall. How dare you lay a finger on me?"

"My master has spoken." Ultán wasn't a great conversationalist at the best of times.

Thorkell faced Asger who had followed behind him. "What's the meaning of this?"

"You don't board." Asger's voice was harsh. "Do you think for one second I'd take a traitor back? A man who has tried to undermine my authority? Our crew depends on loyalty for its survival. You, Thorkell Ormson, are no longer a member of the *Sea Serpent*'s crew. You stay here."

"What?"

There was pure incomprehension in Thorkell's question. Nothing in his understanding of a leader's role had prepared him for such a judgement from anyone, let alone from his captain.

Being wary of Asger's malice was one thing. He'd had long enough to get the measure of the man and avoid trouble where he could. This stepped beyond anything he could have expected. For Asger to leave him there was almost certain death, and the excitement of that expectation was written clearly in the grin Asger gave him.

"You can't," he repeated. "You swore an oath."

"I swore to lead this voyage. I have every right to dispose of a rebellious, disobedient crew member. You are condemned by the words everyone on this ship heard."

"You know that's not true," Thorkell protested.

Asger smiled again. "You are no longer part of the *Sea Serpent*'s crew," he reasserted. It was hard to miss the gloating tone. Somehow, without meaning to, Thorkell had provided Asger with the motive he'd needed to dispose of Orm's son.

Later, Thorkell realised the extent of shock he'd suffered when those words were pronounced and how dangerous his hesitation had been. He could have challenged Asger to a duel on the spot; should have declared a blood feud on his uncle and insisted on immediate reparation, regardless of favourable winds and tides. There was enough tradition and legality behind him to have ensured he received his rights. Instead, his mind and limbs turned unreliably unsteady by the charge and by the callous, attendant judgement, he simply watched in numb horror as the *Sea Serpent* slipped from shore and its crew rowed forward to engage with the sea. He thought Arne turned once to look at him, his gaze confused and sympathetic, as the ship pulled away from the beach.

There was silence in the cove where once there had been noise, whether cursing, snoring, singing, shouting or barking. Even the cheeky seabirds were mute.

The quietness was oppressive. Thorkell looked briefly around at the cliffs surrounding him. They'd already proved the futility of attempting to climb them. There was nothing for it then. The only possible hope of survival for him and Ulf was to chance their fortunes to the sea.

He stood on the shoreline as the ship slipped further away. Ulf leaned against his leg, and Thorkell's hand reached down to caress the hound's ears. His breathing seemed harsh. The two of them would live or die according to the will of the sea.

He studied it carefully. The waves were gentle here in the cove, and the booming roar of distant surf crashing on headland rocks that had been a constant this last week was gone. Even so, the sea had been churned to an opaque, muddy grey. Flecks of seaweed floated on each wave, and sticks of driftwood bobbed along the tide line.

He prayed—but only in the haphazard fashion he knew. His religion had been subsumed in the power of being a Viking, and an ambition to die valiantly in battle. You didn't need religion when you had enough force. He'd learned that.

Thorkell watched as the *Sea Serpent* turned the headland, heading for the open sea, before he gazed around at the prison to which he'd been sentenced. It was a form of farewell and a confirmation there was no alternative to his plan.

He gave Ulf's ear a final squeeze, then walked towards the sea. "Come," he instructed as he entered the cold water. There was a whine from onshore. Ulf hated water.

Thorkell forced himself to continue without a backward glance. Their only hope lay in escaping the beach and finding a more hospitable shore.

CHAPTER
THIRTY THREE

IT WAS COLD. MIND-NUMBINGLY SO, and yet, perversely, Thorkell felt freer than he had in weeks. It was only him and Ulf now, and Thorkell already knew he intended to endure whatever was needed to survive. His previous responsibilities lifted from his shoulders; his only task was to live, and if that involved discomfort, then so be it.

The driftwood made his path through the water difficult. The storm-churned water hid twigs which snarled in his hair and slapped his face, forcing him to break his rhythm and swerve to avoid them. He cursed and kept swimming.

It wasn't long before he discovered the tide had turned and, coupled with a strong current, was steering him away from the path of the *Sea Serpent* and towards the headland to the south.

Thorkell knew enough not to resist the power pulling him. He recognised too well the cold that sucked strength and power from his limbs. The waves, though more gentle than in recent days, were still boisterous enough to slap him in the face and catch him if he took an unwary breath.

At least the current was now pushing him towards land. Under most conditions, the distance would be no more than a five-minute swim away, but this wasn't a dip in the fjord at home, and he was no longer confident he could keep himself afloat long enough to reach the shore.

Thorkell could feel the weight of his waterlogged clothing and the sword he still wore, pulling him deeper into the water's depths. All he could do was relax into the arms of the ocean god and pray he would hold him up until he reached safety.

Somewhere behind him, he imagined Ulf battling the waves on his own. The hound had always hated swimming.

Thorkell didn't see the lump of driftwood floating in the water before him until a moment before a massive wave bore him up then crushed him against its hard surface. His arms grabbed for it reflexively, and he pulled himself up until he was half out of the water, draped over the log.

As he struggled into position, another wave with its burden of driftwood, slammed into him, catching him on the temple.

The head injury completed the wearying work of time and tide. Thorkell succumbed. He floated unconscious, supported only by the drifting wood and directed by the wind and tide.

CHAPTER
THIRTY FOUR

Ciarnat

Ninth Century, Ireland

IT WAS EARLY MORNING. THE WIND and sea, so wild the night before, had finally settled their quarrel and subsided. Now the silvery first light of the sky promised a beautiful day ahead.

Ferocious late spring storms had battered the coast for the past week, and not even the cliffs protecting their cove could keep out all the sea's fury.

As Ciarnat clambered down the rocky track, she paused in confusion, making no sense of what she saw below her. Both water and beach were an indistinguishable white. Familiar landmarks had disappeared, and the bay was the wrong shape.

Only when she stepped from the path onto the beach did she discover that a thick layer of white foam covered the sand and most of the bay. Sea spume, churned and forced through the narrow channel that connected the cove to the sea, had been stranded and, now the wind had changed direction, there no way for it to escape.

It was as light and fluffy as the egg whites her gran whipped up. When she stepped into it, the foam came as high as the hem of her tunic. Pretty as it was, the foam was treacherous, hiding storm-wrack strewn across the ground beneath it. Ciarnat discovered that the hard way when she hit her shin on hidden driftwood and then scraped herself badly enough to draw blood as she tried to clamber free.

She'd come to gather dulse for her gran who used it to flavour her soda bread. After such a wild storm, she'd expected there would be plenty freshly ripped from deeper water and abandoned on the rocks along the high-water mark, but she'd never be able to find the seaweed beneath this foam coverlet.

She looked about. To the north of the bay, there seemed to be a clearer area. The track to it was above the tide line and uncluttered. It would take several minutes to walk there, but it would be better than climbing up the hill empty-handed, and explaining why to her grandmother.

Once clear of the foam, it was an easy walk around the cove. The surrounding cliffs sheltered Ciarnat from the sea breeze, and the rising sun was beginning to throw out some heat. Her cloak was already too hot to wear.

With no hidden obstacles, she stepped out freely along the track, swinging her basket as she went. Now and then a snippet of a song sprang to her mind and her lips. She was content to sing a phrase or two that amused her, or maybe the chorus, but made no attempt to fashion the whole song.

The rhythm of her strides set the pace for the lyrics. It occurred to her no bard yet had written a walking song for women. A pity, she thought. Women walked so much every day—farming, weeding, washing, milking, cleaning, chasing children. Men wrote songs for men—war songs, love songs, exotic tales of High Kings, faraway lands with strange monsters and faeries. No one wrote songs about women's lives.

When eventually the track brought her down to the beach at the north end of the cove, she saw she had been right. There was little foam here—a few clumps caught in rock pools and some marking where the high tide had reached. Otherwise, the beach was clear, and the red dulse she sought was there in plenty.

She took her time filling her basket. After the week of foul weather, it was pleasant to be alone outside and away from the smoky house and her gran's complaining. The sun warmed her back as she bent and picked the weed. She slipped the shoes from her feet and paddled in the cold water.

When the basket was full, she straightened her back and stretched, easing the stiffness, and looked around. The sun had climbed in the sky, and the tide had started to turn. It was time to go. A rock made a convenient place to sit as she brushed the sand from her feet and tied her shoes on.

She lifted the basket strap over her shoulder to make it easier to carry, picking her way around driftwood and rocky outcrops. Her head had been bent while she'd picked the seaweed, and only now did she take in her surroundings. This end of the cove had been protected from the line of foam marking the far side of the bay, but it had still received its share of driftwood that now lay tossed in untidy piles along the high-tide line.

Other flotsam had been caught up in the debris. Seagulls screamed and argued as they rummaged in the pile, scavenging for small snails and other sea creatures thrown up by the tide. Among the kelp and tangle of sticks, a broken sandal lay abandoned.

Further ahead, Ciarnat saw a bundle of dark cloth had been swept ashore. She hadn't even noticed it when she passed by earlier, the colour of the material blending in with the rocks and timber. She walked over to see if it was worth saving.

As Ciarnat got closer, she saw the bundle was large, but it wasn't until she bent to touch the fabric that she realised it was a body washed up on the sand. She gave a soft cry of distress and took an involuntary step back as she studied the man before her. He lay on his belly, face turned away from her, dark blond hair matted with sand and weed. The bundle of cloth was a cloak that still covered most of him.

She stood staring for a few minutes, uncertain what to do. She could hear the soft sound of the sea behind her, already starting its climb back up the beach. Above, the seagulls called and swooped. She couldn't just walk away and leave him to the fate of the incoming tide or predatory birds and animals. For decency's sake, he needed to be buried, to have words said over him to mark his passing, but there was no one to call for help. The solitude she'd been enjoying now posed a problem.

She knelt and tugged the cloak from where it tangled between his legs. She tried to turn him, but her repeated efforts simply served to shake him, which made seawater stream from his mouth but wasn't enough to shift his position.

Frustrated, she went across to his far side to gain a purchase on his shoulder and lever him over. He was heavy, and the wet fabric hard to hold on to, but at last, she felt him move. She gave one more push, and he rolled, landing with a thump on his back.

She was breathless from her exertions. Shifting him had been hard work. While she caught her breath, she sat beside him on the beach and studied his face. With relief, she discovered he wasn't from their village.

He had taken a blow to the forehead, the mark livid on his pale brow. Ciarnat winced in sympathy and reached to brush sand from the wound. His skin had a bluish tinge and was cold beneath her fingers. She felt a surge of pity. It seemed cruel fate had left such a young man dead and stranded on a strange shore.

She had made her decision. She would leave and get help. Padraig the herdsman would be out with the cattle, but with luck, he might not be too far away from the farm. If she hurried, she might just be back before the high tide washed the poor man back into the sea. In the meantime, all she could do to protect his body against predators was cover his face with the cloak.

She was fumbling with the pin at his shoulder when he suddenly moved and coughed. She shrieked with terror and jumped back. He coughed again, then slowly rolled back onto his side in a paroxysm of coughing that only ended when he vomited.

It was this last event that reassured Ciarnat. Ghosts could, no doubt, come back from the dead to frighten the living, but she'd never heard of one who threw up in front of the person they'd come to haunt.

The foul smell made her queasy, and her stomach roiled in sympathy as her mouth filled with saliva and her body retched.

With a soft groan, the man collapsed back into unconsciousness again. His face was half-buried in the wet mess he'd spewed up. Ciarnat used one of her father's curses. This stupid man would suffocate in his vomit if she left him.

Gingerly she reached out and tugged at his shoulder. Her patience had evaporated. Reassured that he was unconscious once more, she stood up, marched back to his far side and once more used his shoulder as a lever. She was much less cautious this time as she rolled him over.

Remnants of vomit clung in small pieces to his face, and the smell was nauseating.

Ciarnat steeled her stomach to stillness, lifted a corner of the cloak from around his knees and wiped his face clean. At least he wouldn't die face down in his vomitus now.

She sat back and considered her options. She no longer had to worry about disposing of a corpse, but that raised other problems. She couldn't abandon him, helpless on the beach, particularly if there was some way to save his life, but she also needed to get back home before Gran wound herself into a frenzy of worry.

She was trying to balance these two imperatives when she realised the man's eyes had opened and he was watching her. "Hello," she said.

His mouth worked, but no sound emerged. He frowned, before trying again to speak—which started another round of coughing and gagging. After the spasm passed, he lay with his eyes shut for so long that Ciarnat wondered whether he'd lost consciousness again.

"If I can get you safely up off the beach to dry land, then I can leave you and get help," she explained to his unresponsive form. "I can't drag you up there, so you *have* to move."

His eyes opened.

Ciarnat had no idea whether he'd understood, but he began to twist his body. She realised he was trying to free his arms, which were trapped in his cloak.

"Wait." Ciarnat reached again for the pin at his shoulder and pulled it free. The cloth was tucked tightly under his body. She tugged as hard as she could, and when he realised what she was doing, he shifted his weight and rolled to help her it free.

She pulled the sodden fabric back, discovering it was snagged on his sword hilt. Free to use his arms, the man struggled to push himself up.

Ciarnat helped until he sat steadily with his head drooped and resting on his bent knee. He looked exhausted. He spent long minutes recovering his breath. Occasionally he coughed, and Ciarnat didn't like the rasping sound of his breathing. She got to her feet and stood in front of him, reaching out her hand. "You've got to come with me to above the high-tide line. You can rest then. There's even a cave if you can make it that far."

At least he'd lifted his head and appeared to be listening.

"Once I know you are safe, I can go home, fetch the donkey. Then when you're ready, you can ride home with me, and Gran can look after you. She's a healer. But you *must* get up."

He recognised the purpose of her outstretched hand. Slowly he struggled up, first to his knees, then to his feet and stood, leaning heavily on her for support.

"Good, that's good." Ciarnat smiled to find herself using the same phrase she used to encourage Asal, the donkey. "Come on," she urged.

Slowly they shuffled up the beach, stopping frequently when more attacks of coughing consumed him, but at last, they were above the high-water mark.

Ciarnat pointed to the mouth of the cave. "Can you keep going? It's not far."

He followed the line of her finger and nodded.

It was easier going here, free of the rubble that littered the beach, and Ciarnat was aware he was carrying more of his weight as he became more confident and less dependent on her support. She eased her shoulders gratefully. He was a tall man, and he'd been heavy and uncomfortable, particularly as she was also burdened with her basket and his cloak.

The cave floor was sandy, with some free-standing rocks

at the entrance. Ciarnat steered him towards one of these and helped him sit down.

Once again, he sat with his head slumped forward, and his eyes closed. He was taking quick short breaths, and Ciarnat could hear a wheeze as he tried to get enough air. She hoped her gran would know what to do for him.

"Here," she said, "I'm putting my cloak around your shoulders. It's dry in here, but if the sea breeze springs up, you'll need it. Or you could lie down on it if you want."

She spread his cloak over the rocks in the sunshine to dry.

He'd opened his eyes again.

"I'm going now," said Ciarnat. She pointed up the track. "I need to organise some help. You stay here, and I'll be back as soon as I can."

She felt she was saying things for her comfort rather than his. There was no sign he understood her, but she gave a small wave as she walked away, and he lifted his hand in response.

CHAPTER THIRTY FIVE

C IARNAT MADE GOOD TIME HEADING HOME. The long, low farmhouse nestled in the lea of the hill, well below the reach of the sea breeze that coiled over the ridge. A few scraggly, twisted trees were a testament to the force of the wind which regularly buffeted the ridgeline.

As she'd expected, Gran's worry expressed itself as anger. "Where have you been? I've been waiting for you. You should have been back ages ago."

"Sorry. I got the dulse for you." Ciarnat lowered her basket to the floor. "But I found a man washed ashore. He needs your help." She knew her gran would be intrigued and unable to resist an appeal to her healing skills. "I thought I could bring him back here on Asal. He'll never be able to walk up the hill. His breathing sounds terrible, and he coughed so badly he made himself sick."

"Washed ashore, you say. What happened to the boat he was on? Was it wrecked?"

Ciarnat shook her head. "I don't know. He either couldn't talk because his voice has gone, or he didn't understand me. He looks different. He has fine clothes and a good sword, but not like any I have seen before."

"Different? How different? Is it safe to bring him here?"

"He can't hurt us," Ciarnat laughed. "He can barely stand."

"Yes, but when he recovers... Still, your da is due home tonight. He may know who or what he is. All right. Take the donkey and fetch him. I'll make up a bed in the byre."

Ciarnat smiled. She'd known her gran wouldn't resist a challenge.

The donkey made short work of the trail down to the beach. When they reached the cave, Ciarnat dismounted and tethered Asal to a log. The man was nowhere in sight.

She saw the footprints they'd made in the sand, and his cloak was still spread out on the rock as she'd left it, but he seemed to have disappeared.

If he was on the beach, she was sure she would have seen him.

The only other option was he'd gone further into the cave. She felt a shiver of alarm. It had been easy to discount her gran's concern when the man had been unconscious and vulnerable. It was a different matter to be seeking an armed stranger, in the dark, with no way of judging his intentions towards her.

She'd never explored the cave in any depth. As a small child she played there when she came to the bay to swim or to gather dulse, but she'd never ventured in beyond the daylight. She hesitated before stepping to the edge of the darkness and calling out. She held her breath as her cry echoed around the cave. If the man didn't reply, she had no idea what to do.

Several moments of the most intense silence passed—quite long enough for her courage to shatter into humiliatingly small pieces. She decided to count, as her father had taught her, to one hundred. If there was no reply, she would turn and run.

The plan made her braver, and she started her count with some confidence. She reached forty two before there was a disturbance in the darkness ahead of her. A form detached itself from the shadows and grew larger as it approached into the light. She stepped back.

When he'd been helpless, it had been her instinct to aid him. Now she was wary. As he stepped forward, she saw he was armed. His unsheathed sword was in his hand, and his eyes were over-bright as he studied her.

Ciarnat stood frozen, too terrified even to breathe for the time it took him to identify her. Then the febrile brightness faded from his eyes. His sword hand lowered, evidently weighed down by the weapon it carried. Their eyes met, and he nodded as he recognised her.

As she held his gaze, it came to Ciarnat that he had been as afraid as she, and she gave a wry smile of relief. "Come," she said and led the way out of the cave.

She helped him onto Asal's back. He was a big man and looked ridiculous with his long legs almost dragging on the ground each side of the animal.

"Hold on to the mane," she indicated and saw him make a wild clutch at it as they started to move. He didn't look very comfortable or happy, perched there, but there was no alternative if she was to get him home. He'd stood to challenge her in the cave, but she had seen it had taken all his strength and he'd been wavering as she helped him mount.

Ciarnat didn't imagine poor Asal was thrilled either. It was a long trudge up the hill for the over-burdened animal.

When they reached the farm, Gran had already prepared for her patient. Water heated on the fire, and her oaken kist, with its store of dried herbs and healing simples, was open in readiness beside the bed she'd made up in the byre.

Ciarnat was shocked at how much the donkey ride had cost the man. He'd left the last of his energy at the cave. It took both her and Gran's combined strength to get him from Asal's back. He could hardly move unaided.

She helped him onto the bracken bed. His face was deathly pale, and he looked barely alive. He leaned back against the wall with his eyes closed. The rasp of his breathing was heavy in the enclosed space.

"Here, help me with his tunic. You'll have to give me a hand to roll him so we can get it off."

Between the two of them, they managed to strip him. Ciarnat thought he might complain as they bared him, but he made no response as the women examined him.

"There doesn't seem to be any other injury apart from his head," said Gran. "But he's certainly a warrior." She indicated a couple of scars, one on his shoulder and the other over his ribs. "These are old, but he's been in a fight before." Gran picked up his right hand. "Yes, see the calluses? He got these training with a sword."

Ciarnat said nothing. For the last five years, she had helped Gran with her healing work, and she knew the examination was necessary. Even so, she found the sight of his exposed chest rather unsettling and intrusive. She wondered if he would have permitted it had he been more conscious and aware.

"We'll clean him up first, while he's lying still," said Gran. "He'll be more comfortable if we get the salt and sand off him. Bring the bowl of water and the clouts."

Between them, they rinsed his hair and washed his body.

"That's better," said Gran as she looked down at him critically. "He's not bad looking, whoever he is. It'll be a pity if he doesn't make it." She sat and listened to his laboured breathing for some minutes. "Fetch me the pot from the shelf. He's got water in his lungs. You usually see it with fishermen who get into trouble and nearly drown."

"He'll be all right, though, won't he?" asked Ciarnat. "He's in the air now and can breathe."

"Maybe." Gran's voice was discouraging. "Most likely, this will bring on a sickness in the lungs. We'll know in two days if that is going to happen. If it does, then his survival is up to fate. He's already frail; there won't be much fight left in him. You will have to hold him," Gran instructed. "Lean him against your shoulder so I can reach his back."

Ciarnat pulled the man into an awkward embrace while Gran rubbed a thick paste on and covered it with a cloth. "You can let him lie now," Gran said as she rubbed the remaining paste onto his chest and again pressed a soft cloth on top to cover it.

Ciarnat could smell the pungent green herbs ground into the grease of the ointment

"It help him breathe easier," Gran said. "The paste warms his chest and loosens the phlegm so he can cough up the water that is still trapped. The scent opens the air routes. The herbs are also soporific, which means he should sleep for a while now. We'll reapply it when he wakes."

They watched for a few minutes. Already the man's breathing seemed softer, more regular, and some of the tension left his face.

"We'll leave him to rest now. He won't need us for a while, and you've still got chores to do, my girl. Get that dulse spread out to dry, but cut me off a small bit first and I'll make white soda bread. When he wakes, he'll need feeding."

CHAPTER THIRTY SIX

GRAN BROUGHT FILAN TO THE BYRE to see her patient. Ciarnat followed, eager to see what her father would make of the stranger.

The man lifted his head when they entered and hurriedly pushed himself up until he was sitting. Ciarnat saw his hand automatically scrabble at his side as he searched for the sword now hanging from a peg on the wall above him. His eyes flickered nervously as he watched them approach.

"Hello," Da said, and when that greeting failed, tried another in a language Ciarnat didn't know.

That had more success. The stranger nodded.

Da's next words sounded like a question, to which the man replied.

"He's a Norseman," Da informed Gran after a few minutes' stilted conversation. "I've met them when a trade delegation came to Áed's court. I spent some time trying to learn their language. They're pagan, of course, from some northern land. I think he is saying he fell from his ship, but my understanding is rudimentary. His name is Thorkell."

"What do you want us to do with him?" Gran asked. "Is he dangerous?"

Filan rubbed his chin. "The pair I met were traders, or so they said, but there have been other reports of shiploads of Norsemen raiding villages in the north." Da was thoughtful. "However this man came to be in the water, he must have come from a boat, which means somewhere off our coast, not very far away, there'll be more of them. You need Padraig to send his boy down to the village to warn them to keep watch in case of an attack."

"Should I let him die?"

"Is that a possibility?" Da studied the man on the bed.

"Probably so. There's seawater in his lungs. By tomorrow he will have a fever. If I don't treat him, it's likely to be fatal."

Ciarnat was horrified; they couldn't abandon him to die. She'd put so much effort into saving this man's life. "He's our guest!" she exclaimed. "We can't kill him."

"I didn't say we would," Gran said calmly. "Letting him die in peace is something else and in the hands of God. Let your father decide."

Thorkell watched Da's face. Ciarnat was sure he knew what they were discussing.

"Da," she appealed.

Filan studied his daughter and smiled slightly. Her eagerness, compassion and interest in the man were writ large in every expression on her ardent young face. But Filan hadn't earned his position as the king's *ollamh* by being foolish. His high status was a tribute both to his learning and his wisdom, and he knew the man on the bed was dangerous. Not in the sense that meant he'd murder them as they slept. It was what the stranger represented that was dangerous. The northern men might be traders or raiders, but whichever it was, they came to Ireland for profit. Why else, Filan considered, would Thorkell's ship have been at sea? He was a warrior, not a fisherman.

"He will stay as our guest, and you will care for him," Filan eventually pronounced, and was rewarded by the warmth of his daughter's smile.

Thorkell could be a useful bargaining chip if there were going to be conflict. Better to have him as a friend, or as a trade, if needed. There was no value in a dead man.

Gran gave a soft approving grunt. "Welcome, Thorkell," she said formally. "My name is Betha."

Thorkell nodded.

Betha pointed to her granddaughter. "Ciarnat. She will help care for you."

Thorkell smiled at the girl as he spoke to Filan.

"He thanks us for our hospitality," Filan translated. "The sooner he learns our language, the easier it's going to be for us all," he commented.

True to Gran's prediction, by the next day, Thorkell's condition had deteriorated and he was running a temperature. His breathing was fast and shallow, and the rattle in his chest sounded worse.

"Why doesn't the ointment work anymore?" asked Ciarnat as she wiped a cold sponge over his hot forehead.

"It can only do so much," replied Gran. "It works wonders for a slight cough or a cold, but this sickness has gone deep inside him where ointment can't reach. All we can do now is keep him clean, cool him when he gets too hot by sponging him, and try to make him drink some broth while he's awake. He won't want to eat."

Ciarnat could see beneath the surface tan that Thorkell's face had an unhealthy, sallow pallor. The bruise on his forehead was an ugly black stain, vivid against his pale skin. He looked much worse than when she'd rescued him from the sea.

She smoothed goose fat over his dry, cracked lips. "Will he die?" she asked as she studied him.

"That is in the hands of fate." Gran's voice was gruff and uncompromising. "It's no use getting too attached to him," she warned. "We can only do so much for the sick, and sometimes it's not enough to save them."

Thorkell drifted in and out of consciousness as Gran and Ciarnat attended to his needs. When Filan visited him in the evening, he was tossing restlessly from side to side, utterly unaware of Filan's presence.

Gran shook her head in reply to her son's unspoken question. "The fever is burning him up and stripping his strength away.

Ciarnat and I will take turns sitting with him tonight. We'll keep him as comfortable as we can, but there's no more we can do. The outcome depends on him."

Later that night, Ciarnat kept watch. Thorkell was less restless, but she couldn't deceive herself that this was an improvement. The flesh of his face had sunk into hollows beneath his cheekbones. Ciarnat remembered his solid weight and the trouble she'd had trying to move him the day before. Now his long frame looked frail. It seemed to her he had shrunk over the day. "Don't die," she begged. "You must fight this and win." His hand was hot and dry beneath hers. She closed her fingers and squeezed it. "You're strong," she urged. "Don't let me down." She gave a small laugh. "I've put too much effort into you already."

There was no response. Ciarnat hadn't expected any.

The night was quiet and still around them. Daybreak was still some time away. Gran had taught her most people pass into death at the hour when night wanes, slipping away into the darkness before the light of the new dawn.

"Don't go," she whispered. "You're much too young to die. I want you to get well again. I want you to get better so you can tell me who you are and how you came here. You can't die here as a stranger among us. That would be sad."

She bowed her head and prayed, as the priest had taught her, although she wasn't sure the saints would intercede to save the life of a man who was almost undoubtedly pagan.

CHAPTER
THIRTY SEVEN

WHEN SHE OPENED HER EYES, SHE saw Thorkell looking at her.

"You're awake!" she exclaimed. "Welcome back. Would you like something to drink?" She mimed, holding a cup to her mouth and drinking to make sure he understood. When he nodded, she poured a mug of water. She had to support him to sit up and held the cup to his lips as he sipped. He drank thirstily, but the task seemed to exhaust him. He slumped back on the bed as soon as Ciarnat let him go. She eased him onto his side so he was comfortable.

"Is there anything else you need?" she asked hopefully, but he was unresponsive. Ciarnat tidied his bedding, tucking the blanket up under his neck, and resumed her vigil.

Gran came in just after the dawn. "How is he?"

"He had a drink but then drifted off again."

Gran sniffed. "Well, at least he made it through the night. All we can do is wait. You go and have a break. I'll stay with him for now."

Later, Ciarnat found her father on the bench outside the cottage. She sat beside him and passed him a slice of bread and honey. "I thought you'd like some."

"Thanks," he smiled.

She ate her breakfast. "What do you know of Thorkell's people?" Her tongue stumbled as she pronounced the strange name.

"They come from a cold land across the sea somewhere to the north," Filan said. "Many years ago a band of them raided Reachlainn Island, murdered the priests and people, pillaged the church and burned the buildings. Then they disappeared. A few years back, they returned, and since then they've established a pattern of coming to our shores every spring and summer. They loot the villages, raid the churches and take what they want. They are a dangerous, pagan people."

"But you said you met some at court?"

"Yes. But those men had come legitimately. They wanted Áed's assistance to expand their presence in Dublin. There's quite a settlement of them, wintering over each year. A *longphort*, they call it. The place they rest their longboats for the winter. They control the slave market in Dublin—which is the main commodity they trade." .

"So you learned their language?"

Filan smiled. "Very poorly. I was trying to understand the distinction between the raiders and the traders. *Are* they the same people, or are they different tribes? One of the men was friendly, and I spent some time with him. My music interested him, and he taught me a couple of their drinking songs."

"So, what did they say? Are they two different peoples?"

Filan shrugged. "I couldn't discover it. I didn't have enough language for any deep sort of discussion. Perhaps the Norsemen are both—if they can trade for goods, they do. Otherwise, they steal them in their raids."

Her usual chores kept Ciarnat busy while Gran and Filan took turns watching their patient. Much as she loved having her da home, his presence added to her daily work. More washing, more cooking, more cleaning.

To Ciarnat's surprise, Thorkell was still alive that evening.

And the next evening.

And the one after that.

By which time even Gran admitted, albeit grudgingly, that he was likely to survive, and consequently redoubled her efforts to ensure it.

The house filled with the fumes of medicinal herbs simmering over the fire, and Ciarnat was kept busy applying warming poultices to Thorkell's chest and back as Gran fought the congestion that still lingered in his chest.

"He has to cough it up," she told Ciarnat, showing her how to position Thorkell over the edge of the bed so his head was lower than his torso. "If bad humours linger in his chest he'll have a relapse. He will only be safe when we get all the seawater out of him. Rub his back," she instructed. "No, harder, like this," she said, demonstrating the technique. "You want to push any fluid up and out of him," she explained as she vigorously pushed and pummelled the poor man's flesh. She was so matter of fact she might have been kneading bread.

It wasn't an indifference Ciarnat shared. Despite Gran's teachings, she felt self-conscious whenever she touched Thorkell. It was one thing to care for him when he was asleep or unconscious, but it was downright embarrassing to have to do it while he was awake.

Thorkell coughed and spluttered, his body heaving with the paroxysm.

"There you go," Gran said encouragingly, patting him on the shoulder as if she was encouraging a young dog. "We'll do this a few times, and you'll soon feel better."

A week later Gran pronounced Thorkell well enough to be allowed out of bed, and Filan helped support him as he took the few short wavering steps from the bed to a seat by the door.

"Is he well now?" asked Ciarnat.

"As well as we can make him." Gran smiled. "From now on, he just has to get his strength back. Good food and rest will do the work for us. It's always a grand feeling when we win a fight against death."

CHAPTER THIRTY EIGHT

❝WHEN WILL HE BE FIT ENOUGH to travel?" Filan asked.

Gran glanced across the yard to where Thorkell rested in the sun. A small pile of shavings had collected around his feet from the wood he was whittling.

"Not for a while," she said.

"How long is that?" Filan was impatient. "I've stayed here too long as it is because of him. I need to return to court."

Gran shrugged. "Then you'll go without him, my lad. He won't be fit enough to travel at least until the seasons change. You've seen how weak he is."

Filan's jaw dropped. "He has to stay here that long? That's ages away."

"He's got no other home to go to that I know of," said Gran tartly.

"But ..."

"There are no 'buts'." Gran was firm. "He tried to help me in the herb garden yesterday. He hoed half a row and had to stop. He was pale and sweating."

"Even so."

"He lost an enormous amount of condition when he had that

fever. He's a walking skeleton. Look at him. A slight breeze could knock him over. Regaining good health takes time."

"But I have to go. Áed needs me, and my place is beside him. But how can I leave you and Ciarnat here without protection?"

Gran made an impatient noise. "Protection. From *him*? Don't be daft; he's so weak he's no threat to anyone. Besides which, he seems friendly and helpful enough."

Filan sighed. "I hope you're right. At least you have Padraig if you needed some support."

"Ciarnat and I will manage just fine," Gran assured him. Her gaze focused on where Ciarnat had come into the yard and taken a seat beside Thorkell.

"I can't understand a word he's saying," she said, "but Ciarnat seems to be making progress with his language, and I've heard Thorkell trying out some words in ours."

"She has a quick ear," said Filan. "She always did. When she was with me, she'd pick up a tune or the words to a song in no time."

"You still miss having her with you," Gran stated flatly.

"Aye, I do. But she's safer here, even with a Norseman for company," Filan sighed. "If there's no help for it, then I'll leave tomorrow."

⁙

Ciarnat breathed a sigh of relief when Filan left. She still hadn't forgiven him for abandoning her with Gran five years ago. There was a barrier between them now, and the easy communication they had once shared was a distant memory.

They loved each other, of course, but there were things that she would never now discuss with her father. It went without saying that there were things she'd never talk about with Gran, either. The two generations separating them ensured that.

As summer advanced, the residents of the farm grew into a comfortable routine together. In the early morning, Ciarnat would rise, milk the cow, collect the eggs and feed the pigs. By the time she returned to the house, Gran had made the morning meal. Padraig always joined them. It allowed him and Gran to discuss issues with the cattle and ensured, as Gran said, 'the man has one decent meal a day—those boys of his are useless'.

It also meant Padraig got to spend time with Gran. In the time Ciarnat had spent there, the matter of Gran's relationship with the man had never again been discussed. Sometimes, when Gran went to 'visit a patient' but left her behind, Ciarnat imagined Gran and Padraig had found a quiet place together.

Anyway, the current arrangement fed Padraig and permitted him to feel he was doing his bit to supervise and protect Filan's women, particularly concerning Thorkell.

Ciarnat wondered if Thorkell resented this. Padraig made little attempt to hide his animosity. He said plainly Thorkell was 'an outlander' and accordingly treated him with a suspicion that verged on insulting rudeness.

After the meal, came the ordinary tasks of the day—laundry, cleaning, sewing, weaving and spinning, maintaining Gran's precious herb garden and caring for the food crops.

Padraig and his sons completed the heavy work with the cattle, ploughing or planting oats and grain, but there was more than enough work for Gran and Ciarnat.

Filan had spoken truly when he'd said his mother could have enjoyed a life of quiet rest and luxury had she chosen, but that wasn't her way. She enjoyed her work and expected Ciarnat to work alongside her.

When Gran wasn't at work on the farm, she'd walk to the village below the valley, where she served as a midwife and healer woman, and she usually took Ciarnat with her to increase her skills.

Ciarnat didn't dislike the work—there was a satisfaction every time a mother and baby came through childbirth well and safely. She'd seen many, and tears came to Ciarnat's eyes with each successful new birth. She was interested enough watching what Gran prescribed for illnesses and was happy to gather herbs or brew up potions to Gran's specifications. But she was bored. That was the trouble. The people in the village were polite enough, and she was even related to some of them, but she'd spent her formative years in an environment which was dissimilar enough to prevent her forming close friendships with girls reared differently. She sensed she made them uncomfortable and suspected that, without Gran's protection, they'd have rejected her.

She still pined for the days she'd spent with her da, for the musicianship they'd shared, for the excitement of performing, for the variety of being a guest in a new hall. She still sang when she was alone. She couldn't help herself. Singing was as comfortable as speaking and sometimes expressed things more obliquely and subtly than mere words. She missed the harp, now lost to her while Filan was away.

Gran loved her but didn't have that thread of music in her; she couldn't hear the notes and words floating in the air the way Ciarnat could.

Above all, living with Gran was very dull.

Thorkell was a relief. He helped with those chores he could— chopping wood, stacking firewood or cutting and gathering peat. He'd help carry her milk pail or the buckets of pig swill. Most importantly, he was a fresh face, a man, and one near enough to her age.

"Thanks," she said as he lifted the heavy pail for her.

He smiled at her. "I'm stronger than you."

It took her a second to understand his heavily accented words. "You speak our language!" she'd said delightedly.

"A little," he admitted.

"More than I understand yours," she said. "I must practise more."

He gave her another warm smile. "There is time."

When he grew tired, for he still wearied quickly, it was nothing but courtesy for her to sit beside him and entertain him. Her hands were busy, for Gran despised idle hands, but they would be spinning or stitching, which left plenty of time to talk.

She was curious about his background. Apart from defining him as a Norseman, Filan had left specifics vague. It didn't take much imagination to realise Thorkell, whom she instinctively liked, was one of the foreign raiders.

To Ciarnat's surprise, she realised Thorkell could understand almost everything she said. He'd had some trouble with her family's accent, he explained, but once his ear tuned to her speech, he knew enough to be able to talk to her.

As she still struggled with the basic pronunciation of his tongue, she was mortified he was a more able scholar, until he explained he'd been reared by a nurse who had taught him her language.

"Was your nurse one of our people?"

Thorkell nodded, suddenly reluctant to expand on how the woman had come to his home fjord. His unease was apparent on his face.

Ciarnat looked away. She was surprised at the spurt of anger she felt for the unfortunate woman's fate. It was time to discover the truth about Thorkell. So far, he'd been too ill, or else courtesy to a guest had prevented her probing. She suspected Filan had a shrewd idea about the man they were harbouring but had said little. "She was a captive, wasn't she?" The challenge in her voice made Thorkell wince. He nodded again.

"Was that why you were here? Were you coming to raid us?"

Thorkell opened his mouth, then shut it. What was he supposed to say?

"It was, wasn't it."

"*Já*," he said reluctantly.

"I see." She focused on a place on the wall where a stone had fallen loose. A long silence fell between them.

"I must go," she said at last. "There's butter to churn." She stood up.

"It's been our way for years," Thorkell blurted out. "We are traders. That's our way of life."

Ciarnat spun to stare at him. "Are you saying you traded for your nurse?" Ciarnat did not attempt to disguise her anger.

Thorkell turned his head away.

"I didn't think so. There was no trade, was there? You raided an innocent settlement and took what you want. Just like your people have burned and stolen from our churches and monasteries. Even here, in our remote little valley, I've heard of you 'traders'. As far as I can see, your people are thieves."

That got a reaction!

"We're no more thieves than you." Thorkell's anger matched hers. "It's our way of life, and *já*, if we can, we trade. If we can't, we raid. How is that any different from the fighting between every petty tribe on your island? I've met your High King. Every season he's at war with the rest of the tribes until they acknowledge his supremacy."

"Aye, but that's just because he's the High King! The tribes must recognise that. He wouldn't attack them if they accepted him."

"And paid him taxes and tribute?"

Ciarnat swallowed. She hadn't thought about this and nodded reluctantly. "Aye, I suppose."

"Maybe they would prefer to be independent," Thorkell snapped. "Have you considered that?"

"That's not the same as what your people do to us." Ciarnat paused. "You dare to come from over the sea, neither kith nor kin to our people, wreck our homes, steal our people, our food and our goods."

"We need trade goods to earn gold. We send them deep into the continent across the sea. It's how the trade survives. Slaves, hides, metalwork—where do you think we get our stock from?" Damn it; she'd got under his skin.

"So, we're just 'stock' to you? So many cattle to be raided at your pleasure?" Ciarnat's outrage was palpable.

They glared at each other.

"Maybe your people are 'just stock' to us, but you don't help your own cause. I tell you honestly, if your tribes came together in unity to stop our raids, we wouldn't be able to sustain them. It's your own tribes' stupid, childish war games that leave your people vulnerable."

"So now you blame us? We suffer, and you say it's our fault? How dare you! A murrain upon you, Thorkell, and the devil take your kind." Ciarnat stalked off, anger radiating from her like a cloud.

Thorkell sighed.

CHAPTER
THIRTY NINE

THEIR QUARREL LASTED SOME DAYS. NEITHER Thorkell nor Ciarnat had previously questioned the rules they lived by, or whether they were universal. They just were—as immutable as the tides and reinforced by everyone around you as you grew up. Having a stranger cast their critical eye over the way you lived was offensive, uncomfortable and bitterly resented by each of them.

Gran raised her eyebrows when she realised neither was speaking to the other, but said nothing.

"About time. That girl of yours was getting much too friendly with him," said Padraig. "It would pay you to keep them apart."

"Hush up," said Gran. "They can sort things out for themselves. Until then, Thorkell's a guest here, approved by Filan," she reminded him. "He's to be treated with courtesy."

Padraig muttered something rude under his breath.

"Don't be so grumpy," Gran chided. "He's a nice boy, and helpful around the place. I've watched him helping you as well."

Padraig nodded slowly. "It's the only decent thing I can say about him. He's a good worker, even if he's weak. He knows his way around a farm."

"Well, there you are then."

"He says our soil is richer than their land at home. Told me his farm has thin, poor soil. It'll be why the man is here. He'll want to steal our land!"

Gran shrugged in impatience. "*Sa!* He is at least in part a farmer. It's good for Ciarnat to have company, and he'll be gone soon enough when he recovers his strength. Leave him in peace."

Gran had every intention of following her own advice, but two days later, she came across Thorkell leaning against a wall. Unaware she was behind him, she watched as the arm by his side reached out, and his fingers moved as if searching for something beside him.

Gran frowned. She had seen Thorkell do this before—each time absent-mindedly. She'd assumed he flexed his fingers to restore suppleness to his sword arm. "How are you feeling today?" she asked.

Thorkell spun around, clearly startled. "Oh, well, thank you," he mumbled dismissively. And that would have been the end of it if Gran hadn't seen his eyes were wet.

"What is it?" she asked.

"Nothing, I'm fine. Just catching my breath before Padraig finds me more work to do."

"Nonsense, my boy. I'm not blind; I can see something is upsetting you. What is it?"

"No, it's ..."

She sat down and patted the place beside her on the bench. "Tell me what it is. Are you missing your home? You haven't told me your story yet. How did you end up in the sea?"

Thorkell let out a long sigh, and with no other courteous option available, he unwillingly took the seat beside her, but said nothing. This pushy, competent woman who had saved his life was, he supposed, entitled to an explanation, but he had no idea where to start. He didn't want a repeat of the conversation he'd had with Ciarnat. He had thought she was his friend, but now she wouldn't talk to him.

"I think it's time for you to tell us about yourself," Gran prompted. Perhaps she understood Thorkell's hesitation because she softened her tone. "Where is your place, and who are your people?"

That at least was easy to answer. "I come from the northern lands across the sea. My father is jarl, that is to say, chief of his clan, and I'm his only son—his only child—and heir."

Gran nodded. "So what happened that you were washed up on our shores?"

"My father, Orm, captained our summer trading voyages. But this season, a few weeks before we launched, he was injured and his leg badly crushed. He appointed his younger brother Asger, my uncle, to lead this season's campaign in his place."

Thorkell fell silent. The enormity of Asger's betrayal still left him numb with a sick horror, and he found it hard to speak about it. Ulf was dead, and Thorkell would never forgive Asger for that loss. He'd survived, but only because of Ciarnat and her gran. His teeth ground together. By Odin's balls, Asger was going to pay dearly for his betrayal.

Gran watched as her guest stared into space. The grim set of his jaw didn't encourage interruption.

"Ach, ach," she cleared her throat. Thorkell glanced at her. "So, what happened?"

He took a deep breath. "Asger and I never got on. I don't know why, it's just the way it was. My father warned me he could be dangerous and, before the voyage, made Asger and me vow to work together for the sake of the crew and the *Sea Serpent*. He even made Asger agree my hound would come with us as usual."

He gave a wan smile. "For the first few weeks, everything went fine. I was determined to work with Asger, and in fairness, he was polite to me. Then the storm hit."

He fell silent again and stared at his feet.

Gran rolled her eyes. "What happened when the storm hit?" She didn't bother hiding her irritation. From the corner of her eye, she caught a flicker of movement. Ciarnat had come to lean against the wall behind her.

"This is worse than plucking a chicken," Gran remarked. "What happened next?"

"When the storm passed, and the wind changed in our favour

we packed up the *Sea Serpent* and the men clambered aboard."
Thorkell's hand clenched into a fist of remembered frustration.
"Asger wouldn't let me, or my hound, board with them. They
rolled my father's ship into the tide and sailed away, leaving us
stranded on the beach of that mean little cove, with no way out.
I watched as they disappeared. Part of me thought they'd come
back, that the crew at least would protest."

Thorkell shook his head. "There was no choice. We couldn't
stay on the beach and starve, so we took to the water. The sea was
still rough, and there was debris churned up by the storm. My
poor hound always hated water, but he followed me." Thorkell
took a deep breath. "The rest you know. When Ciarnat found
me, she saved my life. My dog didn't make it and must have
drowned. He'd never have left me otherwise."

"Is that why your hand is always reaching for something?"

"What do you mean?"

"I've watched your arm stretch out as if you were seeking
something. Would that be your dog?"

Thorkell looked down at his hands as if he'd never seen them
before. "I suppose that's so. I never realised. He was always by
my side, and I'd stroke his ears."

Gran shook her head. "That's sad. I'm sorry for your loss. It's
always hard to lose a companion."

Time and quiet are the best healers, she thought as the silence
dragged on.

"What was his name? I mean your hound. What did you call
him?"

Thorkell looked shocked, and his head snapped around as if
he'd just registered Ciarnat's presence. A slight flush coloured
his cheekbones. "Ulf. I named him for a wolf."

"Ulf," Ciarnat repeated. "I'm sorry he didn't make it."

The conversation ended Ciarnat's hostility. From then on, she
made a point of stopping beside Thorkell for a chat when she
passed him during the day. She knew the pain of losing a loved
one, and she didn't make the mistake of assuming Thorkell's
mourning for his hound was any less than hers had been for
Rian. Grief is grief, and guilt is guilt, she thought, then realised

it was a comment Gran might have made, and giggled.

"What amuses you so?" Thorkell asked.

"Nothing. I just realised I am becoming like my gran," she said

With their quarrel behind them, their earlier easy rapport was re-established. Ciarnat was fascinated when Thorkell spoke of his love of the sea.

"You see, the ship isn't a solid object sitting on the water. When the sea moves, the ship bends and flexes with the motion. It's why our ships are so seaworthy. They don't oppose the power of the sea; they take that power and dance with it, so the ship feels alive under your feet."

"Did you always want to be a ..." Ciarnat paused, seeking a non-inflammatory term. "... a warrior?"

"Not necessarily," Thorkell said. "I like the sea and sailing. I like travelling and exploring. Being a warrior is just part of being able to do those things, and it's what was expected of me."

"So if you could choose for yourself what you wanted, what would you do?"

"I'd still be a warrior because those skills are important; but really, I'd want to travel. I listened to a trader many years ago, speaking of the Far Eastern countries. The rivers are deep enough to navigate for hundreds of miles. I thought then I would like to see strange places and people for myself." He gave an amused chuckle. "I was excited enough the first time I came to Dublin and saw men of different colours. Black men, brown men. I hadn't known there were such people. Now imagine seeing for yourself where they live."

Ciarnat nodded. "I understand that. I'd like to travel and see things as well." She sighed. "When I was a little girl, Da used to take me with him on his travels. He was training me to be a bard," she explained. "Then one day I was attacked, and Da decided my gender made me a risk for him. That's when he brought me here to Gran. I miss the excitement, the different places, different people. Sometimes I get so frustrated being stuck in this valley day after day."

"Maybe we should sail away together," Thorkell joked,

"and see all these foreign places. Maybe we could even reach Miklagard."

"Miklagard? Where's that?"

"Your people call it Byzantium. It's far to the east of my home."

"That would be wonderful," Ciarnat sighed. "What a dream to have."

"Ciarnat," Gran called, "can you bring in the washing? It's going to rain."

"And *this* is my reality," Ciarnat added.

CHAPTER FORTY

Erin

Present Day, New Zealand

ERIN PULLED AT THE WEEDS BENEATH the roses. It was late summer and the season was on the turn, the last rose petals almost ready to drop. She'd left them in place when she pruned back the rest of the plants, a splash of colour in the garden. The sun warmed her shoulders as she knelt on the lawn, fossicking for weeds in the flowerbed. She liked feeling the soil between her fingers, releasing its damp, earthy scent. The warm afternoon scent of old roses and the texture of fertile soil in her hands held a sense of harmony—a feeling the world was somehow correct, and she was a part of it.

Which was just as well, Erin thought, because other areas of her world weren't nearly as satisfactory. The prospect of a baby should surely be bringing her and Luke closer together; instead, they seemed to be drifting apart. Luke was becoming more and more wrapped up in his job and showed little interest in discussing their child. When Erin tried to involve him in planning, whether it be antenatal classes or buying baby clothes, he sidestepped the conversation. He returned to his obsession with world markets, the effects of tariffs or, for a change, the fluctuating politics in his workplace.

Tonight they were going out to dinner with his firm, and Erin would meet Luke's new colleague. 'You'll like Alwyn,' Luke had assured her.

Erin sniffed. She'd have much preferred to have the evening to herself. On top of which, she didn't feel particularly well. She was behaving like a sulky child; she scolded herself. Adults went to functions like this all the time. Her mother used to refer to them as 'command performances', a traditional part of supporting your partner. It came with the territory, and a good wife took a keen interest in her husband's profession. (But he isn't interested in either *your* job or your pregnancy, whispered a voice in her ear.)

She tried to shrug it off, but she'd become increasingly irritated by Luke's self-absorption. Was it pregnancy that was making her so sensitive, or had he always been this way?

Their relationship had always been 'relaxed', and Erin had even prided herself on their maturity. They had few arguments, enjoyed each other's company in bed, and shared a common goal of working towards building a prosperous life together. When they'd become a couple, discussing what was important to each of them, there had been little to warn of any future problems. Their professional interests and ambitions seemed synchronous, and they'd agreed that children would eventually be part of the deal.

Their life was tranquil, lacking in the passionate highs and lows she'd observed in other relationships. And, Erin assured herself, that was just the way she liked it. No dramas for her, thank you very much.

They'd bought a lovely house they could just about afford to pay for, they both had modern cars, and they'd enjoyed a couple of overseas holidays. 'We'd better get some travelling in before we're tied up with kids,' Luke had said before they'd gone to Vietnam. They even travelled well together, thought Erin.

The common denominator had been their jobs. They were both hard workers, and their shared interest in financial matters meant there was always something to discuss and share. If Luke's gossip was more interesting than her own experiences at the bank, that figured, didn't it? He was closer to the cut and thrust of international trading, a state that meant politics and policies were his meat and drink. It had been one of the things that fascinated her and drew her to him.

Now Erin was beginning to wonder whether that was enough. She was proud of the work she did, proud of the awards and accolades she'd won, proud of helping her clients, but now she was setting sail for a host of new challenges as a mother. Already she felt herself mentally withdrawing from her workmates—or perhaps they were withdrawing from her. There was an elegiac sense of farewell surrounding her daily duties. She loved her job and would perform her tasks diligently until the day she left, but other interests had entered her focus, centred around her pregnancy. She'd assumed Luke would share that shift with her.

⁘

Two hours later, Luke hooked her elbow through his and led her on his arm into the Hippopotamus restaurant. Most of the others were already seated at their table, having come straight from work. They were, Erin estimated, at least two drinks ahead of Luke who'd had to leave work early to get home to pick her up. She knew she'd be the sober driver tonight once he caught up with them.

David Kittering, Luke's boss, stood up to greet her. "Goodness, Erin, you look more beautiful than ever," he exclaimed. His hand held hers as he leaned forward to kiss her on the cheek. She caught a whiff of Scotch on his breath.

"Thank you, I believe it's something to do with the hormones during pregnancy," Erin said lightly. She'd long suspected David was a 'player', and she kept a wary distance between her, his person and his compliments. Not that she expected him to do anything inappropriate, but Luke's firm circulated scandal as quickly as it did balance sheets, and she'd always taken care to be cautious at these work dos.

Erin was conscious her own thickened waist would be construed as a disadvantage as measured by the professional young women present that she dubbed the 'shark pool'. They all shared a standard look: thirtyish, whippet-slender, serious— or was that seriously inebriated? If not yet, Erin knew from experience they soon would be.

They were all snappily dressed in business suits of black, charcoal, grey or navy, their white shirts unbuttoned just sufficiently to reveal a mere glimpse of curved breast and lacy underwear. It was a style Erin herself had perfected for years and been proud to wear as a professional uniform. Now she was grateful for the empire line of her simple dress that fitted comfortably under her bust and minimised the baby bulge.

She gave a warm smile to David's wife Marg, a woman she admired.

"May I sit here?" she asked.

"Of course, dear. And David is, for once, right. You look lovely. Pregnant women shouldn't look as radiant as you do."

"Thank you," Erin murmured, taking her place. "I can't help but be aware some of the women view my extra weight, let alone my condition, as almost leprous. They're avoiding me in case they get infected."

Marg gave a hoot of unconstrained laughter. "I know, and isn't it funny? I wouldn't let it bother you, my dear. You look great, and I hope that husband of yours is looking after you."

"He is," Erin assured her, although there was a hollow ring to her words.

Luke chose that moment to join them. "Come, darling," he said, reaching again for her elbow. "I want to introduce you to the newest member of the team."

She rose, smiled at Marg and complied as Luke steered her across the floor. She felt her tolerance slipping. Whether he intended it or not, Luke was, quite literally, pushing her around. She was within a nanosecond of digging her heels in and refusing to budge when Luke brought her to a halt.

"Erin, may I introduce you to Alwyn Bishop," he said formally. "Alwyn, my wife."

Erin stared at the man in front of her. Luke's behaviour had alerted her to the importance of this meeting, so she smiled, said something nondescript and continued to scrutinise him. Average height, average weight, and, as far as Erin was concerned, fairly average looks. Whatever drew Luke to him was going to remain a mystery.

She thought he looked a cocky little bastard with not a lot going for him, but there you are. If he was Luke's friend, she would have to try and at least tolerate him.

Alwyn did little to recommend himself. She felt his eyes travel over her and immediately lose interest as he took in the thickness at her waist. His 'delighted to meet you' was phrased so unemotively it was clear he was speaking the words by rote.

Erin inclined her head but felt no need to start a conversation.

Luke seemed oblivious to the tension between them and smiled happily, now that his wife and new best friend had met.

Erin prayed this introduction wouldn't lead to invitations for Alwyn to visit them at home.

"We need to take our place at the table," she prompted. Was she imagining it, or was there a cruel cast to Alwyn's face as Luke rambled apologies as they separated? Perhaps it was ungenerous, but she couldn't help thinking Luke appeared weakened by his obvious infatuation with Alwyn.

The waiter seated her at the table. Erin smiled at the people on either side of her. She'd known Geoff, the company's financial controller, for years and rather liked him. On the other side was Sally, the receptionist whom she'd met before but had never spoken to.

Sally, it seemed, was cheerful, chatty and into her third glass of wine. "Hi," she said. "I heard you were having a baby. When's it due?"

"About three months," Erin said. "Which seems like forever at the moment."

"I bet it does. Still, it's all worth it in the end, or so I hear," Sally smiled. "Luke must be happy about it."

Erin smiled. "He's happy, but then, of course, he's not doing the hard work of actually carrying the baby."

"Yeah, men have it easy," Sally agreed. "Mind you, he and Alwyn have been pretty busy with the new business they're setting up, so he's not sitting around doing nothing."

Erin glanced up from the menu she was studying. New business? She didn't think Luke had mentioned it to her.

"He's always loved his job," she said. "Although I haven't quite worked out what this new venture is about."

"Well, I'm not sure I understand it entirely, but it's something to do with Bitcoin and setting up a company that looks after all the far-out, speculative brokering stuff that Kittering and Hodges won't do. We're a pretty conservative company."

"It's always seemed a sensible approach to me, particularly when they're responsible for other people's money," Erin said.

"Yes, but I guess it's not that exciting for the guys that are real go-getters. So Alwyn and Luke are running their own show now, using our premises as a base to help them start up. If their operation is successful, they'll get bought out by Kittering and Hodges, and of course, they'll be full partners then."

"What happens if they fail?"

Sally looked surprised. "Um, pass? I don't know. I don't imagine they will. Alwyn's very competent and persuasive, and Luke's experienced in the industry. I understand their early results are encouraging."

And I'm pregnant and now is not the time for a speculative venture, Erin thought. She knew Luke hadn't explained any of this to her. He'd let her think things were rolling on as usual and that his job was secure. They'd always discussed things together as a couple—jobs, goals, savings. This new-found secrecy was deeply disturbing.

"Let's hope you're right," she said, glancing down the table to where Alwyn was sitting.

As if he felt her gaze, Alwyn looked up.

Erin was sure he smirked when he realised she was watching him.

CHAPTER
FORTY ONE

ERIN WAS QUIET AS SHE DROVE HOME.

"You OK?" Luke asked.

"Mmm, sure. Just tired." Erin took a breath. "When were you going to tell me you'd gone into business with Alwyn?"

"Ah." Luke shot her a glance. "Well, it's not so much 'gone into business', you know, it's just a subset of what we've been doing all along."

"So are you still employed by Kittering and Hodges?"

"Yes, sort of. Well, not exactly. They're helping us get started because when we're successful, they'll acquire a whole new arm to their business. But no, technically we're self-employed at the moment."

"You didn't think you should discuss this with me first?" She was fighting for control, but there was anger in her tone. She couldn't avoid it.

She didn't need the light from the dashboard to see Luke's face set into sulky lines. She could hear it in his voice.

"I was pretty sure you'd make a fuss about it, and see, you are."

"I'm pregnant, for fuck's sake. We're going to be dropping down to one income in a couple of months—your income.

What's going to happen when the money stops coming in? What are we supposed to live on if this venture fails?"

"You're always so damned negative about everything. I knew I was right not to tell you. You're upset and unreasonable. But you know what will happen? You'll be the first one to be pleased when the money starts rolling in. So it might be nice if you were supportive now."

"Of course I'm bloody upset. We've always discussed everything together. What's changed that you had to keep this secret from me?"

"I knew you'd throw a fit, that's all. What's the point? I was going to do this anyway, and an argument wouldn't have stopped me."

"Don't you think, at the very least, we should have discussed the timing of this venture? Couldn't it have waited until I'd had the baby and was back at work? At least we'd have some form of security then."

"Alwyn wouldn't have been prepared to wait. He wanted to move on this straight away, and he's right. There's a place for what we're doing right now. If we waited, we'd probably have missed the boat. So no, we couldn't wait."

"This is all about Alwyn and what he wants? What about what your wife and family *need*?"

"It's nothing to do with Alwyn. I knew you wouldn't listen, let alone understand. All you want to talk about these days is your bloody pregnancy. Well, that's your thing, fair enough, but I've got a future to make for us. You don't even listen when I tell you how my day has gone when I come in at night. If you had, maybe I'd have told you about this sooner, but there it is."

Erin stared at him. "It's not *my* bloody pregnancy, it's *ours*. It's the pregnancy *we* planned and discussed together. This isn't something I took upon myself to do alone. We're supposed to be sharing the experience." Just like we're supposed to be sharing everything else, she thought.

"Look, I'm sorry you're upset, but it will all work out, you'll see." Luke's voice was soothing. "You know I'm thrilled about the baby. I just don't show it the same way as you, that's all.

Trust me; things will be OK."

It's not OK now. What makes you think it's going to get better?

Erin wanted to scream, but she clenched her jaw and left the words unspoken.

They finished the journey in silence.

Somewhat to her surprise, Erin was tired enough to fall asleep quickly but woke up two hours later. Of all the indignities of pregnancy, wanting to pee all the time was the worst.

She managed not to disturb Luke, who was peacefully snoring, as she slipped back into bed.

What on earth were they going to do? she asked herself as she lay beside him.

She'd prided herself—had thought they both prided themselves—on taking a sensible, well-planned approach to their lives. They shared their objectives and discussed the best way to achieve them. The pregnancy was a case in point. They had both agreed they wouldn't start a family until they were financially stable and could support a child on one income.

Now Luke had blown that apart. Not only were they going to be insecure financially, but she wondered what else he might be planning or doing that he hadn't shared with her.

It would be easy to lay the blame on Alwyn, but Luke was an adult, capable of making his own decisions.

Erin shifted restlessly on the bed. Luke had been doing a few odd things recently. She hadn't allowed herself to dwell on it, but she'd been disturbed the night she woke to find him trying to make love while she was asleep. He'd been drunk and randy, of course, and she *had* woken up, so she could hardly claim the sex was non-consensual, but she wondered how far Luke would have taken things if she hadn't.

Perhaps it had been a harbinger of what was to come. Luke had put his desires before hers and considered her opinion and consent as irrelevant.

She rolled onto her back. Beside her, Luke grunted and repositioned himself, facing her. As he wriggled over, his arm lifted and fell back so it rested on her stomach.

Erin pulled a face. The last thing she wanted was any contact with him tonight. She was just about to push his hand off when, unexpectedly, her abdomen gave a sharp lurch, and Luke's hand slid away.

Erin gasped and clapped her own hands to her stomach. She was rewarded with another wriggly movement from inside.

Her baby was kicking!

For the moment at least, Erin's worries disappeared in a wave of pleasure.

CHAPTER
FORTY TWO

Thorkell

Ninth Century, Ireland

ONE DAY IN EARLY AUTUMN, WHEN cicadas were singing in the hedgerows and thistle seeds flew in twirling clusters over busy fields, the whole village had joined together. Men scythed the grain, the first harvest of the season, while the women walked behind them gathering it into sheaves. Small children ran about, playing and falling in the stubble left behind.

It wasn't so very different from the way they organised things back home, thought Thorkell. The work was hard, but there was plenty of laughter in the voices he heard around him. A couple of younger women smiled at him as they bent to gather stalks he'd cut.

He was a foreigner here and still regarded as such, but slowly, the villagers were warming to him. Thorkell rested his scythe on the ground. Along the row, others were working their way through the field of barley. Sweat trickled down his forehead, and the sleeve he used to wipe it away was almost as wet as his skin.

Ciarnat walked towards him. "Have some light beer," she said, offering him a mug.

Thorkell nodded his thanks as he took a deep draught. "Is it always this hot in summer?"

Ciarnat smiled. "Yes. Harvest time is always like this. Drink plenty. You'll need it to keep your strength up."

Thorkell looked up at the bright blue sky. "I didn't expect to say this, but I'm almost missing the rain."

As usual, Ciarnat couldn't resist challenging him. "You've complained about our rain non-stop the whole time you've been here; now you complain about our sunshine? You're a hard man to please."

Thorkell grinned and watched Ciarnat's hips swing as she walked away down the line to offer a drink to the next man. They'd repaired their friendship, and he supposed he had Ulf to thank for that. The story of his dog's death had opened a route into Ciarnat's soft heart.

He still wasn't sure what to make of her. She could be as haughty as the ladies in the High King's court. Then again, she could be as cheeky and common as any urchin brat in the village. She was as independent and self-reliant as any shield-maiden, but although she protected herself with a wall of sarcasm, at her core she was as kind and sweet as warm honey.

He thought of Odell's stern, chilly loveliness. She'd once been the most exquisite woman he'd seen, and as an impressionable boy, he'd taken her as a measure of ideal beauty.

Thorkell tried to rationalise why Ciarnat now seemed the more attractive woman. He'd decided it was because her external features, lovely as they were, wrapped a woman more vital than any he'd known.

Her eyes, of course, were exceptional—a blue so deep that in some lights they were the deep purple of iolite, the compass stone Vikings used to travel the seas. Matched with her lightly tanned skin, a smattering of freckles on her nose, her long, dark, wavy hair and feminine shape, she was beautiful by any standards.

When Ciarnat laughed, there was no artifice, and her happiness was contagious. When she stooped to help a patient, her care was genuine, her instinct focused on support. When she was angry, there was no avoiding her wrath. She didn't hide what she was. Her warmth, her energy and her emotions were shared unsparingly. Even the quirky, acidic relationship she had with her gran was a thin veil over the closeness between them. A beautiful woman, with a singing voice these Christian people described as 'angelic'.

Thorkell shook his head and took a tighter grip on his scythe as he returned to swinging at the wall of barley in front of him. It was no good dwelling on Ciarnat and her endlessly challenging, teasing mien. His duty was clear before him. He had a blood feud to settle when he returned home. This was no time to start courting a woman, however much she moved him.

He was almost back to his full strength. Long days helping Padraig mend the barn's roof, or hoeing Gran's herb garden had rebuilt his muscles, and good food had filled his frame out again. He'd recently started practising the training drills with spear and axe to regain his speed and skills. If the glances he pretended not to notice from the village girls were anything to go by, he was looking just fine as well.

Thorkell sighed. The barley would be cleared today, and if so, the harvest festival would be tomorrow night. It was time for him to leave, and he would have to say so tonight. He dreaded telling Ciarnat.

He'd been scrupulously careful in his behaviour towards her; he'd made no advances, and limited opportunities for intimacy between them. He was a guest in her home; she and her gran had saved his life. Filan, his host, a man of some reputation, had trusted him enough to let him stay with his women when he couldn't be there. No man of honour, regardless of race or breeding, would attempt to seduce the daughter of the house in such circumstances.

Ciarnat herself was always circumspect. She'd offered friendship and companionship, and nothing more—her laughter, often at his expense, her explanations when he didn't understand, her kindness and, above all, her friendship had been a large part of his recovery. Thorkell recognised his debt to her and her family.

Was he foolish to think there was more to the glances they shared? More meaning to the jokes Ciarnat made, something more than friendship in the pleasure with which she greeted him each morning? It seemed to him they were both careful never to touch, even by accident. Once he'd reached for a spade just as she'd picked the tool up, their hands had collided, and Ciarnat had jumped back like a startled horse. He'd immediately snatched his hand away, and the spade dropped to the ground. They'd shared a moment's embarrassed laughter, and then a more extended, self-conscious period of silence as they returned to their work.

It had felt significant to him, but it was impossible to tell what the woman was thinking. She guarded herself well. He simply knew that Ciarnat had become the focus of his days.

He swung his scythe viciously at the plants in front of him. Why was nothing in his life ever simple?

That night, when they sat at supper, he broached the matter. He spoke to Gran. It was more comfortable if he didn't have to look at Ciarnat. "You've been more than hospitable. I know full well I owe you all my life, but I am recovered now, and I need to return to my home. My father is old and infirm, and some scores need settling. If I don't leave now, it will be too late in the season for me to catch a boat plying the sea to the north country. Thor knows I have no desire to leave you all, but I must."

To his relief, Gran nodded. "I know lad. I know." She reached over and patted his knee. "You're looking fit and well, boy. We'll miss you and the work you help us with, but we know it's time for you to go." She sighed. "I had hoped Filan would have returned by now. He usually visits for the harvest, and then you could have travelled north with him. But the season is waning. You are right to leave now. At least you'll be able to celebrate Lughnasa with us tomorrow before you leave."

"Lughnasa?"

"The celebration for the harvest. It's named for one of our old gods."

Thorkell took one swift glance at Ciarnat. As far as he could tell, she hadn't moved. No expression crossed her face; no sharp movement indicated her feelings. But she'd stopped eating.

He risked a closer look. Ciarnat was disciplined to her core and gave no hint of her thoughts—but her face had turned unhealthily pale beneath its light summer tan. The otherwise charming freckles stood out, small dots of distress in her pale, frozen face.

Thorkell bowed his head, unable to watch her. He excused himself shortly after and made his way to his bed in the barn. His grief seemed unbearable. He couldn't cope if he were causing her the same pain.

The next day Ciarnat and Gran were busy preparing food for the feast that evening, so he spent the day with Padraig doing chores. It wasn't until dusk, as they made their way towards the village, that Thorkell got a chance to talk to her and judge her mood. "Are you looking forward to the feast tonight?"

"Yes, it's always fun, and there will be dancing later." Ciarnat seemed as relaxed and friendly as ever.

Perhaps he'd imagined her distress last night. Perversely, he was disappointed and annoyed with himself. "Dancing?"

Ciarnat grinned at him. "Yes. Dancing. You'll enjoy it."

"I don't know your dances. I'd likely make a fool of myself."

"No, you won't. Everyone joins in, particularly the younger ones. Most of the village romances start on the dance floor at harvest time, so it's very popular. You'll have to take a care who you dance with tonight; they might get ideas about you."

"Now I'm afraid for my safety."

He heard her chuckle. She stopped. "Here, I made this for you. It's traditional; you need to wear it to celebrate Lughnasa."

She drew a strand of threaded bright red berries from her pocket. "You can put it around your neck, or in your hair like a crown. I made one for myself as well."

Thorkell bent his head to allow her to settle the string around his neck. He was acutely aware of the touch of her light fingers on his skin.

"There, now you look as if you are one of us."

She stepped back and smiled as she threaded her strand through the braid in her hair. The bright berries were vivid against her dark hair, and there was a slight flush in her cheeks. Her prettiness took his breath away. For a brief moment, their eyes met, then she stepped away.

.÷.

The village was lit up with the flare of firebrands and the bonfire already alight by the time they arrived. Trestles had been set up, their legs almost buckling beneath the weight of food. Men turned a spit from which the rich scent of roasting meat hung in the air. Ale was being poured freely. Before he knew it, Thorkell and Padraig had been handed mugs by the Christian priest.

"Drink up, lads," he urged. "It's been a bumper harvest this year. We've been truly blessed."

"Thank you," Padraig said as he downed his drink. "The man takes good care of us," he explained to Thorkell. "Not just our poor, penitent souls, but he cares for our bodies, too. Isn't that right, Father Niall?"

"All things in moderation," replied the priest. He nodded to Thorkell. "I saw you working yesterday. You've been a great help to us this season."

Thorkell smiled as the priest turned away to serve others.

"Go and help yourself to some food," Padraig suggested. "There's plenty for everyone. We'll all have sore heads and sorer stomachs tomorrow, but it will have been worth it."

As night darkened, music began. One man started playing a jaunty tune on a small whistle, then another joined in with a larger flute. A drummer soon settled into the rhythm, and still another musician began to play an extraordinary instrument such as Thorkell had never seen before. It had a bladder which he inflated, then squeezed under his arm while his fingers played the tune on two whistle-like pipes protruding from the bag. The drone produced from the contraption was powerfully sonorous and easily heard over the crowd's cheerful chatter.

Thorkell turned to a man beside him. "What is that?"

His companion grinned. "Ye've no heard the uilleann pipes before?"

Thorkell shook his head. "Never."

"Once heard, never to be forgotten, aye, Norseman?"

Thorkell nodded.

After a few tunes, the musicians paused for a break, and the noisy crowd settled into silence as a woman's clear voice soared over the crowd.

The bonfire's blaze illuminated her—a girl all in gold, as precious as the metal itself.

Thorkell had heard Ciarnat sing around the farm, but he'd never seen her perform for a crowd. He watched how completely she held her audience's attention. Her first song was a prayer of thanks for the harvest. She sang it simply, sweetly and reverently, although Thorkell wasn't sure whether she praised Christ or Lugh. He glanced across at the priest who didn't seem to be disturbed.

Then Ciarnat moved to secular songs, with love songs and humorous verses for the crowd's amusement. They applauded noisily and called for more when she bowed and finished. She smiled, but shook her head, indicating the other musicians waiting to play.

"You were wonderful," he said sincerely when Ciarnat made her way through the throng to stand beside him.

"The dance music is starting," she said. "Will you dance with me once I've had something to eat? I never like to eat before a performance."

He followed her over to the feast trestles. "I'll help you carry it," he offered. "There's a space over there on the wall where we can sit while you eat, and if I'm going to have to dance, I'd better have another few drinks."

CHAPTER
FORTY THREE

IT WAS A BEAUTIFUL NIGHT TO be outdoors, although all the light from the blazing bonfire and flaring torches eclipsed the moon and stars. The temperature had dropped at sunset, but the fire threw out a fierce heat, so they were warm enough, even though Ciarnat was only wearing a summer dress.

Thorkell would have been content to sit beside her like this forever, enjoying the scent of her soft hair and her closeness, but Ciarnat had other plans.

"Are you ready?" she asked.

"Ready?"

"To dance, stupid."

Thorkell groaned. "I haven't had enough to drink yet."

"You've had more than your fill. You'll fall over if you have much more." It wasn't true, but Thorkell could tell she was enjoying teasing him.

"Surely you shouldn't dance right after eating all that food? You'll get a cramp. We need to give it time to settle."

"Don't be silly," she said, reaching for his hand and pulling him to his feet. "Come on."

Older couples swayed sedately on the perimeter of the dancing floor while in the middle the younger pairings were having a more vigorous time. Ciarnat led Thorkell into place. She'd been right. The dance steps were easy to pick up, and no one cared if you got them right or not.

The women formed an inner circle which the men surrounded with their own. The dance was lively, with a good deal of banter between the couples. Men strutted while women dipped and swayed, graceful and proud in response, until the men seized their waists and swung them around. Then there was laughter and shrieking as the girls lost their balance and fell against their partners.

The first time this move took place, Thorkell was startled and uncertain, and twirled Ciarnat cautiously, but he was soon made to understand that enthusiasm and vigour were expected in the dance. Before long he'd mastered the manoeuvre and was spinning her with flamboyance, enjoying the feel of her when she landed in his arms. A part of his brain tugged at his memory, cautioning him this was a perilous game to play, but he'd had sufficient drink to mute it—and he was so very much enjoying himself.

Dance followed dance until Thorkell was grateful whenever the musicians stopped to allow the dancers to catch their breath and refresh themselves.

"I'm exhausted," Ciarnat said as she sat down on the wall again. "My feet are going to be sore tomorrow."

"Are you saying you want to stop? Are you too tired?"

Ciarnat looked at him with narrowed eyes, completely understanding what lay behind the caring words. "You'll give up before I will," she shot back at him and watched his eyes crinkle as she rose to his challenge.

They sat together in silence for a few minutes. The musicians had paused for a supper break.

"You should know I don't ever give up," Ciarnat said eventually.

Thorkell looked sideways at her. "I don't either."

Ciarnat took a deep breath, then turned and faced him. "Are we still discussing dancing?"

For the longest moment, Thorkell looked into her eyes. All his good intentions, wise decisions, sensible solutions, all crumbled under her steady gaze. He gave a slight sigh. "No."

The word said, they both looked away. Honesty is sometimes too great a burden.

"It's impossible. I have duties ..."

Ciarnat gave a short laugh. "And so do I."

"You know I have to go ..."

"The question is, will you come back, or am I just a silly green girl?"

Thorkell's gasp suddenly seemed to fill his mouth with words. "No. Never. I have to go, you know that, but my heart is here. I want you in my life, to be my wife... to be my love." His voice faltered and faded on the last four words.

"It wouldn't be easy." Ciarnat spoke carefully. "Your people and my people are not at peace. I know what you Norsemen do when you pillage a settlement."

"And yet the villagers here have been kind to me."

"They're too stupid to know any better." Ciarnat's voice was suddenly angry. "When they find out, what do you think they'll want to do? Drive out the Norseman is my guess."

"You could come to my father's house. He would welcome you." Thorkell smiled. "He has a taste for beautiful women."

"Wonderful! I'd be your wife in a land where women of my race are regarded as slaves," Ciarnat's said viciously. "I'd rather be a free woman than any man's slave."

Thorkell bowed his head. It was true. Neither of them were children. Both knew enough to see the problems ahead. "And yet," he whispered, reaching out to put his hand on top of hers.

Without hesitation, her hand turned and curled into his. "And yet," she murmured.

For a while they sat quietly, allowing what they'd both acknowledged to seed and grow.

The music began again.

"Once more?" Thorkell smiled as Ciarnat nodded.

"Once more," she echoed.

The music was softer now, the tempo slower. The musicians, winding up for the night, knew their audience. These lads and lasses, so full of energy, lust and youth, would still have to get up in the morning to milk the house cow, feed the chickens and do a full day's work in the fields. Best to steer them home quietly.

Those still on the floor had little taste now for flinging their partners around in the dance. Most of the older people had long since gone home. Gran and Padraig had left a couple of hours earlier. There was no one left to interfere, and it *was* Lughnasa, the festival of fertility and ripeness. The bonfire had burned down and shed little light on the couples clasped together in the last few dances. Kisses were stolen, soft willing bodies caressed under the safe cover of darkness. In a few months there would be a rash of hasty weddings, and who cared?

The priest took a tolerant view of his parishioners' sins. Who was he to take a severe approach to the misdeeds of his flock? God was kind, and Jesus had already died to forgive all mankind.

Ciarnat and Thorkell walked home hand in hand. Away from the burning torches and firelight, the deep blue dome of the sky held enough light from the moon and stars for them to find their way up the track to the valley.

It seemed there was little to speak of between them, and yet everything needed saying. For now, it was enough to walk together, so close their bodies bumped at regular intervals. Thorkell felt Ciarnat shivering and drew the cloak from his shoulder to wrap around her.

"We can share it," she said and waited while he repinned it on his shoulder and spread the length over her shoulders as well. Now they walked nearer each other, a quiet, gentle pace, suiting their strides to each other. Thorkell wrapped his arm around Ciarnat's waist and pulled her even nearer. For a moment, her step faltered before she caught the new rhythm and moved beside him, their steps as close and matching as a dance.

At the top of the rise, where the track descended to the broad pasture of their valley, large patches of gorse and broom edged the trail and threw deep pools of shadow on the ground. Thorkell stopped. The night was gentle around them. In the distance, an occasional cattle beast lowed; nearer still there were small night creatures that rustled the grass. No human sound intruded on their privacy.

They took the time to explore each other's mouths. Ciarnat ran her fingers over his face, and he leaned his face into the palm cradling his cheek.

"That feels good," he murmured.

Ciarnat stood still as his thumb caressed her lips. Oh, her mouth was soft and yielding.

They walked on, moving ever slower.

Thorkell turned towards her. "Your hair in the moonlight," he said softly. "I will always remember that—how beautiful you are, how beautiful the light is on your hair." He reached out to stroke the soft braid. "You are my moon-maiden."

"You'll forget me when you return home," she said, forcing herself to speak lightly. For pride's sake, she thought, don't shame yourself in front of him by begging him not to go.

As if he'd read her mind, he answered her unasked question. "When I've completed my task, when I've seen Orm and taken my full revenge on Asger, I promise I will return here."

"Return?"

"A year ago, my father had thought to establish a permanent winter camp in Dublin. He wanted to rid himself of my thrice-cursed uncle. Now, maybe I'll be the one to settle there."

"You'd leave your home?"

Thorkell nodded slowly. "A man, a sensible man, looks for treasure. When he finds it, he should stop searching and cherish it."

Ciarnat felt the tears she'd been battling fill her eyes. "Yes, perhaps that's what a sensible man would do," she agreed as she gave him a shaky smile.

He reached for her hand again, and they continued walking.

Neither of them felt any need to rush their exploration, nor progress matters too far.

Thorkell would still have to leave, and they both knew whatever happened tonight would only make the parting harder.

CHAPTER
FORTY FOUR

Ciarnat

Ninth Century, Ireland

THEY COULD SEE THE FAINT GLIMMER of light around the edge of the shutters when they reached the farm.

"They must be waiting for you," Thorkell said, sounding amused.

"Why would they do that?" Ciarnat asked, puzzled.

By the time they reached the barn, the soft rustle of animals inside moving on the straw had given them their answer.

"There are horses inside," she exclaimed. "Da must have returned." She gave Thorkell a radiant smile and ran towards the door.

He followed more slowly and entered the house to hear her cry of joy as she rushed forward to greet her father.

"You've come back. You've missed Lughnasa this year, though. Did Gran tell you?"

Filan stood up from his feet and hugged her. "My bonny girl," he said at last, holding her at arm's length. "Have you got taller?"

"Oh Da, you know full well I've been full-grown for a year or more," she said in exasperation. "Why are you so late you missed the harvest festival?"

"Hush, child. I'll tell you in a moment. But first of all, I've got a present for you."

"For me?" Ciarnat was startled. Filan rarely brought gifts for either her or Gran.

From beneath the table, Filan drew out a large package wrapped in oilskin.

"Happy Lughnasa," he said as he set it down on the table.

The wrapping covered the present entirely, but Ciarnat had no difficulty in identifying the object inside.

"A harp. You've brought me a harp?" she exclaimed. She could imagine no better present. When Filan had left her with Gran, she'd missed being able to play his harp almost as much as she'd missed her da. She could borrow his instrument when he visited, but there was as much grief as there was pleasure in the experience. Her fingers were no longer nimble on the strings and technique that had been as natural as her gift for song felt clumsy, forced, and her practice ended all too often in frustration and misery.

Her fingers hurried as she worked the knots on the package.

You'd do better if you slowed down," Gran remarked watching her struggle to free the binding.

Ciarnat looked up with a grin as the knot finally loosened. "I want to see what's inside."

Free of the binding, the wrapping came away readily.

"Ah."

Filan smiled at Ciarnat's deep intake of breath. "Do you like it?" he asked.

"It's wonderful," she breathed, running her hand down the intricately carved body. "What are they?" she asked as her fingers traced the petals of an exotic flower unknown to her.

"Who knows?" Filan answered. "The man I bought it from had no use for it. I told him I would give it to you."

Ciarnat gave a slight smile. Her hands caressed the curve of the harp's neck and then stroked the pillar. "How could anyone not want to keep this? It's so beautiful." She ran her hand lightly across the strings. "Ugh," she said. "It's out of tune."

"Here's the key."

"Thank you." Ciarnat gave her father a warm smile. "It's a wonderful present. I'll treasure it forever."

Filan nodded in satisfaction. "I thought you'd like it."

He looked up as Thorkell entered, shutting the door behind him. Filan raised a hand and smiled. "You look well, my friend," he said, clasping Thorkell's arm. "Come and join us. Now that you're here and Ciarnat has her present, we can get back to what Padraig here was just telling us. Carry on," he urged the cattleman.

Padraig frowned at Thorkell. "As I was saying, I was talking to old Diathi tonight, and it's looking like a harsh season ahead. They've already got a wolf prowling the woods above their valley. It will be a long, bitter winter when wolves start coming in so early in the season. I told him he was lucky; at least it was only one beast."

"It's not likely to be one wolf on its own, though, is it?" Filan asked. "They're pack animals. It wouldn't be alone."

"Unless it's a young male pushed from the pack to make its way," Thorkell suggested.

"Diathi swears it's alone. He's seen it—a big grey beast. He thought it was a lost hound at first, but it wouldn't let him approach. So far no stock has been lost, but that'll be only a matter of time, of course. I suppose we will have to go up there and help him flush it out soon."

"What did you say?" There was an urgency to Thorkell's voice that startled Padraig.

"You don't need to be afraid, Northman," he taunted. "No wolf is coming for you. You're safe here."

Ciarnat saw Thorkell's bright blue eyes turn icy. "You accuse me of fear, you fool? When Ciarnat found me, I had lost a hound. If that animal is mine, I have to find it."

"Oh." Padraig was silenced.

"Do you think it could be?" asked Ciarnat.

Padraig shrugged. "I'm only repeating what Diathi said."

"Then let us hope it is yours," Gran said. "Poor animal if it is lost and surviving on its own."

"Indeed," Filan added. "That would be an excellent outcome if it were so. Come and sit beside me, Thorkell. I am pleased you are looking much better than when I saw you last."

"I am, thanks to the good care I've received. I'm glad to see you before I leave. I owe you and your family a great debt of gratitude for your hospitality," Thorkell replied. "I was planning on leaving tomorrow—or maybe," he gave a grin, "later today, but what Padraig has told us changes things. I must check on this animal to make sure it's not Ulf before I leave here. Either way, I'm glad you're here so I can thank you in person."

Filan's face fell. "Ach, there's a problem. That's what I need to tell you, and it is what held me up, so I was late for Lughnasa." Filan settled himself on his seat. "Áed's campaign moved south this summer against Leinster. So far south, his war-host has reached Glenn dá Locha and is doing a fine job burning up the countryside all around. As a result, Leinster's men and any allied warrior bands have been pushed even further south. They are now no more than five days' march north of us, if that. We're now completely cut off from Áed's force. I had to take my time slipping past enemy forces unseen. A lot of time I travelled by night, skirting picket lines and camps."

"Would your authority from the High King not give you safe passage?" asked Thorkell.

Filan gave a short bark of amusement. "It would if Leinster admitted Áed's sovereignty. As they're his sworn enemies, and I am well known to be Áed's man, I didn't want to find myself murdered, or captured as a hostile spy and interrogated. Even if they traded me as a hostage to enrich some petty lordling's holding, it would be too humiliating for Áed's *ollamh* to endure."

"Thankfully you made it through unscathed," Gran commented dryly.

Filan gave her a cheeky grin. "Not quite unscathed. I bear the scars from hiding in scrubby coppices and gorse bushes. It will take days to brush the burrs and prickles from my saddle and cloak."

Thorkell was frowning. "But I was planning on leaving tomorrow! Which route would you recommend I take? I'd planned to travel overland to Dublin. I must return to my father's hall, so I need a ship to take me. Dublin is a large port, and if I'm there before the season ends, I'm bound to find a trader or another longship that could use an extra crewman across the northern sea." He stopped as Filan shook his head decisively.

"There's no way now. Not by land, anyway," Filan said. "The lines were closed as I came through. It is because I know the country so well I was able to use hidden tracks that usually only locals know. But the situation has changed. In the days since I passed through, I've heard the bands have joined together into one armed force, roaming freely across the breadth of the land. With all the protection my craft and my position afford me, I can't get through until Áed retakes control, and neither can you. We're both prisoners here until the fortunes of war change."

There was silence as his audience considered his news and its impact on their plans.

"Just as well it's been a good harvest then," Gran said briskly. "At least we've plenty of food for everyone, and extra hands to thresh and mill the grain is always a good thing. Padraig can use more help." She nodded at the stockman who'd been sitting quietly at the back of the room.

He nodded dourly.

He won't be pleased Filan's home, Ciarnat thought with amusement before turning her thoughts towards Thorkell. *He'd be frustrated.* She knew how driven he was to reach his home and avenge being cast away in that inlet. But would he also be pleased to have more time to spend with her? She looked at him under her eyelashes. It was hard to judge his mood, but his face was grim.

It was his wyrd, Thorkell thought. Predetermined, ordained and devised by the Norns. As useless to oppose or be enraged by it as it was to try and row a small boat against a strong wind. Thorkell sighed and bowed his head. There were so many questions that could have been avoided if he had left this valley today.

What did Ciarnat expect from him? What did he want to offer her? What could he offer her? This last consideration vexed him. In his land, in his father's hall, he was son and heir to a fine steading. The *Sea Serpent* would eventually be his; its men would serve at his command. He had status, wealth, pride and an honourable family name. Without false modesty, he knew he could offer much to his bride.

Filan had been generous in hosting a man stolen back from the sea. More than generous. He had given his guest a home, a purpose and his health back. But it left Thorkell in his debt, a situation that chafed him badly. In his dreams, he'd repaid that debt with gold and jewels. More, he had offered a high and noble place as his wife to Ciarnat. All that was now delayed. Thorkell cursed at the twisted path the fates had designed for him.

Then he looked across the room at Ciarnat who, he noted, was carefully not looking back, and smiled. What harm in a few extra days, even a few additional weeks? She loved him, he knew, and knowing he loved her back made this tolerable. If this was his wyrd, then who was he to argue?

"Well, if I can't travel to Dublin at the moment, I suppose I can at least go and search for my hound. How far away does Diathi live?"

"A morning's walk, no more," said Padraig. "If you leave early, you'll be back by late afternoon."

They fell silent then, each of them thinking of what Filan had said.

At last, Padraig broke the silence. "I'm for bed, and any wain amongst us with work to do later today needs to do the same, else they'll be no use."

"You're staying in the barn?" Filan asked.

"Aye. Too late now to head up the valley to my place." Padraig nodded to Gran and went to the door.

"I'm for bed as well. Wait for me, Padraig. I need you to give me directions to find Diathi. Thank you all for sharing Lughnasa." Thorkell smiled at Ciarnat. "It seems I must be your guest for a while longer."

Gran rose to her feet and went to bank the fire. "We've all got chores tomorrow. Sleep well."

"Tomorrow," Ciarnat echoed as she headed for bed.

CHAPTER FORTY FIVE

Thorkell

Ninth Century, Ireland

HOURS EARLIER, HE AND CIARNAT HAD WALKED home beneath a starry sky. In the intervening time, the temperature had dropped, and the valley was now shrouded in a thin, wispy mist that clung in drops to his hair and cloak and rendered the hills surrounding him invisible. It wasn't the most inviting morning for travelling a land he was unfamiliar with, but Thorkell had already felt the faint stirring of a sea breeze on his cheek. Unless he were much mistaken, that would strengthen as the sun rose and, as the morning warmed, would clear the mist away.

He'd managed to get the directions to Diathi's holding from Padraig before they went to sleep. Padraig had offered to come with him, but mindful of Filan's news of marauding men not far away, Thorkell elected to travel alone. Padraig was fit and competent, but he wasn't a warrior. By Thorkell's reckoning, whatever happened, whether he had to hide or fight, he'd be better off alone than trying to protect the feisty old farmer.

The path along the clifftop led to the north, although, Thorkell sighed, 'path' was an overly optimistic description of a muddy sheep track that meandered along the edge of the cliff. Only the sight of occasional cattle and horse droppings convinced Thorkell he was on the right course. Not many travellers came this way.

Some two hours later, as Padraig had mentioned, the track descended into a steep, wooded valley. He'd expected a stream bed, but the bottom of the gully was dry. Nothing softened or sweetened the dusty track between the trees, and he was glad when his path led up the far side into the open country at the top.

Thorkell sat on the grass, took the stopper from his flask and drank deeply of Ciarnat's home-brewed ale. He searched the countryside ahead but saw no visible signs of a dwelling, although in the distance there was a high grassy bank which concealed some of the views. The light was in his eyes as he squinted to make out any details, but the late morning sun was against him. At least the path was clear to follow. Thorkell stood and continued down the track.

Half an hour later, he reached the bank and realised it was a man-made curved wall, protecting a settlement behind the barrier. He followed it around until he reached the gates—formidable wooden barriers, double the height of a man—that filled the space between the arms of the embankment. Inexplicably, they were shut and barred on the inside.

Thorkell frowned. Surely at this time of day these would generally stand open? Herders should be with their animals, men and women be at work in the kale plots and cattle byres beyond the walls, and children tumbling in the grass around the gateway. There was something very wrong here.

He approached the gates cautiously. Just because I can't see anybody doesn't mean I'm unobserved, he reminded himself. If the hair rising at the back of his neck was any indication, there must be several pairs of eyes watching his progress.

He stopped in front of the gates—far enough away, he hoped, to be beyond the range of spear throw of an overzealous defender.

"Ho there," he called. "Is there anyone here?"

It took some time, and he nearly called again, but at last a man's head appeared over the top of the gate. Thorkell took him to be on the later side of middle age. His dark hair was flecked with grey. The torc about his neck denoted his status. "Who calls?" he yelled down. "Who are you, and what is your business here?"

"My name is Thorkell Ormson. I am a guest of Filan the *ollamh*. His man Padraig sent me here to find Diathi."

"What do you want with Diathi?"

"He told Padraig he'd seen a beast in the woods. I've lost a hound. I'm hoping this is him."

The man's head disappeared down behind the rampart, and Thorkell spent long moments waiting. He was too far away to hear anything said behind the gates, and in any event, it would be drowned out by the background noise he'd finally identified as cattle and sheep behind the barricade.

What were they protecting themselves from? Filan's warning of armed bands roving the land seemed the likely cause, although they were supposed to be some days' march away. He raked the surrounding country with his gaze. There was no sign of enemy forces yet, but a sensible village was wise to be careful.

It took a while, but finally the man returned with another whom Thorkell took to be Diathi, as he was of a similar age and appearance to Padraig. He tried to recognise him from Lughnasa the night before, but he'd paid little attention to the people talking to Padraig. His whole focus had been on Ciarnat.

Diathi, it seemed, had been more observant. Thorkell saw him nodding agreement to his companion and imagined his identification had been confirmed. In fairness, it was probably easier for Diathi to remember a tall, fair foreigner, who would stand out, than for him to identify yet another Irish farmer.

"Come closer," the leader shouted.

Thorkell hesitated, instinctively scanning the gates and top of the walls for weapons trained on him.

"You're safe." The leader's voice was impatient. "Diathi confirms he spoke to Padraig and that he saw you at Lughnasa.

If our *ollamh* vouches for you, then that is enough for us."

"Who am I speaking with?"

"I'm named Owen Ó Súílleabháin. I lead the people here in the absence of our chief and warriors who are away fighting. Approach the gate. I give you my word; you won't suffer harm. We'll let you in."

Thorkell strode towards the gates as they opened. Although he kept a wary eye out for danger, it seemed Owen was honest.

The man came to meet him at the gate and grasped him by the arm as he greeted him. "I regret our hospitality is so poor," he apologised. "Come with me and let me find refreshment for you. Then you can tell us what brings you here. We are usually more welcoming, but Eoin, our cattle-master, reported seeing armed strangers crossing our lands at twilight yesterday. Our chief allies with Áed, and the men we saw were foreigners."

"Filan told us Leinster wars with Áed this season. These may be his forces, although Filan reckoned them several days march away."

"Hmm. Whoever they are, we thought it prudent to bring our people and animals into shelter. We sent scouts out early this morning, but none have returned yet with news of where those men are now. At least the grain has been harvested and stored, so we don't have to worry about it being stolen or burned."

He led the way to a bench set outside. A woman approached with a jug of ale and poured it into mugs for them. "God's greeting to you, stranger," she murmured formally.

Thorkell nodded his thanks.

He studied the neat, well-constructed settlement. There was an air of cheerfulness as people walked purposefully about their business. A regular rhythm of hammering indicated the forge was in operation. Washing hung on lines, and he could hear cries from the animals penned in the long barn. "Your health," he said as he drank. "You have a fine village here."

Owen smiled. "We are lucky in our chief, and in the lands he holds. We don't need some ambitious little chieftain coming down here and stirring trouble for everyone. Áed may not be to everyone's taste, but he's better than a mass of petty lordlings warring and pillaging throughout the land. I'm only sorry you don't see us at our best."

"Any prudent settlement would take precautions," Thorkell agreed.

"You said you were looking for a hound?" Diathi questioned. "How did you come to lose it?"

It took time for Thorkell to tell his story, and the sun was high in the sky by the time he finished. "I'd planned to start travelling north, to Dublin, today, but Filan cautioned against it. In the meantime, Padraig reported that Diathi had seen some beast in the woods. If there is any chance it's my animal, then I have to take it. If Diathi can show me where the creature has been seen, or at least point me there, I can search for it myself."

He waited expectantly. Owen and Diathi looked at each other.

After a moment, Owen nodded. "It will probably be safe enough, Diathi, as long as you take care," he pronounced. "Show the man the way; it will be quicker and safer because you know the country well."

CHAPTER
FORTY SIX

DIATHI LED THEM AWAY FROM THE coast towards the wooded hills Thorkell had seen beyond the harvested fields. The sun beat down as they trudged across the stubbly, uneven ground, the dry stalks crackling beneath their feet.

"Thor's blood, it's hot out here," Thorkell commented, wiping the sweat from his forehead. "Whereabouts did you spot the strangers yesterday?"

"Just about here," Diathi answered. "Eoin saw them against the backdrop of those trees ahead of us. Frankly, the sooner we're under their cover, the better," he said. "I feel exposed when they could be watching us, but we can't see them."

Thorkell grunted agreement and Diathi set a brisk pace across the paddocks.

It was a relief when they reached the woods and ducked into the cool shade away from the sun's glare. Light filtered through the leaves and dappled the ground and the tangle of undergrowth barring their way which they had to step around.

"No sign of your strangers," Thorkell remarked as Diathi studied the ground.

"No, but they've been here. Look." He pointed to a couple of footprints crossing the dusty bottom of a long dried-up puddle. "With luck, they were just passing through and are now a day's march away."

He led the way, past stands of birch, oak, ash and holly, heading ever deeper into the wood where the trees were taller, and the canopy eventually blocked out the light, so they walked on through a muted twilight. The ground climbed as they proceeded until they reached the banks of a stream tumbling down over rocks from its source further up the steep, rocky hill that rose in front of them.

"Up there?" Thorkell asked, studying the rough terrain.

"That's where I saw it," Diathi replied. "Up there, on the rocks. It's a good place for any animal to have its den. Not many people come this way." He walked upstream, studying the mud edging the water. "Let's see if I can find some sign."

He prowled for some time, occasionally scuffing at the soil with his foot. He shook his head. "The ground's too hard and dry this late in the summer, even here on the bank," he admitted in defeat. "Sorry, Norseman, there's not a lot to read. Let's climb."

Thorkell nodded, trying to control the surge of his emotions. The hope that had filled him since Padraig first mentioned Diathi's sighting of the beast burned like a fever. He'd been certain Ulf would come running to him as soon as the dog caught his scent, so all he needed to do was arrive within the vicinity of his den for them to be reunited. He'd focused so much on a happy ending he'd forgotten to consider how improbable such an outcome was.

Now, as they clambered up, over and around the boulders littering the hillside, he had to confront the dismal possibility they might not see the elusive, wolf-like creature at all, let alone find the animal was Ulf.

The sound of the rushing stream on their left grew louder as they climbed. From this height, the water fell down the hill in a series of small waterfalls that tumbled into rock pools, the noise of which drowned the sound of their passage.

Thorkell, absorbed in his thoughts, had lost interest in searching for itinerant warriors. They were taking a rugged route up the hill, and he concentrated on placing his feet securely among the treacherous rocks. It would be all too easy to twist a knee or ankle in this terrain, so he followed Diathi closely and carefully

They were reaching the top when Diathi stopped abruptly, taking Thorkell by surprise. Another step forward and he'd have collided with him. Diathi put a hand up to ward him off then touched a finger to his lips to caution silence.

Thorkell lifted his head but heard nothing over the constant babble of water. He looked at Diathi again and realised the man was sniffing the air—gently turning his head as he followed a thread of scent carried on the breeze.

Thorkell breathed in cautiously, searching for whatever had caught Diathi's attention. He registered the warm, dry smell of dusty rocks beneath his feet and the richer damp scents carried by water splashing against hot stones, but nothing more. He assumed they were searching for a feral animal odour that would locate the beast's den and was surprised when Diathi indicated he should get to his knees and crawl behind him to the edge of the rocks that shielded them from the valley floor beneath.

It was only when he reached the brink of the uneven platform they occupied that Thorkell realised Diathi had caught a whiff of smoke lifted by the air rising against the heated rocks. He looked at Diathi and nodded confirmation that he, too, had picked up the smell.

Diathi pointed down the hill, indicating a route through the boulders that curled down the slope, turning towards what seemed to be a gully disappearing out of sight around the edge of the hill.

Diathi waited, his eyebrows lifted in an unspoken question until Thorkell nodded his understanding, then led them along the way he'd indicated down the hill. Thorkell saw he'd picked a track that allowed them to move with some speed while being hidden from any observer in the gully. It increased his respect for the local skill and knowledge of the wiry hunter who guided him.

CHAPTER
FORTY SEVEN

AT FIRST, THE NOISE FROM THE brook suppressed any sounds the two of them were making, but as they approached the mouth of the gully, Diathi indicated the need for greater stealth as he led them to the downwind side of the entranceway. There was plenty of low brush and grass here to hide them. Once again, Diathi dropped to his knees and led the way at a crawl into the gully itself. It soon became apparent there was no need for concealment. The men who had camped here had gone. Whatever their possessions, they'd taken them with them. Their fire smouldered dangerously under the hot sun, but there was no sign or sound of human activity.

Diathi tutted at the carelessness of people who would leave a fire undoused in the middle of a summer-dry woodland but made no move to cover it over himself. Instead, he busied himself studying the earth around it and the ground around the clearing.

"Five men, maybe six," he reported at last. "They slept and ate here last night. Rabbit, probably." He indicated some bones thrown away on one side of the gully.

"Should we smother the fire?" Thorkell asked.

Diathi slowly shook his head. "Usually, of course, aye. But why did these men not kill their fire? Was there a reason? Are they coming back?" he asked rhetorically.

"Or did they plan an ambush?" Thorkell asked as three men stepped from the trees a few feet ahead of them.

Thorkell automatically reached for his shield and held it in front of him; his other hand rested on the hilt of the sword at his belt.

Diathi had whirled around. "There are two men behind us," he said. "It's a trap."

Thorkell swore under his breath. So much for admiring the local guide, he reflected bitterly. The recent months of peace and leisure had softened his senses and reflexes. Worse, he'd allowed himself to be careless by putting his safety in the care of another man. Now he'd pay the price.

Filan's words came back to him: 'I didn't want to find myself murdered, or captured as a hostile spy and interrogated. Even if they traded me as a hostage to enrich some petty lordling's holding, it would be too humiliating.' If they captured Thorkell, there'd be no king's protection for him, and he could well imagine how Irish warriors would enjoy having a Viking to torment.

He grabbed Diathi by the shoulder and yanked him close as he backed them both towards the rocky walls that lined the sides of the gully. "Can you fight? Have you a weapon?" he asked.

"Only my hunting spear." Diathi indicated the tall weapon he'd carried all day. "I'm a hunter, not a fighter, but I can kill."

"Then make every poke of that spear count. And don't throw it at them; otherwise, you'll lose your only weapon. Keep a step behind me, so I don't hit you with my sword. That spear's long enough to reach the enemy from there, so you'll be fine."

Out of the corner of his eye, Thorkell saw Diathi retreat until his back was pressed hard against the rock. If the man pushed back any harder, he'd become part of the wall himself, he thought with grim humour as he unsheathed his sword.

Then there was no time for humour at all as a dark-haired warrior came closer. Nothing about his dress separated him from his fellows, but it was evident he was in control. He grinned as he closed the gap between them. "Caught. Just like coneys in a trap," he mocked. "I'd always heard Vikings were fierce warriors. It turns out they're less skilled than our silliest young boys. Still, I'll take your torc home as a trophy for my woman." He drew his sword. "It will look good on my walls."

Thorkell didn't bother replying as he watched the men fall into a rough arrowhead behind their leader. He crouched and waited for their first strike. "Let them come to you," he counselled himself as much as Diathi. "Don't get drawn away from the wall at your back."

A grunt told him Diathi understood.

Then they closed. The leader was fast and powerful, but shorter than Thorkell with a lesser reach. Thorkell had little trouble getting through his guard and scoring first blood in a wound to the man's sword arm. Swift as Thorkell's action was, the second fighter swung at him with an axe, and Thorkell dodged rapidly aside and into the path of yet another warrior's sword.

Thorkell parried, thrust forward when he could, ducked and swayed around their attacks and inflicted as much damage on them as he was able. Occasionally he saw Diathi making good use of his spear. He watched gratefully as the point drove deep into the thigh of a man staging a brutal attack and saved him from almost certain injury.

He knew he was tiring and had to finish the fight fast. The weight of his sword pulled at arm muscles grown recently more used to farming tasks. If he were to control the battle, he would have to be bold. He clasped his sword in both hands and took the leader by surprise when he stepped forward beside him. As the man, taken off balance, tried to adjust his stance, Thorkell repeated the blow behind the knee he'd given Asger all those years ago.

The results were satisfactorily similar. The leader gave a yell as his knees collapsed beneath him, and sank to the ground. It was unfortunate the man beside him had chosen that moment to make a wild swipe at Thorkell with his sword. The arc of his stroke connected with the skull of his falling leader.

Thorkell stepped back and drew a deep breath. There was a stunned silence from his attackers as they looked at the body on the ground. Then they stared at Thorkell.

It could, he thought, have gone either way—they could have accepted the death of their leader meant defeat and retreated. It very nearly happened. Then one man, braver or perhaps more frightened, than his companions, gave an ear-piercing shout and charged at Thorkell with his short, stabbing dagger.

The force of his attack was much too powerful for Diathi to respond to, and penetrated Thorkell's defence. Although he tried to dodge, Thorkell felt the blade cut a blaze of fire across his chest. It was only the head of his axe, still stuck in his belt, that deflected the rest of the blow and saved him from being disembowelled.

"Odin!" he shrieked in rage as he lifted his sword and swung it hard against his opponent. The man staggered and wavered but managed to keep his balance, and jumped clear, only for his place to be taken by his comrades. Vicious, welcome anger re-energised Thorkell. His sword struck once, then twice. He barely noticed where the blows fell as his sword rose and fell in a trained, automatic rhythm. He no longer worried about his lack of current training, no longer cared he was older and less fit than any warrior from a ship like the *Sea Serpent* ought to be. He was a Viking warrior, and true to that code, he would die a warrior.

In the end, when he stopped, there were only two men left in front of him.

Blood from his wound ran down his side and fell to earth, making the ground slippery. Diathi had been quiet for some time. Thorkell cast a glance in his direction and saw him crumpled on the ground. That at least should have stoked his anger. He tried to summon the rage, the fire he'd had, but the moment had passed. He would have to manage the rest of it by himself.

His sword pommel was slick with his blood. He assumed it was his own, but it could have been from the others. The ground felt uncertain beneath his feet, his wound hurt. He could die here, he realised; no Ciarnat, no farewell to his father, no revenge on Asger, no justice for himself and Ulf. He wondered how long it would take for news of this fight to reach Gran, Filan and Ciarnat. Some days, he supposed.

The thought steadied him. He would die on his feet. "Odin!"

he cried again. Even to him, the call sounded feeble, a pale shadow of his earlier war shout. "Thor's hammer!" It was a little louder this time and would have to do. May Odin and his Valkyries send him straight to Valhalla.

He took a two-handed grip on his sword, lifted it and waited for their attack.

It was hard to focus on them. The men blurred and blended in his vision, and he had to shake his head to clear the sweat and hair from his eyes. Even then, there was no attack, although it should have been obvious he was swaying where he stood, and a babe could have disarmed him.

He looked at the two remaining warriors. The closest had his mouth open in a terrible rictus. Thorkell stared at him, confused to find the man was looking beyond him. Was the man wounded?

A low growl came from somewhere behind him. In unison, his two opponents gave almost maidenly shrieks, turned and ran. Thorkell let his sword point touch the ground and bowed his head. Without shame, he leaned his weight on the mighty weapon as an older man would use a wooden crutch.

He shuffled around to see what had so frightened his enemy. There was another louder growl from above his head as he moved. Thorkell froze. He'd turned enough to be able to see up the bank that had protected his back. A full man's height above his head, it crouched on a ledge looking down at him.

This then was the animal Diathi had reported, although it didn't appear to be timid or afraid of humans.

The sun was behind the creature, making it difficult for him to make it out. It was large, but hound or wolf, it was impossible to tell. Carefully and slowly Thorkell raised his arm and wiped the sweat from his eyes. It made little difference, and his action elicited another angry warning growl.

"Ulf?" Thorkell's voice cracked annoyingly on the word. "Ulf?" he tried again.

He thought the animal cocked its head to listen.

"Ulf, is that you?" *I'm going to look right silly if I'm summoning a wolf,* Thorkell thought.

The animal didn't move, but at least it had stopped growling at him.

"Ulf," he called more urgently. "Here, boy, it's me."

Without warning the beast launched itself down the slope towards him. Involuntarily, Thorkell started back, the movement jarring the wound on his chest. "Thor!" he gasped as he absorbed the pain.

Two bounds and the animal was in front of him.

With the light now in his favour, he studied it, trying to match the memories of his hound with the shaggy creature before him. It seemed bigger and darker than he remembered, and there was a line of grey hair marking what must have been a scar on its muzzle.

"Ulf?" he asked again. He could have sworn the animal had his lips curled back from his teeth in a smile of recognition.

Ears pricked, and with his tail wagging, it jumped up at him, standing on hind legs, its paws on Thorkell's shoulders, in an almost human embrace.

Thorkell grunted as the sudden weight knocked him off balance. The sword he'd been supporting himself with fell from his hand as hound and human tumbled to the ground. The pain was indescribable. The wound stretched further. He could feel it tear as he fell, and the hard ground knocked the wind from him.

He didn't care. Ulf was enthusiastically licking his face.

It took some time but at last Thorkell freed himself sufficiently from the excited dog to be able to push himself painfully to a sitting position. He looked across to where the body of Diathi lay, only to find the man staring back at him. "You're alive!" he said. "I thought they'd killed you."

"Knocked unconscious," Diathi replied tersely. "That whoreson got me a knock on the head with his shield. I was lucky he didn't gut me while I was out to it."

"He probably would have if Ulf hadn't turned up. They scarpered fast enough when he started growling."

Diathi gave a short bark of laughter. "They didn't run that far—just enough to get out of sight. They were standing in the bushes over there waiting to see what happened. They didn't leave until they saw you playing with the wolf. They'll have a fine tale to tell when they get back to their homes—a giant Norseman playing with his wild beast companion. You'll be the stuff of legends."

Thorkell snorted, then winced at pain the movement caused his abdomen.

Ulf had wandered off to inspect the dead men, sniffing them carefully before returning to Thorkell.

"Can you stand?" Thorkell asked Diathi.

"I'll be wobbly, but I'm fine. How about you?"

"Sore. If you're really all right, could you get me the fine woollen wrap our friend over there is wearing?" He pointed towards the dead leader. "It'll make a fine bandage to hold me together for our walk home."

Ulf came over to see what was going on and studied Diathi carefully.

"I won't hurt him," Diathi said when Ulf's nose got in the way of his bandaging.

Ulf seemed to understand, as he sat back on his haunches and watched.

Thorkell waited patiently while Diathi bound the cloth tightly around him and pinned it in place with the dead man's cloak pin. He winced a few times. Diathi was efficient rather than gentle, and once the task was complete, Thorkell sighed with relief.

"That feels better," he said thankfully. "Give me a hand up, and we'll be on our way."

"Do you think they've gone?" he asked Diathi, staring further down the gully where the men had fled.

"They left the moment they saw the wolf wasn't going to eat you," Diathi chuckled. "My guess is they'll still be running."

"Just as well, I couldn't fight off one of Ulf's fleas at the moment. Do we have to climb up there again?" Thorkell eyed the hill above them with concern.

Diathi shook his head. "We can follow our running friends and skirt around it. It'll be quicker as well. I only took us up there because it's where I saw your hound."

Diathi led the way down the track with Thorkell behind him. At the end of the small clearing, he realised Ulf wasn't with him.

Thorkell turned and saw Ulf still sitting where they'd been. "Ulf?" The hound didn't move, just sat and watched him.

In his wildest imagination, it had never occurred to Thorkell that, if he found him, Ulf wouldn't automatically follow him. It seemed he'd been wrong. "Ulf. Here boy."

The large hound cocked his head at the familiar command, then looked at the rocks above him. It was quite clear to Thorkell he was considering his options. "I can't wait for you, my old friend," he said. "If you choose not to come, then this is farewell."

He swallowed a lump in his throat. Men didn't cry at partings.

Ulf still didn't move, and Thorkell bit his lip. He waited a few minutes to be sure, then turned and walked back to the hound.

"You want to stay here and be free?" The conversation with Ciarnat crossed his mind. What sort of cursed country was this where women and dogs prized freedom for themselves above aught else?

Ulf watched him but made no move to get up.

Despite himself, Thorkell's voice wobbled a little. The burning pain of the wound to his abdomen was nothing compared to the wrenching pain of his grief at this parting. To have come so close to regaining his friend and then failed so magnificently.

"Go in peace then, my friend," he said at last. For all the world, this felt like a funeral. "I set you free to choose your life. May Odin guide you and Thor protect you." He allowed himself one final caress of Ulf's head to which the hound replied with a brief lick of his hand.

Thorkell turned away to where Diathi waited. Lingering wouldn't make this pain any easier. He made a point of not looking back, not even when he heard the soft whimper Ulf gave as he walked away.

CHAPTER
FORTY EIGHT

Erin

Present Day, New Zealand

SHE STARED AT THE SMUDGE IN DISMAY. Just a smear of blood in the crotch of her panties—a small, monthly tribute to the gods of feminine business that women deal with regularly as a matter of course. Except she was six months' pregnant, and any sign of bleeding must surely be a bad thing?

Erin tried reaching the midwife but her phone was switched off, and the call went directly to voicemail. If she was assisting a woman in labour, she could be out of contact for hours, and Erin needed advice now.

A receptionist and the practice nurse shielded her GP, and Erin became increasingly frantic and panicky as she pleaded with them for an urgent appointment.

The nurse was soothing. "No other pains? No tummy cramps? It's almost certainly nothing to worry about, but I can fit you in at two o'clock if that suits?"

Relieved, Erin put the phone down and tried to steady her

breathing. She cuddled her belly protectively, trying to send out messages of love and support. "Hold on, little one," she murmured. "Kia kaha, be strong."

A stressed-out mum certainly wouldn't help her baby's chances. She didn't think she could bear it if she lost this child. Not now, so far into the pregnancy. Particularly now that she'd felt him kick, he was already a real person to her.

She tried to phone Luke, but he wasn't answering. Erin suspected he was deliberately blocking her. Since the night of the office party, they'd been tiptoeing around each other, neither prepared to break the stalemate.

Luke wore a hangdog look whenever he thought Erin was watching, making it clear he felt hard done by.

Erin, bitterly conscious she'd been manipulated, felt dragged powerlessly into a dangerous financial situation. She felt utterly betrayed, vulnerable and disinclined to offer her husband an olive branch.

Even so, she'd have appreciated support from him now. Whatever their current differences, they'd embarked on 'project baby' together. She had to assume he'd be distraught if something went wrong. As it was, she felt abandoned and alone, and desolation swept over her. Could it be she was going to fail at motherhood as well as marriage?

Perhaps it was as well that she was working that morning and the job kept her busy. It didn't lessen her worry, but if she'd been at home, she would have gone to bed, curled up in a foetal position and sucked her thumb all day. She gave a wry smile. Even she could see that wasn't the best approach to take. It wasn't like her to crumple under pressure. *Just tackle each problem, one at a time, and you'll get through.* And now she was channelling her mother! Although she admitted to agreeing in principle with the advice.

Dr McIvor was admirably calm and matter of fact as he examined her. "Have you had any abdominal pain? Any other discharge? Cramps?" he asked. "No?" He palpated her abdomen. "Everything feels in order. Were you sexually active last night or anytime recently?"

Erin blinked. It was a sensible question, of course, but she'd mentally kept her sex life and her pregnant life in such separate silos, she'd almost forgotten the obvious connection.

"Er, no, I don't think so," she stammered, for all the world like a guilty child. Then she remembered. She and Luke were quarrelling, and sex wasn't on either of their minds at the moment. "Not last night. No." It was a relief to be able to answer definitely. At least they hadn't harmed the baby by anything she and Luke had done.

He grunted, then smiled at her. "I don't think you need to worry too much about this," he said. "Sometimes women develop some spotting mid-pregnancy. It isn't significant unless it happens again. If it does, let me know straight away. Otherwise, you look like a fine, fit mum-to-be, and baby seems sound and well."

"Thank you." There were no words to express her relief. Surely Luke would be relieved as well when she told him. Which thought led, inevitably, to the next awkward question. "Is it still OK for us to have sex?" she asked. Not that she intended to share anything with Luke.

"Oh yes," Dr McIvor said. "There should be no problem there. Just don't be too vigorous. The baby is well protected inside you, you know. If there are any further problems with bleeding, we'd have to reconsider, but otherwise, you should have nothing to worry about."

⁙

"I ended up feeling like a fraud," Erin told Petra a few hours later. "I was panicking, and it turns out there was nothing wrong. Plus, I had to have a dodgy conversation about sex with a man I don't know."

"Ah, the joys of motherhood," Petra teased.

"You can keep it." Erin was morose. "Things have become so tricky between Luke and me that even talking about sex with him is uncomfortable. It's added a complication to what started as a straightforward 'starting a family' scenario."

"Do you think Luke's new venture is that risky? I mean, he's sort of a financial hotshot, isn't he?"

"I don't know what to think." Erin stirred her coffee moodily then looked away to other tables and the young students occupying them. "There's added risk. Yes, I know he's good at what he does, but it still means we haven't got a regular income, and that's scary at this time, particularly as I don't understand the ins and outs of what he's doing. But there's the big issue that he didn't talk about it with me first, and he should have done. I thought that was the way we did things."

She put her spoon down and glanced at her Petra. "You see, I'm trying to interpret what's happening. Luke's always been ambitious. So have I. It's probably why we get on so well, and why it was easy to decide together to make wise financial decisions and put off having a family until we had a house and car; make sure we have financial security before we have a baby. That sort of thing. But now Luke's ambition is outpacing his caution, and when I oppose him he turns nasty."

Petra smiled. "Well, you two were always our *capitalist* friends."

Erin frowned. "What do you mean?"

"You and Luke made, as you say, grown-up financial decisions. It's why you're the wealthiest couple of all of us. Doug and I are the *nerdy* friends. Doug's a geeky scientist, and I work with dodgy, untalented rock groups. And Fergal, well he's our *hero*, isn't he? Competent action man and all-round good guy."

"Wow," Erin said, running over the idea. "I'd never have decided to describe us like that, but... maybe, I guess."

Petra narrowed her eyes as she studied her friend. "Is that all that's bugging you? I mean, I can see it's a problem and all that, but there's something else, isn't there?"

"What do you mean?" Erin turned back to her friend. "My marriage is falling apart, and I thought I was losing the baby. Why should there be something else?"

"Because you're avoiding eye contact with me and that's a warning sign," Petra said bluntly.

"OK. Yes, there is something else, but it sounds silly. You know a few weeks ago I told you I had horrible dreams?" Petra nodded. "Well, I told Brianna about them." Petra's eyebrows rose. "I know what you're thinking. And maybe you're right, and it's all a load of mumbo jumbo, but perhaps there is something in it. Anyway, I told Brianna, and she gave me this to wear."

Erin pointed to the iolite ring on her finger. "It was her grandmother's. She dabbled in the occult, or whatever this is, as well. Brianna told me it would help, and it has. I haven't had a nightmare since, although I still dream. Only now they're..." Erin paused.

"Now they're what?"

"Well, not erotic, precisely, but there's someone in these dreams I seem to be in love with."

"You're getting wet dreams? Jeez, what a crack-up," Petra laughed. "Is this all pregnancy hormone stuff?"

"Don't be an idiot. No, they're not *wet dreams*, thank you very much."

"So, what are they?"

"That's what I don't know. There's a big fire, but it's not frightening; there's a celebration going on, so it's party time. Then this man shows up, and it's obvious I know him very well, I feel such happiness seeing him there. I think he must have been away and just got back, because I feel surprised as well as this jolt of joy." Erin screwed her face up in frustration. It mattered that Petra understood how deeply this was affecting her, but it took a great deal of effort to describe the experience accurately. Even trying her best to be truthful, her words fell miserably short of the actuality. "It all feels so real. I'm not watching this happening to someone else. In the dream, I *am* me, and I'm the one with the feelings. The emotions are still there the next day. It's not like an ordinary dream where you forget everything as soon as you wake up."

"So what makes you say the dream is erotic?"

"What happens afterwards," Erin said, stirring her coffee again rather briskly.

Petra gave a short choke of laughter. "You mean you have it off in your dreams with some sort of dream guy? As in, actual infidelity? Have you discussed this with Luke?"

"Hell no," Erin said with feeling. "Things are difficult enough as they are, without this to muddy the waters. Anyway, when I first saw the man, I thought he *was* Luke."

"And he wasn't?"

Erin shook her head slowly. "When he got closer, I realised it wasn't him, but someone else." She flicked a glance at Petra. "Also, someone I knew," she said quietly, staring into her cup.

"Fuck-me-days. Who?"

Erin hesitated, biting down on her bottom lip.

"Hi, ladies!"

Both women jumped and looked around. A couple of paces away Brianna stood smiling at them. "Sorry, I startled you. You were both so absorbed in your conversation."

"Hi, Brianna." Petra recovered faster than Erin. "Come and join us. Have you been to lectures?" she asked, indicating the laptop and books Brianna held in her arms.

"Not today. I had an exam earlier, and a bunch of us came down here to share the pain."

"You weren't happy with how it went?" Erin asked.

Brianna smiled and shook her head. "I'm hopeless at judging these things. I thought I'd done all right until I heard what everyone else answered. Now I doubt myself."

"Grab a seat," Erin said. "I'm sure you're too hard on yourself," she said as Brianna sat down. "I was never very good at exams, but somehow I muddled through."

"Anyway," Petra said impatiently. "You've arrived at an opportune time. Erin was just about to tell us about the dream she's been having."

"You're still getting them then?"

Erin shook her head. "I'm still getting them, but they aren't terrifying nightmares any more. They are much gentler."

"So, who is this guy?" Petra asked. "Erin's met a man in these dreams. She thought it was Luke at first, but it turned out to be someone else she knows," Petra explained to Brianna with glee. "Come on, Erin, spill!"

Erin glared at her friend, willing her not to persist with her questioning, but Petra was on a roll. "Come on," she urged.

"You can't leave us hanging now."

"Shut up, Petra," Erin said. "This will only bore Brianna."

"Not at all. I've got a vested interest in your dreams, remember? I'm glad the ring seems to have helped."

"Put us out of our misery," begged Petra.

Erin gave an exasperated sigh. "If you must have an answer, it was Fergal."

CHAPTER
FORTY NINE

THERE WAS A MOMENT OF SILENCE. Erin was aware Brianna was sitting stiffly beside her, while Petra's mouth had fallen open. Mercifully, for once her friend was silent.

"Well, you did ask," Erin said accusingly. "And it *is* only a dream. It's not like it's real life or anything. Nothing's happened. It's just a dream," she repeated.

"Are you reassuring yourself or us?" Petra asked, and Erin winced at the all-too-shrewd question. "Bloody hell. Freud would have a field day working with your mind." Petra sat back and stared at her. Erin felt her face go hot.

"I've said it's not real, OK?" Erin snapped. "I'm not making this up, and I can't control what happens in my dreams. Shit, I wouldn't have told you if I thought you'd be this judgemental over something I can't control. At least Brianna has already tried to help with these frigging dreams."

She turned to the girl sitting motionless beside her. "Brianna, I'm so sorry. You shouldn't have heard that. Stupid of me to say anything while you were here. Petra kind of got inside my head and stupidly I blurted it out. Please understand, I don't know where this stuff is coming from, and I promise I'm not making a move on Fergal. I hope you realise I wouldn't."

As she watched, soft colour flushed into the pale skin of the younger woman's face. Those beautiful blue eyes opened fully and settled their focus on Erin's face. Brianna gave her a wry smile. "I know you aren't making any of this up," she assured Erin. "And no, I don't believe you're deliberately trying to make a pass at Fergal." She sighed. "Not that Fergal is mine anyway."

Erin's brows came together in a frown as she tried to interpret the oblique comment. She glanced at Petra, who looked equally confused.

"Let's assess your dreams rationally. What you're experiencing isn't about what you want now, or what you're planning for the future, is it?" Brianna asked.

"What do you mean?" Petra sounded as lost as Erin felt.

Brianna continued to study Erin. "Think about what you've told us. Everything in your dreams is archaic. You've mentioned clothing and so on. But what about the situation—bonfires, weapons, people wearing cloaks. There's no technology in any of your visions, is there? No mobile phones, no electricity, nothing to suggest a close historical match in time."

"I haven't been anywhere near as clear-sighted," Erin admitted, "but you're right. Whatever, and whenever, my dream is about, it's ancient. It feels ancient. I'm certain this isn't something about the future."

"So forget whether you fancy Luke, Fergal or anyone else today," Brianna said firmly. "The players in this particular scene are gone, their fate and fortune long dead and forgotten. Whatever happened to them was a long time ago."

"You surely don't believe that what Erin is saying is real?"

Petra looked rattled, thought Erin, with some satisfaction. Why should she be the only one here disturbed by her dreams?

"I'm beginning to believe it is real—or was real," Brianna said. "What I don't understand is what confluence of events has made Erin suddenly receptive to these stories that must be hundreds of years old, when it's perfectly obvious she has no latent psychic ability at all?"

"You can say that again. Erin's a down-to-earth type," Petra supplied. "She always has been. She never even got scared on the ghost train at the fair."

"Do you think that's what happening? That I'm a reincarnation or something." Erin was grateful for any exoneration. There was guilt, and shame, of course, for the moments, however involuntarily, she'd spent with the historical Fergal, even though those moments had formed some of the most intense bursts of emotion she'd ever known. She paused for thought. "Nah, that wouldn't work, because Luke and Fergal wouldn't reincarnate along with me, would they?"

Brianna shook her head. "I don't think it's reincarnation as such. Do you remember that night I first met you? You had just received your DNA results, and we were discussing them?"

"Yeah, vaguely," answered Erin.

"I thought what Doug said was interesting, and maybe it has some bearing on what's happening."

"As in?" asked Petra.

"He was talking about something called epigenesis. Which, if I understood him rightly, meant traumatic experiences could affect expressions of our DNA, and this could be inheritable. It's a fairly new scientific field, and the idea fascinated me enough that I've read up a little on it since. Maybe there's something traumatic in your ancestral bloodline that's causing these flashbacks."

"Really?" Petra said. "I remember the conversation that night. I don't think Doug meant anything this far off the wall." She chuckled. "He's very staid and correct in his views, you know."

"Maybe he didn't," Brianna answered. "But can you at least see this might be an explanation for what's happening?"

"Even if that were so, it still doesn't explain what Luke or Fergal were doing in my dream," objected Erin.

Brianna grimaced. "This is where I'm departing from the script. But suppose the same event or trauma also affected Luke and Fergal's ancestors. Their ancestors may have been caught up in the same scenario. Who knows?"

"Hardly," Erin was adamant. "Are you suggesting we're all descendants of a group of people who happened to share a historical event? What are the odds on that?"

"Better than you think," Brianna said. "Do you know how many lifespans separate us from our ancestors of, say, a thousand years ago?"

"I don't know," said Petra. "Hundreds, I suppose."

Brianna shook her head. "Nowhere near. I did the maths on it. Say the average age at which a woman gives birth is twenty-five. Sometimes older, sometimes much younger, of course, but let's assume that's the average. That makes four mothers every hundred years. That's all. Forty in a thousand years! Let's face it; you could easily have that number in your living room at a small private party and not be crowded. So you see, not many women stand between us and the dark ages. Only forty."

"I'm impressed." Erin smiled. "I hadn't ever thought it through like that."

"The point I'm trying to make is if Doug is right, and experiences can modify DNA, then forty generations isn't very long in terms of evolution, mutation or any other of the natural processes we've discovered."

"It still doesn't explain the appearance of Luke and Fergal in my dreams."

"Doesn't it? The same arithmetic applies to men."

"I don't mean that. OK, let's accept an ancestor of mine had something occur, triggering a racial—if that's the word—memory of an event or a time. How does that apply to Luke and Fergal? It's unlikely their ancestors have had descendants who just happened to meet up again in the present. What, as Petra asked before, are the odds?"

"I'm working on it. I don't think it's impossible; I just haven't got an answer to that question yet. Watch this space." Brianna gave a cheeky grin that suddenly made her look about ten years old. "Anyway, I forgot to say what I stopped to tell you about. Fergal and I are going to choose a puppy this afternoon. You'll both have to come round and see it once it's settled in."

Erin rolled her eyes. Brianna was just a kid after all. For a moment she'd almost made a believer of her!

CHAPTER
FIFTY

Ciarnat

Ninth Century, Ireland

HE'D COME BACK! EXHAUSTED, WOUNDED and, as Gran put it, with his clothing and skin once again in shreds. But he was here, safe, and with him had come his great hound, Ulf.

Ulf's size was startling, even to a girl used to animals. She was familiar with the dogs that worked the cattle with Padraig, and she'd seen war hounds before in the great halls she'd visited. Ulf would be one of the biggest she'd ever seen. She didn't even have to lean over to pat him—his head reached as high as her waist.

Gran, of course, took it in her stride, completely unfazed that a hound the size of a pony had taken up residence in her yard. Her focus was on treating Thorkell's wound.

"Just keep that animal out of the house," she ordered. "He's so big he wipes everything off the table every time he turns around. I can't be dealing with it."

She tutted in disapproval over Thorkell's new injuries. "This is getting to be a habit," she grumbled as, over Thorkell's protests, she stripped off his shirt and examined the gash, ignoring his flinching. "That was very nearly nasty," she remarked as she prodded around with grim satisfaction. "Whatever gods protect you, my lad, they were working especially hard to save you this time. See," she showed Ciarnat, "a hair's breadth deeper and he'd have been gutted like a fish."

It was ugly, and Ciarnat winced when she saw the cut. She held the bowl, then passed the needle to Gran as she cleansed and stitched the wound with linen thread, all the while keeping her face studiously neutral. It was a skill Gran had taught her at the beginning of her training. 'You have no right to screw your face up at a foul smell, or look sick, or revolted, or burst into tears when you're looking after a patient. They're quite afeared enough without adding to their distress. If you're going to be a healer, you will have to learn to discipline your expression. What the patient needs from you is quiet confidence. Nought else, do you understand?' Ciarnat *had* understood, and as her experience grew, she'd found it increasingly easy to adopt her 'healer mask' when dealing with the ill and injured.

She hadn't anticipated how hard it would be to maintain that poise while Gran forced her needle through Thorkell's shrinking flesh, nor how watching his white face and gritted teeth would whittle away at her self-control. Any doubts about her true feelings for Thorkell were dispelled. Her visceral reaction to seeing him suffer was sufficient to assure her emotions for him were sincere and genuine.

It was hard to know which one of them was the most relieved when it was over, and Gran tied off the last stitch and wrapped a bandage around Thorkell's torso.

Ciarnat turned away to hide her face and lifted the bubbling kettle onto the trivet, ready to wash up the bowls and needles Gran had used. She was a girl who valued reason, and the tumbling turmoil of her emotions felt like the fast, wild run of notes in some dance music, accelerating so rapidly out of control there was no time for breathing or even thinking. She found the torrent of feeling as terrifying as it was exhilarating.

Sometime later, Thorkell joined her in the sun-drenched courtyard where she sat idly picking the strings of the harp.

He was moving carefully and sat down cautiously. Ulf followed and lay down at his feet with a sigh.

"Painful?" Ciarnat asked, smiling at him.

"Not bad. Your gran gave me a foul drink and assured me it would soon ease my soreness." He grinned. "She didn't give me the option of not swallowing the horrible stuff, otherwise, I might have told her I preferred the pain."

"Gran would have told you to stop being a silly boy and do what you were told."

"I know." Thorkell nodded at the harp. "How are you getting on with it?"

"It's a lovely instrument. I can't help but feel sorry its last owner didn't value it properly."

"But you'll make up for that?"

"I will. But my playing needs to improve before I can make her sing. It's been years since I've been able to practise properly every day, and my fingers are sluggish and fumble on the strings." She held her hand up for Thorkell's inspection. "The tips of my fingers are soft. Yesterday I played until they were so sore I had to stop. I've got a blister on my thumb."

Thorkell grasped the hand and inspected the reddened fingers. "Ow!" he said, running his thumb lightly over the tips.

Ciarnat chuckled. "I have it in mind that it's a very small 'ow' compared to yours. They'll toughen up in a few days."

"Maybe you should let them heal before you play again."

"How will they grow calluses then? No, they'll be fine."

"Will you play for me?"

"Play badly, you mean?"

Thorkell rolled his eyes. "Play anything. I want to hear your music." And I want to watch you, he thought. I want to store this memory of you for when I leave.

Ciarnat pulled the harp against her shoulder. "It's a beginner's tune," she warned, "but probably all I can safely play for you until I regain my skills."

Thorkell nodded and leaned back against the wall to listen.

The tune was simple and straightforward. The notes rippled from the strings as Ciarnat set them free. Thorkell had no way of judging the quality of her playing, but as he watched, it seemed to him she relaxed into the music until even her breathing was in time with the phrasing. A soft smile played on her lips as if the act of coaxing melody from the harp gave her pleasure.

Filan, who was crossing the courtyard, stopped to listen and smiled. "Keep your thumbs up," he reminded his daughter, who promptly stuck her tongue out at him. He chuckled as he walked into the house.

"I thought you were so wrapped up in your music you wouldn't have heard him," Thorkell laughed.

Ciarnat sniffed. "If it were anyone else but Da, perhaps, but he's always had a way of getting under my skin, particularly if it involves my musical failings. You should have heard him yesterday when I played for the first time. My hands were in the wrong position; I was too rigid with my elbows; my rhythms weren't accurate. I love my da, but sometimes I want to kill him."

"Then maybe it's as well I wasn't here to witness it." He tried to laugh but caught his breath and winced as the stitches pulled.

"You'll have to behave, else Gran will give you another dose of her medicine," Ciarnat smiled.

⁜

They had two weeks together while Thorkell's wound healed. The injury confined him to the farm, and Gran and Filan were usually close by, but despite these limitations, their romance blossomed. There was a particular pleasure to be had in shared moments when their eyes met, or when Thorkell lightly brushed against her arm in passing. Their need for discretion intensified their emotional connection, and when they *were* able to sit together in the yard and talk, it seemed to Ciarnat that, for those in love, words became a clumsy tool. It wasn't a thought she'd considered before. Words framed and limited ideas and emotions, but a shared smile or glance could unlock a universe.

Gran checked Thorkell's stitches. "You've been lucky, my lad. I thought there might be an infection, but you're healing cleanly," she said in satisfaction. "Give it another week, and you'll be fit to travel."

"Travel." The word fell like a weight into Ciarnat's happiness. Each day brought Thorkell's departure closer. She supposed that knowledge made their romance more intense and sweeter—a thought that did nothing to shape a less bleak future. She tried to imagine her life when he was gone, and failed. An endless round of nothing, she supposed—an experience of helping Gran, household chores and... nothing. For the first time, she feared for herself and for what the years ahead could hold.

She was turning these thoughts over in her head while her hands absently skimmed the strings of the harp.

"Your playing is getting better," Thorkell complimented her.

"Maybe." Ciarnat lifted the harp from her shoulder and straightened up. "I realised something the day you went to find Ulf," she said.

"What?"

"You'd left before I was up, so I didn't have a chance to say goodbye."

Thorkell's brows drew together. "I needed an early start so I could find Diathi, search for Ulf then come back here. I only stayed away that night because it was so late by the time we got back to his village, and I was sore."

"I wasn't complaining you didn't see me before you left," Ciarnat wanted him to understand, "and I knew you were only a few hours away, so if aught happened to you, the news would travel back here. But here's the thing: once you leave to go to your land, if you are injured, or even killed, I will likely never learn about it. I will never know what happened to you." She turned her head away, and the silence stretched between them.

Eventually, Thorkell glanced to where she was sitting, her head drooped, her hands clasped in her lap.

"*Já*, there is no answer to that," he said. "Each year, when the *Sea Serpent* goes voyaging, women are left behind. Sometimes their men do not return. It is a risk we all take."

"At least those widows are told how their husbands died when the rest of the crew come home," Ciarnat cried. "But if something happens to you, there will be no one to send the news to me. You were badly wounded the other day. A little deeper and you could have died then."

Thorkell nodded. "That is why, however much I love you, I haven't asked you to wait for me. And why I cannot promise to return, although I intend to."

"You love me?"

"You know I do."

"Aye." She gave a wry smile. "I love you as well, of course." At a different time, in a different place they'd have kissed now, Ciarnat thought. Maybe they'd even go further. She gave a little sigh. "Do you want me to wait?" she asked.

"I have no right to ask you to do so," he said gravely. "How can I go to your father and make an offer for your hand when my future is still uncertain? He would rightly laugh at me. Our only hope is for me to reclaim the life Asger tried to steal and make sure my father knows I am alive."

Ciarnat turned until she was gazing straight into his eyes. "Aye, but do you *want* me to?"

"You know I do, but it would not be fair on you."

"Then I will." Her voice was confident, but after she spoke, she looked away from him again, and her sad little smile nearly broke his heart.

CHAPTER FIFTY ONE

Erin

Present Day, New Zealand

THE SOUND OF THE FRONT DOOR closing alerted Erin that Luke was home. The immediate increase in tension was now familiar. Once, his presence had brought her joy; now she felt she was treading on eggshells whenever he was around. She wondered if he thought the same.

"I'm in the laundry," she called. Some things never changed. It was Saturday morning and whatever the state of her marriage, sheets still needed to be washed, dried and folded. She thought about Brianna's comment about forty generations of women reaching back to the Dark Ages. She snorted. *I bet each and every one of those poor suckers had to do the chores for their households as well,* she thought. Which wasn't to say that Luke *didn't* help out, he was just selective about the tasks he did, and laundry-related activities were outside his job description.

A few seconds later, Luke appeared in the doorway. She glanced at his face and was surprised to see him grinning.

"Great news!" he exclaimed.

"What's happened?"

"We've got a new client, a young guy, and guess what? He took out that massive Lotto win a few weeks ago and wants us to invest it for him. All eighteen million of it."

"Invest with who? Do you mean Kittering and Hodges?"

"Nah. Alwyn and me. He's looking for a high rate of return. I explained we didn't operate at the conservative end of the market, and he was happy with that. He's realised there's not a lot of point in putting it in a savings account and getting some piddling amount of interest on it. I told him he'd come to the right place."

"Jeez! What happens if he loses it all?"

Luke shrugged. "That's unlikely, but all markets go up and down, you know that. Worst-case scenario, he loses it—but we'll spread it out quite widely, so all his eggs aren't all in one basket. The best thing for us is that the fees for managing his account will bring in a tidy sum, and you can stop being nervous about our financial future."

"That's excellent news." Erin smiled, determined not to spoil the moment by expressing concern. Realistically, if an overly optimistic young man wanted to risk his windfall, it wasn't her business. As long as there were no repercussions for Luke if things went wrong, she thought. "So, is he signing a contract with you and Alwyn?"

"Of course. We'd hardly take him on as a client otherwise. His lawyer's drawing it up, and we'll get it checked out by Kittering and Hodges' legal team before we sign anything." He studied Erin's expression, and she saw his smile fade. "You don't have to be worried, you know. We've thought of everything."

"I'm sure you have," she said and was rewarded when his face lit up again. She hadn't seen him this happy in months, and in response, she made a conscious effort to relax, determined to celebrate the moment with him. "You remember we're due at Fergal's to see their new puppy?"

"Yeah. On the way home I picked up bread and stuff for nibbles, seeing as it will be lunchtime."

"Great."

"One other thing." Luke suddenly looked guilty. "Alwyn and I are booked to be speakers at a conference in Frankfurt."

"You are? You were invited?"

Luke nodded.

"Hey, you're famous. When is it?"

"In two months."

"When?" Erin's voice rose in shock. "But I'll be eight months pregnant!"

"Well, I didn't expect you to come with me."

"No, of course not. I couldn't, no airline would allow me on board. But what happens if the baby arrives early or something? I want you here with me." Even she could hear the panic in her voice.

"I know you do, babe, but this is important for our future. And if your dates are right, I'll be back in plenty of time to support you. Anyway, it's a first baby. I've heard they're always late."

He pulled her into his arms so that she rested her head against him. His voice was calm and reasonable. *What a silly girl she was* clearly implied in his tone. "You mustn't worry about everything all the time," he said chidingly. "It'll all work out, you'll see."

Unwilling to sacrifice the temporary accord they'd established, Erin allowed Luke to hold and soothe her. Maybe he was right, and it was the regular vulnerability of pregnancy making her such a coward, but in her heart, she knew it was more. Underneath lay the more deep-seated fear that Luke no longer cared for her sufficiently to set his life aside, even temporarily, and put her first. She hid her face against her husband's shoulder as a wave of loneliness engulfed her.

❖

An hour later, she sat in Fergal's living room, watching his new puppy.

"What the hell do you call that?" Luke asked.

"Hush," Erin tried to deflect his rudeness. "It's a puppy."

"That's not a puppy. It's a pony. How old is it?"

Fergal looked amused. "Twelve weeks. He's only a baby at the moment." He reached down and caressed the pup.

"Jeez. How big is it going to grow?"

"He'll probably be about a metre tall when he's fully grown."

"What breed is he?" asked Erin.

"An Irish wolfhound."

"What on earth possessed you to get an animal that big? He's ginormous," Luke asked.

Erin detected disapproval. Was that directed at the puppy's size, the breed, or at the general idea of owning a dog? She couldn't recall whether they'd ever had a conversation about having pets. She'd just assumed cats and dogs, like having children, were part of being a family.

"Have you seen the size of me? I'm a big guy. Can you imagine me with a chihuahua or a Jack Russell? I'd break my neck tripping over them. At least I've got a dog that fits me," said Fergal.

"What're you going to call him?" Erin asked.

"Brianna and I have been discussing it. She suggested Murphy because he's Irish, or perhaps Paddy. So far, I'm not a fan. We'll wait a few days to know him more and see what sort of name fits him. He's a bright little guy and seems very confident." Fergal sounded for all the world like a proud father and Erin smiled.

"Got any ideas?"

"Well..." Fergal looked suddenly self-conscious. "I'd been thinking of calling him 'Dog'."

"Dog? What sort of a name's that?" Luke asked.

Erin rolled her eyes. Nothing was going to please her husband this afternoon.

"Have you guys seen *Good Omens*?" Fergal asked in response to their blank looks. "No? In it, the Hound of Hell's destructive force is defused because the boy who owns him calls him 'Dog', rather than 'Satanus', 'Armageddon' or something. I think they said naming something would define its character. So, Dog."

"Maybe something a little more subtle? How about 'Hound', 'Wolf' or even 'Irish' if you want to go down that track?" asked Erin.

Fergal shrugged. "We'll see."

Erin slid off the sofa to sit on the floor. The puppy came over to investigate, and she ran her hands over his coat and rubbed his chest and back. "Who's a lovely boy?" she crooned as she petted him.

Luke rolled his eyes.

"Does the coat get softer as he gets older?" she asked.

"No. They're rough-coated, shaggy, dogs. Easy care, as far as the coat goes or—as I prefer to put it—ruggedly handsome." Fergal grinned. "I believe dogs and owners tend to look alike."

Erin lifted her eyes heavenward, although the claim amused her.

Luke was still fixated on its size. "Jeez, man, wouldn't a Labrador have been a better choice? What happens when it grows? Will Brianna even be able to control it or walk it on a lead?"

"She'll be able to cope quite well, thank you," said Brianna, who'd just walked into the lounge. "Anyway, he's Fergal's dog. Fergal's going to be responsible for the care and training. I'm simply a surrogate in his absence."

Luke looked as if he wanted to argue, but Brianna's presence curbed him, and soon the conversation had shifted to other topics, although the pup continued to break up the chat with its antics. It was difficult not to laugh when he chased his tail, and equally hard not to give a sentimental sigh when at last he collapsed into a deep sleep on Fergal's feet.

"I hope none of you expects me to be a good host," Fergal said. "Because I can't move from here."

"We'll manage," Erin chuckled, and eased herself up onto her feet to help Brianna bring in plates of olives, tomatoes, cheese and bread.

"Just spread the plates out on the table," Brianna instructed, "and everyone can help themselves. Petra and Doug are coming over at some stage, but we can start without them. I don't see Fergal providing silver service for his guests this lunchtime." Her fond smile took the sting out of her words.

"Can I get you something, Fergal?" Erin asked.

"I'll fill a plate up for him," Brianna said. "You guys help yourselves. If you want a beer or something, Luke, would you mind helping yourself from the fridge? Do you want him to get you one, Fergal?"

"Nah, I'm fine," Fergal said. "As a responsible dog owner, I shouldn't be DIC."

Luke snorted. "That thought won't last long! Are you certain?"

For a second Fergal appeared to be considering the offer. "What the hell, you've twisted my arm, you sod. Yes, please," he said, laughing. "A beer would be good."

When Doug and Petra arrived, Brianna and Erin were laughing at the puppy's antics. He'd woken from his nap and, after a prudent trip to the garden, he was ready to play again. Naturally, Petra joined in, and the three women sat on the floor while the excited puppy ran between them.

Luke was smiling and relaxed as he and Fergal dissected last weekend's rugby match and agreed the referee's decision had been wrong. Doug joined them at the table, leaving the women to sit with the puppy romping on the floor.

"How's it going?" Fergal asked him.

"Quite well until Petra saw your puppy, thank you. You realise they'll all want one of their own now?" Doug said, indicating the women. "I'm imagining the conversation we'll be having in the car going home. 'Can I have one? We need a puppy! Oh puh-lease.'"

Fergal gave a smile of pure malice. "One small move towards domesticity for you both. Anyway, Luke's already stolen a march on us. He's the one who's going to be a daddy. Naturally, they'll need a dog and a cat."

"Hell, no!" Luke looked appalled. "It's bad enough we'll have to cope with a baby."

Doug and Fergal stared at him, and Luke realised he'd made a blunder.

"I don't want Erin running around after a puppy *and* a baby, that's all," he explained. "It would be too much for her."

"You might want to let her decide that for herself, mate," Doug said.

There was nothing offensive about the comment, but Doug was never rude. When the usually easy-going Doug made it, in that surgically dry tone, Luke felt he'd been punched. He said nothing, but his face tightened, and two patches of red flushed high on his cheeks.

CHAPTER
FIFTY TWO

ERGAL FELT IT WISE TO CHANGE the subject. Like Doug, he'd been concerned about the change in Luke since he and Erin had announced their impending parenthood. He fully intended to have a word with him about it, but now wasn't the time. "Did you see on the news about the aircraft that went down in Martin's Bay?" he asked.

"Yeah," Luke grasped the lifeline he'd been handed. "Do you know what happened?"

Fergal shook his head. "The accident investigators are looking at it. Their report will come out in a few months; but it's a sad, sad business. Six people dead."

"Isn't it obvious it was the pilot's fault?" Luke asked. "After all, he's the guy flying the damn plane. Surely it's his fault." There was an unpleasantly aggressive edge in his voice that Fergal chose to ignore.

He shook his head. "Not so. Anything could have happened. It's much too early to make any kind of judgement."

"Did you know the pilot?" Doug's voice was quiet.

"Nah. Thankfully I didn't this time." Fergal gave a short bark of laughter. "You know, when I was training, my boss said to me, 'If you carry on this career path, you'll bury a lot of friends.'

Well, at the time I was twenty-two, bulletproof and arrogant. I let his words brush over me. Now I know what he meant."

"And have you?" Luke asked crudely.

Fergal looked at him, refusing to be baited. Only a slight frown showed he registered the patent offensiveness of the question. "Yup," he said quietly. "A damn sight too many friends. And a damn sight too many funerals. It's always the same. Weeping widows, crying partners, devastated parents and fatherless children." He sighed. "Aviation's no industry for happy families."

There was a pause before Doug said cautiously, "Surely, though, it's error or inexperience on the pilot's part? I've heard you explain often enough what happens when an aircraft stalls. Surely it's safe to assume that's what happened. Pilot error? It wouldn't happen to someone like you, of course. You must have thousands of flight hours behind you."

Brianna climbed up from the floor and came to join the conversation. She stood at Fergal's shoulder, in time to watch him shake his head.

"Doug, I'd like to say you're right. The truth is, so many things can contribute to a crash. It would be hard to know where to begin."

"Well, who else would cause it, but the pilot?" Luke wasn't going to give way. If anything, the beer had made him more aggressive.

"No," Fergal said firmly. "It isn't necessarily the pilot. There's a methodology that investigators use when they try to untangle the cause of an incident. It's called the Reason model."

"What? They reason it out? Isn't that what they're paid for?" asked Luke.

"Let Fergal explain," Doug said, his irritation evident.

"The model's named after its creator. It's got nothing to do with reasoning per se, that's just a coincidence."

Luke shrugged.

"Imagine a block of Swiss cheese. You know, the sort with holes all through it?"

"Gruyère," murmured Brianna.

"Yeah, Gruyère. The block gets cut into slices, and a skewer runs through the middle of them holding it all together. So you've still got the block, but each slice of it can, and does, rotate individually and at different speeds."

"What's that got to do with anything?" asked Luke. "You've lost me."

"I'm explaining it. In aviation terms, each slice represents an element which might represent a risk. Slice one could be the pilot. Is he tired, going through a divorce, unwell? The next slice could be the integrity and safety of the aircraft and its engine. Slice three could be weather conditions. Slice four could be something completely random like a flock of birds in the flight path." Fergal paused for a drink. "Remember the holes in the cheese? As the slices rotate, the holes fall out of alignment. So today our unwell or stressed pilot copes with his problem without it affecting anything else, and nothing untoward happens. Same with the weather. Gusty, cloudy conditions with unexpected downdrafts don't cause an accident on this particular flight. And that's pretty much the story day in, day out. Petty, individual issues, almost unnoticeable in the scheme of things. Until one day, as the slices rotate, the holes *do* line up, and all those little incidents, minor in themselves, aggregate and you get an accident."

"Is that so?" Doug looked amused. "I'd never have thought of accident causes that way, but it's a great image."

"Well, I've simplified things a bit," Fergal admitted, "but you get the gist. Usually investigations aren't about establishing blame so much as understanding what went wrong and fixing procedures and practices to prevent it happening again."

"Can the model be used elsewhere?" Doug wondered. "Medical practice might work. Nursing care?"

"I suppose so." Fergal reached to pick an olive from the dish.

"I still say the pilot has to be to blame," said Luke. "OK, there are contributory factors, but only one guy flies the aircraft." He seemed keen to continue the argument, but Doug and Fergal had moved on, and he got no traction.

Soon their talk shifted to the local by-election.

Brianna left the men and returned to the floor and the puppy. "I think I might have found the answer to the question we were discussing last time," she said.

"Mm?" Erin was busy playing tug-of-war with the puppy who was ferociously defending his squeaky toy.

"The probability that a group of people experiencing an event together would have descendants who meet by chance hundreds of years later."

"And?" Erin was sceptical.

"You heard Fergal describe the sliced Gruyère?" Erin nodded. "Suppose, in this case, each slice represents a person who was part of the initial experience or trauma. As Fergal said, each slice rotates. Each individual's children take their place on the skewer when their parent dies. Some fail to reproduce and fall off the skewer as well. The slices rotate as each generation goes through life. Some stay in place and others travel; some are successful, some aren't. It all looks quite random; the only connection between the survivors is some long-forgotten history."

"I don't follow how that helps."

"Don't you see? The descendants don't necessarily meet in each generation, just like the Swiss cheese holes don't align all the time. But suppose one day those holes *do* line up. It's quite possible. Human beings travel all over the world. It's quite conceivable that eventually those descendants could end up here in New Zealand. Hell, everyone in New Zealand came from somewhere else if you go back far enough. Even Māori. Then you've got the descendants of the original protagonists together in one place – all sharing individual ancestral DNA, which we know, thanks to Doug, will have been affected by past traumatic experiences."

"That's freaky." Petra had been listening. "Then what happens? Are they doomed to repeat the original event or something?"

"Jeez, I hope not!" exclaimed Erin. "Most of my dreams have involved fire, although they're a lot happier since Brianna gave me her grandmother's ring."

"I don't know what could happen, if anything," Brianna admitted. "I just thought it might be an explanation for Erin's vivid bad dreams, and why Luke and/or Fergal were in them as well. Maybe, fate being what it is, this could be an opportunity to put right some wrong that happened to your ancestors. Maybe it's meant to be."

Erin pulled a face. "This is getting far too *X-Files* and on the fringe for me. I prefer simple explanations."

"Yeah, but it's an intriguing thought, you must admit," said Petra. "I'm a bit jealous I don't appear in your dreams. After all, I could have been someone important in a past life."

"For all I know, you may be one of the people there," said Erin. "I'm not sure I even correctly identified Luke or Fergal. Maybe I just assumed any man I was attracted to would be Luke. That was my interpretation, not necessarily something real."

Brianna waved a hand dismissively. "I guess we'll see. There may be nothing in the idea. It just came to me as Fergal was talking, that's all."

"Just came to you?" Luke suddenly broke in on their conversation. "Are you saying the planets suddenly all aligned to suit your theory? Just like the mumbo jumbo that our baby would be a boy? Is this more of your psychic garbage? I don't buy it."

"Luke!" Erin was shocked. She hadn't realised the men had been listening. "Don't be so rude. And remember, Brianna was right about the baby."

"Big deal. It was a 50–50 chance, OK? She got lucky, that's all," he sneered.

Erin felt her jaw drop. Luke had been getting more and more impossible at home, but he'd never been openly rude in front of their friends before. She glanced at Brianna, who was staring wide-eyed at him. Erin saw she was shaking.

Bastard, Erin thought. Her fury warred with good manners while she struggled to think of what to say.

"So how far along are you now, Erin?" Doug asked. He nodded at the pup trying to climb into Petra's lap. "It'll alter the tone of our socialising once we have a new baby as well as a new puppy to play with."

"I still have more than two months to go," Erin answered

gratefully. You could always rely on Doug to be the peacemaker. "Frankly, I'm a bit over the whole process. I can't comfortably bend in the middle anymore, and doing my shoelaces up is becoming a real mission."

"You *look* well," Doug smiled. "You must be doing something right."

"It still seems like a long time to wait," Erin complained.

"I told you so," Luke said. "Plenty of time for me to have my trip and be back for the birth."

"You're going away? Now?" Fergal's tone was sharp.

"Not for a couple of weeks. It's just a business trip." Luke was casual. "My business partner and I have been invited to speak at a conference about cryptocurrency. As I say, I'll be safely back in time for the birth, and Erin's a big girl. She'll manage without me for a couple of weeks. You're the independent type, aren't you, babe? She always has been."

"In two weeks, Erin will be that much closer to delivery," Fergal said.

Luke shrugged. "There's plenty of time."

Erin was aware of Fergal's quick scrutiny flicking across her face before he looked away. Luke's remarks had fallen into an uneasy pool of silence. Erin noted no one made eye contact with either her or Luke. Jeez! How much had Luke had to drink? It amazed Erin he seemed so unaware of the disapproval swirling around him. Their friends were polite, but Luke was pushing their tolerance levels. Time to leave, she thought, before the situation became even more embarrassing. "Hey, we'd better head off," she said, awkwardly scrambling to her feet. "We've got things to do."

She ignored Luke's surprise. "Thank you for lunch, and I love your puppy, guys. Can't wait to see how big he gets. Maybe my baby can ride him when they both get older."

"That would be something to see." Fergal gave her a light kiss on the cheek. "Keep well," he said, giving them a small wave as Erin steered Luke out of the house to their car.

"My turn to drive," she said.

CHAPTER
FIFTY THREE

THE PHONE RANG AT NINE-THIRTY. An hour earlier, Luke had left for the office, leaving Erin to enjoy the solitude of an empty house.

She'd had her final day at the bank last Friday. There had been a celebratory morning tea, and her colleagues had clubbed together and given her a lovely pair of opal earrings. She'd been a little teary when the speeches were made. These people had been her colleagues for years. She regarded many of them as friends. Then again, the knowledge she carried in her brain had served the job she'd loved for years as well. Now, overnight, that knowledge would be unimportant. Realising how redundant these things would be had shaken her and stirred a mild sense of panic as she realised what a significant step she was taking away from the life she'd always known.

Now she was alone, pregnant and unemployed. There would be compensations, though. She smiled. This was a rare moment of privileged comfort. Sitting with her back supported by the pillows behind her, she reflected that moments of solitude would be a rare event in the months or even years ahead. Once their baby son occupied the bedroom down the hallway, there would be little opportunity for long, lazy lie-ins.

Consequently, when the phone rang, she picked it up and checked the caller ID with some irritation. Fergal. She wondered whether to ignore the call. She was still embarrassed by Luke's behaviour yesterday. She'd sensed a general air of disapproval from her friends—and although it had been directed at her husband, well, she was his wife, and her innate sense of loyalty triggered an urge to find a socially acceptable excuse for his behaviour.

"Hi, Fergal. Thanks for a nice lunch yesterday."

"Yeah." There was a pause before Fergal, direct as ever, continued. "Erin, what's up with Luke?"

"What do you mean?" The vapid words had escaped her without thought. Of course, she knew what he was asking.

"Come off it," Fergal commanded. "He was brash and a prize arse yesterday. That's not the Luke I know. What's going on? Is everything all right at home?"

Erin heaved a sigh. "I don't know what's going on, Fergal. Luke's changed is all I can say. I worry it's because of the baby, but who knows what's driving it?"

"The baby?" There was silence while Fergal considered this. "But he was delighted the night you told us you were pregnant. I know I'm not wrong. He was one proud father-to-be."

"Yeah, he was," Erin said sadly. "I thought he was happy, that we were both happy. But gradually that's gone, and he's doing increasingly crazy things. You know he walked away from his job to start a company with a new colleague of his?"

"Well, he said something about work, but I didn't take it in. What's happened there?"

"He's started a new, high-risk investment company. It's sort of under the umbrella of Kittering and Hodges, except Luke and his partner—whom I don't trust, by the way—carry all the risk. I'm scared silly because we're just about to drop down to one income and Luke's just thrown all our security away on this gamble." She heard her voice rising in panic and made a determined effort to get back in control. "Part of the problem is Luke knows I don't support him in this, and thinks I don't trust him any more—which is partly true. He never discussed his plans with me, and I'm worried. If I ask him anything, he becomes defensive and belligerent. All of which probably means he's under massive stress, as well, and can't discuss it with me. The result is I'm worried and he's either aggressive or sulky."

"He was a right git to everyone yesterday," Fergal said. "Everything about him seemed off. Angry, aggressive, I don't know. We've been friends for years, but he's never been like this."

"I know." Erin eased her back against the pillows. "I'm beginning to think I've made a mistake going ahead with this pregnancy, but it was something we both wanted and planned. I'm sure of that. Now it's as if he resents the baby, and me, and I don't understand it at all." She sniffed. "Sometimes I think the baby dislikes him as well. When Luke touches me or even comes near, the baby starts squirming and kicking until I feel like a punching bag."

"What a mess. I'm sorry, Erin, it must be shitty for you. And he says he's going overseas?"

"He and Alwyn. It's a business trip. I panicked when he told me, just in case I go into labour while he's away. Now I wonder whether I wouldn't be better off without him." She gave a sad laugh. "I don't need husband complications when I'm giving birth."

She heard Fergal sigh.

"Well look, you know you can always count on me if you need help or support. I promise I'll be there if you want me to; Brianna as well. She was distraught yesterday—not for herself, but for the effect she thinks Luke is having on you."

"Thank you, Fergal." Unbidden tears welled in Erin's eyes. It felt like forever since someone had cared for her. It made her realise just what a toll Luke's ghastly attitude was taking on her happiness. "I appreciate it. If I need you, I'll call. Hopefully, this is just a marital phase we're going through, and we'll adjust sooner or later."

"Make sure you do call. No excuses." Fergal was gruff.

"I promise. And thank you again."

She shut her eyes and leaned back, wondering what she should do. Erin felt tears trying to well up not far below the surface and strove to keep her face serene. She couldn't allow herself to despair. Soon there would be a baby to protect and care for, and it was too soon to write Luke off. There must be something she could do to restore their relationship. Counselling, therapy, marriage guidance?

She probably needed to have a serious conversation with him. Luke might not even realise just how worried and unhappy she was. She hadn't directly mentioned it to him, so perhaps he thought everything was all right.

Tonight, Erin thought. *Tonight I'll raise the matter and insist we talk about it.*

But Luke came home late, his conversation centred on how civil unrest in Hong Kong was affecting the world's stock markets. He looked stressed and tired.

She'd bring the matter up another evening, she decided. There was no point forcing the issue when Luke was so clearly already tense and distracted.

It was only as she lay in bed that she admitted to herself she'd chickened out; that she was afraid putting words to their alienation would cement it and make it real. She felt she was treading on eggshells as it was. Naming their problem could precipitate an argument where the things said between them might be irrevocable, and she wasn't yet prepared to admit their marriage was over.

CHAPTER
FIFTY FOUR

Thorkell

Ninth Century, Ireland

THE RAIN THAT HAD BEEN THREATENING all day set in as the last light of evening left the sky. The weather suited Thorkell's mood, which had been increasingly dour since he parted from Filan a day ago. They'd had no trouble on the road, nor seen any sign of the army or straggling warriors. They'd parted company when Filan had taken the western route to Tara. He'd left with the horses as well, so Thorkell had to walk the last miles to Dublin.

While he'd had the older man for company, he'd been able to distance himself from his problems, but alone, his thoughts ran in circles. Even Ulf padding beside him couldn't lift his spirits, although periodically Thorkell reached out to stroke his friend's wet coat.

He'd been away from Ormsfjord since late spring. Who knew what Asger had been doing in his absence? Thorkell hoped to return home before the *Sea Serpent* returned from its summer campaign, but recent delays made that unlikely. In which case, given Asger's probable explanation for Thorkell's absence, Orm was almost certainly mourning him as dead. Thorkell thought it unlikely Orm would accept a tale that involved his son deserting the *Sea Serpent*.

The thought of his father's grief was upsetting. Nearly as distressing as Ciarnat's had been when he left the farm.

Gran, uncharacteristically, had hugged him. 'I've invested so much time and effort in getting you well, so you take care of yourself,' she had ordered. 'I've taken the stitches out, but that wound needs another month to heal properly. Don't lift anything heavy, or do any physical labour until it is, otherwise it could open up again.' 'I won't,' he'd promised, wondering what she would say if she realised he was planning to sign on as a crew member with a ship heading north, which would most certainly involve heavy lifting and rowing.

Ciarnat had behaved with dignity as she farewelled him. No tears or outpouring of grief, of course—she wasn't that sort of woman—but there had been no missing the sorrow in her eyes, or the twist of misery on her lips as she wished him a safe journey.

He'd wanted to hold and comfort her, but he couldn't see his way forward clearly. To be together, one of them would have to give up their home and their country. That wasn't necessarily prohibitive, except both had lives they couldn't lightly cast aside. He was his father's heir, and Ormsfjord and its people would one day be his responsibility.

Ciarnat could elect to move to Ormsfjord, but it would be a hard decision for her. Aside from her reluctance to travel to a land where her people were usually thralls, Thorkell thought it unlikely Filan would consent to a match that would take his daughter so far away from her home and her family.

All in all, it's a right mess, Thorkell thought miserably, and was only diverted when he reached the outskirts of the township.

It was dark, and he had to pick his way through the narrow streets, careful not to trip on the planks that provided a walkway above the mud. In the five years since he'd first come here with

Hagen, the town had expanded inland. He passed the lodging house they'd stayed in then, hardly recognising it now other wooden or wattle-and-daub dwellings surrounded it. Behind some of the walls, he heard livestock snuffling and scuffling as he made his way towards the waterfront.

Most of the shops and workshops he passed had already shut up for the night. The rain had driven householders inside, but occasional chinks of light escaped between the planks of slabbed timber walls. From the Christian monastery, on a small rise to the south, he heard a bell summoning the monks to service. Despite the good works of Ciarnat's village priest, Thorkell still found their religion incomprehensible. When the Norse gods spoke, a man understood their message.

He needed a tavern. Somewhere he could enjoy a meal and a bed for the night, and with a clientele of sailors who could put him in touch with a ship heading in his direction.

He saw a Norseman enter a sturdy building down by the quay and followed him. He opened the door and scented the aroma of beer mixed with wet wool and the unmistakable briny tang of men who made their living from the sea. He pushed his way through to the front of the room and found an empty place at a table. A boy came to take his order.

"Beer, and whatever you have that's hot," he said. He had to repeat his request twice.

The lad had caught sight of Ulf and was staring at him. "Is that your hound?" he asked. Thorkell nodded. "He's enormous. Is it dangerous?"

"Only if he has to be," Thorkell chuckled. "Like when a man can't get a boy to fetch him his dinner."

The boy gulped, took the order and left, although Thorkell noticed he kept his eye on Ulf as he went about his work.

While he waited, he took in the room half hoping, half afraid, the crew of the *Sea Serpent* would be there. While he had a blood feud with his uncle, he was less confident how he'd have to deal with the crew who had been under Asger's orders. It seemed reasonable they would assume he had died. How would they react when the man they'd marooned reappeared? And what retribution might they expect from Orm for abandoning his only son as a castaway?

"Where are you from?" The question broke into his thoughts. Thorkell turned to the man beside him.

Tall, fair-haired and sturdily built, his companion was a quintessential Norseman, from his size to the rich cloak of wolfskin slung across his shoulders. It occurred to Thorkell that he'd become used to the smaller physique of the local people. It came as a jolt to see a man this size. A man who probably looked a good deal like he did himself. A comfortable sense of familiarity overrode his initial surprise.

"Ormsfjord. Do you know of it?"

The man shook his head. "*Nei*."

"What about you?"

"A small settlement just north of Hafrsfjord. I'm a crewman on the *Trana*. We arrived in port yesterday."

"Ah, then Ormsfjord is to the north of there. I heard of Hafrsfjord from a trader who came by our hall some years back. He was working his way there down the coast."

Something about this man appealed to Thorkell. His immediate liking surprised him.

"What brought you to Dublin?" the man was asking.

"I was injured early in the season. It's taken me some time to recover. Now I'm looking to find my way home. It is my hope there will be a ship that needs an extra oarsman so I can work my passage."

"You should go down to the pier tomorrow. Our ship will be leaving then. We have a consignment of hides to take north before we turn for home. Maybe there'll be a place for you."

"Many thanks. My name is Thorkell."

"Sigurd." The men clasped arms. There was a pause while each weighed the other up.

Eventually, Sigurd gave a sharp nod indicating a judgement made, and smiled.

Thorkell returned the smile cautiously as the boy returned with a mug of beer, a plate of richly scented hot stew and a large bannock.

"I need somewhere to sleep tonight," Thorkell said to the lad. "Well, me and my hound, that is. I'm hoping this place will have somewhere to stay?"

"I can ask my master," the boy said. "There were men in here last week telling a tale of a Norseman they'd fought a fierce battle with who had a huge wolf as a partner. Was that you?"

"Is that so?" Thorkell laughed. "Well, they might have been talking about us, at that." He gave Ulf's head a rub. "If it is the men I think they are, it is lucky they aren't here tonight. I have got a score to settle with them."

"Come back with me," said Sigurd. "Some of my shipmates have lodging in town. There's room for one more on the floor tonight, and tomorrow you can find a ship to take you home. I'll introduce you to Sven, our leader; maybe he can help."

"You are certain your friends won't mind?"

Sigurd snorted. "They're on their last night of leave. Likely they'll be too far gone in drink even to notice you're there."

"Then, many thanks. I won't need your hospitality after all," he told the boy, who shrugged and returned to his work.

Sigurd's help didn't limit itself to finding him lodging for the night, either. And he'd been right about his fellow shipmates' reaction. For the first time in months, Thorkell found himself accepted for what he was—a Viking warrior at the end of the season who needed a passage home.

The next morning he and Sigurd walked down to the pier together.

"That's the *Trana*," Sigurd pointed proudly.

"A fine ship," Thorkell agreed, casting a knowledgeable glance over the vessel. A brisk breeze was blowing up the river carrying the fresh ozone tang of sea air. Thorkell breathed in deeply. He'd missed the ocean. His blood needed the salt, the smell, colour, movement and above all, the freedom of open water.

Even here, shielded from the open sea by the river and estuary beyond, he could feel the tingle of the call. It was his element—always had been.

Manannán was the name Ciarnat had used for the ocean's god that had spat him out onto the shore, and Thorkell had taken the time, during his travels with Filan, to find out more about this watery god. The bard had explained Manannán drove a chariot drawn by Enbarr of the flowing mane who pulled the *Wavesweeper*, and could gallop over water as if it were solid land. It was as useful a description of an ocean deity as any other, and Thorkell was happy to accept it at face value.

Thorkell knew Filan professed to be a Christian, so he was amused when the man's words suggested the old pagan gods were still dear to him. Thorkell had received the same confusing message from Gran, and although not discussed, from Ciarnat's behaviour at Lughnasa. It seemed the people lived between two worlds, the Christian and what they described as Pagan. Thorkell did not argue with this. His faith centred around a sound ship, a good captain and a friendly crew.

He followed Sigurd onto the pier until they were standing alongside the *Trana*.

"Sven," Sigurd called. "I have a friend here wanting a word with you."

Thorkell studied the man who approached them. He was probably twenty summers older than Sigurd, Thorkell judged, with a weathered face and grizzled beard.

"Who wants to speak with me?"

"Thorkell Ormson," he replied. "I'm looking for passage to return to Ormsfjord."

"Hmm." Sven's pale blue eyes scrutinised Thorkell. "Where is your own ship and crew? How does a man such as yourself come to be alone in Dublin?"

Thorkell had wondered how to answer this obvious question. He'd evaded going into details the night before when Sigurd was a chance-met stranger, but now he resolved to tell them both the truth and hope it served him well.

"When my father Orm was injured the charge of his ship this season was given to his brother. Orm cautioned me to be careful of my uncle's ambitions, but for a while, all was well. But then, Asger abandoned my hound and me on the shore and refused to let us back on board. I had to swim for my life and nearly drowned. Local people nursed me to health. But now I need to return home. My father may already be grieving for a lost son, and I have a blood feud to settle with my treacherous uncle."

Sven said nothing for a long moment, and Thorkell was mindful of the shrewd eyes taking his measure.

"The crew didn't protest your uncle's decision?" Sven asked.

Thorkell shook his head. "It took everyone by surprise. Ulf and I were the last to board, so the ship was already in the water and ready. Asger gave the order to sail and had his thrall hold me off at sword point until they were under way. If anything was said later, I don't know. It's one of many things I need to get home to find out."

Sven nodded. "What had you done to annoy your uncle?"

"He claimed I'd interfered in his control of the crew. It wasn't true, but he used it as a reason. More likely, it was because I'm my father's only son and his heir. With me dead, Asger would inherit my father's land and holdings."

"What do you know of this man?" Sven asked Sigurd.

"Only that I met him last evening and offered him lodging with our crew for the night. He seems a good man. When he said he needed to work his way back home, I brought him to you."

"I've heard of Orm. He has a reputation as a strong leader," Sven remarked. "His current wife is kin to me."

"Odell? They have been married for six years or so?"

Sven rubbed his chin. "That would be about right. Odell, yes, that was her name." He drew a deep breath. "By that token, we're kin of a sort. All right, Thorkell, son of Orm, you can have a place on the *Trana*. Does the hound come?"

Thorkell beamed with relief. "My thanks to you. *Já*, Ulf comes with me."

"Get your things then. We sail on this afternoon's tide. You too, Sigurd. Tell the crew as well. There's a steady westerly wind, and I sense good sailing weather for the next few days."

As the men walked away, Thorkell thanked his friend. "You've done so much for me. I've become so used to delays and frustrations I can hardly accept how easy you've made it all."

Sigurd clapped him on the back. "You've been away from

your kind too long, that's all. I knew my father would take you."

"Sven's your father?"

Sigurd nodded. "*Já*. He's a good man when he's not annoyed."

Thorkell laughed. "So's my own father."

CHAPTER
FIFTY FIVE

THEY SIGHTED LAND AT FIRST LIGHT and by mid-morning had left the open ocean for the calm waters of the fjord. Above them, the seabirds screamed a welcome, and Thorkell smiled.

Sven stopped beside Thorkell's bench. "You're nearly home," he remarked.

Two small boys playing on the rocks caught sight of them and went running along the shore to the settlement.

Sven waved to them. "There go the heralds," he said with a grin.

"I used to do the same thing when I was a child," Thorkell smiled. "We've made very good time. You were right about the winds being favourable."

"That, and the *Trana* is a good ship. Speedy but stable."

Thorkell nodded. He'd come to respect Sven, liking his easy control of both the ship and his men. He imagined Orm would approve of him. "Will you stay a few days?" Thorkell asked.

"Tonight, *já*. It will be good to meet your father and see my kinswoman."

Thorkell watched the familiar shoreline sliding past their ship. "It feels very good to be home," he said.

"It always does." Sven carried on his way to the prow.

Sven was right, it always did feel good to return home, but this time felt special. Orm's leg should have healed by now. Would he want to lead next season's campaign on the *Sea Serpent*? If he didn't, that left either Asger or Thorkell to captain the ship, and Asger wasn't going to be alive by then, about that Thorkell was determined.

Sven called orders from the prow, keeping the ship well clear of the seaweed-clad rocks as they steered around the last point. The settlement lay straight ahead of them. Thorkell squinted, trying to make out whether *Sea Serpent* lay in port. The low angle of the morning light made seeing detail difficult, but although he scanned carefully, there was no sign of his father's ship.

He breathed a sigh of relief. He'd been preparing himself for an immediate confrontation when he reached the shore. Now it looked as if he'd have time to develop a welcome for Asger, and if the *Trana* arrived before the *Sea Serpent*, it was unlikely Orm had been told he was dead.

He was smiling with anticipation as he shipped oars and helped take the heavy rollers from beneath the thwarts while the *Trana* glided the last distance towards the beach. He was first to leap into the sea and wade to shore where the rest of the crew joined him. Between them, they pulled the *Trana* over the rollers and far enough up the beach for safety. The next few minutes were spent busy with ropes and securing the longship.

It was only then Thorkell looked around in puzzlement. A visit by a ship was always an exciting event and usually collected an audience to welcome the vessel, but today there was no one on the path coming down from the hall to greet them. Even the usual gaggle of small children running around, getting in the way, were missing.

He frowned.

"What's the matter?" Sigurd asked.

"I don't know. Something's wrong. Where is everybody?"

Sven came across to join them. "Is it always this quiet here?" he asked.

"Never. I didn't see the *Sea Serpent* as we sailed in, so I hoped we'd made it back before they arrived. But perhaps I was wrong. It's never this deserted." Thorkell gestured towards the empty stretch of water. "There should be fishing boats out there, and people on the shore. I'll go up to the hall and see what's happening. If nothing else, those children must have carried news of our arrival by now."

Sven put a hand out to stop him. "Wait, man. We'll come with you. You may need back-up if that uncle of yours is there."

So Thorkell Ormson returned to his father's hall with thirty seasoned warriors following him.

They had cleared the steepest part of the track, and the great Hall lay ahead of them. Hearth smoke rose blue above the ridgeline, but the doors were closed, and no people were to be seen. Nor were there workers in the gardens; the weaving hut door was shut, and no sounds came from the smithy.

Thorkell's frown deepened. "*Sa*, something is amiss."

Suddenly the doors before them were thrust open and a man stepped through. Behind him, a straggle of others spilt out from the room and clustered in the doorway.

Thorkell was close enough to recognise their leader. He stopped in his tracks. "Arne?"

Arne nodded. "Thorkell," he acknowledged. He barely glanced at Sven or the others. "You have returned at a bad time."

Thorkell felt his stomach lurch. "What has happened? Where's Orm?" he demanded.

He didn't wait for a reply but strode up the path and pushed past Arne. Sven's men followed him through the doors.

People were standing in the hall. They fell silent when Thorkell entered. Some stared, others looked at the ground, avoiding Thorkell's gaze, but all gave way before him as he made his way through.

To his relief, there was no sign of Asger, although he spotted Toke who'd been with him on the last voyage. The man hunched his shoulder and stared at his feet. Thorkell would deal with him later. His focus, for now, was Orm's chair at the head of the hall.

It was empty.

Thorkell looked around. Orm wasn't here, nor could he see

Odell. He turned and faced the crowd. "What has happened? Where is my father?"

CHAPTER
FIFTY SIX

ARNE PUSHED HIS WAY THROUGH THE press of people. Their sigh of relief was palpable. "Orm is dead." Arne dropped the words like weights into the pool of silence.

Thorkell shook his head. Such a thing was incomprehensible. "Orm?" It was too absurd an idea for him to absorb. He'd focused on killing Asger, he'd considered what to do with the rest of the crew, but he'd never considered returning to a home without Orm's steady presence. Whatever happened, Orm would be there, and now Arne denied him that? "He can't be," he said flatly, but Arne's face showed only grief and sympathy.

"I'm sorry, Thorkell. Orm was buried three days ago. We thought you were dead as well. It is wonderful to have you return to us," Arne said with apparent sincerity.

A woman in the audience gave a quiet sob. Aileen. Thorkell identified her as she lifted the hem of her apron dress to her face to wipe her eyes. He'd half expected she'd have been sold on by now.

"How did he die?" Thorkell asked, impatient of the courtesies. Arne had been part of a crew that deserted him, leaving him to die. Time enough for social niceties when he understood what had happened here.

Arne hesitated, then addressed the crowd. "Thank all the gods that Thorkell has returned, and that changes everything. We'll meet later, once we know his wishes. Now there's food and accommodation to prepare for our guests. The rest of you have work to do."

Thorkell narrowed his eyes as everyone filed out quietly. Arne had become a figure of authority if he could so easily direct the villagers.

Sven and his warriors remained to flank Thorkell.

"Please," Arne gestured to the benches around the walls.

"What happened? How did my father die?" Thorkell asked.

"We think Asger murdered him."

Thorkell froze. There were soft gasps from the listening men.

"We arrived back ten days ago. It wasn't a successful voyage for the *Sea Serpent*, and we were glad to be home." Arne spoke directly to Thorkell. "When Asger abandoned you, it divided the crew. His friends, and some younger men, held that Asger must have had reason to punish you so. The rest of us were furious. We knew you'd done nothing to justify such treatment, and Asger's actions had made us complicit in what we thought was your death."

"How did Asger kill my father?"

"When Orm welcomed us back, Asger told him you'd been killed. He made it sound as if you'd died fighting." Arne shook his head. "It was a bad business. Orm was frantic with grief at your loss."

"And you didn't tell him the truth?" Thorkell was incredulous.

"Not then, *nei*. Truth to tell, I wasn't sure how to proceed. If I'd stood and spoken, there'd have been a bloody fight, kin against kin, in this hall. It seemed a kindness to let the old man believe his son was in Valhalla. I'd intended to tell Orm the truth the following day and let him summon the Thing to pass judgement on Asger. None of us realised what Asger's intentions were."

"That night we ate together in the hall. With Orm grieving, it wasn't a celebration, but the crew were at least happy to be home. Orm didn't eat, but Asger poured him wine and urged him to drink it." Arne stopped.

"Go on, man," Thorkell said impatiently.

"The next morning, we woke to be told Orm was dead. We could hear women wailing, and we assumed Orm, grieving for you, had died of a broken heart." Arne shook his head. "Rowena was summoned to prepare him for burial. Within a few minutes, she came running from Orm's chamber, her eyes wild, and told us he had been murdered. She claimed he'd died of poisoning. She'd checked her kist of medicine, and some potion was missing. Someone, she claimed, had stolen it and given it to Orm. His body showed the signs."

"Odin's eye! This Asger was your father's brother?" Sigurd asked Thorkell. "How could any man be so base?"

Thorkell shook his head in incomprehension.

"Then," Arne continued, "Asger came in. He heard what she was saying and went white with anger. 'You evil old *völva*,' he shouted at her. '*You* murdered him, you treacherous foreign witch. You're the only one here who would know what poison to use.' She stood her ground. 'Not so, Asger,' she said—and believe me, you couldn't mistake the passion and accusation in her voice. She stood proud and firm. 'When Orm injured his leg, you saw the potion I gave him for his pain. I even, Christ help me, told you it would kill a man if he took too much. Now the bottle is empty. Someone used it without my knowledge because I keep records of what I use. The drug is a healer and a killer, a two-headed blessing, so I was always careful with it. But you would have known where to find it and what to do with it. You killed Orm.'

"The rest of us were still trying to process that Rowena was accusing Asger of murder. We all knew she was no witch. Just a woman who knew the ways of healing. And with that came the realisation that Orm's death meant Asger would inherit Ormsfjord.

"We never had a chance to act, because Asger gave a mighty shout of rage, grabbed the axe from his belt and split her head in half. She died, right in this hall," Arne explained, indicating a spot on the floor.

"He murdered Rowena as well?" asked Thorkell.

Arne sighed. "Asger claimed he'd sentenced her to death for killing Orm. I think he expected a cheer, but we were shocked and silent. He cannot have liked what he saw when he looked at us. If we had to choose which of them told the truth—her or Asger—then we believed Rowena.

"I stepped forward. 'Asger, you've killed your accuser. At the very least, this matter must go to our courts—to the Thing, for judgement. We will send for old Halfgar to be our law-speaker. We've all heard him before. He will make a fair trial of this.' I heard a rumble of agreement from the men with me. Asger's face was a berserker mask of fury. I braced myself for a blow, but it never came. He swore at us in the vilest language, accusing us of cowardice, before turning and leaving the hall. We let him go. For the moment we had work to do, so we left Asger to cool his temper on his own."

"So where is he now?" Thorkell asked.

Arne stretched his hands. "By the time we'd arranged for Rowena's body to be decently cleaned and had laid Orm out, we realised the *Sea Serpent* had flown. The younger men had spent the night camped on the shore. They followed Asger. There was nothing we could do to stop them."

"So you let a murderer and kin-slayer go?" Sigurd's tone was incredulous.

"What could we do?" Arne shook his head. "We buried Rowena and Orm up on the hill, near where your mother lies."

"With no jarl left in Ormsfjord, it fell to the freemen of this settlement to discuss and decide what to do. We assembled here today for the Thing. Then the children came running and reported seeing your ship. We thought it was Asger returning." Arne breathed out a deep sigh. "You can have no idea how thankful we are that you have come back to us, Thorkell, although we know how terrible this is for you."

Thorkell nodded slightly in acknowledgement. "Then, tell me, where is Odell? I haven't seen her."

⋅⁝⋅

He found where they'd buried Orm. The sky was clear, and the full moon gave enough light to follow the track up the hill easily. They'd surrounded the grave with stones that shone pale in the moonlight. He could smell the moistness of the high pile of freshly turned earth.

"Oh, my poor father," Thorkell murmured.

If Arne was correct, then Orm's death was also fratricide. Not just dead, but foully murdered. It would be hard to find a more despicable cowardly way to kill such an honourable warrior. Orm would have wanted to die bravely in battle and be transported to Valhalla, not shuffled out of life as a victim. Sheer fury raged with Thorkell's grief.

Asger had fled, stealing the *Sea Serpent*, and Odell had gone with him. Thor's hammer! Orm's body had barely cooled before his wife ran off with his murderer. Had she known what Asger would do? Had they planned the murder together?

"I swear by Thor and Odin that I will avenge you," he promised his father. "I'll kill that treacherous woman and make Asger's death as painful as possible. He'll take a long time dying."

Had Asger challenged Orm, that would have been a different matter. Orm would have had a chance to defend himself, to fight his enemy. He had been a great warrior. Even crippled and lame, he would be a hard man to defeat. But Asger had stolen Orm's life.

Murder by stealth, by deceit! Thorkell groaned with rage and disgust. Such a foul act wasn't the Viking way.

Some distance away was another mounded pile of earth. Rowena. Thorkell walked across to pay his respects.

She had been his nurse and his second mother. He had loved her for her kindness and her wisdom, and he'd not been alone in that regard. She was the community's healer. Her knowledge of herbs and their properties had been vast. Men lived today because of her medicine. Many women had borne their child safely because of Rowena's skill and care.

Thorkell didn't for one moment doubt her testimony. Arne

said she had stood proud when she challenged Asger. Thorkell could well believe it. And she died for it.

"May Odin's curse fall on you, Asger."

He returned to Orm's grave and sat beside it. Ulf settled next to him, and Thorkell leaned his head against the great hound's shoulder for comfort. He spoke to Orm a little, but mostly he was quiet and reflective. Bitter regret for things he'd never said to his father consumed him. He grieved he hadn't got the chance to see him once more before he died.

His father's death meant he was now jarl of Ormsfjord.

He gazed down at the settlement clustered along the seashore below him. He'd spent his childhood here, and he knew its secret ways—where to find the first berries in autumn; the best spot for swimming; the sweetest pastures for cattle; the hidden tracks in the birch and pine forests which you could follow to hunt for wolf and deer. Now the place was his to rule. If he so chose.

He wondered if there was anything worthwhile to keep him here. Orm and Rowena were gone. Half the district's fighting men had left with Asger. The others, belatedly swearing their loyalty to him last night in their relief at his return, had once abandoned him on a seashore to die. Such a thing could not easily be forgotten.

In Ireland, Ciarnat waited for him. He could have a good life with her, and he'd leave Ormsfjord behind with no regrets.

He gave a shuddering sigh. First, he had to find Asger. He owed Asger one death already for abandoning him on that rocky shore. Now, avenging his father's death was a duty, and by the gods, it would be his pleasure to deal it out. But to kill Asger, he first had to find him.

He sniffed the wind, sensing a sea change. It was getting lighter. The moon had sunk below the hills, and a breeze was beginning to stir. Dawn wasn't far off, and with it came a new day and a new direction. Thorkell rose to his feet and faced his father's grave. He lightly pressed his right hand over his heart and then raised his arm in salute to Orm. "Farewell," he said quietly.

CHAPTER
FIFTY SEVEN

Erin

Present Day, New Zealand

"LOOK AFTER YOURSELF. TAKE CARE." LUKE had been cheerful and breezy as he planted a light kiss on Erin's cheek. "I'll be back so soon you won't even notice I've left."

Erin waved mechanically as he climbed into the car beside Alwyn.

"Cheers, Erin," Alwyn called out before Luke slammed the door.

Now she was alone, with the house to herself for two whole weeks, and she'd have been lying if she said she hadn't been looking forward to it. Silence folded in around her as she briefly closed her eyes and felt her accumulated tension loosen across her shoulders, slide off and follow Luke down the road.

She walked into the baby's room and sat down in the armchair she'd positioned beside the window. 'For breastfeeding,' she'd explained to Luke, who'd helped her carry it in. He'd been miffed that part of their living-room furniture had been repurposed in such a fashion, but Erin had been insistent, and he'd reluctantly agreed.

She was right to insist, Erin reflected. The chair was comfy and sufficiently large; she could curl her legs up on it. Dappled sunlight filtered through the branches of the laburnum tree outside the window and warmed the room, and the breeze through the leaves cast softly moving shadows on the wall.

I can sit here and watch the baby sleeping, she thought happily. She'd already made up the bassinet, so it stood empty, waiting for her son. On the opposite wall was the cot. Even though she knew it would be some time before the baby was old enough to use it, she'd already tucked in the sheets and blankets he'd need. The whole room was neat, tidy and, above all, ready. 'Should we be green and use cloth nappies instead of disposables?' she'd asked Luke a few weeks ago. He'd stared at her blankly before giving a short laugh. 'Well, you probably won't care about the environment at two in the morning when you're changing the fucking things. Do what you want, but I'd get the easiest to use.'

Erin wasn't sure how she felt about that. A guilty part of her recognised the practicality of his comment. More depressing was the implication it wouldn't be Luke up in the middle of the night doing the red-eye shift.

As so often these days, Erin felt her mind give a palpable twitch as it flinched away from considering her husband. Dammit. The man was already at the airport, but he still sent her blood pressure skyrocketing.

Two weeks! Two weeks of blissful serenity, just me and the baby.

She leaned back, quietly contemplating the Wedgwood blue walls and white furniture. She focused on her breathing as the midwife had shown her and felt it grow less jagged.

After a while, she felt the baby move—a gentle, soft repositioning of limbs within her. Her hands cradled her belly. It will all be well, she assured her child. I will always be here for you. Rest, you are safe, little one.

Was it her imagination, or did the baby dislike his father?

There'd been several instances when it had almost felt as if he'd responded to things Luke had said or done. Perhaps the latent hostility between his parents distressed him, which was a troubling thought.

She'd wondered how well she would sleep without Luke in the bed beside her. Since their marriage, they'd slept apart a mere handful of nights. Whatever the current quality of their relationship, bodies got used to sharing the warmth and comfort of a marital bed. Under different circumstances, she'd undoubtedly have helped herself to sleep that night with a glass or two of wine. That avenue being barred, she anticipated a restless night.

She needn't have worried. She fell asleep quickly—which made the shock of being woken by the phone at 2 am particularly unsettling. Shit, phone calls at this hour of the night were rarely good news, and Luke was travelling overseas! Panicked thoughts of aircraft crashes, terrorists and other emergencies ran through Erin's mind as she jolted awake.

The call came through on their landline and Erin had to wriggle across to Luke's side of the bed to pick up the receiver. "Hello?"

"Who is this? Are you Mrs Power?" It was a man's voice. She didn't recognise it, nor did the caller introduce himself.

"Yes. What's this about?"

"Is Luke there?"

Erin breathed a sigh of relief. It wasn't a call to tell her Luke had died in a crash, or the plane had disappeared. "What? No. He's not." Erin squinted at the clock to confirm the time. Who the hell called at this hour?

"I need to get hold of him urgently."

"I'm sorry, he's not here. He's overseas. You'll have to call him at the office when he gets back."

"You don't understand! He's lost all my money," the man wailed. "I'm ruined. I'll be bankrupt. Where's your husband? I need him now." Panic radiated down the telephone line. "What am I to do? I'm fucked. I'm sitting here thinking about killing myself. I can't sleep."

Shock rendered Erin speechless. She felt her heart lurch as the adrenaline kicked in. Oh, shit! What had Luke done? More to the point, what was she supposed to do about it? There was nothing she *could* do.

She drew on years of professional banking work to stiffen her spine. "I'm sorry, but you'll have to take that up with Luke when he gets back. I can't help you," she said firmly. She wondered whether to suggest he phoned the suicide watch line, then decided it would be inappropriate.

"But I'm desperate." The man's voice rose to a wail. "I have to speak to Luke now!"

"I'm sorry, but he's not here. Do you have his cell phone number?"

"Yes, but it's switched off."

"He's overseas. I imagine he'll check it from time to time if you want to email or leave him a message."

"I need help now!"

Erin felt herself growing irritated. Whatever issues this man had, whether Luke was responsible or not, there was nothing she could do about it. It was late, she wanted to sleep, and this conversation was going nowhere. "Look, I'm sorry, but there's nothing I can do for you. You'll have to get hold of Luke and talk to him."

The voice turned menacing. "Listen, lady, your husband has ruined my life. You need to do something about it. I'm not having my life destroyed because of your filthy scumbag husband. I'll get my own back."

She had endured abuse before in the course of her job when she'd had to turn down mortgage and loan applications— customers weren't happy, and some had taken it out on her. Still, she'd always known she had the protection and support of the bank behind her.

This was different. It was a personal attack, and Erin was here alone. She took a deep breath. "I know nothing about this," she repeated, as calmly as she could. "It's no use trying to abuse me. I can't help you. You will have to talk to Luke either when he switches his phone on, or when he's back in the country. Try texting him."

"You soulless bitch, he's destroyed my life..."

And mine, Erin thought. She shook her head. She had her own problems. "I'm hanging up now. Goodnight," she interrupted. The receiver rattled as she placed it back in its cradle and she realised her hands were shaking.

Carefully she dragged her heavy body back to her side of the bed and switched the light on. She was far too rattled to go back to sleep. She rearranged the pillows behind her and sat up, leaning back against the headboard. Her heart was pounding wildly, and she unconsciously rested her hands protectively on her abdomen, cradling her unborn son.

Damn you, Luke, she thought, although, she admitted fairly, she didn't know how responsible he was for the man's distress. But damn him anyway. He'd gone away and left her to cope with everything. She certainly didn't need his professional life causing her extra worries.

If she hadn't been woken abruptly from such a deep sleep and so shaken by the call, she'd never have admitted Luke was away. Certainly not to a stranger. She hoped there wouldn't be repercussions while she was there on her own. She didn't imagine it would be difficult for someone to track down Luke's address.

"Goddammit," she muttered at last as she swung her legs over the side of the bed. She hated feeling vulnerable. It wasn't a state she was used to, and she resented it.

She might as well get up and make herself a cup of tea. She wasn't going to get back to sleep in a hurry.

Later, sitting back in bed sipping her tea, she wondered how genuine the caller's threat of suicide had been. It would be awful if some action of Luke's led to the man's death. She wondered how her husband would cope with it.

CHAPTER
FIFTY EIGHT

"YOU CAN'T STAY THERE ALONE. GOD knows what could happen. He sounds like a right nutcase." Petra was adamant. "I'll come and stay with you until Luke gets back."

Erin smiled at her phone. "Nah. Truly, I'll be fine," she reassured her friend.

"Yeah, but you weren't that certain in the wee small hours of the night, were you?" Petra was positively squawking her outrage across the network. Erin held her mobile further from her ear. Petra knew just how to project her voice for dramatic effect, and was disturbed enough to be utilising that skill to its full extent.

Despite herself, Erin grinned. They did not need a phone. Anyone within a five-kilometre radius of her friend would hear her in full war cry. "I'll be OK," she said. "Last night I had a shock, that's all."

It wasn't quite 'all'. Erin had spent the rest of the night sleepless, and only good manners had dictated she wait until eight-thirty to call her friend. But talking to Petra had put things into perspective. "It was the shock of it, that's all," she said. "I was barely awake, after the best sleep I'd had in ages." Resentment coloured her tone—what a bastard he'd been. How easy was it for a pregnant woman to get a decent night's sleep at the best of times? "Because I assumed the call meant Luke was in an air accident or some other disaster, it took me longer than it should to respond to this guy. At least now he knows he'll have to wait until Luke's back to talk to him."

"But wouldn't you say he was kind of threatening?" asked Petra, sounding doubtful.

"Yes, but I've had plenty worse when I worked in the bank," Erin said. "People don't like being told they can't extend their overdraft, or whatever. Some people got nasty."

"Hmm." Petra was unconvinced. "I still think I should come and stay. At least you'd have back-up and a witness if he calls again."

Erin had a sudden vision of bright-eyed, positive Petra living with her for two weeks—the precious two weeks of peace, solitude and tranquillity she'd promised herself as preparation for motherhood. She shuddered. "How likely is that?" Erin scoffed, determined to stop Petra foisting herself on her. In the bright light of a new day, it was easy to dismiss the shock and worry she'd had last night as just that, 'night fears'.

"Suppose he's on P?" asked Petra. "You wouldn't know what he's capable of."

"He seemed remarkably coherent for someone on heavy drugs. I suppose he might have been drunk, although he was speaking clearly enough. He won't call again."

It took a while, but eventually Petra was placated with the assurance that Erin had her mobile number on speed dial. "You will call if this idiot contacts you again?" she pleaded.

"Shall do," Erin promised and then diverted her friend's attention to the Six60 concert that weekend in Lower Hutt. "What time will you guys be leaving?" Usually Erin and Luke would have been going as well, but Erin had been unwilling to face a concert in her heavily pregnant state.

From there, it was easy to chat about Petra's job, as she was responsible for a number of the band's requirements. Petra reminded Erin that she would be working behind the scenes, so her tickets to the show were complimentary.

"You lucky bitch," Erin murmured.

There was a choke of laughter from her friend. "These guys are brilliant to work with. Be grateful you never get to deal with the other bands I have to nursemaid."

"Fergal and Brianna are coming as well," Petra said. "We'll miss you two."

"Well, Luke's a long way away, and I'm in no condition to battle with crowds."

"Fair enough." There was a pause before Petra asked, "Do you think there was anything in what that guy last night was claiming? About Luke, I mean?"

Erin sighed softly. Deflecting Petra was never going to be an easy task. "I don't know. Some weeks ago, Luke told me a youngish guy won Lotto and asked Luke to invest his winnings. I don't even know whether this is the same person."

"But Luke's good at his job, right?"

I wish I knew, thought Erin, before she said, "I've always believed so. Kittering and Hodges always valued him and trusted his judgements. It's why they backed this new venture. I don't imagine his skills have changed."

But she *did* wonder. She didn't like Alwyn and mistrusted his influence on her husband. Was it possible that Luke's skills, disciplined by his old company's conservative policies and staidness, had been nurtured, and flowered safely, in that environment? Free of those restrictions, had he done something reckless?

"I'll have to go," Petra said. "I need to get to work. You enjoy your day, and remember, if you want a friend to stay, I'm your girl."

Erin smiled. "Thanks, but I think I'll be fine. I've got a fulfilling day ahead, catching up on my reading, arranging flowers and checking my potential birthing dates."

"Good on you," Petra laughed.

CHAPTER
FIFTY NINE

Thorkell

Ninth Century, Norway

THORKELL ACCEPTED SVEN'S OFFER TO LEAVE Ormsfjord with them. To find news of Asger and the *Sea Serpent*'s crew, he needed to follow them, and they might have called into Hafrsfjord for supplies. At the very least, he'd hoped to hear some word of them or their intentions.

There had been nothing to keep him in his old home for the winter. Worse, he'd be tied to the land when spring opened the seaways again. It had been the work of moments to overrule Arne's objections and appoint him as the steward of Ormsfjord during his absence.

"Arne, the people here trust you. I've watched you with them. You'll do a fine job of caring for Ormsfjord."

"*Nei.* That cannot be! Ormsfjord needs its jarl," Arne protested. "Your home and your people need you. Every free-born karl in our settlement wants you to be our jarl. Your father would have wanted it. I'm a poor substitute at best."

"They respect you, and that's a great place to start." He looked at Arne's unhappy face. "I have to go, you know that. Asger may have evaded me, but I must find him and avenge my father. There'll be no ships into Ormsfjord now until next spring, and by then, Asger's trail will be cold. At least at Hafrsfjord, they may have news of him and his intentions. If I don't go now, I may never find him. He knows full well he can't return here. He's a murderer and kin-slayer. Our laws and courts have sentenced him as an outcast. Once the Thing passed judgement, the people wouldn't accept him."

Arne had sighed and bowed his head, accepting the inevitable. "May Odin guide you," he said as he clasped the younger man's arm in farewell.

As they rowed the *Trana* slowly seaward past the familiar landmarks of his birthplace, Thorkell wondered whether he'd ever see Arne or Ormsfjord again.

By the time they reached the open ocean, the change in the weather was evident. Heavy squalls marched far out at sea along the horizon, the waves were fierce, and the fair sailing they'd enjoyed since leaving Dublin was behind them.

They ran south before the wind until Sven ordered them to drop the sail and they turned east, picking their way through the treacherous straits separating the many rocky islands guarding the entrance to Hafrsfjord. The relief the crew felt as they entered the long, protected waterway of their home fjord was palpable. Sheltered by the hills either side of them, the *Trana* rowed the length of the fjord in calm water.

They emerged from the narrow confines of the fjord into a large, natural rectangular harbour.

Sigurd saw Thorkell looking around in amazement and clapped him on the shoulder. "Welcome to my home," he shouted, a big grin

"We think of our home as a hammer—the fjord is the handle, and this harbour is the head. Thor himself protects us."

Around them, the men stretched, swore and exchanged jokes. They were safely home. Theirs was the last ship to make landing that season. The weather closed in behind them ushering in an unusually long, hard winter with a sequence of wild storms buffeting the coast. There would be no traffic in and out of that harbour until the spring thaw.

Sven's wife was a small, thin woman, who made up for her lack of inches by the generosity of her smile and her apparent affection for her husband. "God's greeting to you. Welcome to Hafrsfjord and to our hall. Drink and forget the trials of the journey," she greeted Thorkell as she brought him an elaborately decorated mug of ale.

"*Skål*," he said, bowing his head in acknowledgement. "Your health, my lady."

He was sitting beside Sigurd later that evening when a man approached them.

"Sven says you are looking for the *Sea Serpent*?"

Sigurd looked across. "*Já*. You have news? Sit down, man." He moved over to give him room. "Thorkell, this is Ander."

Thorkell nodded. "You know something about the *Sea Serpent*? She's been here?"

Ander nodded. "Maybe a week ago. They brought a woman with them, Odell, who claimed kin to our jarl. So we welcomed them as guests and gave them our hospitality. Their leader Asger was in a hurry and wanted supplies. We were surprised. It was late in the season for a voyage, and we discovered from his thrall that his home port was only a day or two to the north. It would have been more usual for him to reprovision there."

"He had to leave Ormsfjord in a hurry. He's outcast," Sigurd answered.

"Ah. We thought there was something wrong, but the woman seemed sick, and our lady is kind."

"She was ill?" Thorkell asked.

"Nothing serious," Ander explained. "Seasickness. She's the sort that feels ill just looking at the waves moving."

"She's getting what she deserves then," said Thorkell with malicious pleasure. Ander raised an eyebrow.

"She was my father's wife," Thorkell explained, "and she's run off with the man who murdered him. I hope she dies vomiting in misery. Did they say where they were bound?"

Ander shook his head slowly. "Asger was vague, and we didn't press him. Now I understand the reason; I wish we'd made more effort to find out. He could be going anywhere. All I can say is he won't get far now the storms have set in. He'll have to hunker down and put the ship to rest for the winter, just like you. I can't see him crossing the North Sea now, and even keeping to the coast will be treacherous."

"The man will be desperate," Sigurd objected. "Fear puts strange pressures on a man. He might try the sea crossing anyway."

"And he might die in the effort," Ander shrugged.

"There's nothing more Ander can tell us, and the sea lanes are impassable until spring," Sigurd said later. "You'll have to spend the winter with us. Are you any good at hunting?"

Thorkell grinned at him, recognising the implicit challenge. "I can tell the difference between a wolf and a deer's tracks," he teased.

Sigurd snorted. "Prove it."

It was good to have a friend, Thorkell reflected. He hadn't called a man 'brother' since Hagen died all those years ago, and they'd been boys together, not men.

Sigurd had an uncomplicated appreciation of the pleasures of life and unfailing good humour which made him a comfortable companion. As with his mother, it was his instinct to be generous, and he shared that with those around him.

When the men played at sport, Thorkell enjoyed the uncomplicated physical competition. Frequently Sigurd was his opponent as they wrestled and sparred, or tried to pull each other over in tug of war. They were well matched in weight and reach.

There were the usual indoor tasks of winter—nets and ropes to be woven or mended; weapons to be burnished; leather to be patched and polished. Then, when the snow was firm enough, they hunted together in the low hills to the east of the harbour.

Hafrsfjord's hills and valleys had a softer contour than those further north at Thorkell's home, and the nature of the hunt changed accordingly. Wild animals were wilier, and faster over this open ground, and a successful hunt depended on carefully stalking prey until you were close enough to almost touch them. Ulf and Thorkell took to it with relish, the big hound creeping through the snow beside his master until he received the signal to charge forward and seize the quarry. Thorkell's proudest moment came when, with Ulf's help, he brought down a full-grown wolf with his spear.

"Not bad for a northerner," Sigurd conceded as he ran his fingers through the animal's thick pelt. "You'd never have managed without that hound of yours, though."

Thorkell laughed. "True enough, but whatever the reason, I now have the makings of a thick cloak like yours."

Sigurd smiled. "I'll help you prepare the skin," he said.

⁘

The thaw came late, flooding the land with meltwater and turning the ground to mud. Routine tasks became difficult, tempers flared and even Sigurd looked tired and tense. Adding to their misery, the change of season provided fertile ground for the spread of colds. Sufferers sniffed through chafed noses, and the nights were punctuated with the sound of coughing.

Working with the ship provided an escape for those chosen to be its crew, and taking her out to sea charged their spirits and blew away the megrims.

The *Trana* bounced over the choppy sea running under her keel, and a spray of ice-cold water spattered Thorkell's face, making him gasp as he leaned forward into the next stroke of the oar.

Sigurd, seated beside him, roared with laughter as his friend shook the droplets from his hair. "You needed a bath anyway," he joked.

For both of them, it was a relief to be on the ocean after long months on land.

CHAPTER
SIXTY

SOME DAYS EARLIER, THORKELL HAD SAT at the table with Sven and Sigurd.

"We'll be leaving next week," Sven said. "You can have passage with us, of course, or you'd be welcome to join as part of the *Trana*'s crew for the season."

Thorkell considered. "You've been a generous host and your offer is kind, but I need to make decisions now. I will seek word of Asger and his crew." Thorkell gave a helpless gesture with his hands. "If I know where he is, I can kill him, but the sea is wide. If I can't find him, then I'll set my course for Dublin."

"Why Dublin?" Sven asked.

"The town is growing, and our own folk are settling there. There is good, fertile land. When I was injured last year and had to live with the local people, I realised how poor the soil at Ormsfjord was, and how much work it took to harvest even a meagre crop from our land in the short growing season. There have been years when we have gone hungry through the winter, years where the crops never ripened. It's a different story when the ground is rich. A man could do well there, and I believe a man such as myself, who already has friends with the Irish, will have many opportunities to prosper."

"How could you have friends among the Irish?" Sven looked confused.

"Because he has a woman there," Sigurd grinned. Thorkell looked at him sharply. "No, you haven't spoken of her, but it's been obvious. I've watched too many of our local girls try and catch your eye, and yet you don't see them. I'll swear an oath on Odin's eye you're not one of those gelded monks whose monasteries we raid. So the only reasonable conclusion is you have a girl hidden somewhere." Sigurd was watching Thorkell's face and gave a crow of triumph. "I'm right, aren't I?"

Thorkell opened his mouth to speak, then shut it hurriedly.

"Is that right, lad? Are you thinking of marrying a native and living over there?" Sven's face furrowed with anxiety. "Do you think your father would have given you his blessing?"

Thorkell gave a short laugh. "Well, I didn't approve when Orm brought Odell home, but that was because she was young and beautiful and I desired her. Now I know how treacherous she turned out to be; I was right in my assessment." Thorkell gave an impatient shake of his head. "Orm would have wanted me to stay at Ormsfjord, and if he were still alive, I'd have made an effort to persuade Ciarnat to live there with me. But Orm's gone." Just saying the words made the enormity of his loss apparent to him. He blinked rapidly.

Sigurd flicked a look at Sven then tactfully looked away. Fathers die, it was the nature of things, but Sigurd knew he wasn't ready to lose Sven yet.

"Since I came here, I've been thinking about the future. Orm's death changes things. I wasn't exaggerating when I said my family land is poor—beautiful, I grant you, but poor in quality. Our soil produces a scant harvest, and the weather limits its productivity. My father was jarl, and our family has an honourable lineage. Now I inherit the title, but to what end if each year is a struggle? Our land barely produces enough for our people. Harald the Fairhead promised we could retain one-third of the taxes we raise each year if we supported his cause to become High King, and Orm *did* support him. But how do we levy taxes when our people struggle to raise enough food to keep them through the winter? We began raiding Britain and each summer, a generation or more ago, to gather the wealth needed to pay our dues to the king. And each new king imposes fresh taxes. Who knows what the future brings?"

Sven pursed his lips. "I think most voyages are made for that necessity, however rich the land we own."

"Last summer, I stayed with people in Ireland. I saw how they lived. They harvested two cuts of hay each season from their land and were surprised when I queried this. Their cattle grow plump and sleek, grazing in their pastures; their horses the same. The forests are rich with game, the rivers with fish. It's a fair land." Thorkell stopped abruptly.

"And is she pretty?" Sigurd asked, with a mischievous grin on his face.

"What?" Thorkell was startled, then gave a self-conscious smile. "Ciarnat, you mean? I would say she was beautiful."

"There you have it," Sigurd declared to Sven. "Thorkell needs to return to his bride as soon as possible. Otherwise some bolder warrior will sweep her up and ride off with her to marry her himself."

"There is the little matter of a blood feud," Sven murmured.

"So that's where I must start," Thorkell stated. "Will you let me be part of your crew until I hear word of Asger's plans? If not, then let me stay until Dublin. From there I can travel south by land."

"Wouldn't you rather sail there?" Sigurd asked.

Thorkell shifted uncomfortably. "I don't have the bearings to take us to their harbour, and..."

"And what?" Sigurd asked, his impatience evident.

Thorkell gave a short laugh. "It is in my mind that arriving on a Viking longship may not the best way to win my woman. Our race is not much loved in Eire. While I was vulnerable, the station of the women who nursed me protected me. Otherwise, I'd have received scant charity. Later, the villagers learnt to tolerate me because I was willing to work. But the largest part of my safety was because I was the guest of one of their skalds. They call them 'bards' and hold them in the highest esteem in

306 | Penelope Haines

that land."

Sven rose to his feet. "So be it," he declared. "You sail with us until you need to leave."

He gave Thorkell a glinting smile from beneath his heavy brows. "Your hound comes with you?" he asked innocently, then laughed as Thorkell automatically reached a protective hand to caress Ulf's neck. "I jest, lad," he smiled. "I know full well the hound comes too."

⁙

It was a strange departure for Thorkell. His previous voyages had involved farewells—to Rowena, Orm, old friends, even Aileen. It was as much a part of the rituals of casting off as loosening the ropes and pushing her down the rollers. Today there was no one there for him. He stood awkwardly by the *Trana*'s stern as others of the crew embraced their children and wives. Some wiped tears from the eyes of their loved ones as they said goodbye.

Eventually, a woman separated herself from the rest and approached him. "Fare you well, Thorkell Ormson," she said.

Thorkell smiled at his hostess. He'd learned to both like and respect her quiet skill in making the hall comfortable and welcoming. "You have been a most gracious lady, and this guest thanks you for your care. May the gods protect you and Hafrsfjord."

Sven's wife smiled, reached forward and kissed him on the cheek. "May Thor and Odin fill your sails with kind winds and give you a safe journey."

Ander, Sven's second in command, blew the horn summoning the crew on board, among cheers and waves. They took their seats, unshipped their oars and waited as the ship was pushed deeper into the tide. A minute later, the rhythm of the drum began to pound the beat for the strokes. In unison, oar blades flashed to the water, cutting the surface, before digging deep and driving the ship out into the bay.

Stroke by stroke they crossed the mighty harbour and headed for the fjord that led to the sea.

Thorkell leaned into the work with enthusiasm. The next part of his journey had begun.

CHAPTER SIXTY ONE

Ciarnat

Ninth Century, Ireland

"I'M LONELY," CIARNAT REFLECTED.

Thorkell had left three days earlier. Long enough, as Gran had remarked with some satisfaction, for life to return to 'normal'. 'Normal' was not having a large man cluttering up her cottage. 'Normal' was only preparing sufficient for two women to eat. 'Normal' meant the daily household tasks of laundry, mending and making were easier and quicker. Regrettably, it also meant no one to help carry the milking pail, or chop peat, or stack the firewood. Ciarnat had enjoyed the luxury of having help.

Worse, when Ciarnat looked up from a task, no laughing blue eyes were waiting to intercept her glance; no moments of shared amusement at some absurd pronouncement Gran might make; no teasing; no more silly laughter. She was hollow with the loss.

She had promised to wait for him and had poured all her love into that vow. He'd promised to return—if he could. Now, as she considered the bleak wasteland of the years ahead, she wondered at the futility of her words. It had seemed a fine, romantic thing to affirm her love—but to what end? she asked.

A soft, surprised gasp made her turn her head in time to see Gran suddenly slump and, very slowly, topple sideways.

"Gran?" Ciarnat leapt to her feet and ran to where her gran had fallen among the plants of her herb garden.

Ciarnat flung herself to her knees beside her. "Gran, are you all right? What happened?" At least Gran's eyes were open.

Her hands moved automatically, checking Gran's breathing, feeling the pulsing blood at her wrists. She laid the back of her hand on Gran's forehead. Her skin was overly hot. "You're burning up!" she exclaimed. "Can you talk?"

"I'm fine." Gran's voice came out in an uncharacteristically croaky whisper. "Don't just kneel there, girl. Help me up."

"In a second. Tell me why you fell."

Gran frowned. "Help me," she demanded as her hands scrabbled at the ground trying to push herself up.

Ciarnat made no move to aid her.

Gran frowned. "I've got a headache. I felt a little dizzy and lost my balance. That's all. It's not serious."

"It *is* serious. You've got a fever. I'll get you up on your feet, but you're going to bed."

Gran opened her mouth to protest, but Ciarnat interrupted. "You are going to lie down, and I'll make an infusion for you. Don't be foolish about this."

Gran scowled but tried to nod her head. She flinched as she attempted the movement. "My head hurts," she whispered.

"Give me your arm." Ciarnat was shocked at how little Gran weighed. How could she have lived with her for years and not appreciated how frail her body was? She'd considered her a tough, sturdy woman. It occurred to her now that had more to do with Gran's personality than any physical robustness.

She helped her into the house and got Gran onto her bed, piling on as many blankets as she could find, because she had started to shiver. She shook so severely Ciarnat could hear her teeth chattering.

She made a brew of feverfew, and while she waited for the kettle to boil, Ciarnat put a stone on the stove to heat. She put it at Gran's feet, wrapped in a rug, to help warm her. "Here," she said. "I'll help you sit up. You need to drink this."

Gran went to sleep soon after, with Ciarnat sitting beside her, wondering what she was going to do.

She was severely shaken. Gran had never once been ill. In all the years she'd lived there, Ciarnat had never known such a thing could happen. Gran seemed indestructible—she never sickened, never complained. She'd trained her granddaughter well in the skills of a healer. Neither of them had considered a time when those skills might be needed to care for Gran herself.

In the short term, they'd manage well enough, Ciarnat thought. She could run the farm and home by herself; there were sufficient provisions already laid up for winter and hay stacked in the barn for the animals. No doubt Padraig would drop by in the next few days, and she could ask him to tell the priest in the village of Gran's sickness, for there would be no healing help for the villagers while Gran needed nursing. Ciarnat's place was at her side, looking after her.

Ciarnat remembered how long Thorkell's convalescence had been, and he'd been a young, fit man. Gran, although robust and active, was not young, and would likely take longer to recover. Ciarnat grimaced. Gran was unlikely to be an easy patient to care for, particularly once she started feeling better.

Gran slept for most of the afternoon. On the occasions when she woke, Ciarnat made her fresh feverfew tea and rubbed her temples gently with a cooling herbal mixture.

"My head hurts," Gran told her again.

Ciarnat was more worried than she cared to admit. Nothing she did seemed to bring Gran relief, and her skin felt hotter than ever, although she complained of the cold.

"Let me sponge you," Ciarnat begged. "It will help bring the fever down."

"No," Gran muttered, tossing her head restlessly from side to side.

"It will help," Ciarnat insisted. "Let me do it. Here." She

placed a damp cloth to Gran's forehead.

Gran screamed, and Ciarnat jumped back.

"I said, no! You're trying to kill me. I know what you're about." Gran's eyes narrowed in hatred as she looked at her granddaughter. "You leave me alone, you murderous demon."

"Gran!" Ciarnat protested. The accusation rattled her severely, but it was clear Gran's mind was wandering in a different reality. Ciarnat was grateful when she dropped off to sleep again.

She had little choice but to leave Gran alone while she went outside to milk the cow and feed the animals and chickens. Some tasks had to be done, regardless, but Ciarnat hurried through the work as fast as she could and was grateful to find Gran still asleep on her return.

If she saw Padraig, she'd ask if one of his sons could come and help with the outside chores. Indeed, she wondered whether she should go and fetch Padraig now. But if Gran's mind was wandering, it wasn't safe to leave her.

Ciarnat made a light meal for herself, then left it uneaten. She had no appetite. Gran's bout of delirium was a terrifying indication of how serious her condition was, and Ciarnat was aware how little she could do to aid her.

She brought her bedding down from the loft and set it out beside Gran's bed. She didn't expect to be able to sleep, but if she did doze off, she was a light enough sleeper to wake if Gran stirred.

As night came on, Gran became restless, tossing and turning. The sheets were soaked with sweat, and Ciarnat changed the bedding. Gran protested feebly as Ciarnat rolled her over, but there was no strength to her complaint. She seemed barely conscious, and Ciarnat took the opportunity to bathe her. Gran was frighteningly hot, and Ciarnat knew how vital it was to cool her down.

Afterwards, Gran seemed a little quieter and more comfortable, and allowed Ciarnat to spoon medicine into her mouth. Ciarnat took a comb and gently smoothed Gran's hair, which seemed to calm her. Her breathing grew quieter, and her movements less restive.

It was natural for Ciarnat to put the harp to her shoulder and play quietly. Music was soothing; she knew that and hoped the tunes would calm Gran. Soft lullabies, simple compositions of her own or Filan's making. At last, Gran lay quietly, her breathing seemed more comfortable, her sleep deeper.

When she'd put the harp away, Ciarnat sat for a long time holding Gran's hand. She was frightened and very alone. She'd sat beside other sickbeds, of course. Sometimes alone, if Gran was busy elsewhere. And she'd sat alongside those who were dying—even some who died while she was with them. It was part of being a healer—you helped with births, you eased deaths and every condition between.

No one had ever told her it was different when your kin was involved, that there was a crippling terror to understanding all your skill, determination and knowledge might not be enough to win the fight.

She closed her eyes for a while, half-awake, half-sleeping, but came fully alert when Gran wrenched her hand away. She glanced at the candle to see how far it had burned down. Ciarnat must have been dozing for an hour. She turned her attention to Gran and shot to her feet, terrified by what she was seeing. Her grandmother's face was now flushed a deep shade of red. Even as Ciarnat watched helplessly, Gran's back arched abruptly, and her arms began to twitch uncontrollably.

Ciarnat was horrified. She had no idea what to do. She reached out to rub Gran's arms, but the cramping muscles were too powerful for her to ease. Ciarnat managed to grab a wrist and felt the wild pounding of Gran's elevated pulse rushing beneath the overheated skin. Gran was burning up.

For the space of a few minutes, Gran's arms flailed, while her back cramped unnaturally, then, as suddenly as the attack had begun, her body relaxed.

Relieved, Ciarnat bent forward to straighten her—and stopped. Gran was lying quietly now, but not in the gentle stillness of peaceful sleep.

Ciarnat slowly straightened up and clapped her hands over her mouth to stifle the involuntary moan she couldn't help making.

She backed away from the bed until her legs hit the edge of her chair. Her limbs gave way and she fell onto it. The jolt freed her voice.

"Ohhhhh!" she wailed, careless of the noise she made as her cries bounced back at her from the walls of the small cottage. She, so good with words, could not express the turmoil that suffocated her. Her only release was to produce those terrible, animalistic cries again and again and again.

The twin strands of shock and guilt threatened to strangle her. She wrapped her arms about herself and hunched over, howling out her grief. She'd never even said goodbye. Worse, the sickness had progressed so rapidly there had been no time to tell Filan.

Now his mother was dead.

CHAPTER
SIXTY TWO

Thorkell

Ninth Century, Ireland

THEY ASKED QUESTIONS OF OTHER SHIPS they met as they passed through the Shetland Islands and Orkney. No one had news of Asger or the *Sea Serpent*.

Sven shrugged. "Sooner or later someone will have seen or heard of them," he said to Thorkell consolingly.

Sven and Ander had plotted a course down the east coast of Britain, an area new to Thorkell, but one Sven and the *Trana* had visited some years earlier. They stopped twice to raid coastal villages but got little reward for their efforts. There had been raiding parties through late the previous year, and scant time for the residents to recover. Even the small church at the second village was reduced to using an earthenware chalice.

Sven spat in disgust when he surveyed the quality of goods his crew brought on board. "A couple of hides, a poorly balanced knife. Two silver coins, one woman's bracelet. Is that it?" he asked in disbelief.

"They were so poor, they made us look like kings," Sigurd answered.

"Odin's eye!" Sven muttered.

That evening he announced a revised plan for the season. They would turn north, retracing their steps, and then work their way through the island chain known as Nordreys, following down the western side of Britain until they reached the Isle of Man. Situated midway between Ireland and Britain, it was a perfectly placed spot to decide which country they'd concentrate their raids on this season.

Thorkell tried to put himself in Asger's place.

Which way would the fugitive go? Friendless and without family, he would need to choose his moves carefully. The news of his crime would already have spread throughout the Viking brotherhood. Few would have sympathy for a treacherous fratricide and, being an outcast, any man was free to kill him.

Would Asger choose the routes he was familiar with from previous seasons and explore the coast of Ireland? The settlement at Dublin was expanding quickly, an ideal place for a younger son or brother to settle, acquire land of their own and begin trading.

The drawback for Asger was he and the *Sea Serpent* were well known. It wouldn't be easy for him to remain anonymous and escape the consequences of his actions.

"If it were me," Thorkell said to Sigurd, "I'd have gone eastwards when I left Hafrsfjord."

"East?"

"I'd follow the route I've heard the traders tell of. Eastwards past the coast of Denmark and up into the cold northern sea. Somewhere on the eastern side, there is a mighty river that a ship can follow to the city of Miklagard. When I was a lad, I had dreams of going there myself."

"But he has your father's wife with him," Sigurd objected. "Surely he wouldn't take a woman on that journey?"

"Maybe," Thorkell said. "It would be safer than plying local waters. Asger may think I'm dead, but he must know someone will come after him one day seeking revenge." A thought occurred to him. "Odell still has family as well who are likely to want answers."

"We are her family, come to that," said Sven. "The only answer I would want from such a murderous woman is a knife drawn across her throat. She has dishonoured us all."

Thorkell flicked a quick look at his friend. He had overlooked that point.

Sigurd's mouth was thin and rigid with disapproval.

They both took a moment to consider his bald statement.

"If they have gone east, they're likely well beyond your reach by now," Sigurd said at last, "and it could be years before you hear where they have gone."

Thorkell nodded. "*Já*. We can only keep on asking other crews if they've seen or heard of them."

Without further information to guide him, Thorkell was content for the moment to go wherever Sven decided and let the gods determine Asger's fate. Each day they sailed westward was a day nearer to Dublin and, eventually, to Ciarnat.

When they reached the Isle of Man, they turned westward, Sven's decision dictated by the winds. "I smell clear weather coming in from the west," he announced. "If we go east, we'll be caught up in a storm surge. We head for Dublin."

Thorkell, remembering how close he'd come to drowning a year earlier, was grateful for Sven's caution.

They reached the Dublin Bay shortly after dawn. Dropping their sail, they rowed the final stages into the port, picking their way cautiously through the shoals and sandbanks protecting the river's mouth. A brisk onshore wind had roiled the water into a succession of choppy waves that splashed and heaved against the *Trana* as they made their way through them and into the smooth waters of the harbour.

Thorkell looked at the low-lying hills surrounding the town. As the sun rose over the bay, wild geese took flight, heading eastwards, with the morning light on their wings. He nodded to himself. For better or worse, his wyrd lay in this land. If he got news of Asger and Odell, then his course was clear until he'd taken his revenge. If there was no word of the man, then he was free to travel south to Ciarnat.

The harbour was busy even at this early hour. Sven gave a grunt of pleasure when he picked out a familiar vessel. "The *Visund* is here! This is good news. Eric knows more gossip than any man I know," he explained. "If anyone has news of your fugitives, it will be him. Not much happens that he doesn't hear about."

They made their way to the tavern. It was early, but the doors were already open, with a brisk trade in hot ale and porridge.

The proprietor nodded at Thorkell. "You're back, then? You are famous in these parts, you know. The boy hasn't stopped talking about your hound since he saw it. He must have told everyone about the giant of a man and his enormous hound. It seems you're a bit of a hero."

Sigurd slapped him on the back. "A hero, no less," he teased. "Who would have known?"

Thorkell reddened. "To your boy, perhaps," he said to the innkeeper. "Let's hope he hasn't told too many people otherwise it is going to be embarrassing."

"He's told a few," chuckled the man. "Now, what can I serve you men?"

They asked after Asger and the *Sea Serpent*. The innkeeper shook his head. "I remember the man and his crew, but they haven't been here for a while. I couldn't tell you the last time they were in port."

"Which could mean anything," Thorkell said in irritation as they ate their breakfast. "Does it mean they came here after they'd killed my father?" The man had been unable to recall when he'd seen them.

"It would have been unlikely they made it back here from Norway at the tail end of last season. Remember the weather turned rough? It would have been a dangerous gamble, even for a desperate man. In which case, they haven't been here this year," Sigurd replied. "He would have remembered that."

Thorkell gave an impatient grunt. He wanted certainty and a clear direction to follow.

Sven had declared a two-day rest at Dublin, but after that

the *Trana* would depart for a season of raiding along the coast. Thorkell was going to have to make his mind up soon. If Asger was still in these waters, his best chance of meeting him was to sail with the *Trana*, and he knew Sven and Sigurd would be happy to help him. He ran his hand through his hair in frustration. Why was his life so complicated?

Sigurd was watching him with shrewd eyes. "Don't look so downhearted," he advised. "Either way, you win, don't you?"

Thorkell gave him a hard stare. "How so?"

"If you hear of Asger, you get to kill him. If you don't, you win the girl. If you're fortunate, you get both. So cheer up."

Put like that, the odds suddenly looked decidedly cheerful. Thorkell grinned. "You have a way with words."

"I know."

"You're a smug bastard, you know that as well?"

Sigurd laughed. "Come on. We have lodgings to find."

As they wandered through the market, Thorkell lingered at the shops selling metalwork. In the past few years, Dublin had seen a fusion between Norse craftsmanship and Irish metals, resulting in the production of elaborately crafted jewellery. Many of the stalls sold torcs, brooches and rings, some made from the local Irish gold which the Vikings prized highly.

Thorkell settled eventually on a finely wrought clasp for Ciarnat's hair. As a secondary thought, he purchased a well-made cooking knife as well. "For my girl's grandmother," he explained. "It always pays to be nice to the family of the woman you're courting, don't you think?"

CHAPTER
SIXTY THREE

EVERYWHERE THEY WENT THEY ASKED FOR news about the *Sea Serpent* and heard nothing. Those who recalled the ship and her crew said she hadn't been in port for months. They headed uphill through the town in search of a room for the night.

"They might know of one." Sigurd pointed to women washing clothes in the open basin that ran alongside a well. He walked over to ask them.

Thorkell followed him across the square. One of the women gave a startled gasp, and Thorkell, assuming she was nervous of Ulf, turned to reassure her. She spun swiftly away and lifted her shawl to cover her face, but too late.

"Odell!" Surprise made Thorkell shout the name.

"What?" Sigurd swung around, grabbing the woman as she turned to flee. "Oh no you don't. Let's have a look at you," Sigurd said as he ripped away the shawl to see the woman clearly. "By Odin's eye, it *is* her." Sigurd ran his eyes over her. "She's in pup," he added in disgust as he registered her swollen belly.

The other women scattered, leaving Odell alone with them. She stared at Thorkell, her face ashen in terror.

"Where's Asger?" he demanded, but got no reply.

Sigurd shook her by the arm. "Speak, woman."

"Where's Asger?" Thorkell asked again.

"I don't know." Her words were whispered as her eyes filled with tears.

"What do you mean? Where is he?" Thorkell pressed. "Don't even think of lying to me."

"He left me here. I don't know where he is."

Odell's eyes were darting from side to side, looking for help. It was clear she'd have bolted if Sigurd hadn't kept a firm grip on her.

"I think we should take this discussion somewhere quieter," Sigurd cautioned. The group of women had disappeared, but they had attracted the interested attention of a few men. "This is a family matter; let's keep it that way. Where do you live?" Sigurd asked. When he didn't get an answer, he shook Odell again.

"Take us to where you stay," Thorkell ordered her.

When she still didn't move, Sigurd gave an exasperated 'tch' and twisted her arm up behind her back until she cried out.

"Right. If you don't want me to break your arm, you'll lead us to where you live."

Odell's face twisted in pain, and she looked from Sigurd to Thorkell, finding no sympathy or kindness in either of them. Heavy tears rolled down her face as she shuffled around, while Sigurd kept the pressure on the arm lock. She led them into a narrow alley between the buildings. Some way along they reached a gate. "Here," she indicated with her chin, and waited while Thorkell released the catch. The gate opened into an enclosed area, home to some chickens and a pig. Against the rear wall leaned a small shed—a shack really, nothing more. Odell led them to it. "I stay here," she said.

Sigurd released her arm and stepped back as Odell fumbled to untie the rope that held the door to the bothy closed. The door swung open, allowing light to fall into the tiny room. A rough bed of twigs and bracken lay against the back wall. A cloak hung from a peg on the wall, and a narrow shelf held a small tallow candle and a plate.

"This is where you live?" Thorkell asked, taking in the poverty of the place.

Odell nodded. An ambitious chicken ran over her foot and into the shack.

Sigurd shoved Odell forward so that she stumbled across to the bed. "Sit down," he said and stood over her as she eased herself down on to it. He looked around, making no attempt to disguise his disgust. "You left your husband and home in Ormsfjord for this?" he asked incredulously.

Odell bowed her head, saying nothing. The men could see her body shaking with fear.

"Get out of here," Thorkell kicked the chicken out and closed the door. There was barely enough room for the three of them. Both men had to bend their heads to avoid hitting the roof.

Thorkell studied Odell in silence. She was thin and drawn. Her hair hung flat and lifeless, and her face, once so fair and bright, was sallow and lined. An ugly sore sat beside her mouth.

"Where's Asger," he asked at last. "Why are you here?"

"He left me," Odell said.

"Why? Did you betray him as well?" Sigurd sneered.

Odell glanced up at him. "No." She shook her head. "He knew he was outcast. He wanted to leave here before other Vikings arrived in the spring. He thought you were dead," she said to Thorkell.

"Why didn't he take you with him?" Thorkell asked.

"He thought it was best if I stayed here. I don't travel well. I was sick all the time on the ship when we came here. Asger planned to cross the sea to the east, and it would be a long journey. He talked to a merchant who had travelled that way before and was returning. They agreed the *Sea Serpent* would follow the merchant's ship when it sailed. Asger could give the *knörr* armed protection and in return get a guide into waters he didn't know."

"And you agreed to that? To stay here alone?"

"He didn't ask me."

Thorkell gave a harsh laugh. "So Asger abandoned you here? In this dump?"

"It's still better than she deserves," Sigurd observed.

"You killed Orm," Thorkell stated baldly. "You killed my father."

"*Nei*, I did not!" she cried. For the first time, she looked at Thorkell directly. "I did not kill Orm, and I didn't know that was what Asger intended to do. I swear it." She registered his scepticism. "You must believe me. I thought Orm's death was natural. He was an old man."

"So why did you leave with Asger? Why run away with your husband's murderer?"

"You don't understand. Orm was dead. I was sitting beside him, still in shock, when Asger rushed in. He grabbed my hand. 'You need to come with me,' he said. 'Pack a bag, quickly.' I wasn't thinking clearly, but with Orm and you dead, Asger was the new jarl. I did what he told me and followed him down to the *Sea Serpent*. It was only later I learnt Rowena had accused him of murder. When I asked him directly if he had killed Orm, he denied it. Anyway, by then it was too late. I had gone with him."

"I don't believe her," Sigurd said. "Let's get this over with. Will you kill her, or shall I?"

"No!" Odell scuttled back on the bed and cowered in the corner. "No, I beg you. Don't kill me. I haven't done anything," she cried.

"Ach," Sigurd said in annoyance. "I'll do it." He reached for Odell's arm and yanked her to her feet.

"When's the baby due?" Thorkell interrupted.

"What?" Odell stared at him with terrified eyes. It took her some moments to unscramble her thoughts. "Oh, in late summer."

"What does that signify?" Sigurd asked.

"Who fathered it?" Thorkell asked quietly. He watched Odell closely. Did something flicker in her eyes?

"Orm," she said. "Orm is the father."

The men looked at each other. Thorkell counted back the months. It was just possible, he supposed.

"You've been barren since you married my father. Do you expect us to believe that now, after all these years, an ageing man with a damaged leg, managed to father a child on you?"

Thorkell was openly scathing.

"It is the truth."

"Surely he would have been too injured."

"Orm was confined to bed for a long time. Once the leg started healing, he'd get bored and difficult. It was the easiest way to keep him happy."

Sigurd snorted crudely. "Now I've heard more than I needed to know."

"It is the truth," Odell repeated.

"She's lying," Sigurd told Thorkell. "You aren't going to believe her, surely?"

"I think she's lying as well," Thorkell agreed. "But I can't take the chance. If that babe in her *is* Orm's, I can't kill it. I'd be killing my kin."

Sigurd dropped his grip on Odell. "So what? You intend to let her go; to live? Despite what she's done?" he asked in disbelief.

Thorkell gestured around the hovel. "If you call this living." He pointed to the ill-fitting door. "That doesn't even keep the light out. It won't keep the cold out, let alone rain and snow. She'll be lucky to survive next winter."

Sigurd spat in disgust. "So, just like that, you forgive her?"

"Never," Thorkell said, his voice curt. "But I will not kill her with that child in her. If she lives, I can find her again, after I've killed Asger."

He kicked the door open and stepped through. Behind him, he heard the hard crack of a hand against skin. "Keep that bruise in remembrance of me," his friend said, before following Thorkell.

∴

"So that's it," Sven said.

They had gathered at the tavern. "The *Sea Serpent* has gone eastwards after all. You may hear news of them when some merchant from those lands reaches Dublin. Otherwise, the trail has gone cold."

"I still can't believe you let Odell go," Sigurd grumbled. "She's dishonoured both your family and mine."

"He had no choice," Sven snapped. "I'm not happy either, but would you have Thorkell kill his brother?"

"If it was Orm's. I didn't believe her."

"It wasn't a risk he could take," Sven said.

Sigurd shrugged. "What will you do now?" he asked. "We sail on the morrow."

Thorkell rubbed his chin. "I will stay here." He gave a short huff of frustration. "It's a hard choice. I want to kill Asger, but with no idea where to look, it's a fool's quest. I could sail for years and never find him."

Sven nodded. "Well, there's always a place for you on the *Trana* if you want it."

Thorkell gave him a grateful smile. "I hate leaving the task undone," he confessed. "The truth is I'm more likely to hear news of Asger in a port town like Dublin than anywhere else. Gossip from visiting crews filters through a place like this. I'll leave word of my interest in news of the *Sea Serpent* with the innkeeper and offer a reward for information. Sooner or later, if Asger is found, someone will get word to me."

"You'll go and court your girl?" Sigurd asked.

Thorkell nodded. "The situation is likely to be complicated. Ciarnat's father is the High King's bard, so he's powerful. Ciarnat will be an heiress, and I have no idea how Filan would feel about his only child wedding a Norseman. Then again, she lives with her grandmother, and although the old lady is fit and healthy, I don't know that Ciarnat would choose to come with me and leave her to live on her own." He shrugged. "As I say, it's going to be complicated."

"You'll manage," Sigurd laughed.

CHAPTER
SIXTY FOUR

Ciarnat

Ninth Century, Ireland

"YOU MUST REALISE YOU CAN'T STAY here on your own," Father Niall said. "Thank you, my child," he added as Ciarnat poured ale into his mug.

"Where else should I be?" Ciarnat asked. "This is my father's house, and these are my father's lands. Where else should I be?" she asked again. Her tone was sweet and conciliatory, but Gran would have recognised the steely set to her jaw.

"Ciarnat, you're a young woman. Hardly more than a girl. You can't live so alone and isolated. Who is there to protect you, all the way out here? You're two miles from the village. If something untoward happened, there'd be no one around to help."

"Padraig is just up the valley if I need someone, and he or one of his sons comes by most days. I'm not completely on my own. Gran taught me well; I'm fully able to run the farm by myself."

"I'm sure you can, my dear. But you must see that it is not

proper, living alone like this. For one thing, you'll be lonely. If your father were here, it would be a different matter."

"Well, he's not here," Ciarnat said, "and in his absence, the responsibility to care for his lands and holdings falls to me." She felt her hold on her temper slipping. Gran had been laid to rest a fortnight earlier, and all Ciarnat wanted now was to be left in peace to get on with things and mourn her grandmother in her own way.

"Maybe I could ask Grainne to move in with you," Father Niall mused.

Ciarnat stared at him. She knew Grainne as an elderly, idle widow. She had the role of village busybody and was the source of much malicious gossip. "No, Father. No one is going to move in with me, least of all, Grainne. I'm sorry, but we wouldn't suit."

"Well, what do you suggest?" For the first time, the priest looked irritated.

"I suggest you let me get on with my chores in peace," Ciarnat said flatly. "I appreciate your care, but I'm well able to fend for myself. Most certainly I'm not having anyone else moving in with me."

"My child!" the priest protested.

Ciarnat had heard enough. "But I'm not a child, Father. Tell me, did you have this same conversation with Gran? Did you try telling her it was inappropriate for her to live alone out here?"

The priest gave a short laugh. "Your grandmother was a force of nature. We often sparred, and over many issues." He shook his head ruefully. "I don't think I ever made her change her mind on any matter."

"Well, there you have it," Ciarnat said. "I will live here, in my father's house, and carry on Gran's work as a healer in the village, as she would expect me to. Young Maeve's baby is due any day, so I'll be attending her when her time comes. You needn't worry about me, Father."

"Ah, yes. Maeve," the priest murmured, before smiling at Ciarnat. "Very well then, I concede defeat. I won't press you on this matter any more, although your situation does worry me."

"I'll be fine," she reassured him.

She watched as he walked away from the cottage, and waved when he turned before rounding the corner and disappearing out of sight.

The conversation had rattled her, although she wouldn't admit it to Father Niall. She wasn't afraid to live alone, and she wasn't going to leave her father's house, but there had been moments since Gran died when acute loneliness had oppressed her and she didn't know how to deal with it.

She'd taken it for granted that Gran would be there forever, so the speed of the brain-fever that killed her had left Ciarnat in shock. She'd spent the days after Gran's death in a dream-like state, barely noticing the priest and villagers who came to pay their respects and to help prepare for the funeral. Now they'd gone, and she had to adjust to her new life.

She missed Gran terribly, missed the acid comments and brisk manner that had concealed her warmth and care.

Padraig's son, Connor, had been sent to find Filan and tell him of Gran's passing but there had been no word from either her father or Connor.

Gran was here alone before she'd come to live with her, Ciarnat reassured herself. If Gran had been self-sufficient then she could be as well.

But Gran had Padraig, said a voice in her head, and you have no one. Thorkell was miles away, and Gran's sudden death had carved such a hole in Ciarnat's life that it seemed years, not just a matter of weeks, since Thorkell had lived with them.

She turned away from the door. Father Niall meant well, but she had to take care of herself. Winter was coming in fast, and there was work to be done—cream to be churned, chickens to feed, an evening meal to prepare. Loneliness and introspection were luxuries she couldn't afford.

Padraig came around later that afternoon, and she told him of the priest's visit.

"Ah, well now, the man has a point," he said after some thought.

"What? I can look after myself perfectly well."

Padraig grunted. "That's not what I meant, and it's probably not what the good father was trying to say, but he'd be too shy to tell you outright."

"What?" Ciarnat was impatient.

"You're a wealthy young woman living without protection. You're vulnerable to any man who sees an opportunity to better their condition by marrying you. It's only respect for your Gran's passing that has kept the lads from the village away from here until now. But there are some already making plans to court you. I've heard them talk."

"That's daft. I'm not going to marry anyone. Not at the moment, anyway."

"I didn't say you would consent to such a thing. It is not unknown for women to be forced," Padraig said bluntly.

"You jest!"

"Nay, I do not. It's only been a few weeks since Thorkell tangled with those soldiers. They were barely a day's march away from here. I'm not saying the village lads would hurt you, although they'll surely pester you. But there will be others who wouldn't mind an alliance with the *ollamh's* daughter and might not be scrupulous about how they achieve it."

Ciarnat stared at the old man, her certainties crumbling as she considered his words. Her concerns had been practical: running the farm —whether she would be strong enough; would she need help for some of the more onerous tasks like chopping peat and firewood? Padraig and his sons would help, of course, but perhaps she would need to hire in additional labour.

She'd never had any worries about her safety. It occurred to her that Padraig had made a point of visiting every day since Gran had died. She thought he had been grieving, and visiting her had been part of his mourning. "Is that why you have been coming here? To check on me?"

"Aye."

Ciarnat sat down with a thump. "Gran was all right here on her own," she said.

"I kept an eye on her. Besides, she wasn't a young woman, nor was she Filan's daughter. Also, she could look after herself."

"And you don't think I can?" she asked. She tried to sound confident, but an uneasy memory of Ultán's attack surfaced. She shuddered. She'd only been a child then, much weaker and less confident.

"No," Padraig said. "You'd stand up for yourself, I give you that. But against a determined man? Nay, you would not stand a chance."

CHAPTER
SIXTY FIVE

Erin

Present Day, New Zealand

TWO MORNINGS LATER, THE PHONE RANG. Erin had been lying awake. Sleeping wasn't simple to achieve when you couldn't roll over comfortably or shift position readily. She checked the time as she pushed herself into a place where she could read the clock. 2.30 am.

"Yes?" she said warily, as she picked up. She supposed it could be Luke calling; he hadn't contacted her since he'd left home. She'd tried to call him, but his cell phone was switched off. Surely it was unlikely the anonymous caller from the other night would call again?

"Is Luke there?"

It *was* that bloody man again. "No. I told you last time. Luke's away. You'll have to wait until he comes back, then you can phone him at his office. Please don't call here."

"He's ruined me. I need to talk to him." Short, sharp sentences spoken in a hard voice.

"He's not here, and harassing me isn't going to help you. Don't call again."

"I'm going to kill myself." This time the disembodied voice climbed into a wail.

Erin had had enough. "Oh, for fuck's sake, just go away," she shouted as she slammed the phone down.

She switched the light on and sat up in bed, thoroughly enraged. Her response to a potentially suicidal man had been completely inappropriate, but frankly, she didn't care. How dare he take his problems out on her. She shuffled her pillow, stuffing it behind her to support the small of her back. She realised, in the process, that her hands were shaking.

Bastard! She wasn't sure whether she meant her late-night caller or her husband. Either. Both. Damn them all to hell. She had to worry about her baby. The last thing she needed was bloody men trying to dump their problems on her.

She picked up the phone and dialled Luke's number. She had no idea what the time was in Frankfurt. If she disturbed him at an inappropriate time, so much the better. Erin was completely awake now and thoroughly unsettled.

Luke's phone was still off.

"Fuck it!" she swore in frustration. Was Luke deliberately trying to avoid her?

She padded down to the kitchen and made a cup of tea. As she carried it back to bed, it occurred to her that she had no idea where Luke was staying. She hadn't cared enough to remember or even keep a copy of his itinerary. For all she knew, he might not even be in Frankfurt.

She toyed with that as a thought. Maybe Luke had run away and was hiding. Perhaps he was a missing person—a modern-day Lord Lucan. All she'd have to do was wait seven years and he'd be declared dead. She rather relished that idea. No need for the effort and decisions involved in getting a divorce; no acrimonious break-up; no expensive lawyers to pay. She'd be a solo mum, which wasn't what she and Luke had once planned, but given the way things were going, she could be one soon anyway.

Considerably cheered by her fantasy and soothed by her tea, she switched the light off and settled back into bed. Sleep came quickly.

A pale line marked the track she was walking on through the grass. It was too dark to see much else. The brisk wind blowing into her face had pushed the hood back off her head. An annoying wisp of hair kept flapping into her eyes, but she didn't have a spare hand to push it away. One held the front of the cloak closed, the other carried her grandmother's old medicine bag. She flicked her head irritably trying to shift the hair, a pointless effort, as the wind simply blew it back across her face again.

A few yards ahead she could just make out the child they'd sent to fetch her. She'd have liked him to walk beside her and chatter as they went, but his mission completed, the boy was making for home as fast as he could go.

The strident ring of the telephone broke through.

The rapid transition from the dream world to reality was disorienting. A surge of loneliness was still sweeping through her, picked up from the woman in her dream. Goddammit, she'd only just got back to sleep as well!

She switched on the light, reached for the pen and notepad she'd prepared, and wrote down the caller's number. She looked thoughtfully at the digits. It was a local number, so he lived somewhere nearby.

Her clock informed her it was three forty-five.

She let the phone carry on ringing, without picking up. When it eventually stopped, she switched the light off and lay in the dark planning her next move. She'd had enough of being a passive victim. This guy wasn't going to use her as an emotional punching bag. If necessary, she'd report him to the police, but hopefully, her failure to answer his call might have put him off.

If he did call again... well, two could play at that game. How would he like being woken in the middle of the night? And if he lived with someone, how would he explain such a call?

It was particularly irritating that he'd interrupted her sleep when he did. Now she wouldn't know where the woman in her dream was going, or why. Could it be true, as Brianna had suggested, that this was an ancestor of hers? Someone who'd left a thumbprint on Erin's DNA? In which case, her baby would inherit it as well. And what sort of trauma had happened to this ancestor to leave an inheritable trace on DNA anyway?

Erin cradled her belly protectively. The first few times she'd entered the dream had been terrifying. She remembered the vision of fire and the anguish of watching the terror this woman had felt. If it had been an actual occurrence, the woman had suffered terribly. She shuddered. It was even more disturbing if Brianna's theory was correct and the ancestors of Luke and Fergal were part of this story as well. What did it mean? Was this some sort of psychic warning she was receiving?

Erin gave a wry smile. That, at least, was probably pushing things too far. Following Doug's explanation, she could accept, given her sketchy understanding of DNA, that genuine science could be behind the phenomenon. But she didn't believe in ghosts, Ouija boards, tarot cards or crystals. Erin prided herself on being a realist and a sceptic.

CHAPTER
SIXTY SIX

Ciarnat

Ninth Century, Ireland

A MONTH HAD PASSED SINCE GRAN WAS buried. Ciarnat knelt at the foot of her grave. Despite the biting wind that blew in from the sea, frail shoots of green grass were already defying the onset of winter and struggling to live on the mounded earth. When spring came, Gran would sleep beneath a soft green canopy. Ciarnat had brought bulbs from her garden to plant around the edge of the grave. That garden, with its carefully collected store of herbs, had been essential to the old woman. It was right, thought Ciarnat, that a memory of it should flourish here, with Gran.

At her funeral, Father had spoken of Gran being in heaven for eternity. Ciarnat thought Gran would instead prefer to be in her garden with her plants.

"It's peaceful," her father said. "She'll rest here easy enough."

Ciarnat nodded. Filan had arrived home only yesterday. He'd been away from the High King's hall when Connor came seeking him, and it had taken the boy another two weeks to track him down. 'In the end, it was pure chance led to us meeting on the road. I was returning to the Hill of Tara, and he was travelling out to the west to find me. He recognised me, and gave me the news,' Filan had told her the previous night. Ciarnat had nodded, grateful she hadn't been the one to tell him his mother had died. It was hard enough watching him stand beside the grave today. His grief and loss were written on his face.

"I should have been here," he whispered, as if to himself. He lifted his face to the sky, and Ciarnat could see the tears in his eyes. She turned her head away and busied herself with her planting. Such moments should be private.

"Did she suffer?" Filan asked at last.

"It was swift," Ciarnat temporised. Truth to tell, she was bearing a significant burden of guilt herself. Had she known more, done something else, could she have saved Gran? Foolish questions, perhaps, but they haunted her. She brushed the damp earth from her fingers as she stood up. "I did my best," she tried to explain, "but the fever was fierce. It burned her up until she went into a fit. She complained her head hurt, but nothing would soothe it."

Filan's eyes narrowed as he studied his daughter. She'd become very thin. Her face was pale, the dark purple smudges under her eyes a testament to her tiredness. His heart went out to her. She was as beautiful as ever, but there was a new maturity about her.

"Come," he said, putting his arm around her shoulders. "I know you did your best for your gran, and far more besides. It was her time to go, and she'd be proud of all you did for her, and for the way you've managed since." He pulled her to him, so her head rested against his shoulder. "*I'm* proud of you. It's been a hard time, and I wish I had been here for both of you."

Ciarnat gave a sad smile. "Father Niall would say things happen as God commands."

Filan gave a derisive snort. "No doubt he would, but God works his commands through imperfect men and women who struggle to do the best they can."

Sharing meals was necessary, and Ciarnat realised that evening just how much she'd missed it. Cooking for herself had bored her. The impulse and effort to eat had seemed too much with no one else there. That night, the simple meal of stew and soda bread she'd baked earlier tasted better than anything she'd eaten since Gran died.

Of course, it helped that Filan had completed the evening tasks, leaving her free to cook. He'd filled water buckets for the horse and donkey, carried the milk pail for her, brought in firewood and chopped fresh kindling.

His labour gave her welcome relief from the endless cycle of work she'd been doing. Most nights, she had been so tired she barely had the energy to play the harp after her meal.

"Good food," he mumbled around a slice of bread.

She smiled, pleased with the compliment. It was nice to have someone to share the evening with. Later Filan sat beside her as she played her harp.

"I haven't played much recently," she confessed.

Filan shot her a sharp look but nodded. "Sometimes it's like that. Music can ease our sorrows, but there are times when pain swamps us so much we lose our way. But tonight, play a little for me. It will soften the grief of your gran's leaving."

He spoke truly. As her fingers moved over the strings, Ciarnat felt some of the tangled grief unravel. A faint smile she was unaware of played on her lips as the sound tumbled from her hands. Filan saw it with sadness, recognising both the release the music afforded his daughter and the emotional depth she now brought to her instrument. He registered the small stiffnesses and lack of fluency in her fingering, but what she'd lost was more than compensated for in the cadence and phrasing of the melody.

At last, she sang a lullaby, a simple child's song that Filan recognised. When she finished, there were tears in her eyes. "I sang that for Gran, just before she died," she explained. There was deep sadness as she spoke. "Even my singing couldn't soothe her at the end." Her hands rested in her lap, and Filan reached across and covered them with his own. "I used to think my music was some sort of magic," Ciarnat confessed. "When I was a child, there didn't seem to be anything there wasn't music for—songs for happiness, songs for sadness. I used to think playing the right music would make everything I wanted to happen be real. But it doesn't work like that when you grow up."

"Oh, sweeting." Filan's voice was warm with sorrow. "The magic is always there, and one day you'll find it again. The fault is our own. Sometimes our human needs and emotions swamp us, and we lose the quietness in ourselves. To find the magic, we have to find peace so we can listen to it and let it flow through us."

"But it's gone," Ciarnat said. "There's an emptiness inside me. I can feel it."

"That emptiness won't always be there," Filan assured her. "You're human, and you're grieving for your gran; that puts a veil of sorrow between you and the magic. But in time you will heal. You won't forget Gran—I don't mean that — but in time you will see things happen for a reason, and that reason is good. It was Gran's time to go, and your time to grow up. Of course you're hurting. But you're a child who has lived with music, with that magic place in you that song comes from. You've already been there, and when you are ready, you will find your way back to that place."

He gave her hands a squeeze of sympathy. "Your grief is a measure of how much you loved Gran. If you hadn't, it wouldn't hurt you now. Grief is the price we pay for love."

"Was it like that when you lost Ma?"

"Yes. The darkness stayed with me for a long time." Filan smiled at her. "I only found my way back when my daughter began to travel with me. Then I learnt that love is the best cure for grief."

They sat in silence, both occupied with their thoughts. Ciarnat looked as she considered his statement.

"Which brings me to something I need to raise with you," Filan said eventually. "You are old enough for me to find you a husband. You are a fully grown woman, and it is time to find a man who can offer you a home and a life you can share."

"Nay!" The word was forced out of her before Ciarnat had time to soften it.

Filan stared at her. "What do you mean, 'nay'? Do you mean you are opposed to marriage generally?"

"I'm not against marriage," Ciarnat hastened to explain. "But it is too soon. I'm not ready. I want to live here and mind the farm for you."

"You have made a brave fist of it, Ciarnat, but you must see that is not possible." He raised his hand for silence as she tried to reply. "I know how much work you've had to do here. But it is not suitable for a young woman to live alone. You need companions, friends, a life that is more than just work. Most of all, you need a life and a future of your own."

"But I don't want to," Ciarnat cried. "I don't want just any husband."

"Ah!" Filan said. "I understand. Nay, of course, I wouldn't find you 'just any husband'. I'll make sure he's a good man who can look after you and give you a good life. You are my daughter, and you are beautiful. We can aim high in our search for a suitable match. There's no hurry about it. We have got the time to choose wisely. I would not let you go to just anybody. Trust me on that."

CHAPTER
SIXTY SEVEN

CIARNAT BIT HER LIP AND LOOKED down at her hands.

"What's the problem? I've said I would find a good man for you." Filan frowned trying to master his irritation. His daughter had inherited her grandmother's stubbornness.

As Ciarnat remained silent, Filan's eyes narrowed as an unwelcome suspicion began to grow. "Is there someone you already favour?" he asked cautiously. "Have you formed an attachment?"

At this, Ciarnat took a deep breath and raised her eyes to his. "I told Thorkell I would wait for him," she admitted.

"Thorkell? The Norseman?" Filan was outraged. "Do you mean that whoreson seduced you? When he was my guest?" Shock consumed him. "What have you done, you wretched girl?"

Ciarnat jumped to her feet, her eyes blazing. "I haven't done anything," she retorted, "and neither did Thorkell. I haven't betrayed your trust. Nor did he. You should know me better than that."

"Oh." Filan's shoulders slumped in relief. "Then, what?"

"We..." Ciarnat stopped. How to distil, for her father, the

importance of words spoken on a summer's night? How to explain those few words that meant nothing and everything? "We agreed there was something between us that we both wanted to explore." Ciarnat forestalled Filan's objections. "Yes, we understood how difficult such a choice would be for us. But we both knew we wanted to try. Thorkell had to go home to his father, for he feared he would think Thorkell was dead. Then again, Thorkell wants revenge on the man who abandoned him to die. In his own country, Thorkell is the son of a chief, a jarl, he called it. His standing is at least the equal of my own. He promised to return when he could. He didn't ask me to promise to wait for him. It was my choice to do so."

"You realise he's pagan?" asked Filan. "He worships false gods. When he washed up on our beach, it was from a Viking warship. He's a Viking warrior. They weren't sailing our coastline on a fishing trip, Ciarnat. These are raiders, come to prey on our people. It was only luck that kept them from our village, else they would likely have sacked it, like all the others over the years. Likely they would have slaughtered Father Niall and your kin in the village."

"You gave him help and shelter," Ciarnat retorted. "Gran nursed him back to health."

"Yes, and I agreed to let him live because I thought knowledge of his people's ways could be useful. I agreed because such as he has been coming to the High King's court seeking trading rights, and helping him might earn more in the way of favours long term from his kin than letting him die. That was all."

"Well, you *did* let him live. For half a year he stayed with Gran and me. He helped me, and he helped Gran. When Padraig needed someone to work with him and the cattle, he was there. When the harvest came, he worked with the villagers. Thorkell learnt our ways more than we learnt his. We came to know him well, and if we were cautious of him at first, we came to see he was a good man, no different from the rest of us. Even Padraig grudgingly conceded that. Gran was no fool. Did you think she would have let him stay if he hadn't been worthy? So when you talk about arranging a marriage for me, you can't. I've promised to wait for Thorkell."

Filan sniffed. "My daughter, you may have forgotten that you owe your filial duty to me. If I say you marry, then you will."

"But I won't. You can't force me," Ciarnat cried.

Filan stood and arched his back, stretching. "As to that, I probably could if I had to." He straightened up and looked Ciarnat square in the eye. "I am a reasonable man, and it is not my intent to cause you grief. But nor will I allow you to waste your youth on a children's fairy tale. I give you twelve months to honour your pledge. During that time, I will seek out a good match for you. If in a year Thorkell has not returned, you will marry the man of my choosing."

He saw Ciarnat about to argue and held his hand up. "You will say no more. I have given you a grace period, that is all. There will be no more discussion on this point. Go to bed," he ordered.

Ciarnat ground her teeth in frustration but decided it was prudent to obey.

She'd thought to begin the argument again over breakfast the next day, but Filan pre-empted her.

"I have said all that is needed. We won't discuss it again," he said, dismissing the conversation with a wave of his hand. "However, we must organise a suitable woman to live with you and help with the work. The king will want me back once the spring arrives. He only released me because my mother had died. I will ask Father Niall if he knows of someone who can help."

"You can't!" Ciarnat's voice rose in a wail of protest. "Father Niall suggested Grainne. I'd die rather than have her here!"

"Grainne? The Father suggested Grainne live here?" Filan's horror matched his daughter's. They stared at each other, sharing a moment of complete agreement.

Filan started laughing. "At least we are in harmony on that point. I wouldn't let the woman over the threshold. We'd never get rid of her. What a horror! Gran would turn in her grave at the thought of her being in our house."

Ciarnat giggled.

"I'll go down to the village today and see if I can find someone more suitable. Have no fear, I won't inflict Grainne on you."

Ciarnat rolled her eyes as he walked away down the track. It had been nice to have his help, for the all-too-brief period he'd felt he should offer it. She was now on her own again. In his absence, she worked her way through the chores.

They had passed the shortest day, and it was good to see the evenings growing longer. She hated the early sunset, which left her still outside working in the cold when darkness fell. It took her all day to get the work done, and she was tired by the end. If—and it was a big if, she conceded—Filan could find suitable help, it would be nice to share the load with someone.

Filan was gone the whole day. By the time he returned, she'd made a fresh loaf of soda bread. A pot of thick stock lived all winter at the back of the hearth. Ciarnat added to it each day with any leftovers and heated it into a warm, aromatic soup.

Filan grunted satisfaction as he took his first mouthful of the hot potage. "You're a clever cook, Ciarnat."

"Gran taught me," she said. She hadn't intended to be terse, but she was too bone-weary to carry on a polite conversation.

Filan frowned slightly but let the comment slide as he continued to eat his meal. When he'd finished, he pushed the bowl aside. "I've reached an agreement with Aoife. She'll move in here when I leave."

"Aoife?" Ciarnat asked. The name was familiar, but she couldn't place it.

"She's Oisin's widow. She's doing it hard, what with a young daughter and all. She's been staying with Oisin's family, but they don't get on and have made it clear she and the child are unwelcome extra mouths to feed."

"Ah," Ciarnat had identified the woman. "Oisin drowned, didn't he? I remember Gran and I went to the funeral. I must have met Aoife there, but I don't know her otherwise."

Filan shrugged. "She knows who you are, and needs the work. She's willing to live here with the child and help run the farm. I made it clear she needed to follow your instructions, that you are the mistress here, so you should have no trouble with her."

"Where will she stay?" Ciarnat asked. The farmhouse had been large enough for her and Gran, but they'd been kinsfolk.

"How old is her daughter?"

"I would say about seven or eight. Aoife was very firm; the child will be no trouble and will work for her keep as well. Where will they stay? I thought you could move down here and let Aoife and the girl have the loft. That way, you could have some peace."

Ciarnat looked at Gran's bed. She'd avoided moving from the loft when Gran died. Sleeping in her bed seemed to underline the finality of her death, although Filan was using it now with no apparent qualms. She supposed her reluctance was foolish. Gran was gone, and there was no changing that.

She nodded, wondering what it would be like to have a child in the house, whether it would brighten the place up. Before Thorkell arrived, she'd frequently felt lonely. Gran had been company, but she was ancient, set in her ways and often grumpy. She hadn't appreciated the scale of her isolation until she had to return to it when Thorkell left.

As long as Aoife was reasonably pleasant to live with, it might be nice to have a companion—as long as it wasn't old Grainne!

CHAPTER SIXTY EIGHT

Erin

Present Day, New Zealand

❝I THOUGHT WE SHOULD HAVE A retro evening. Fergal suggested a games evening, but I wanted to try a fondue which was something my grandparents told me about. First a cheese fondue, then a chocolate fondue."

There was silence around the table as everyone considered Brianna's words.

Erin sneaked a glance at Fergal whose face was strictly neutral.

"I inherited a couple of fondue sets from the grandies," Brianna said cheerily.

It took a second or so before Doug was brave enough to say what the rest of them thought. "Um. That would be my parents' generation, not the grandparents."

It wasn't hard to see Brianna's disappointment, although she was too brave to say so.

There was a brief moment before Petra broke the awkward silence. "I think it's a brilliant idea. Tradition, family values and all that stuff." She wavered slightly before her partner's stare.

"Absolutely," Erin added. "My folks had a set, and I always wanted to try it. I thought it sounded quite exotic. But we never got around to it."

Brianna perked up with their support. "I've read the recipe books, and we do it in two courses. First the cheese dip, then chocolate. You guys sit there while I lay the table."

The thing was, Erin thought, idly pulling Wolf's ears as they waited, even if Brianna occasionally made them all feel old by her casual assumptions, she was a great hostess.

"Hey, Fergal, this dog's getting enormous."

Fergal grinned. "He's a growing boy. Aren't you, Wolf. He'll be up to my size soon."

"Just as well he's nice natured," Doug commented.

Brianna called them to the table as she spread trays of food in front of them. There were chunks of bread, sliced salamis, crackers, an array of vegetables and pickles.

"Dig in, Erin. You're eating for two," Petra said as she passed her a platter.

"Not for much longer, I hope," Erin said. "I'm a wee bit over this whole pregnancy thing. I'm so large I can barely fit behind the steering wheel. It's becoming quite a job to climb in and out of the car."

She was well aware the meal her friends had organised tonight was to look after her and give her company while Luke was overseas. She was torn between amusement that they were treating her as fragile, and gratitude at not having to spend another evening alone.

"Have you heard from Luke yet?" Doug asked.

Erin shook her head. "No. It's very odd. We've been tiptoeing around each other for the last little while. Even so, I would have expected him to ring, at least."

"When's he back?" asked Fergal.

"I'm embarrassed to say, but I don't know. Luke may have given me his flight details, but if so, I've mislaid them, and I didn't write anything down."

"Would his work know?"

"I don't like to ask; it makes me look such an idiot. Besides, he's not working for Kittering and Hodges anymore, so they probably wouldn't know what he's doing. Alwyn, his partner, is away with him, and I don't have contact details for him either."

"This is lovely, Brianna," Petra said, twisting her bread in the cheese sauce. "I don't know why fondue fell out of fashion. It's a lot of fun."

"Particularly when you lose your piece of bread in the pot," Doug said. "I believe you owe me a kiss for that."

"Is that so?" Petra asked. "Who wrote that rule?" she said as she kissed Doug.

"It's worse for men. I've heard if they drop their bread they have to buy everyone a drink," Erin remembered. "I'm sure that's what my mum told me." She was glad to have the conversation shift away from Luke's failures and their troubled marriage.

It was just as irritating when Petra asked, "What happened about your phantom late-night caller?"

"Caller?" asked Brianna.

"He's a guy who's been waking me up in the middle of the night because he's got some beef with Luke. He knows Luke's away, but it doesn't stop him calling me."

"Have you reported him to the police?" Fergal asked. "It's an offence to harass people by phone."

"Not yet. I've got a better idea that I reckon will fix him," said Erin. "Tonight I'm going to call him instead."

Doug looked puzzled. "Why?"

"I'll phone at two or three am. I'm hoping it will be right in the middle of his sleep. I took the number down last time. For one thing, if he lives with someone else, they're going to be peeved by a late-night caller, and he'll have to explain himself to them. I'll tell him I've got his number, and if he calls again for any reason, I'll set the police on him. I'm betting that will sort him."

"Sounds a bit dodgy to me," Fergal said. "You'd be better off contacting the police, or get the phone company to put a block on his number."

"Particularly if he's a nutcase," added Petra. "Fergal's right."

Erin smiled. "I'll do it my way, guys. He's annoyed me enough for me to want some revenge. He can have his night's sleep broken by me for a change."

It was late when Erin finally reached home. The meal had been leisurely, and conversation had flourished throughout the evening. Her friends cared for her and had insisted she also come to the movies with them the following week. 'If I'm still here,' Erin had said. 'It'll be getting close to 'B' day.' 'We'll pick you up,' Fergal had suggested. 'There's no point taking two cars.'

An enjoyable evening, even if she'd overeaten, thought Erin. She got ready for bed but was too excited to sleep at first. The more she watched her clock, however, the slower it seemed to go. She lay in bed, half dozing, waiting for the time to pass. By the time the numbers rolled around to two o'clock, she had almost given up. It took some effort to wake herself up. For a moment Fergal's caution resurfaced, but she was determined on her course.

She punched the numbers into the phone and waited, counting the number of times it rang. It was over a dozen before someone picked up.

"Hello," said a sleepy voice.

"Hi," Erin said. "There's been a guy calling me from this number in the middle of the night and harassing me. Could you put him on please?"

"What?" The disembodied voice was sharp. The woman had woken up.

"There's a man, calling from your number, who has recently phoned me several times in the middle of the night. Please could you put him on? I need to talk to him."

The phone was muffled—Erin imagined the woman's hand smothering the handset—but she could faintly hear agitated voices.

The pause lasted a few minutes.

"Hello?"

She recognised her late-night caller's voice. "Hi," Erin said, in the most cheerful tone she could muster. "I thought I'd pre-empt your call tonight and let you find out what it's like to get woken up in the middle of the night." Revenge felt sweet when she heard him gasp.

Her voice hardened. "Now, you bastard. I have your number, and if you ever fucking call me again, I'll give it to the police and report you. Got it? I'm not putting up with you and your stupid games. Not anymore." With that, she briskly ended the call.

Her heart was pounding as she relaxed back into her pillows. She'd love to be a fly on the wall at his place. A strange woman phoning in the middle of the night with accusations would surely raise some interesting questions. With any luck, it would curb the wretched git.

She was smiling as she turned off the light and settled herself for sleep.

CHAPTER
SIXTY NINE

Ciarnat

Ninth Century, Ireland

C IARNAT LIFTED HER HEAD FROM HER mending as a peal of childish laughter rang out. Clodagh had been gathering eggs, lifting the chickens to search the straw beneath them. Now the child was cuddling a plump brown hen who clucked in contentment as Clodagh stroked her feathers.

"She's enjoying herself far too much," Aoife grumbled. "She's supposed to be working." Aoife's grin softened her words. Ciarnat smiled.

Aoife and her daughter were proving to be ideal, not just as helpers, but as companions. Filan had chosen well when he picked the young widow.

At first, Ciarnat and Aoife had been wary around each other as they tested the boundaries of the arrangement Filan had put in place. Soon they discovered they liked each other, and having Clodagh in the house had introduced a new element. Ciarnat found she enjoyed having the child around.

Aoife was a fond but firm mother and the child nicely behaved, but she brought more with her than simple good manners. Her enthusiasm and intelligence reminded Ciarnat of her own childhood. She had begun showing Clodagh how to hold the harp and pick notes from the strings. Soon she would teach the girl the simple songs Ciarnat had learnt as a child.

Aoife had been harder to get to know. She had been very wary of Ciarnat initially and had kept her distance as far as was practicable.

"Why were your husband's family unkind to you?" Ciarnat asked eventually. She'd been exasperated at first by Aoife's diffidence but soon came to realise it was the result of mistreatment.

Aoife took her time answering. "I wasn't the girl they had wanted their son to marry," she said.

"How did you meet?"

A reminiscent smile played on Aoife's lips. "I'd gone with my family to the Aenach Colmain. Do you know of it? The big fair on the Curragh of Kildare? My father bred horses, and he'd taken a stallion and two mares to sell. I met Oisin there." She gave a small laugh. "The festivities only lasted ten days, but in that time we decided we wanted each other. When the time came to go home, I went with Oisin."

"Weren't your parents worried?"

"They were furious. My mother told me no good would come of wedding a fisherman, and my father disowned me." She gave a sad smile. "In the end, my mother was right. Oisin drowned. We were together long enough to have Clodagh, and then he died."

"So you lived with Oisin's parents?"

"There was nowhere else to go. And they only let me and Clodagh stay because Father Niall threatened them with eternal hell if they weren't good to me. But they made it clear we were a drain on their family."

Ciarnat nodded. She also knew what it was like to feel unwanted. She had forgiven Filan a long time ago for abandoning her to Gran's care, but she'd never forgotten the pain and betrayal.

Now the women counted each other as friends. It amused Ciarnat that she was almost as close to Clodagh's age as she was to Aoife's. It had the happy effect of allowing her to act like a child with the little girl while discussing more womanly things with her mother.

It was midsummer, and that night they would be celebrating the celebration of Litha, the solstice, with the rest of the village.

Aoife unsuccessfully tried to encourage Clodagh to take an afternoon nap so she was fresh for the festivities, but the little girl was too excited. She'd wriggled from her bed to lean out of the loft to ask, "Is it true that tonight you might see a vision of your true-husband if you stare into the flames?"

"You're much too young to worry about that," was Aoife's firm retort.

"Well then, can I dance tonight? Can I stay up to see the sunrise? Will they roll the fire-wheels down the hill?"

Ciarnat snorted.

Aoife glared at her. "It's not funny," she told Ciarnat, before replying to her daughter. "Maybe, but only if you get some rest, Clodagh. Close your eyes and try to sleep; otherwise tonight one of the evil spirits will grab you for being naughty." Aoife rolled her eyes. "Little brat," she muttered. "If she doesn't get some sleep now, there'll be tears tonight when she gets tired."

Ciarnat chuckled. "We've all been like her when we were little."

Some hours later the three of them followed the procession climbing the hill sheltering the southern bay of their little harbour. Father Niall and his cross led the way, the children skipping behind him with excitement.

Ciarnat smiled as she watched the priest bless the congregation and welcome them to the celebration of St John's night.

"Gran would have had a thing or two to say to that," she murmured to Aoife. "She always told me the ancient Druids taught us to observe this eve as a celebration of the victory of light over dark. As well, of course, to acknowledge the nights will now get longer, so the sun and moon will be brought together."

"Was she pagan, your gran?" Aoife asked.

"Nay. Just cynical and practical. She told me never to believe too easily, regardless of who told me a thing was true."

Aoife laughed appreciatively. "She used to scare me when she came into the village, even though she was a healer. She seemed to know far too much for any woman. My mother-in-law called her a witch but wasn't too proud to call for her help when Oisin drowned."

"She wasn't a witch," Ciarnat confirmed, "but *was* a wise woman."

The feasting and dancing started early, and Clodagh joined in with the other children.

Ciarnat watched her dip and spin in the steps of the dance. "She'll be a bonny girl one day," she observed.

"I hope she takes her time," Aoife answered. "The longer she stays a child, the longer she'll be safe."

Later the men took torches from the bonfire and lit the large wheels set in place high on the slope earlier in the day. Covered in dried brush and furze, they burst into flames within seconds. The cry came to release the chocks that held them. The wheels raced down the hill towards the field behind the village. The watching crowd cheered and yelled their encouragement. Both wheels blazed the entire way down the hillside.

"It will be a good year and a good harvest," Padraig said. "Remember three years ago, when one of them blew out? It was a bad, wet season, followed by a colder winter. You can always tell from watching the wheels."

Ciarnat smiled and wondered what Father Niall would make of that.

There was a collective sigh as the church bell began to toll in the village below. She counted as it spoke twelve times. As the last chime rang out, the crowd cheered. Friends, husbands, wives, neighbours greeted each other, and there was happy chatter as they all milled around the bonfire. People embraced

The night would run into the morning. Ciarnat saw young women staring into the flames and smiled at the memory of Clodagh wanting to search for her elusive future love.

Aoife had found Clodagh some minutes before, crumpled into

a small, exhausted pile beneath one of the trestles.

"I'll bid you goodnight, Ciarnat," she said. "I think it's time I took this one home."

Ciarnat waved goodbye. She had resisted the temptation all evening, but now, with no one to watch or comment, she also took the time to gaze into the bonfire.

The fire itself was burning lower now, its earlier fury having settled into a steady glow. Young couples jumped the flames together to mark their bonding.

Many settled on blankets on the ground to keep the vigil through to the dawn.

Someone thrust a warm drink into her hand. She smiled her thanks and sipped the mead. She looked across the fire and saw... *him*... watching her. An unambiguous jolt of pure joy surged through her. If she'd doubted her feelings before, she couldn't now, not when every part of her rejoiced so wholly. She couldn't lie to herself.

He'd come back!

Thorkell was wearing travel clothes. A hood covered his head, shadowing his face. She would have known him anywhere, though, even if Ulf hadn't been at his side. Thorkell began to walk around the fire to her, and she moved to meet him, her eagerness making her clumsy as she pushed past other revellers. Some stared at the stranger in their midst or gazed at Ciarnat critically. She made no effort to conceal her joy. No more than a pace away from him, her hands were already eagerly extended to grasp his.

Thorkell had come to claim her.

He pulled her into his arms, and she went willingly, her body accepting him. For a long moment, they stood together in silence.

"You came back..." she began.

"I promised."

She heard the rumble of low laughter in his voice as his arms tightened around her. As it always had, the timbre of his deep voice melted the path to her heart.

She lifted her head to look at him and smiled.

His lips met hers, and she closed her eyes, savouring the

sensation and cherishing the familiarity of the scent and texture of his skin against hers.

"This time I've come to claim you." His words were rough against her hair. He pulled a little away from her so he could see her face. "If you'll have me?"

He studied her carefully, but there was no artifice in her. She wore her emotion clearly written in every feature—in her sparkling eyes, her smiling lips and the small crinkles that gathered at the corner of her eyes.

"Are you free to ask?" she said.

He nodded. "Are you free to answer?"

All thoughts of Filan, of duty, of waiting for parental permission fled. There was no denying what her heart and her body were clamouring. For better or worse, this man was her choice.

"I am," she said, lifting her face to his, inviting his kiss.

They held each other so for some moments before they were interrupted by a cough.

Ciarnat stepped back and turned her head. "Padraig?" she said. "Thorkell has returned."

"So I see. And you are making a fine spectacle of yourself in front of the entire village." Padraig expressed his disapproval in every line of his being.

Ciarnat drew a deep breath. "He is my betrothed," she announced.

A woman behind her, hearing, gasped. Padraig couldn't have looked more shocked if she'd stabbed him.

She turned back to Thorkell, sudden doubt striking her. "That is so, isn't it?"

He lifted her hand to his lips. "You are mine, and I yours."

She smiled. "Then will you dare leap the flames with me?"

"With pleasure."

Clasping their hands together they ran towards the hot embers. For a frightening moment the leap seemed enormous—much further than she'd imagined—but Thorkell was beside her, his grip firm, as they lifted into the air and made it safely over the flames. She felt a bump against her leg as they leapt and realised

Ulf had jumped beside them.

When they landed, Thorkell pulled her close into his arms again. "For now, and forever," he repeated.

Ciarnat echoed his words back to him. "For now, and forever."

CHAPTER SEVENTY

THE RAIN, A STEADY MIZZLE OF moisture had now set in. Without its fall being particularly intense, summer dust had turned to mud, long grass carried enough moisture to soak the hem of a tunic to the knees within minutes, and a mist lay low in the valley, obscuring the hills beyond.

"My gran used to call this a 'soft day'," Ciarnat explained to Clodagh who was grumbling about being sent out to feed the chickens.

"But..."

"But nothing," Aoife told her. "You go out and do the chores you're assigned."

"A little rain won't hurt you," Ciarnat assured her. "Put the hood up on your cloak."

Clodagh huffed, and pouted, demonstrating in every line of her body that she was mistreated, as she stamped slowly towards the door.

Ciarnat laughed, which brought her a scowl from the child.

"Get outside now, missy," instructed her mother.

The women looked at each other as the door slammed behind Clodagh. Ciarnat rolled her eyes.

"It's fine for you to think it's funny," Aoife said. "She's turning out to be a right handful."

A few minutes later, they heard Clodagh cry out and a crash as a bucket hit the ground.

"Clodagh?" Ciarnat called, jumping to her feet.

Aoife had already made it through the door; Ciarnat was close behind. They found the child standing by the barn door staring out into the mist.

"What is it?" Aoife asked. "What happened?"

"It's a banshee," the child whispered. "I've seen a banshee."

"Where?" asked Ciarnat, peering into the mist. The white-out smothered everything.

Clodagh pointed to the cloud-covered valley that ran to the north of the cottage. "There," she whispered. "It moved over there. I saw it."

"It's all right, sweeting." Aoife cuddled her daughter. "It's all right."

"It almost certainly isn't a banshee," Ciarnat said reassuringly, picking up the fallen bucket. She wasn't as sure as she sounded. Gran had respected the old ways, and her stories had been full of the fairies and spirits with which they shared the land. A shiver went down her spine. Maybe it was the ghost of Gran come back to haunt them because Ciarnat had failed to save her life?

She peered into the mist and gave an involuntary gasp. There *was* something out there. A shape, darker grey than the surrounding cloud, was coming towards her.

She stood her ground, although her heart pounded, watching as the apparition came nearer.

It was a mere handful of paces from her when she recognised who it was and gave a gasp of pleasure. "Da!" she cried in relief, running forward to embrace him.

Aoife went to heat ale for Filan, drawing her daughter along with her. "The mist makes things look spooky," she reassured Clodagh. "I'm not surprised you were afraid, but you're quite safe here."

⁕

In the evenings, after Clodagh had been sent to the loft to sleep, Aoife and Ciarnat had fallen into the habit of sitting together and talking. Tonight, Aoife excused herself after the meal had been cleared away, and left Filan and Ciarnat alone. They sat in silence for a while, staring into the fire.

"What has been happening since I left you last?" Filan eventually asked his daughter. His voice was calm and controlled.

Ciarnat licked her lips. Although her da had not referred to Thorkell, Ciarnat was almost certain Filan had already heard about the events at Litha. His face gave nothing away, but that wasn't unusual for her da.

Ciarnat wished she'd had more warning of his visit so she could have rehearsed what she had to say. She needed to find the perfect words, ones that would guarantee his agreement to, and support of, her marriage to Thorkell. Her tongue, usually so fluent, felt heavy in her mouth. If she searched for inspiration, she searched in vain. In the end, she spoke plainly. "Thorkell has returned. The night we were on the hill celebrating Litha." Even now, the memory brought an unconscious smile to her face. She turned to her father, straightening her shoulders as she spoke. "We leapt the flames and pledged ourselves to each other."

Filan said nothing for a moment, just looked at her steadily. "And where is Thorkell now? He's not here," he said, indicating the cottage.

She shook her head. "He's been with Padraig and his boys for the last sennight helping build the wattle panels for the new stretch of fencing in the lea meadow."

"Padraig let him stay with them?"

Ciarnat sniffed. "Padraig disapproves of him on principle. It's nothing personal, mark you. Thorkell's from foreign lands. Worse, he's a Norseman, and we've all heard about them! But Padraig is not stupid. He knows Thorkell works faster and better than his sons ever do, even as a pair together. So he accepts him. I think he might even like him, not that Padraig would admit it."

"Where was Thorkell staying between his arrival on the night of Litha and going up to Padraig's?"

"In his old bed in the barn," Ciarnat said evenly.

Filan pursed his lips and nodded. He said nothing more.

Sometime later Ciarnat excused herself and pulled shut the doors that gave Gran's, or rather, *her* bed, privacy from the rest of the room. Filan's bed was in his usual place against the opposite wall.

She lay awake for some time. Filan had not challenged her statement, which she supposed was a good thing, but she was sure that didn't mean she had won his approval for her unusual choice of suitor. She guessed Filan intended to have a long talk with Aoife the next morning and find out what had been going on since Thorkell arrived.

Two afternoons later, Ciarnat was at the far end of the garden harvesting herbs, tying them into sprigs ready to be hung and slowly dried over the hearth for winter. The scent of crushed leaves on her stained hands pleased her, and she breathed the pungent aroma with pleasure as she worked carefully and steadily at her task.

Filan was sitting outside the front door, playing a sequence of rippling runs and plangent chords on his harp. As Thorkell approached him, his hound at his heels, Filan looked up.

"God's greeting to you, Thorkell Ormson," Filan said.

There was the barest hesitation in Thorkell's stride. "*Filan na Cláirseach*," he replied, bowing his head in salutation. "And to you. It is good to see you again."

"I see you are well," Filan stated grimly. "I regret I was not here to receive you when you arrived. I hope my household have made your stay here comfortable." His words were formally courteous but his tone chill.

If Thorkell noticed, he gave no sign. "They have, I thank you. I grieved to hear of your mother's death. She was a great lady who saved my life on two occasions. I admired her skill, and I am forever in her debt. I am sorry for your loss."

For a moment, Filan looked away. "Aye, well. As you say, a great lady," he replied, returning his attention to Thorkell.

Aoife, looking out the window as she kneaded dough, had seen what was happening, and came bustling out of the cottage with Clodagh close behind her.

"Thorkell," she exclaimed. "I didn't know you were back. I'll bring you both some ale."

Ulf trotted over to Clodagh who flung her arms around his neck. "Ulfie, did you miss me?" she crooned into his neck as she embraced the hound.

Thorkell's fierce war hound wagged his tail and managed to wriggle free enough to lick the child's face vigorously. Clodagh giggled.

Aoife came back with a pitcher of ale and two mugs for Filan and Thorkell, setting them down on the bench beside Filan.

"Leave Ulf alone, sweeting," she instructed, but with no great urgency to her command.

Both hound and child ignored her.

Aoife looked at Thorkell who grinned at her. "Leave them be," he advised. "She's turned my hound into a puppy dog. I never realised his ferocious coat hid such a soft heart."

Aoife shrugged and went back into the house. A satisfied smile lingered on her lips.

Thorkell poured ale for himself and Filan.

Filan had watched the scene, one eyebrow raised. "It appears you and your hound have won hearts here," he observed. This time the sarcasm and anger were impossible to miss.

Thorkell turned and handed the mug to the older man. "I hope so," he said carefully.

Filan glared at him, but Thorkell returned his gaze steadily. "My purpose here is to seek..."

"Thorkell!" A shriek arose from the gardens as Ciarnat registered his presence and ran towards him over the turfed path. Thorkell strode to intercept her.

"Sweetheart," Thorkell murmured into her hair as she embraced him. "Your father is here, and not as fond of me as he might be."

"Really?" Ciarnat exclaimed, fight in her eyes, as she released herself from his arms and turned towards her father.

Thorkell clung on to her upper arm and swung her back to face him. "No. This matter is for your father and me to sort out," he warned. He felt her body go rigid. "No," he warned again as he sensed her preparing to fight.

"But..." Ciarnat's muted wail was an agonised whisper.

"No." Thorkell was unswayed. "Return to your herbs," he urged. "This is between men. If you interfere now, you'll cause lasting damage for all of us. I know you want to sort it out, but you cannot. Trust me."

She remained there, rigid with anger, a minute longer.

"Go," Thorkell insisted. Ciarnat continued to resist. "Now!"

Ciarnat glared at him but backed off.

Thorkell breathed a sigh of relief. His feisty, passionate girl could blow his planning apart with one unwary comment. Any chance of reconciliation with Filan depended on cool reason, a quality he judged Filan to have in good measure.

CHAPTER
SEVENTY ONE

“SO, WHAT WERE YOU TRYING TO SAY?” Filan prompted. He had watched the interplay between his daughter and the Norseman, a sardonic gleam in his eye.

“I seek your daughter's hand in marriage,” Thorkell said.

“And what possible reason makes you think I would consent to such a thing?” Filan made no effort to disguise his anger. “You were thrown upon our shores—a half-drowned rat of a man—and given every aid we could offer you. In return, you steal my daughter's affection and seduce her into an illicit relationship. What sort of repayment is that for the help we gave you?”

“I have stolen nothing.” Thorkell's voice was flat and carefully modulated. This was no time for him to lose his temper. “Nor have I, in any way, dishonoured Ciarnat or suborned your rights as a father. There is no 'illicit' relationship, as you choose to call it. I am making an honourable proposal of marriage. That is all.”

Filan's eyes narrowed. “Then what bride-price do you intend to offer me? She's *Filan na Cláirseach*'s daughter, not some village girl, easily bought with a boat-hold of fish. She could marry the best in the land. I've already rejected offers for her hand, from better men than you. What can a man such as you possibly give her? I will not let her wed until I know her future welfare and happiness are assured. You have no place, no kin, no means to keep or protect my daughter. You and your people are pagan interlopers. What you ask is impossible. You are a foreign man and should return to your land. There is nothing for you here."

Thorkell was angry and even angrier at himself that he should have to deal so with Filan's apparent contempt. He didn't think of himself as proud; he'd never needed to be. He was what he was, and no one could dispute it. No man, not even Filan, would be allowed to disparage his lineage.

Unconsciously he stood straighter, his fists tight against his side. "*Já*? And why not? My lineage is as honourable as any man's. I am a warrior, from a line of noble warrior chieftains. I'm the Jarl of Ormsfjord, with men at my command, a hall, and lands of my own, more than equal to any of your petty Irish kingships. Ciarnat will want for nothing when she weds me."

"What use is all that to Ciarnat? Or to me? Whatever you claim, you have no land, men or riches here in Ireland, do you? You stand before me as a landless man, seeking to marry Ciarnat. You must see that it is impossible."

"That can be easily remedied by my taking Ciarnat to Ormsfjord with me and making her my lady. She'll live richly there with servants to do her bidding, and rich furs and jewels, if that is her desire. What does she have here? A life of constant toil, a small cottage—it's not a lord's hall, is it?"

Filan's cheeks flooded with angry colour. Irate words crowded his mouth, but before he could utter them, Aoife had come to the door.

"There is food prepared if you will come inside and eat."

Filan's mouth snapped shut on his unspoken words, but neither man moved. They stayed, their eyes locked on each other, until Ciarnat walked by and took Thorkell's arm to lead him inside.

She could feel the rigidity in his body as she walked beside him. She had expected Filan to raise objections—Thorkell's proposal wasn't what he wanted for his daughter—but she was certain Filan liked Thorkell and that matters would be quickly resolved between them. Now the air between the two men fair crackled with animosity.

For the first time, she was afraid of the outcome. If Filan forced her to choose between Thorkell and himself, it would tear her apart.

Both men had drawn blood in their duel.

It was inconceivable to Filan that Ciarnat might leave and go with Thorkell; the threat of such a thing had jolted him severely.

Offended pride burned Thorkell. How dare *anyone* dismiss his father, his home and heritage with such contempt?

Both men were aware they had strayed into dangerous territory, but neither man would back down.

They sat down to eat.

"Get that dog out of here," Filan ordered sharply. "There's not enough room for it inside."

Thorkell ordered Ulf out, then sat in silence.

Aoife appeared unaware of the tensions around the table. "Did you get Padraig's fence finished?" she asked Thorkell.

Thorkell nodded. Then, as Aoife evidently expected a more coherent response, he added, "*Já.*"

"Last time he was here, Padraig talked about a remarkable young bull he had bred. Did you see it, Thorkell? What did you think of it?"

"Um, it's a fine-looking beast." Thorkell seemed confused.

"What colour is it?"

"Brown." Thorkell's voice was flat.

Ciarnat was listening, a slight frown creasing her forehead. She wanted to scream her frustration at Thorkell and Filan. What was Aoife up to with her inane questions?

"So, do we have a new *Donn Cuailnge?*" Aoife asked. Her amusement was apparent.

At that, Filan turned his head, his interest sparked. "A new Brown Bull of Ulster?" he pondered.

"Maybe there's a song for you to write in that?" Aoife asked mischievously.

"You might want to wait and see how the animal develops," Thorkell warned. "He's still only a yearling."

"Still, it would be something if we had such a creature in our herd," Filan said. "Imagine the songs and stories I could spin."

"To make the story complete you'd need its rival, though," Aoife remarked. "Remember, in the tale, there are two bulls, the brown, and *Fionnbheannach*, the White Bull of Connacht. Didn't they fight for dominance?"

"Indeed, they did. There's nothing an audience likes better than tales of heroes fighting. In the story, they fight to the death, and both die gloriously of their wounds. You are right, Aoife, maybe I should rework the saga."

Thorkell was trying to follow the conversation. "I don't know this story."

"It's one of the most famous of our sagas," Filan said, temporarily forgetting his anger. "I'll perform it for you someday. You'd like it. Whatever else, Vikings are also great fighters."

"Maybe there's another interpretation," Aoife said in a soft voice. "Is there, perhaps, more to learn from the tale if we look deeper? Could it show that conflict between equals can never end in anything but ruin for both?"

Filan was no fool. He recognised he'd been manipulated and glared at Aoife, who stared back with a serene smile.

It occurred to Ciarnat that Aoife was one of the few people unafraid of Filan. Usually people were nervous of his status, and even more of his wit and sharp tongue. Offending an *ollamh* could have far-reaching consequences. They had an endless supply of weapons to deal with those who opposed them—a sarcastic line of doggerel, a verse in a ballad. All could cause eternal shame to the offender. For all her gentleness, Aoife had a quiet strength, and it was a lesson for Ciarnat in a new skill. Gran had been direct and abrupt in her approach to conflict. Aoife had chosen a softer way and asserted her position with just as much authority.

"Can I go outside and play with Ulf?" Clodagh asked. "I want to teach him a new trick."

"Of course," Aoife smiled. She turned to Thorkell. "If that is all right, of course? Ulf's very tolerant, isn't he?"

"He enjoys the attention."

There had been an indefinable shift in mood around the table. Ciarnat got up to help Aoife clear and wash the platters. The men looked at each other.

Filan jerked his head towards the door. "Shall we go back outside?" he asked Thorkell.

Aoife waited until they had gone. "I think we should make ourselves scarce and stay inside," she murmured. "At least until they've thrashed this one out."

Ciarnat studied her. "You've been managing them all morning, haven't you?"

"Not so much managing them, as preventing them from placing themselves into corners they can't get out of," Aoife smiled. "Sometimes men need a little help with that."

Two hours passed before Filan called for his daughter to join them. He and Thorkell shared the bench with their backs set to the wall. Ciarnat perforce had to stand facing them, like a small child facing discipline. She studied their faces but could read nothing from either one.

"This is your opportunity to speak, daughter," Filan told her, "and we would hear what you have to say. Thorkell has asked for your hand."

Ciarnat started to speak, but Filan overrode her.

"You'll have your chance to speak in a moment. As you know, I have been planning a suitable match for you. One where you would be cherished by the man I give you to, protected by his family, and would want for nothing in your life."

Ciarnat tried to speak again, but Filan waved his hand to shush her.

"Thorkell, as we know, owns no land in Ireland. His wealth is what he carries on his back—a sword and axe. Nothing more. Neither men nor land nor coin. He is poor and landless here. He assures me if you go with him to his own country he has land and men at his command and servants to wait on you. That you could live a prosperous life with him and his people. Is that what you want?"

Ciarnat stared at him in dismay. "Nay. Aye. I mean, I wish to wed Thorkell, but when we talked between us, we agreed it would be best if he settled here. With you. If you allow it."

"If I refused that, then what is your choice?"

There was a long pause. Ciarnat stared at her father, but there was no softening of his expression. Thorkell appeared to be studying the ground.

Ciarnat searched for a subtle answer and found there was none. She took a deep breath. "If you force that choice," she said, with tears standing in her eyes, "then I will go with Thorkell. Father Niall told us the story of what the good wife in his Bible said. 'Where you shall go, I will go; where you lodge, I will lodge; your people shall be my people and your God my God.' I will be that wife if need be."

The men were silent.

After a while, the tears overflowed and trickled down Ciarnat's face. "Please, Da, don't make it this hard for all of us," she begged.

Thorkell scuffed the ground with his feet but did not comment.

The silence stretched forever, and this time there was no Aoife to break it. Ciarnat dropped her head and let the tears fall unashamedly. Her heart twisted with the bitterness of this choice.

At length, Filan stirred and sighed. He looked at his daughter, immense sadness writ clear on his face. "So be it. Ciarnat, if this is your choice, then it shall be as you ask, but I caution you, you may come to regret it bitterly. It is none so easy to marry away from kin, family and all you know. What seems clear and plain to you both now, may change when you find that Irish and Norseman have different ways. What will you do if the two nations are ever at war?"

He shook his head as he stood up. "I hoped for better for you, my daughter." He gazed at her. "You may, as you ask, live here, and Thorkell will be your husband."

"Oh, Da, thank you," Ciarnat cried, rushing into his arms.

Filan hugged her and kissed her forehead. "In the end, sweeting, I cannot bear to cause you pain."

Above her head, Filan looked at Thorkell. "You have won something most precious to me. If you ever hurt her, or fail to care for her, I swear I will kill you."

The men's eyes locked.

Slowly, Thorkell rose to his feet to stand beside Ciarnat. "A moment of your time?" he asked Filan.

"For what?" Filan's pain twisted across his face.

"You have made your pledge," said Thorkell. "Now I will swear my own oath." Without breaking their eye lock, he dropped on one knee. "I swear, by the gods by whom my people swear, to cherish and protect your daughter to my life's end. If I break my oath, may the land open to swallow me, the sea rise to drown me, and the sky fall upon me."

Filan nodded. "So be it."

CHAPTER
SEVENTY TWO

THE WOMEN STUDIED THE RUINED MEADOW. Large areas of pale, flattened grass showed where tents were pitched. Between were worn and rutted tracks where people, carts and horses had driven deep gouges across the sward. Beyond the campsite, where the horse lines had been, piles of manure were black dots on the formally pristine field.

"What a mess!" Ciarnat groaned. "Padraig prides himself on keeping the grass in good condition. I'll be surprised if he's still speaking to Da after he's seen this."

Aoife smiled. "It will heal quicker than you think. Don't forget, we're in the autumn flush of growth. There's still time for the grass to come back before winter. You won't know anyone's been here in a few weeks. And it's been worthwhile; it *was* a grand wedding."

Ciarnat grinned. "It was. But I'm glad it's over. A whole week of celebration! It was more than I ever expected for a wedding."

"It was Filan's chance to show you off," Aoife said. "And having the High King show up as a guest at his daughter's wedding was a fine demonstration to everyone else of how important a man your father is. They are proud of him in the village, of course, but I don't think they had any idea of just how famous he is."

"Ah well, now he's gone with the king, we'll get some peace again," said Ciarnat as they turned to walk back to the house together.

"I didn't think new brides got much peace," Aoife said slyly, "not if they're lucky in their husbands."

Ciarnat scowled at her, as her cheeks flushed pink. The truth was, she was shy but proud of what she was learning and doing each night with Thorkell behind the shut doors of their bed. But it was still too new an experience for her to feel comfortable discussing it, even with Aoife.

Once the doors of the box bed were closed, their world was their own.

"Let down your hair," Thorkell would whisper, and Ciarnat would unplait or unpin the dark weight until it fell, waist length, about her.

Thorkell would twist and wind his fingers in it. "Your hair is alive. It's like the softest silk the merchants sell. You are so beautiful," he told her, as his fingers roved, rejoicing in her warm body and soft skin.

"So are you," she murmured shyly. Ciarnat hadn't expected that. Hadn't fully understood male and female were equal and opposite—in beauty, strength and desire. "Is it the same for all couples?" she asked.

He shrugged. "I suppose so. Maybe." His forehead creased as he thought. "I think we have something special, though."

Ciarnat agreed.

Now, she walked for a while beside Aoife. "Do you miss being married?" she blurted.

It was Aoife's turn to blush. "Yes. Sometimes."

"Would you marry again?"

"I suppose, if I found the right man." Aoife looked at Ciarnat. She spoke with sorrow but no self-pity. "But I'm a widow, I'm older, and I have a child. Most men want children of their own, not some other man's get. And again, I could never make a choice that didn't take account of Clodagh's happiness."

Aoife had never complained; she never indicated she felt

anything other than happiness and contentment with her life. The bleak acceptance of her fate that lay behind Aoife's serene smile appalled Ciarnat.

They walked the rest of the way back in silence.

Late that night Ciarnat lay on her side, Thorkell's body pressed against her back, his form curved into hers, his hand resting lightly on her hip. They were both nearly asleep when Aoife's words floated back into her head and shattered her desire for sleep.

Ciarnat tried to imagine being a widow, inhabiting a world in which Thorkell wasn't always there, lying safely beside her through the years of their lives. The enormity of that fancied loss overwhelmed her, and her hand involuntarily reached to cover his.

"Sweet Christ," she prayed. "Don't ever let that happen to me. Let me be the one who dies first. I couldn't bear to lose him."

Autumn turned to winter, and Aoife's words proved true. The damaged meadow, with its ugly scars, healed and was verdant before the first fall of snow covered everything beneath its white mantle.

Then spring arrived with a series of turbulent storms that kept them confined indoors. Clodagh took the confinement poorly, and tempers became strained. She sulked if they reminded her to go and feed the chickens and fetch the eggs, while simultaneously grumbling she was never allowed outside to play, and it wasn't fair.

Aoife, who bore the brunt of her daughter's behaviour, began to look thin and strained. Ciarnat, worried for her friend, tried to occupy the young girl. She told her stories and worked with her on her harp playing. Unfortunately, Clodagh felt free to treat Ciarnat with as much petulance and bad behaviour as she did Aoife.

Thorkell endured it in silence. There were times when he frowned but said nothing, until the afternoon when Clodagh, when asked to practise a run of notes on the harp, stuck her lip out and refused.

Thorkell put down the wood he had been carving and stood

up slowly, his movement inside the small house emphasising his size. "Clodagh, would you come outside with me please?" His tone was pleasant enough, but something must have given Clodagh pause because she hesitated and took a step towards her mother.

"Clodagh, outside, now!" Thorkell repeated.

She looked to Aoife for protection, but her mother looked up from the bread she was kneading and shook her head. "Thorkell has asked you to go with him. Don't keep him waiting," Aoife cautioned, pointing a floury hand towards the door.

With that, Clodagh bit her lip and did as she was told, her eyes downcast.

Thorkell followed her out.

Ciarnat and Aoife looked at each other.

"What do you think he's going to do?" asked Aoife. "I know she's been a brat, but he's not going to beat her, is he?"

"I don't know," Ciarnat said. And it was true. Disciplining children wasn't a matter that had ever arisen between them.

"He is angry, isn't he?" Aoife asked, her voice frightened.

"I think so. Thorkell gets this furrow in his forehead sometimes. I have sensed he disapproves of Clodagh's behaviour occasionally." Ciarnat didn't add she had often wanted to slap the child herself but had refrained for Aoife's sake.

"He wouldn't hurt her, though, would he?" The dough was taking a punishing as Aoife banged and pounded it in her distress.

Ciarnat was silent. The two women stood and listened but could hear nothing from outside the house.

Time moved slowly as they waited. It was probably only ten minutes before the door opened and Clodagh and Thorkell came back in.

Clodagh's face was puffed with tears, and her lips trembled as she walked across to Ciarnat.

"I'm sorry, mistress, I was rude," she said and gulped on a sob. "I won't do it again."

Ciarnat was startled but pulled herself together sufficiently to reply in a calm voice. "Thank you for your apology, Clodagh. Being stuck inside is difficult for all of us. Being polite to each other makes it easier to bear."

Clodagh nodded and sniffed. A hand crept up to wipe her cheek as she turned to her mother. "I'm sorry, Ma. I didn't mean to be naughty and bad. I'll try to do better."

Aoife would have hugged her, but Clodagh had already spun and was running for the ladder to the loft. She scampered up and disappeared into the darkness. From time to time, they heard a heartbroken sob, or a trumpeting clamour as she blew her nose.

Aoife and Ciarnat looked at Thorkell, but he shook his head and held a finger to his lips.

"That loaf looks almost ready to prove," he said casually.

"What?" Aoife asked. "Oh," and she hurriedly covered the crock and set it aside as she washed her hands.

For the rest of the afternoon, the adults quietly went about their work. Ciarnat tuned the harp, then practised chords and runs. Aoife twirled her spindle, twisting flax into thread, and Thorkell returned to his whittling.

Ciarnat looked up. "I didn't realise how late it is," she said. "It's chore time."

Aoife stood. "I will get the meal going." She looked up towards the loft. "Do you want me to feed the chickens and shut them up?" she whispered to Thorkell.

"*Nei*," he said. "That's Clodagh's job. I'll bring the wood in and fetch the water."

Ciarnat and Aoife looked at each other as Thorkell walked out.

Ciarnat shrugged. "You'd better call her then," she murmured before she, too, went out to feed the animals in the barn.

She had barely lifted the latch on the barn before Clodagh walked past her on the way to the chicken pen. She avoided Ciarnat's eye but went about her work diligently enough.

By the time Ciarnat had finished with the animals, Thorkell had returned with the last pail of water. He looked at the chicken shed as he passed and gave a slight nod of approval.

He held the house door open for Ciarnat. She looked at him as she ducked under his arm and he gave her a cheerful wink but said nothing.

Supper was a quiet affair. Clodagh was subdued, but notably polite and on her best behaviour. Later, she left the table and headed to bed without demur.

"What did you do to her?" Aoife asked softly in amazement. "She's so unlike herself. Did you swap her for a changeling?"

Thorkell chuckled. "We just had a little discussion about her place in the household, and it wasn't as elevated as she had begun to think. That is all. We will see how long this improvement lasts."

CHAPTER
SEVENTY THREE

A FEW DAYS LATER THE SPELL OF bad weather broke, and the morning dawned bright and fine.

"Can you take the day off with me?" Ciarnat asked. "I thought we should celebrate spring together with a picnic."

Thorkell paused as he pulled his tunic over his head. "Just you and me?"

"It's been a long winter. I thought you and I could remember we're still newly-weds and steal a day together."

"I suppose I could." Thorkell ran his mind over his plans for the day. "Nothing I had in mind is so urgent I cannot spend time with my wife."

"Then we'll go, just the two of us." Ciarnat clambered out of bed and went to tell Aoife.

"Can I come to the picnic?" Thorkell heard Clodagh beg.

"Not today, sweeting," Ciarnat said. "Today is a private day for Thorkell and me."

Thorkell heard a mewl of disappointment from the child which elicited a word of warning from Aoife. The girl was silenced, and Thorkell grinned in satisfaction.

It was cold enough outside the farmhouse for Thorkell to be grateful he had brought his wolf-skin cloak. Ciarnat had her shawl wrapped firmly around her shoulders and secured at her waist by her belt.

"I've packed bread, cheese, honeycomb and a flask of ale," she said, smiling at her husband.

He looked particularly dashing, if remarkably barbarian, with his fur over his shoulder and his axe at his waist. "Where are we going?" he asked as he followed her away from the house.

"You'll see," she said, leading him up the rise that protected the farm from the sea winds. It wasn't a route he remembered taking. Usually he headed up the valley towards Padraig's hut.

The wind on the crest of the hill was strong, and they fought against it as they climbed. Once they had reached the summit, he saw the track turned a corner and ran down a cliff on the seaward side.

"What are we doing here?" he asked as they stopped for Ciarnat to tuck her hair back into its plait.

"Having a picnic," she said. "Follow me down, but be careful, the track can be slippery."

The track was too steep for further conversation, so he followed obediently until they reached the bottom. "Now, tell me why we're here? I didn't even know this place existed."

"Didn't you?" She looked at him curiously. "Well, perhaps not."

She put the basket on the ground and hitched herself onto a convenient rock.

Thorkell sat beside her and looked at the bay. "It is beautiful here."

"Aye, it is," she agreed, "and two years ago at this very time of year, a girl came down that track to collect dulse for her grandmother's soda bread." She smiled as she reminisced. "It was a lovely day, just like today. The only thing is, it wasn't just seaweed she took home to her gran that day." Ciarnat turned her head to look at her husband and grinned. "Stranded in the bay, like a beached sea creature, she found a half-dead man at the sea's edge."

Thorkell looked around. "It was here? You found me here? I didn't realise."

"You don't recognise the place?"

"*Nei*. I remember nought. There is a large gap in my memory between swimming from the cove and waking up in bed at the barn with you and your gran caring for me."

"Come on. I'll show you the actual place. That day, all this side of the bay was full of sea spume which covered everything and is the only reason I found you. I had to walk across to the other side to look for seaweed."

They took the path along the foot of the cliff until they came to the great cave.

"Here," she said, putting the basket down again. "Those are the rocks we sat on then, and that's the cave where you hid while I went to get the donkey. Poor Asal wasn't best pleased having to haul your hulk up the track."

"What an amazing place," Thorkell said appreciatively. "This cave is enormous. How far back does it go?"

"I have never explored it. It is too dark, and I've never come down here with a torch. When I came back to pick you up with the donkey you had gone in there so far I couldn't see you." She smiled. "I thought you were going to kill me until I realised you were so weak you were using your sword to prop yourself upright."

Thorkell gave her a hard kiss. "Look how wonderfully it all worked out in the end." He walked further into the cave. "This would be a haven in times of trouble," he said thoughtfully. "No one would ever find it. You could get half the village hidden in here with no effort. People must have used it for shelter in the past. It is well above the high-tide line. Just imagine, some far-distant ancestor of yours may even have lived here."

"Maybe," Ciarnat shrugged, although his words made her uneasy. "It feels dark and haunted to me. Almost as if someone walked across my grave. No one comes here now." She led the way back to the rocks in the bright sunlight and spread their lunch out.

They ate in mutual silence, enjoying the cry of the seabirds and the sound of the waves.

"What did you do to Clodagh the other day?" Ciarnat asked.

"I thought she was going to throw another tantrum when we said she couldn't come with us today, but she didn't."

"Pretty much what I told you. I asked Clodagh if she knew who you were. She sniped back, 'Ciarnat'. Once we'd sorted out you were the *ollamh*'s daughter and established the land was Filan's and you managed it for him, as mistress of the house, things became clearer for her. I reminded her I was your husband, and what did that make me?" Thorkell chuckled. "She's not stupid. She saw where this was going, and answered 'the master' quickly enough. By the time everyone had their right title and position sorted, including Aoife, she realised she had overstepped the mark and was just a silly little girl at the bottom of the pecking order. I think it was humiliating for her. But I didn't lay a finger on her, if that was what you were asking."

Ciarnat smiled at him. "Very clever of you. Yes, I think both Aoife and I wondered what you had done."

"Good, then pour some more ale for your clever husband." He laughed as Ciarnat stuck her tongue out at him.

"This was a good idea." Thorkell wiped his lips with the back of his hand.

"You've still got foam on your beard," Ciarnat told him, and reached across to dab it off with a cloth.

"I've got something on my mind as well," Thorkell said, drawing her down on top of him.

"I hoped you might," she said, easing herself into a comfortable position against him. "Why do you think I wanted you all to myself for the day?"

"Wanton wench," he teased, although his hand was gentle as he stroked it down her cheek and neck.

"Would you want me to be different?"

"*Nei*," he chuckled. You are my one precious jewel, perfect in every facet."

Ciarnat chuckled. "Now you're a poet," but her words ceased as his hands roved further.

"Oh," she moaned, her lips against his, as her body joined with his.

There was a soothing rhythm to the sea's swell against the

rocks. They lay together resting, enjoying the warm spring sunshine.

Thorkell put his arms behind his head. "I love the sound of the sea. It reminds me of my boyhood."

Ciarnat shifted uneasily beside him. "Do you miss your home? Do you want to go back there?"

"*Nei*. I miss my boyhood sometimes. I miss the expanse of deep green water just beyond the headland, and learning to sail and row, as all us children did. I remember the steep escarpments where my friend and I used to go bird-nesting. I miss my father, and the need to avenge him will never leave me. But there's nothing left at Ormsfjord now that I value. Those days are gone forever." He rolled to face her and propped himself up on an elbow.

"My father lived his life as an honourable man. He was a ferocious fighter, but he was also a man of peace, and he cared deeply for his holding. The truth is, the land barely made enough, in the few short weeks the weather was warm enough to farm it, to keep his people alive. And he was lucky. He only had one brother, so when my grandparents died, the land was portioned between the two of them and worked as one unit. Even then, it was barely enough. It's why Norsemen go reiving. How else can they make enough to pay the king's taxes and keep their households?"

"You said it was much the same here," Ciarnat objected.

"*Já*, it is, but your land is richer. Also, I've married an heiress." A grin split Thorkell's face. "I'd be a fool to throw it all away and insist we go to Ormsfjord. I don't think you'd like the deep cold we have during our northern winters."

"What happens if you hear news of Asger?"

A shadow crossed Thorkell's face. "Then the duty to avenge Orm takes precedence over everything."

"I hope you never, ever come across him again," Ciarnat cried.

Thorkell reached across and pulled her into the comfort of his arm. "Who knows what future the Norns hold for us? But in the meantime, there are other ways we can pass the time."

Two weeks later, Ciarnat missed her monthly courses, and a

month after that, she was confident she had conceived. There was no particular reason for it to be so, but she clung to the whimsy that they had made the baby on the day they'd made love on the beach.

CHAPTER
SEVENTY FOUR

Erin

Present Day, New Zealand

SHE HEARD A KNOCK ON THE DOOR.
She was expecting Petra. They had agreed to 'do' lunch at the Hot Shot café.

"I'm coming," she called. "Bugger," she muttered as she realised she'd left her phone on the bed. "I'll be with you in a second." It was the work of a moment to go back and grab the phone. "Right, I'm ready," she said, smiling, as she opened the door.

She stopped short. "Alwyn?" she asked in disbelief.

"Hi. I've got Luke's luggage." She stood back to let him carry the case into the hall and dump it.

"Where's Luke?" she asked.

"Coming. He's not very fast at the moment."

Erin followed him back to the open door and looked down the path. "Luke?" she said, staring at her husband. "What the hell happened?" His leg was in plaster, and he hobbled towards her on a pair of crutches.

"I'll leave you two to it," Alwyn smirked at her. "See you later, Erin." He stepped lightly down the steps. "Cheers, mate," he said as he passed Luke. "Keep in touch."

Erin watched as Luke manoeuvred himself and his crutches up the front doorstep.

"What the hell happened?" Erin asked again.

"Let me sit down, and I'll tell you all about it," Luke panted. "This is frigging hard work."

She followed him into the lounge and watched him lever himself into a chair.

"There," he said as he settled himself. "Hi, sweetheart. You look more pregnant than ever. Have you got a kiss for me?"

Erin gave him a perfunctory peck. "What happened?"

"I broke my bloody leg the first day we arrived in Frankfurt. It was icy in the airport car park. I slipped and broke both bones in my lower leg. I spent the first day of the conference at the hospital being treated. Frankly, it was a nightmare. I don't remember the first few days. I was high on painkillers."

"But why didn't you phone and tell me?" Erin cried. "Surely you must have realised I'd want to know."

Luke looked sheepish. "Well, in all the drama of them cutting my trousers off so they could set the leg, my phone disappeared at the hospital. I don't know where or how I lost it, or even if someone nicked it."

"Couldn't you have replaced it?"

"There didn't seem much point. All my contacts were lost, so it would have been a hassle setting it up overseas. I'll buy one now I'm home."

"But you didn't call me! I was worried. Suppose I'd gone into labour?"

"Oh."

Erin could tell the thought hadn't occurred to him. "You didn't think?"

"Sorry." To give him his due, Luke looked genuinely apologetic.

Erin rolled her eyes and muttered 'men' under her breath. "I was just going out. Petra's picking me up any second now. We're going to lunch. Do you want to come?"

Luke shook his head. "Sorry, I'm shattered."

Erin studied him. "I can see that. Would you rather I stayed with you? Can I get you a coffee or something to eat?"

"Thanks, but no. They fed me on the plane. I'd as soon you went out, frankly. If I've got the house to myself, I can get to bed and get some sleep."

"Do you need a hand?" Erin indicated his plastered leg. "Can you get around OK?"

"Yes. As long as I take it slowly, I'm fine. I'll need a hand for showering, to get a waterproof covering to protect the plaster, but I won't bother now. I think I'll just hit the sack and crash for as long as I can."

Erin nodded.

"Are you ready, Erin?" Petra called as she walked into the living room. "The front door was open and … shit, Luke! What have you done to yourself?"

"Busted a leg," Luke said tersely.

"I can see that."

"It's a bugger," Luke complained. "It's going to take weeks to heal. I've got to go to the hospital and get checked out now I'm back in New Zealand, which will be a right pain in the arse. I hate those places. God alone knows how long before I can drive again."

"And I'm about to have a baby," Erin supplied. "The timing could hardly be worse."

"You'd be right there," said Petra. "What a mess, for both of you. Well, if you need a hand, let us know. Are you still coming to lunch, Erin?"

"Luke wants to get some rest," she said, "so I'll come with you."

"Are you sure you're going to be OK?" she asked again.

"Yeah, I'm fine."

⁙

"See you tomorrow night," Petra called.

Erin watched her drive away. It had been a delicious lunch, and for an hour she'd been able to push her worries away. Now they were back. To make matters worse, she felt mildly nauseated. "Probably overeaten," she muttered to herself.

Luke's homecoming wasn't what she'd imagined. She'd planned to confront him about his lack of communication; she intended to ask him about the late-night caller, and what Luke to do about it. She even hoped he'd be pleased to see her and excited about how close she was to term. But no. Instead of her pregnancy being the star of the show, Luke's accident had pushed her out of the spotlight and asserted his own medical needs firmly into the mix.

She sighed with frustration.

It was likely she'd be looking after two helpless male creatures for the foreseeable future—a baby and a cranky husband.

Luke wasn't in the living room. He'd managed to make it through to their bedroom, and when she checked, he was asleep in bed. A large mound under the duvet intrigued her until she realised he must have used every available pillow to lift the bedding off his plastered leg.

She watched him for a while. Luke always could sleep profoundly and lost in dreams; his face had relaxed. It was easy for her to see the man with whom she'd fallen in love.

"Ow," she grunted as a vigorous kick in the belly brought her thoughts back to the baby. Once again, she wondered whether the child disliked his father. But that was impossible, surely?

Luke's case still stood in the hallway.

Kneeling was complicated with a swollen belly, but she managed it and emptied the suitcase. She ignored anything that wasn't washing. Luke could surely tidy up after himself. It was enough effort to scoop up the piles of linen and carry them to the machine. Whatever else happened, Erin was going to be very happy when she'd had the baby and returned to having a flat stomach.

Luke slept through the afternoon and into the night, leaving Erin at a loose end. His presence had destroyed the peace of the house. True, he was out for the count, but the uncertainty of when he'd wake, what his mood would be and what she wanted to discuss with him churned around in her head, making her tired.

Eventually, she gave up and climbed into bed beside him. He didn't stir, not even when she helped herself to one of the pillows he'd arranged around his leg.

The light from the early-morning sun shone in her eyes, effectively blinding her, but the man walking towards her seemed familiar. By the way he moved and his overall size and shape, she initially took him for the man she'd come to realise she loved. It was only when he blocked the sun as he came closer she realised it was someone different.

Her eyes narrowed as she studied him. His clothes were unfamiliar—boots and rough trousers instead of jeans. A coarse tunic. He was some paces closer before she recognised it was chain mail. There was a sword at his belt, and he carried a shield like a backpack.

He smiled faintly as he walked towards her. Could this really be Luke?

She tried to puzzle it out. The confusion cost her. Too late she recognised malice in those cold blue eyes. Before she could run, he'd grabbed her around her neck and began to squeeze. He was both strong and tall enough to lift her off her feet, and her toes scrabbled to find purchase on the ground to ease the pressure on her throat.

She was just about to pass out when he dropped her. She fell to her knees, coughing and gasping. He was talking over his shoulder to someone behind him, and while his attention was elsewhere, she gathered herself up. She had no weapon, but her feet would do. She kicked him between his legs with all her force.

There was a bellow of agony, and Erin woke from her dream, gasping with terror.

She lay on her side and looked across to where her husband

had surely been beside her. She had to search until she found where Luke was, writhing on the floor on his side of the bed, shrieking with pain.

"Fuck you," he panted out.

Erin tried to speak, wanted to ask him what had happened, but her throat was raw and burning. Each breath cost her pain as she put her hands to her crushed and aching neck. Words couldn't force themselves through her swollen vocal cords.

"Help me up, you bitch," Luke demanded. "I need help. What did you knee me for?"

"You tried to strangle me." The words came out in a hoarse whisper. "What the hell were you trying to do?"

"What?" Luke stared at her, his hands clutching his groin. "I did nothing of the sort. For fuck's sake. Can't you see I've got a broken leg?"

Very slowly, Erin eased herself up. She was shaking so severely it cost her an enormous amount of effort to make it around the bed. "You tried to strangle me," she rasped again, and when Luke shook his head in denial, she took her hands from her neck.

"Look at what you've done," she demanded. "You did this. No one else."

Her husband stared at the livid marks on her neck. "Holy shit!" he said in horror. "Did I do that? Christ, I didn't know. God, Erin, I'm so sorry! I was having a nightmare. I thought I was fighting an enemy."

He'd managed to lever himself up to a sitting position, "I'd never have touched you in a million years. I hope you know that." He stared at Erin. "Fuck it! I could have killed you."

"You nearly did," Erin whispered, and squatted down beside him.

"It's these fucking painkillers. They're messing with my head. I'm so sorry." Luke stared at his fingers. "My hands ache," he said as he flexed them. "So it's true.

"Erin, I promise I didn't know I was attacking you. The dream was so real, so vivid..." He trailed off in frustration. "I can't even tell you what it was about now; it's fading so quickly."

"I was dreaming as well," Erin said. "I saw you..." She stopped in confusion. "At least, I don't know for certain it was you. You were dressed like someone from a long time ago, but it could have been you. I thought it was you." She shook her head painfully. "Sorry, I don't sound very coherent. And then you attacked me."

They stared at each other.

"So, we were both dreaming," Erin said after a long pause.

"That's bizarre. What the fuck is happening to us?" Luke asked.

CHAPTER SEVENTY FIVE

THEY WERE GOING TO THE LATEST Marvel movie, and Fergal had suggested Erin travelled into town with them, for which she was grateful. With all that was going on, she felt a bit under the weather.

Fergal got out of the car as she approached. She smiled politely. Since she'd blurted out Fergal was in her dreams, Erin had been slightly self-conscious around him and particularly careful not to worry Brianna by seeming too friendly.

"You, OK?" Fergal asked as he opened the door for her.

"Yeah, I'm fine," she said, her mouth set into a grim line. "This pregnancy isn't fulfilling any of the romantic visions I imagined when I started down this track." She manoeuvred herself into the back seat.

"Hang in there, girl," Fergal advised.

"Problems?" Brianna asked, turning around to look at Erin.

"In a manner of speaking. Luke arrived home yesterday."

"And?" Brianna asked cautiously.

"He's broken his right leg. He's in plaster from foot to thigh, and he's on crutches. He can't drive, which means if I go into labour, I guess I'll be driving myself."

"No, you won't," said Fergal as he buckled his seat belt.

"You'll call us, and we'll take you. Also, if you're worried about looking after Luke and a new baby, I'm pretty sure ACC will give him some help. He'll be entitled to it."

"Accident Compensation Corporation? Do they?" Erin asked. "Home help? I've never heard of that."

"You've never had an accident, I guess. If ACC doesn't offer Luke some help, you should ask for it."

"I'll tell him," Erin said.

"Didn't he want to come with us tonight?" Brianna asked.

Erin shook her head. "He says he's still shattered with jet lag. He's still on German time, and of course, the trip back on the plane wasn't a walk in the park for him. He's going to have an early night."

"Did you ask why you didn't hear from him while he was overseas?" asked Brianna.

Erin snorted. "Apparently, in all the drama of breaking his leg, he lost his phone. Possibly it was stolen, or some such. He couldn't be faffed trying to sort out a new phone overseas so didn't replace it."

"Couldn't he have borrowed Alwyn's, or emailed you? I don't know. Used the hotel phone? At least to let you know what had happened to him," asked Brianna.

"Seems it never occurred to him."

"Oh." It was a little comment, but the silence stretched on.

"He caught me on the hop when he arrived home yesterday," Erin said. "And of course, I was going out. I offered to stay, but he said he'd rather go to bed and sleep. He looked exhausted. So I went out to lunch with Petra anyway."

"In fairness, it can't have been easy travelling with a broken leg," Fergal remarked.

Erin shrugged. "Things will sort themselves out, I guess. Just having him back and coping with his injury has put enough strain on both of us at the moment. The medication they gave him has side effects that haven't helped. He has bad dreams."

Reflexively she rubbed her neck. She was wearing a roll-neck collar to cover the marks of Luke's morning attack. She hadn't yet managed to process how she felt about that bizarre episode and certainly didn't want to invite comment from their friends.

"There's a lot we need to talk about, but we haven't had the time. I haven't even got around to telling him about the late-night guy yet."

"What happened with that?" Fergal asked.

Erin bit her lip. "I did what you told me not to. I rang his number. A woman came on the line, and I asked to speak to him. She put him on, and I told him if he called again I'd report him to the police. I haven't heard from him since, and that was five nights ago. So it worked."

"Oh well, fair enough if it got him off your back." Fergal indicated for the turn into the parking building. "Now we can enjoy a good meal and watch the movie in peace."

"I'll second that," said Erin staunchly, trying to ignore how her neck ached.

It *was* a good meal. It had been Petra's turn to choose the restaurant they'd go to, and she'd picked Thai fusion, usually a favourite of Erin's. The food was fresh, tasty and attractively presented, but Erin had no appetite and picked at her food.

The iolite ring on her finger seemed unaccountably tight, and she twisted it uneasily, trying to ease the pressure.

"Are you OK?" Petra asked in surprise, "only you usually fight me for the last roti."

"I do not!" Erin smiled.

"You do so. Aren't you hungry?"

"No, not tonight. But I'm fine." Her friend gave her a sharp look. "I am, truly. Perhaps just a bit rattled about Luke and his leg, that's all."

"You've got a lot going on at the moment," Doug said with his usual diplomacy.

"I have indeed."

It was a short walk from the restaurant to the cinema, and Erin began to feel increasingly unwell. She was nauseated. Her head ached with a steadily building pressure, an affliction she rarely suffered from, and her throat was sore and aching. By halfway through the movie, she was forced to close her eyes as the flickering lights and action on the big screen poked fiery needles into her skull. Her finger was now throbbing intolerably, adding to her misery,

Oedema, she thought. She'd heard about it at prenatal classes. Maybe I've got pre-eclampsia?

When the lights came on, she stumbled behind the others into the light of the foyer. Fergal turned, saw her face and gasped. "Erin. You look terrible. Are you sick? Should we take you to the hospital?"

She could barely shake her head. "Home," she pleaded.

"You should have said something earlier. Come on, we'll get you to the car."

She kept her eyes shut all the way home. Discomfort and pain combined until it was hard to know if the headache or the nausea was worse. The two conditions swirled through her in a maelstrom of sensation until she was dizzy and disorientated. Through it all, her finger throbbed. She tried to yank the ring off, but it was too tight on her swollen finger.

"Do you think Erin's all right?" Brianna whispered to Fergal.

"I don't know. She looks awful. I suppose it might be something like a migraine, but I didn't know she suffered from them. We'll talk to Luke. At the very least she'll need a doctor when she gets home."

They started the turn into Erin's street when she cried out. A colossal force had just kicked her so hard in the belly that she was winded. Bizarrely, this newest discomfort brought her out of the black fog she'd been in throughout the journey, and she sat up and opened her eyes.

"What the fuck?" At the same time, Fergal slammed on the brakes, throwing them all forward in their seats.

Ahead of them, vehicles crowded the road. People gathered on the pavement. At the end of the street, a massive fire threw light on the three fire engines, ambulances and several cars gathered in front of a house that was fully ablaze.

"Oh shit," Fergal said as he pulled over.

"That's our place," Erin cried in horror.

Erin wrenched the car door open and propelled her heavy body out. Without any awareness of her pregnancy, she ran down the road towards the flames.

Fergal ran beside her. "Erin, wait! It's too dangerous!"

"Luke's in there! He's got a broken leg!" she cried.

A police officer stopped her. "You can't go any further."

"It's my husband. He's in there. He was sleeping."

"Stay there," the officer said.

Erin tried to push forward, but he grabbed her arm.

"Ma'am, you must stay here." He looked at Fergal. "Are you with her?" Fergal nodded. "Then keep her here. It's not safe to go further."

"Come, Erin," Fergal urged, pulling her into the circle of his arm. "Just wait."

Erin fought his embrace, but couldn't break it.

"The policeman is radioing someone. Just wait until he comes back."

Just wait, just wait. Erin heard the words. They meant nothing.

The storm that had twisted inside her all evening was back with a vengeance. Pain coiled from her skull to her belly and spun her into a dizzy whirl of nauseating blackness.

Somehow, she'd wet her pants. She felt the water trickling down her leg but was too far gone to care. The last thing she heard was the distant sound of Fergal's voice.

"Her water's broken. Get an ambulance."

Consciousness drifted away as she was sucked down into the black vortex.

CHAPTER
SEVENTY SIX

Ciarnat

Ninth Century, Ireland

"IT'S A QUARE DAY," AOIFE CALLED, as she made her way to the washing line.

Ciarnat smiled at her. The warm weather matched her mood. It seemed her happiness was so overwhelming she couldn't stop smiling. It really couldn't be a more perfect day.

Last night she'd told Thorkell she was pregnant. He'd been overjoyed with the news—then worried for her. She'd laughed gently as she lay in his arms. "I'm young, healthy and happy. Nothing is going to go wrong, and I'll be cautious."

"I'm away up the valley today, to help Padraig shift the herd. Keep yourself safe," he told her that morning.

She smiled as she kissed him goodbye.

Now she knelt in the grass, and the joy they shared wrapped around her like a warm, golden cloak.

Although Gran's grave had long grown green, covered with the wildflowers and herbs Ciarnat had planted, she still felt closest in the old plot by the cottage.

"I've got a secret to tell you," Ciarnat whispered to her gran, sure the plants would pass the news on. She and Thorkell had agreed they'd try and keep the news to themselves until Filan next came home, although Ciarnat doubted it could be kept long from Aoife who washed their linens.

The pungent scents of sage, sorrel and mint melded with the earthy smell of damp soil that clung to her fingers. She breathed in the rich aroma of summer soil and greenery.

She 'tskd' at the mint, already showing signs of bolting through the bed. "We can't have that," she muttered as she ripped lengths of it from the soil and dumped it in her basket. She would dry the leaves she harvested, but the rest of it could be burned.

She stood up, straightening and stretching her back. Her eyes were drawn to a plume of smoke rising beyond the low hills that marked where the track wound down to the village. Someone down there had a giant bonfire. She turned back to her garden.

By the time she looked up again, a large pile of weeds and clippings had accumulated beside her. Time to dispose of them. She stood and stretched again. Her eyes sought out the smoke she'd seen earlier and widened in alarm. Far from dying away, the blaze had grown large and menacing. Black smoke, shot through with an angry red haze, smothered the sky above the hills.

Ciarnat looked around for Aoife. "What is it?" she asked.

"I don't know," her friend replied. "I've been watching it for a while, and it doesn't look good."

"Where's Clodagh?"

"Safely inside."

The women stared at the wall of darkness.

"What do you think we should we do?" Aoife asked at length.

"If it's just a fire that's out of hand, then they need our help. But if..."

Neither wanted to put their fear into words.

A Viking raid?

They'd never experienced such a thing, but they'd heard all about the murderous destruction the godless invaders caused.

"We hide. Now," Ciarnat said, making a decision. "We leave here as quickly as we can. Whatever is happening in the village, there's little help we can give. But perhaps we can protect ourselves. We'll go to the cave by the beach to hide."

"I'll grab food and blankets." Aoife rushed to get supplies and gather up Clodagh. Ciarnat nodded. They had no source of help here. Thorkell had gone out this morning to help Padraig, his only weapon the axe he habitually kept tucked into his belt.

Ciarnat bit her lip and continued to keep watch.

She thought she saw movement on the path across the valley, and the breath caught in her throat as she screwed up her face to make out the details. They were moving quickly. She needed to look to the right of the dark haze. Light from morning sun angled into her eyes, effectively blinding her. The man walking towards her seemed familiar. For a moment, the familiarity was so strong, she took him for Thorkell. His movement and overall height and shape were right. Only as he came closer, blocking the sun, did she realise he was a stranger.

Thorkell had worn the same clothes once. Ciarnat recognised the flanged helmet, the torc and the battle-axe. Behind him, she saw others of his kind.

Futility consumed her. Sweet Jesus! She and Aoife had waited too long.

Her throat closed in fear, and she had to force her voice out.

"God to you this morning," she said. "What man are you?" She hated the tremulous note she heard as she uttered the greeting.

It was too much of a coincidence, the wall of smoke, and now a stranger in their valley.

He smiled faintly and walked towards her with a swagger of confidence. The confusing sense of familiarity grew stronger; she felt she knew, or ought to know, who he was. Too late it occurred to her he must be kin to Thorkell and that could mean only one man...

Terrified, she turned to run, but he grabbed her quickly. His hands went around her neck and began to squeeze. His blue eyes fixed on her face, and she sensed him enjoying her terror as he tightened his grip. Instinctively her hands went to her throat, clawing at his gloved hands, fighting for her life, as she tried to break free from him.

He was both strong and tall enough to lift her off her feet, and her toes scrabbled to find purchase on the ground, seeking to ease the pressure on her throat and let her breathe.

She felt she was about to pass out when he released her. She fell to her knees, coughing and gasping for breath, fighting the swirling confusion in her head. He was talking over his shoulder to someone behind him, and while his attention was elsewhere, she forced herself up. She stumbled as she wavered upright and stood there shaking.

Fury took her. She was mistress here! She knew full well Aoife, Clodagh and Filan depended on her. It was her duty to fight.

She had no weapon, but her feet would do. She kicked her assailant between his legs with all her force. He fell to the ground like a poled-ox, but she had no time to celebrate her victory or glory in his choked scream. There were other hands on her, forcing her face high towards the sun's light.

"Well, would you believe it? I recognise this bitch."

She wrenched her face away from the sun's cruel glare and stared into the face of the man in front of her.

It seemed she was in some sort of nightmare, for a face she had long forbidden from her thoughts loomed in front of her. "Ultán?" Her voice quavered despicably. She licked her lips, desperate to regain some control. Her arms were held, twisted up her back until someone from behind bound her ankles.

Ultán smiled at her. "Soon, sweetheart. I'll be there soon," he said with lascivious promise before he kicked the side of her knee. Unbalanced, she collapsed sideways and fell into the herb garden.

From where she lay, she heard the house cow and Asal bellowing as the raiders drove them from their stalls. Twisting around, she watched men rush inside the house. They emerged moments later. She saw her harp brought out, gripped in a warrior's hand and set in the grass among a growing pile of household objects. Thorkell's sword, lifted from its place above the hearth, joined it. She imagined, buried somewhere in that pile, lay the hair clasp Thorkell had once given her.

Outside, one of the men was trying to set fire to the southern end of the thatched roof, and a small trail of flame crept slowly up towards the ridgeline. Soon, a thin thread of smoke issued out through the front door and flames began to lick, with growing appetite, along the lower edge where thatch met timber.

As she watched, Asal was dragged towards the pile, although he fought wildly, clearly terrified of the fire, and warriors began to pack their loot on the poor donkey's back.

A few seconds later, Aoife and Clodagh were half hauled, half thrust out, through the door. Aoife fell awkwardly. Clodagh, her face streaked with ash, clutched Aoife's skirt on the left side. She slipped as her mother fell to her knees, then rallied, and helped Aoife to her feet. A firm hand in the small of Aoife's back pushed her and Clodagh down to join Ciarnat on the ground in the wreck of the herb garden.

It seemed their leader, Asger, had recovered from her attack on him. He strode down the path and stood over her. She read the anger in his eyes, but for now, he let her be, although his look promised due retribution for the pain she'd caused him. He jabbered at Ciarnat in his language. Was he asking a question? She had no idea what he wanted, so she shrugged her incomprehension.

He repeated the question, but when she still didn't understand, he shouted out to his men. Ultán came to stand beside him.

"He wants to know where your man is," Ultán said. "Thorkell?"

"Was that what he wanted? I don't know where Thorkell is," she said. She spread her hands and shook her head at Asger. "I don't know. He's away."

Asger looked at her and narrowed his eyes as he snapped another command.

"He asks again," Ultán said. "You'd better tell him. He'll hurt you if you don't."

Ciarnat ignored him and looked at Asger, spreading her hands again and lifting her shoulder.

"He's away hunting for a few days," she lied.

She braced herself for pain as Asger stepped forward, but he reached beyond her and pulled Clodagh up by her plaited hair as he snarled some more words at Ultán.

"For the last time, he says, tell him the truth, or he blinds the child," Ultán urged.

There was an anguished moan from Aoife as she watched her terrified daughter twisting in Asger's hold.

Asger's eyes were on Ciarnat's face as he drew a short knife from his belt. He spat a phrase at Ultán.

"It's your last chance," Ultán said.

There was no choice. Thorkell would have to take his chances, Ciarnat couldn't let Asger maim Clodagh. She opened her mouth to answer.

The voice was powerful enough to be heard over the roaring fire and the clamour of man and beast.

"Thorkell, son of Orm, answers. Who seeks him?"

CHAPTER SEVENTY SEVEN

HE WAS THERE, STANDING BY THE corner of the barn, watching them.

Asger's men fell silent as Thorkell strode forwards. In his right hand, he held his axe. His left had a tight grip on Ulf's collar. The great hound was bristling, growling deep in his throat, his ears pricked and his eyes bright as he eyed the men before him.

Asger dropped Clodagh and took a step forward. "I hear tell you've been asking after me," he taunted. "Even offered a reward, so here I am. Asger, the man whom you seek."

"Asger the murderer," Thorkell agreed. "The man outlawed by the Thing for the treacherous slaying of his brother. The outlaw who took his own brother's wife and tried to kill his nephew. That Asger. Asger the disgraced and despised."

There was muttering from among the men. Ciarnat wondered whether they knew of their leader's crimes or if this was news to them. Clodagh took the opportunity to bolt to the safety of her mother's arms.

Thorkell had come to a stop a few feet from the open door of the house. The fire hadn't burned this far, and the slope of the ground gave him a height advantage over his uncle. "I have sworn a blood feud against you," Thorkell said. "I invoke the right to *einvigi*, a duel between us. Will you fight like a warrior, or will I run you down as the outlawed coward you are?"

It was strange, the change his words wrought in the men. Mere minutes ago, their faces were hideous with blood-lust and cruel, jeering laughter. Now they were serious and thoughtful.

Asger licked his lips as he glanced sideways at his men. Some had sailed as crew on the voyage when Asger abandoned Thorkell. Some may not have cared, and others may not have known that Asger killed Orm, but they all knew the law. A man declared an outlaw was outcast—forever. Any man who slew such a one did so with impunity. Asger had no choice.

"I will fight," Asger said tersely.

Thorkell nodded. "We will fight. To the death."

Thorkell ordered a reluctant Ulf from his side and sent him, hunchbacked with disapproval, across to sit beside Ciarnat. Clodagh released Aoife and went to bury her face in Ulf's coat. He gave her face an absent-minded sniff as she approached, but the hound's attention was on his master.

"I'll have my father's sword back," Thorkell said, "and my shield," taking them from the plunder piled beside Asal. He shifted his axe to his belt and hefted the weight of the sheathed sword in his right hand. "*Já*. It is good," he said approvingly, buckling on his sword belt as he gave a reassuring smile across to Ciarnat.

She shuffled herself into a more comfortable sitting position. As her hand pressed into the ground to shift her weight, it found the small knife she'd been using to prune the herbs. She'd no idea when she'd dropped it. Now, with everyone's attention on the coming duel, it was the work of a second to pick it up, slice the bond around her ankle and slip the blade into her belt, so it lay between her tunic and the leather.

The men shuffled back, clearing an ample space around Thorkell and Asger. For long minutes the two antagonists studied each other. Neither seemed in a hurry to begin.

Thorkell was taller and younger than Asger and occupied higher ground. His uncle had the advantage of a protective helmet and armour.

Asger moved first, closing the distance between them, his axe raised high, aiming for a head blow. Thorkell sidestepped the blow quickly, delivering his own buffeting blow which was deflected by his uncle's shield.

It seemed the opening sally had been nothing more than preparation for the main event—a small testing of each other's commitment. The two men closed, and from there, the fighting was fierce. Each man cut and hewed at the other without mercy.

Ciarnat winced as each blow fell. Her whole focus was on Thorkell. She saw him flinch as a massive blow got through his guard, heard his heavy breathing, listened to the grunts both men made as they parried and stabbed.

Ciarnat gave a low moan when first blood went to Asger, who opened a slice across Thorkell's knuckles. It was not serious, but the sight of blood and the realisation of how vulnerable her husband was sickened Ciarnat.

It was hard to tell who had the upper hand. Both men seemed evenly matched. Both knew no quarter would be given in this fight. Asger's need to retain control of his ship and crew equalled Thorkell's determination to avenge his father. Ascendancy swung from one man to the other as the fight continued.

Ciarnat gasped when Thorkell, using the sharp edge of his shield as a weapon, gave a mighty swipe at Asger and knocked him off his feet. Faster than a blink Asger sprang up again, but it seemed he'd twisted something in the fall, hindering his movement. He was noticeably slower to repel Thorkell's next sally.

Thorkell pressed him hard, driving Asger backwards, and Asger stumbled again on the sloping ground.

A grim smile hovered on Thorkell's face as he raised his sword to deliver the death blow over the bowed head of his uncle.

"Aaaaargh!" It was a battle cry. Ultán hurtled from between the watching men, his spear pointed at Thorkell. Before Thorkell could react, Ultán had stabbed the weapon deep into Thorkell's shoulder with such force that his momentum carried them both up the slope until the wall of the house stopped their passage.

Ultán gave one more massive thrust, shoving the spear through yielding flesh until it drove into the farmhouse wall, pinning Thorkell helplessly to the building.

The shocked silence, broken only by Thorkell's involuntary groan, held for a moment.

Ciarnat broke the impasse by scrambling to her feet and bolting up the slope towards her husband. Ulf surged ahead of her, teeth bared. He leapt at Ultán, ready to worry him, but was stopped when the point of Asger's sword entered his throat.

With a small whimper, Ulf staggered and collapsed slowly to the ground, blood streaming from the fatal blow. With his ultimate strength, he dragged himself the few feet across the ground to where his master was pinned and died at Thorkell's feet.

Ciarnat almost made it as far as Thorkell, but Ultán grabbed her by the arm, nearly wrenching it out of its socket.

"Oh, no. I'm going to have my fun with you," Ultán promised her.

She stared at him, her face blank. The shock had so disordered her reactions she barely noticed the threat, so intent was she on reaching her goal. She tried to shake him off as a minor distraction and stared in surprise at the hand on her arm that refused to let go.

"She's mine first. Hold her for me." Asger was on his feet again. For a long moment, he stared at his late adversary, now pinned, helpless, on the wall. Thorkell's body twisted in agony. He tried, in vain, to pull the spear from his shoulder. He even tried to move forward along its shaft, only to be foiled by the carved flange.

Asger's men stared at him in silence, the recent events too shocking to be easily absorbed. Only Asger and Ultán seemed composed, although Asger was breathing heavily.

Thorkell took a shuddering breath and raised his head to look at his tormentors. Watching him, Ciarnat saw the effort it took to gather himself together.

"I call you all," Thorkell cried, his voice surprisingly strong, even through his pain. "By the severed hand of Tyr, I lay this curse on Asger. You and your foul breed are cursed. Your livestock will sicken, your crops will wither, your dogs will roam wild, your daughters will be sold into slavery, and your wives will lie in other men's beds. All you attempt will fail; your name will disappear from memory. Bear witness to this: Asger; you, his thrall, and all who now hear my words—freemen, karls, warriors and all—may Odin and the other gods, Frey and Njord, show their anger to you, my enemies. I name you breakers of the law, breakers of the peace, incurrers of the gods' anger. You are accursed until an heir of mine avenges me."

His words fell into a pool of horrified silence that lasted an appreciable moment until Asger broke it.

"But you have no child, do you, Thorkell?"

Asger smirked before he turned away to face his shaken men. "Men!" he cried. "Warriors of the *Sea Serpent*, I summon you to witness justice. The *einvigi* is complete. You all know the rules of combat. There *are* no rules!" He roared with laughter, and with that, thrust his fist into the air in a sign of triumph.

His voice rose as he declaimed, "The Norns alone decide the day of our death. We can't change it, nor alter it a jot. Today is Thorkell's day to die. Today, the crew of the *Sea Serpent* win the fight. This place, this property, these women, are yours to plunder as you will. My friends, my warriors, my crew! Enjoy all you can find here; take all you can, and our revenge will be complete. But first, bring everything that will burn and lay it at Thorkell's feet. We'll build a great funeral pyre in his honour— one he can enjoy while he's still alive!"

As Ciarnat watched, the men, initially shocked and cautious, caught Asger's mood. One began shouting. "Asger! Asger! Asger!"

The men took up the chant. Smiling, Asger placed one hand over his heart and bowed to them as they began to pile hay and timber in front of Thorkell. Asger gave a mocking laugh before turning towards Ciarnat.

CHAPTER
SEVENTY EIGHT

"HE'S YOUR MAN?" ASGER ASKED HER, indicating Thorkell with a lift of his chin.

"Until my dying day," Ciarnat replied, her voice proud and fierce.

She was numb with shock. For a shining moment, it had appeared Thorkell would save the day, that there would be a happy resolution to their troubles. It was over. Nothing now could save them.

"Oh, you won't die right away," Asger assured her. "Let's get comfortable. Maybe here, on the grass where your man can watch us?"

He dragged her in front of the cottage and pushed her to the ground. Ciarnat could see her husband, pinned against the wall above her, twisting and writhing in desperation at what was unfolding in front of him.

Ciarnat kicked out as vigorously as she could and heard Asger laugh, his laughter joined by other men gathered to watch.

"She's a flighty one, this mare. She'll be different when the stallion has ploughed her furrow!"

Anger gave her additional strength, but it wasn't enough to prevent her rape.

He ripped her tunic and with rough hands parted her thighs, then probed more intimately into the secret folds of her body. Asger's weight kept her pinned to the ground as he thrust inside her. She panicked and screamed as her whole body twisted wildly, resisting the invasion. Neither the scent of the man nor the pain of the intrusion was anything like she had known with her husband.

She could hear Thorkell shouting at Asger to stop.

It seemed to go on forever.

They'd left her hands free—to push at her assailant futilely? To hammer her fists against his shoulder as he took her? To stick the knife, she'd freed from her belt into her rapist as he, at last, released her?

Asger screamed as her knife entered his groin. He writhed away.

Ciarnat looked up at Thorkell. Their eyes locked, and in that brief gaze, they shared an eternity of anguished love. Shame, hopelessness and even pain were subsumed in that glance.

"Well struck," she heard him cry.

"Odin's eye!" Asger swore from behind her. "Kill the vicious bitch."

Ultán smashed a fist into her chin, and Ciarnat slumped, almost insensible, on the grass. She entered into a strange, fugue-like state where reality seemed very far away.

Blood spurted between Asger's fingers as he tried to stem the bleeding from his thigh.

Ciarnat closed her eyes. She had struck true. Whether Asger knew it or not yet, he was bleeding out. Nothing could staunch the flow of that dark arterial blood. Asger was dying. Dying in front of the man who had cursed him.

She heard the men gather around their fading leader, stunned by the rapidly changing events.

"Can we bandage it?" a young man asked. "Shouldn't we at least try to stop the bleeding?"

"*Nei*," replied another. An older man by his voice. "Ye'll not stop that torrent. It's a fatal blow. He'll be gone soon."

There was a murmur from the surrounding men.

Ultán flung himself on his knees beside his master. "Live," he begged. "Don't give up! Live!"

Asger gave a faint chuckle. "*Nei*. The gates of Helheim are already opening for me."

"Then free me," Ultán begged. "You promised to free me if I brought you to Thorkell and you defeated him."

There was a long silence. Ciarnat's curiosity was sufficient for her to open her eyes.

Asger lay silently.

"You promised," Ultán insisted urgently. "Don't go before you pay this final debt."

"Leave him in peace, man," said one of the crew over an angry mutter from the rest. "He's going fast. Leave well alone, or you'll answer to us."

"Please," Ultán implored desperately.

Asger remained silent.

The men surrounding Asger gave a collective sigh.

"He is gone." The older man said a moment later.

Ultán gave a howl of despair and flung himself on the ground, beating the earth in frustration.

From above him, Thorkell, pinned and helpless as he was, added to the man's pain with a vicious burst of humour.

"Even your thrice cursed master refused to free you. A thrall you are, and a slave you remain until your dying day," Thorkell shouted in mockery from where he was pinned.

The Viking men stood in silence for several long minutes, pondering what to do next.

"What do we do?" the younger man asked eventually.

"Send him to the afterlife," the older warrior said. "You want to cremate him? We have a fire already laid and burning. Let Asger lie in state, while the traitor Thorkell writhes in agony. Put Asger on the funeral pyre, and let Thorkell and his hellhound be the sacrifices that go with him."

There was little discussion. Most of the men were in agreement. Ciarnat could hear them going "*Já, Já*," in confirmation of the suggestion.

It was odd, how far removed she felt from what was happening.

Something, perhaps shock, alienated her from the urgency of the moment.

They rolled Asger onto a rough stretcher improvised from spears and blankets she recognised from her home. They bore him up on their shoulders and laid him on the pile of wood in front of Thorkell.

"Watch him as you burn, you scum," a warrior spat at Thorkell. "He was our leader, our captain. Fate stole him from us too soon."

Ciarnat saw the man she loved, still alive, futilely twisting against the spear's shaft at this insult. The pile was mounting higher around him as angry warriors snatched anything burnable to add to the pyre. A warrior grabbed a brand from the burning roof and thrust it deep into the pile of kindling. The flames at Thorkell's feet took hold fast in the dry tinder.

He's like suffering Christ, Ciarnat thought, staring up at Thorkell. *He came to save us, and now he's crucified.*

It was true. Thorkell's anguished position had a lot in common with Father Niall's statues in the village church. A ragged, wind-blown flame was creeping up through the piled timber towards Thorkell's feet.

Ciarnat had almost succeeded in distancing herself from what was happening. In her mind, she was beside her husband, supporting him, healing his wounds. Gran was there, she thought. Gran was holding them up, telling her not to be afraid. Gran would lead them through.

New pain then, as they hauled her upright. Her body protested as she was forced to abandon her trance for more suffering. If they kept interfering with her and disturbing her peace, she wouldn't be able to escape into the pain-free world she'd discovered.

"Tie her to the pole and let her watch," she heard, as rough hands seized her and bound her to the upright that usually supported Aoife's washing line.

She was barely conscious when she heard the order to fire the thatch again.

This time the fire blazed up brightly.

The light disturbed her. Darkness suited her best. She shut her eyes and was nearly back in her trance when she heard Thorkell's first scream.

In anguish, Ciarnat looked towards the house where the men stood, their dark shapes silhouetted against the red glow of the flames, watching as her husband was burned alive.

There was another long scream from Thorkell.

The fire had caught truly now. A light breeze had sprung up, and the inferno was well away, the whole cottage ablaze. She could no longer make out Thorkell, the flames were too dense to see through, but his agonised screams rang clearly over the roar of the fire.

Driven nigh to madness by the sound, she writhed and tore at her bonds like a mad thing until blood covered her wrists and hands. Her shrieks of horror and despair added to the noise.

The flames towered over her head, blocking the clear night sky above as they twisted and writhed, borne on the wild currents of air from the inferno. The wind-tossed sparks showered down, clinging as they landed on her cloak and skin. The sickening scent of roasting meat mingled with the heavy smell of smoke coming from the smouldering thatch.

Later she would find entire lengths of hair from the left of her head missing, scorched away, frizzled to nothing in the fiery heat. Her skin blistered, her eyes dried waterless, and the air in her lungs burned. She fought to reach the pyre, although the post they tied her to held firm against her struggles.

The screams went on forever, each one burning its fiery scar into her mind.

It took a long time for Thorkell to die, but she knew when the moment came, knew when Thorkell ceased to suffer. She felt it in the air when he left her. The sound of the fire was different. Anguish, like an auger, drilled her heart. She gave up fighting her bonds. Her head drooped with intolerable weariness as she sobbed out her endless, wrenching grief and horror.

It was the change in the men's voices that alerted her. Bored with the fire now that Thorkell no longer suffered in its midst, and with Asger duly sent on his way, the warriors were restless.

Ciarnat forced her head up in a sudden panic. Some made

their way down to the herb beds where she'd been sitting. There was a moment's pause before she recalled Aoife had been sitting there beside her.

Once she'd realised, it was obvious what was happening to Aoife.

A tall warrior rushed past, carrying Clodagh in his arms to where Asal was tied. She was shrieking and kicking, but it made no impression on the man. He dumped the child, still screaming her mother's name, face down over the donkey's back and tied her in place.

Ultán returned to her side.

"My turn now," he sneered. "Did you hear your husband sing to you from the fire? Getting you ready for me, he was."

He cut her free from the pole, his blade carelessly scoring her wrist in the process, and flung her to the ground.

Asger had been brutal, but straightforward in his use of her.

"I've wanted to do this to you for years," Ultán hissed as he forced his way into her. "You had me sold into slavery. Now I will have my revenge."

Within Ciarnat, a gulf opened. Shock and confusion separated her from the world.

Ultán delighted in pain. Even through her distancing fog, Ciarnat registered the abuse her flesh received. The knife pricks, the twisted, mangled flesh he took delight in. It infuriated him that she seemed immune, shielded from him, her mind absent. Frustrated, it drove him to greater cruelty. She felt her spirit separate itself from the shell of her body and slip away down the dark path that leads to death.

Towards the end, he rolled her over and sodomised her brutally, forcing a low groan from her.

Other men took his place, pounding her flesh and using her body as their plaything as she was tossed, like a doll, from man to man.

Eventually, the men grew bored. The women now lay like lifeless rags, and the marauders had taken all the bounty they could.

Ultán stood over Ciarnat. He prodded her inert body with his foot and got no response.

"Dead, or nearly so," he sniffed. "Let you bide there and rot."

With Asal dragging his heels on the lead rope, the crew of the *Sea Serpent* left the valley and returned to their longship. Behind them, the valley returned to silence. Nothing moved but the low flames, still guttering, among the burned-out timbers of the house.

CHAPTER SEVENTY NINE

Erin

Present Day, New Zealand

"OH, POOR LOVE!"

Erin could hear them talking about her, but it was too much effort to rouse herself and respond.

Brianna had travelled with her in the ambulance, leaving Fergal to follow in the car. Now Brianna was explaining to the ward sister why she needed to admit Erin that night.

Erin had heard the argument before.

There had been a heated discussion between Fergal and the paramedic before he'd allowed them to put Erin in the ambulance. 'She doesn't need an ambulance just because her waters have broken!' he'd protested. 'Get her home now and take her to the hospital tomorrow morning. They'll induce the labour then.' 'Her home is that house fire you're attending over there. Her husband has a broken leg and is probably trapped inside. Add to that, she's been very ill this evening and her waters have broken. So you're taking her to hospital. Now.'

Fergal won, of course. Given his size and presence, he probably always did. A smile curled Erin's lip. Good old Fergal.

Erin drifted in and out of awareness as they attended to her on the ward. She hurt too much to want to return to reality. Sometime later she discovered a drip inserted into her arm but couldn't remember it being done.

She was a woman who had mostly managed to avoid physical pain. Now she was discovering boundaries and layers within the experience she had no idea existed. The level where she was currently was bearable.

She heard voices around her, but couldn't be bothered breaking out of her bubble to respond. Her throat hurt, her stomach roiled, her head ached, but she was coping. She'd like it to be over with, of course, but at this level, she could handle it.

An irritated voice cut through. "I can't get this bloody ring off. Her fingers are so swollen it's cutting into her. What can I do?"

Later another, saying, "Jesus. What happened to her throat? Look at the state of it! Who did that to her?"

Someone must have replied, but Erin had already lost interest and sunk back into the mist.

The lights were dimmed in the ward, the only illumination coming from the instruments monitoring her and a few floor-level night lights. The darkness made it easier to drift away.

She was in her familiar dream world. The fire again! She'd seen flames in her dreams before but never realised a house was burning at its core.

As she watched, she saw smoke rising along the ridgeline. To her horror, she realised a man stood pinned to the door frame by a spear stuck through his shoulder. She recognised him immediately; she loved him. In desperation, she ran up the slope towards him.

A huge thug of a man stopped her when he grabbed her by the arm and spun her away.

She heard the pinned man shouting at his tormentors. Whatever he said, it quietened the men for a few moments until one replied and laughed at the suffering man. She sought the speaker in the bunch and cringed as she realised it was Luke.

He reached for her and pulled her closer to her lover's feet. It was apparent he was staging her rape to cause the pinned man maximum anguish. The man pinned above them shouted his rage and despair as Luke tore her clothes, and forcibly entered her. Her stomach twisted with nausea. He wasn't gentle with her and took delight in the distress he was causing. Incomprehension collided with familiarity. She pummelled his arms and shoulders, which merely drove him on.

There was fresh grass beneath her back, and she could smell the smoke from the smouldering thatch.

Whoever this man was, he was a dead ringer for her husband. He even smelt a little like Luke, but he was heavier and his muscles more defined and hardened. She closed her eyes to shut out the anguish on the watching man's face. He suffered for her, and that exacerbated her grief and shame.

Luke, or his avatar, finished and began to push himself off her. Her hands went to her belt. She'd found a knife.

With as vicious a thrust as she could muster, she drove it full into the fold of his groin. She'd intended to geld him. Instead, she pierced a vital blood vessel.

Luke shouted in shock as blood welled through the fingers he'd clasped to stem the flood. He rolled away, and she faced the suffering man on the spear.

They hadn't had nearly long enough to share their love. With all her heart, she tried to let her eyes tell him that, to let him know their love was greater than all the horror that surrounded them. There was no hope for them.

She had no protection from the buffeting blow that smashed into her face. Dazed and confused, Erin sprawled on the ground. Her stomach cramped with nausea, and she was so faint and dizzy she wondered if she was concussed. Every part of her body ached.

Men strode past her to attend to the stabbed man.

Ignored for the moment, she lifted her hand to nurse her cheek and paused when she caught sight of her sleeve. She was in another woman's clothes.

She lay back, trying not to panic, and took stock of her body. Her face ached and throbbed, of course, but more thorough checking alerted her to other hurts.

This wasn't a dream. This place was real, and she, Erin, had become the woman she'd seen before. Or had she? Even as she tried to understand, she was aware emotions ran through her that Erin couldn't have engendered alone—terror, terrible fear for the doomed man, grief, horror, frustration.

Erin shook her head against the surging flood that threatened to engulf her. These weren't her feelings. It made no sense. Somehow, she'd melded with the woman whose life she'd been dreaming about.

They shook her awake, pulled her to her feet and tied her upright to watch the burning. While she'd been semi-conscious, it seemed Luke had died.

His men laid him carefully and reverently on the fire at the other man's feet.

The woman that was her avatar fought her bonds like a tiger and cried bitterly as the man she loved died hideously in front of her. Erin screamed her outrage until her throat was lacerated.

She lost consciousness after that. Erin thought, it was best to let go and float away.

Now the fire was dying down. A smudge of greasy soot spread across everything. Erin could feel the taint of it on her lips and felt sickened when her brain informed her it was the last smoky touch of the burnt man's flesh.

She shut her eyes in horror, not needing to see anything more.

⁙

Another voice intruded into her space. "Have you asked her if she wants more pain relief?"

The woman was clearly frustrated. "I've already asked, but she doesn't respond."

The first woman's voice was relaxed, soothing, sympathetic. "If she wanted it, she would have told you. Leave her be now."

She was so surprised by that kindness that Erin opened her eyes. She was on a clean bed, with lights above her. Nothing around her made sense. She sank back into the bed and drifted.

"Her vital signs have dropped to critical!" The shout dragged her back from her safe place.

The information didn't interest her enough to hold her there, so she turned to dive away again, but a monstrous surge of pain stopped her.

She was outraged. Her body was hers to control, and she chose oblivion. For the first time in hours, she was fully conscious, rebelling against this new imperative. This time her body stubbornly refused to let her go.

She lay there, imprisoned by her flesh as it convulsed into a contraction. "Sweet Jesus, that fucking hurt." The words were forced from her in a wail.

"You're doing really well. The contractions are only two minutes apart now. Shall I rub your back?"

Erin registered Petra's voice and reopened her eyes. "What's happening?"

"It's all going just the way it should. You've got a healthy body, and it's behaving perfectly."

Erin flexed her fingers and realised Petra had Erin's hands clasped in her own. A new understanding pushed at her mind. "Was I gripping you? When it hurt?" she asked.

She registered Petra's wry expression.

"Shit. Sorry. I didn't mean to hurt you."

Petra chuckled. "It's no matter." A frown crossed her face. "Are you OK, though? I don't mean the contractions; they seem fine. But you've been out of it. I've been worried. That ring of yours has been glowing like it's lit up with a torch." As she spoke, another wave of pain crawled its way through Erin.

"I've had nightmares," was all she managed until the wave had crashed over her. She groaned in pain.

"You've had nightmares?" Petra prompted.

"Oh, Petra, it was terrible. I think it was a dream; I don't know." Erin tossed her head restlessly from side to side as tears began to fill her eyes. "It seemed so real, and I was there. The Vikings burned alive the man I love. It was hideous to watch. It took a long time, and they raped me. Luke raped me. Fuck!" Tears streamed down Erin's face. "I know it didn't really happen to me, but somehow I was in the body of the woman I've seen, and it was happening to her. It was gang rape and terrible. Man after man took her—took me. Shit, I don't even know what I'm saying."

Another contraction surged through her. "I think it was only this pain that dragged me back here," she moaned. Another wave swept over her. "Fuck! Why did no one ever tell me how much it hurts?" she gasped once the worst of it had passed.

"Because we wouldn't need the contraceptive pill if every thirteen-year-old understood labour," Petra said drily. "No woman would have sex, ever, once she saw this."

Erin smiled at Petra's earnestness. Once she would have felt the same; now she simply wanted all men dead, and Luke in particular.

With that thought, a wave of consciousness came crashing back, bringing the numbing realisation Luke, or the Luke who had been her husband was dead. Even more disturbing, she'd been the one who killed him in her dream.

"I stabbed Luke to death," she told Petra. "I killed him."

"What? No, you didn't. Erin, that's a terrible thing to say."

"But he is dead, isn't he?"

Petra was silent, and Erin turned to look at her.

"Yes, in the fire," Petra confirmed sadly.

"In my dream, I killed him." Tears filled Erin's eyes. "Oh Luke!"

"It was only a dream, for fuck's sake. Let it go, Erin. It's not real life."

Another contraction tore at Erin.

"Keep panting, Mrs Power," the nurse said. "You're doing great! Nearly there."

Erin did her best to pant, but it was damnably hard when there were so many obscenities she needed to utter if only she could stop groaning.

"Steady, steady. Don't push yet," some other woman exhorted her.

What was she? A racehorse? What did '*steady, steady*' even mean?

Her body cramped again, and she felt sweat trickle between her breasts as her body absorbed the pain. Again, she realised her hand had crushed Petra's, and tried to pull free. "Sorry, sorry, sorry," she muttered.

"I told you, it's OK," Petra assured her. "You can return the favour one day."

Erin was sufficiently amused for the next contraction to pass without too much effort.

Now the woman between her legs was urging her to "*Push, push!*"

"What?" Erin asked.

"You can push now. Your body is ready for your baby." It was the reassuring voice again.

She relaxed under the influence of the woman's confident tone.

Erin had no idea whether she was doing the right thing. Presumably her body knew its job. She had always thought her mind controlled her body, but with one casual contraction, it had re-educated her and realigned her thinking forever.

The flesh followed its mysteries and imperatives. If Erin thought she controlled it, then more fool her. Her body did what it had to do, and now it was delivering a baby.

Samuel Luke Power arrived at 15.02 pm.

CHAPTER EIGHTY

Ciarnat

Ninth Century, Ireland

AOIFE'S ROUTE TO THE CONVENT KITCHENS meant she walked against the press of students passing her on the way to their studies. A girl of nine years or so caught her eye, and she quickly turned her face away. Aoife had learnt there was no point giving in to the impulse. Each time, her heart gave a leap of hope, only to break, while claws of visceral pain tore at her. She supposed they always would.

Clodagh was gone, had probably been dead for weeks. But what if she had survived? Aoife yearned to know, even as she dreaded what horrors a living Clodagh might be enduring. The aching hollow inside Aoife was nigh on unendurable. She would spend the rest of her life mourning and worrying about her lost daughter.

Summer was well past. Autumn had settled in with its steady mizzle of misty mornings and damp days. Aoife had watched as the last of the swifts, swallows and martins left for their journey to warmer climes.

When she walked down by the lake, there were new arrivals. Great white-fronted geese had moved in from the north, making it their winter home, and swans now floated majestically across the water. A lesson, Aoife supposed, that life kept moving from season to season.

The busy head cook had the meal ready for her. She never failed to smile and welcome Aoife, who was grateful for her support. "How is your patient today?"

Aoife sighed. "Much the same as always. She eats, sleeps, washes and changes her clothes when I tell her. Otherwise, all she does is pray. I wonder whether I'm right to hope for a change."

"The poor lass. Her husband burned to death in front of her!" The cook shook her head. "It would make anyone go mad with grief."

Aoife nodded. She wasn't certain Ciarnat's affliction was madness. Rather, she had withdrawn so deep within herself it seemed there was no reaching her.

She smiled her thanks to the cook and made her way back to Ciarnat.

·⁚·

Padraig had been the first to reach them after the raid. He'd taken them, damaged as they were in body and mind, into his cottage and his care, ruthlessly dispatching his sons outside to stay in the barn.

The Vikings had destroyed most of the village. There, the few remaining survivors had to focus on rebuilding what was lost. They had nothing left to spare; certainly nothing extra to provide for two sick women.

When Filan heard about the raid, he'd galloped south to find his daughter. Shattered by the damage she'd sustained, he arranged for the women to retreat to the safety and peace of Kildare Monastery, where he hoped, in time, Ciarnat would heal in mind and body. Aoife, though, knew some sorts of damage were beyond healing.

Ciarnat's hair had regrown after it had been burned away by the fire. But the damaged locks had grown back white, a striking, startling contrast to the rest of her dark brown hair. Something similar had happened to Ciarnat's mind.

Aoife wondered whether her own ability to get up each morning, attend her tasks and function as a facsimile of her former self was because the attack on her had been impersonal. However badly she suffered, she'd simply been collateral damage. The attack on Ciarnat and Thorkell had been deliberate and targeted.

Once Asger discovered Thorkell was alive and seeking him, he had no alternative but to find and destroy him. Ultán had sought out Filan's holding, seeking revenge. That his quest had aligned with Asger's had been fortuitous for both of them. It had been a cursed quirk of fate that had brought the two together. Ciarnat's presence there had been an unexpected bonus.

If Aoife was right, Ciarnat's terrible guilt stemmed from her involvement, all those years ago, in Ultán's enslavement and Rian's death. Ciarnat had always been a girl who took her responsibilities seriously. 'Everyone I love dies,' Ciarnat had told Aoife on several occasions in the terrible days after the attack. 'Those who love me most, suffer the most. I am a curse. From now on, I will give my love solely to God.'

Aoife had tried to say such guilt was unnecessary and futile, but Ciarnat ignored her and simply retreated further into the world of prayer and penance.

It seemed such an unlikely path for her to choose. Before the attack, Ciarnat and Aoife had attended the village church, but Ciarnat had never previously displayed any particular faith or interest in religion. Since, she devoted her days to fervent prayer and refused to be moved from her intent to embrace religious austerity.

Aoife herself had prayed to St Brigid, the founder and patron saint of the abbey, asking for guidance and help for Ciarnat, but the saint had been silent.

Somewhat more useful had been the Mother Abbess, who had

taken the two women into her care. She'd spent time with Ciarnat, both talking and praying with her. "She wants to dedicate her life to God," she told Aoife. "You may have to accept that."

"But why?" Aoife demanded. "This devastation was no fault of hers."

The Mother Abbess shook her head. "That must be between her and God, my child."

Which was all very fine, but the weeks were passing, and there was a pressing matter to which Ciarnat needed to attend.

Today, having exhausted other alternatives, Aoife intended to force Ciarnat to face and engage with reality. She'd made a tentative assay a month ago that had resulted in such an explosion of rage from her friend that Aoife had been afraid to continue. This time she was determined not to fail again.

She waited until the meal was over. "Ciarnat, we need to talk." There was no response. Not even a blink to indicate Ciarnat had heard. "I know you don't want to discuss it, but we can't leave it forever." Still nothing. "A child is growing in your belly. Each day you get bigger. You must know that. We need to make plans."

"There is nothing in my belly." Ciarnat's voice came out like a growl. "I'll thank you for leaving me alone."

"Not this time." Aoife was firm. "You cannot keep pretending it isn't happening."

"You lie." Ciarnat's voice was rising. "It is not true."

"Why would I lie? You know the truth as much as I do. You must do."

Ciarnat's reaction was so intense it frightened her. "No, no, no, noooooo," Ciarnat wailed. Her whole body shook with the violence of her rejection.

"But..."

"No." Ciarnat pounded her fists on the table in her fury. "I'll not bear a child for them. I'd rather be dead. I want to be dead. I won't have it."

It took some time and a lot of shrieking from Ciarnat before she quietened. For the first time in weeks, Aoife thought she detected awareness in her friend.

"Do you think I'll bear some barbarian's bastard child? Do

you think I need anything to remember that day by?" Ciarnat asked. Hate and malice twisted her face, but the anguish in the question was terrible.

For a moment, Aoife quailed. Then she considered what Ciarnat had asked and shook her head. "It's not a bastard, though, is it? It's Thorkell's baby."

"How can it be?" Ciarnat's rage was rising again. "You saw what they did to me, what they did to us. How then can you think the child would be Thorkell's?"

"Because you were already with child before the Vikings attacked."

It was Ciarnat's turn to look confused. "You're not suggesting their hate and viciousness didn't destroy everything? Thorkell's child can't possibly have survived what they did to me."

Aoife bit her lip. "Ciarnat, I do your laundry. You haven't bled since the first days of spring. Not even after all they did to you." She walked across to Ciarnat and reached out. "Stand up," she ordered. Somewhat to her surprise, Ciarnat obeyed. "Feel your belly."

"What do you mean? To what end?"

"I mean, place your hands on your belly and tell me what you feel. I want you to realise how big you have grown."

Ciarnat ran her hands uncertainly across her stomach.

"You've delivered enough babies yourself," Aoife said, "to know that is not the belly of a woman 15 weeks' pregnant. You are much further along. You have the belly of a woman at least six months gone, which means your baby can't possibly be the result of rape. This is your husband's child."

Ciarnat rested her hands on her bump. Her hands couldn't deny the evidence she felt. "After the damage they caused? I thought that would have destroyed any possibility of keeping the baby."

"It seems God granted you a small miracle," Aoife said. Her smile was sincere, although it wavered.

Ciarnat was shaking her head. "I'm not so sure. How could I ever be certain?" The despondency was back. She sat down again with every sign of returning to her inertia.

Aoife felt like slapping her. "You owe it to Thorkell to bear this child and bring it up as strong, healthy and bold to honour his father."

When that failed to gain a response, she tried again. "Do you remember what Thorkell said? When he cursed them all?"

Ciarnat looked at her blankly and shook her head.

"He promised Asger that he and his line will be cursed through all eternity until this world is ended. They will amount to nothing; they will fail; their seed will fail; their fame will be as nought until an heir of Thorkell's avenges him and this betrayal. That's why you have to be strong, Ciarnat. Only if you give birth to Thorkell's heir will there be a possibility his death will be avenged. If not now, then in the years to come. Do you not understand that?"

A spark of interest flared in Ciarnat's eyes. "Revenge," she said slowly, savouring the syllables as she spoke them. "Yes," she said finally. "I remember."

"Then you need to wake up from the sleep you've been in and look after yourself and the babe you carry."

Ciarnat said nothing more. Aoife was uneasily aware she'd failed to get a commitment from her friend, but it seemed her words had made an impression on her.

Later that evening, Ciarnat glanced at Aoife. "I killed Asger, didn't I? Does that not count as revenge, even though I'm not a child of Thorkell's?"

"You avenged yourself and Thorkell when you killed that bastard. You may not have been Thorkell's child, but you are Thorkell's heir, so the curse worked rapidly. But Asger's home was not burned and pillaged; his women were not raped; his children have been left unharmed. Maybe that is what Thorkell was thinking when he spoke of vengeance."

"Asger had no home, unless you count Ormsfjord which he stole from Thorkell. But he was an outcast," Ciarnat said. "He could never go back there, and he didn't have a wife."

"What about children?"

Ciarnat shook her head. "I do not know. Thorkell told me once that Asger had run off with his stepmother after they murdered

Thorkell's father. He found her in Dublin, and she was with child. She claimed it was Orm's, making it a half-sibling to Thorkell. He did not believe her but spared her life at the time, in case it was true. It may be that child has been born and is Asger's heir."

"And maybe, as fate works these things out, one day your child, or even your grandchild, will avenge Thorkell by killing Asger's son," Aoife said. She had no truck with such heathen concepts, but if the idea kept Ciarnat happy, she was willing to embrace it.

CHAPTER
EIGHTY ONE

AOIFE HAD HOPED THAT CIARNAT, HAVING accepted the reality of her pregnancy, would embrace the prospect of being a mother and that some emotional connection between mother and child would help her break free of the walls she seemed determined to put up around herself.

It was not to be and became the source of deep, if suppressed, anger and resentment between the two women. Aoife, mourning her daughter, couldn't understand any woman rejecting her own child. Ciarnat's obduracy, by its nature, was a silent criticism of Aoife's grief and eternal attachment to Clodagh.

Ciarnat, adamant no other life would be blighted by the curse her affection brought with it, was determined not to embrace, love or nurture her child in any way lest it, too, died a tragic death. She owed that much to Thorkell. If there were no other way of ensuring his heir's safety, then she would reject the babe.

It was stalemate, and it said much for the affection between the two women that such a fundamental breach didn't destroy their essential faith in each other.

"Who else," Ciarnat asked, "could I ask to rear my child? Who else would love and cherish the babe?"

Aoife didn't reply, confident the act of childbirth itself, and the first sight of her new-born child, would alter Ciarnat's views.

Aoife chose to ignore the hours Ciarnat spent on her knees in front of the high altar. She discounted the plans Ciarnat shared to make the great cave a retreat, and she rejected utterly Ciarnat's plans to immure herself there as a recluse. Aoife comforted herself with the thought that a good deal of nonsense could be forgiven a pregnant woman.

Mother Abbess saw it differently. "You must understand, my child," she cautioned, "that you cannot control your friend's life. Ciarnat, for reasons unique to her and God, wishes to become an anchorite and seclude herself from the world. She has made this very clear to me. You may not understand, but if you love her, you must let her seek her own redemption. She believes she has sinned, and you are not required to absolve her of those sins. Only God can do that. If you love her, do as she asks and care for her baby. It may be God's way of healing your own damage."

Aoife nodded politely, bowed her head for the Mother Abbess's blessing and resolved never to allow such a hideous future for either Ciarnat or her child.

⸭

Filan visited the abbey a month before Ciarnat was due to give birth. Aoife gave them their privacy and went for a walk in the pale spring sunshine. Slowly new life was returning to celebrate the change of season. There were fresh buds on the trees, and the willows were growing young shoots on their bare branches. The seasonal variation of birds had started—house martins, swallows and swifts were returning, and she searched in vain for the stately geese and swans that had brightened the winter.

She had hoped to have words with Filan before he left the abbey and win his agreed opposition to Ciarnat's plans, but he had left before she returned to their cell. Still, she imagined he would be as opposed to those plans to retire from the world as she was.

Three weeks later, Ciarnat went into labour in the early hours of the afternoon.

"Why did I never realise how much pain women went through?" she wailed, as a contraction rippled through her. "I should have been much more sympathetic."

"According to the Mother Abbess, the Church teaches this is God's punishment for Eve's original sin," was Aoife's dry reply.

She was gratified by the string of profanity that issued from Ciarnat's lips, none of which sounded like a woman determined on serving God's will.

Aoife had been secretly worried about the birthing process. That Ciarnat had been able to carry the child to term was a miracle in itself. The Vikings had so severely abused both her and Ciarnat, she had feared internal damage might have occurred which would hinder the baby's delivery.

When the child emerged safely, Aoife had an impulse to kneel and thank God. She didn't, for she had no wish to encourage Ciarnat's delusions, but there were tears in her eyes when she laid him in Ciarnat's arms. "He's strong," she said. "A credit to both his father and mother. You must be very proud."

Ciarnat said nothing, but Aoife watched as her head bent over the babe and smiled. As she'd thought, nature would sort out Ciarnat's fantasies. The pull of motherhood was the strongest in the world.

Cheerfully, Aoife took the linen for washing and proceeded to clean and tidy the room. She brought a hot tisane for Ciarnat to drink. "It's made to your own recipe," she said.

"Take the child from me," Ciarnat said. "Take him away to where I cannot see him."

Aoife stared at her. "Oh, no! You are a mother now. You cannot reject your own wean. He is your responsibility. I'll not help you in your stupidity."

"Take him," Ciarnat repeated. "I give him to your keeping."

"You can't do this!" Aoife cried. "He needs your breast. You must feed him. He needs your care."

Ciarnat stared at her in silence. She settled the child beside her on the bed and rolled over with her back to it.

"He is Thorkell's son! He is the legacy of Thorkell's love for you. Through him, you can keep the memory of the husband you loved alive."

Ciarnat said nothing. No argument Aoife could raise stirred her from her path.

At length, in desperation at the babe's need, Aoife lifted the child into her arms and went to find a wet nurse.

⁙

Filan arrived three weeks later to take them home. Aoife had some idea she could persuade Filan to order his daughter to accept her maternal responsibilities. His refusal stunned her.

"All my decisions for my daughter have been in vain," he told her heavily. "All I have ever wanted is to keep her safe, and I have failed her so terribly. So now, if she wishes to withdraw from the world, and if that keeps her safe and happy, then she has my blessing."

"But..."

"No buts. Not for Ciarnat," he said curtly. "You're a good woman, Aoife, and I hope you care for my grandson as you would your own child. But you must not argue or press my daughter to change her mind."

"She is so young," Aoife protested.

Filan shook his head and walked away.

The farmhouse had been rebuilt in the months they had been gone and looked substantially the same, although the garden had fallen into neglect and no chickens ran around the pen.

Aoife stared at the place she had last seen her daughter; she tried to recall the terrible sight of Thorkell's body pinned against the door frame. The door had been painted green instead of blue. Asal no longer grazed by the barn.

Mercifully, time had intervened and blurred the memories. Aoife shut her eyes. The memories were unbearable, but the farm had been cleansed, and Aoife realised she could endure living there.

She settled the wet nurse into her place in the loft and ensured the child was fed and happy. By the time she had unpacked, Filan had returned from escorting Ciarnat down to the big cave in the bay.

"How is she?" Aoife asked.

"Where she wants to be, or so she assured me," Filan answered.

His voice was as matter-of-fact as ever, but Aoife saw the set of misery to his downturned lips and the shine of unshed tears in his eyes that testified to his pain.

"Oh my dear," she said, instinctively drawing him into her arms and holding him. He leaned his forehead against hers.

"I asked her to reconsider; I told her she could change her mind any time—but she refused," he said. He shut his eyes as a tear rolled down his cheek. "Oh, Aoife! This breaks my heart," he cried.

Filan wrapped his arms around Aoife's waist, and they stood together for a long time, each comforted by the other.

CHAPTER EIGHTY TWO

Erin

Present Day, New Zealand

"HOW'S IT GOING?" PETRA ASKED AS she seated herself at the café. "Brianna texted to say she's running late. She'll be with us soon; said she had news to share."

Erin manoeuvred herself into the seat. Sam was strapped to her chest in a sling arrangement which she was proud to have figured out how to manage by herself.

"What's it like being a mum?" Petra asked.

Erin grinned at her friend. "I'm taking each day as it comes. Everything is a learning curve. There are days when I could use having a mum of my own to help me. Feeding, changing and putting Sam down for his sleep manages to keep me busy for an entire day. And don't even mention the broken nights!"

"You're an inspiration to us all," Petra said, smiling at Sam who was watching her. "Are you a little menace?" she asked dotingly as she wiggled her fingers at him. "Do you make your mum's life difficult?"

Erin chuckled. "You realise you're cooing at him, don't you?" she teased. "If you're not careful, you'll get clucky."

Petra flushed. "That's not such a bad thing to be," she said, turning her attention back to Erin. "Anyway, how's the grown-up stuff going? You know, insurance, the police?"

"I told the police all about my late-night caller. It's hard to know what they think, except they've established the fire was deliberately lit. I think at first they thought I'd caused it because they kept asking about my relationship with Luke and how he felt about the baby." She frowned. "I'm damn sure that bastard Alwyn stirred things up by telling them our marriage was failing." She gave a philosophical shrug.

"In the end, the fact that I was with you guys all that evening was my alibi. The timing of the fire meant I couldn't possibly have lit it. I don't think the police were happy, but it got me off the hook, so now maybe they'll take 'late-night guy' seriously."

"You're kidding me, right? How could they even imagine it was you?"

"They're the police; it's their job to be suspicious. On the other hand, the insurance firm has been reasonable. Luke was well insured thanks to Kittering and Hodges. Even though he'd stepped sideways from them in the last few months, their policy still covered him, so I got money straight up. Enough to tide me over the first few weeks and get me into a rental."

"Will you build again?"

Erin was thoughtful. "I'd like to. Sam is going to need a home, and that section is the nearest he's got to an ancestral pad. I'm not certain whether the insurance will settle totally until the police charge someone with arson. It's all a bit up in the air. But yes, I think building a new home would be a good thing. I always liked living there." She stirred her coffee absently. "Even though it's just a demolished site at the moment, I still feel close to Luke there."

"Are you missing him?"

"Terribly," she said as she put her spoon down. She gave Petra a sad smile. "I know things were going a bit pear-shaped over the last few months, but I still believe, under all the stresses of our lives, that we loved each other." She put her hand up to her mouth. "I don't think I realised just how deeply I loved him until I lost him. I can't stop dwelling on what his last moments must have been like— his leg in plaster, and not able to move around very quickly. The medicine he was on had strange side effects but helped him sleep. I think he went to bed that evening as soon as I went out. Maybe he was even asleep when the fire started. At some point, though, he must have woken and realised what was happening. They discovered his body on the floor by the door. He would have been trying to get out. I can't bear the thought of what his last moments must have been like." Tears filled Erin's eyes.

Petra put her hand over Erin's. "Are you still having nightmares?"

Erin looked puzzled. "What, about Luke?"

Petra stared at her. "No, your dreams. You remember. You complained of vivid dreams during your pregnancy that drew you into them."

Seeing Erin still looked confused, Petra burst out, "Dreams. They were so bloody powerful, Brianna gave you a ring to protect you from them. That ring," she said, pointing to the stone on Erin's finger.

Erin stared at the ring, clearly striving to understand. Eventually, she nodded. "I remember," she said slowly as she twisted the ring on her finger. She lifted her eyes to Petra. "You know, if you hadn't reminded me, I think I might have forgotten about them. So much has happened in between, and I've had so much to sort out and grieve over, they've become irrelevant. They were pretty intense while they lasted, but I haven't had one for ages. I guess, like all dreams, they've faded. I'd be hard-pressed to remember what they were about. Luke always used to say they were because I'd had too much spicy food the night before."

Petra shook her head in amazement. "They were real enough for you to tell us all about them at the time."

Erin smiled. "Well, they say once you have a baby, you forget how much childbirth hurts. At least, you remember it hurt, you just can't remember how bad it felt. I suppose it's the same for those dreams."

Petra gave up. "Well, as long as you're OK now," she said.

Brianna arrived five minutes later. "Sorry I'm late."

"It's no matter," Petra said, studying the menu. "Have you any idea what you want to eat?"

Erin had been looking at Brianna. "You look very pleased with yourself. Have you had good news?"

For a moment, Brianna looked awkward. "Well, yes. Though I wasn't going to say anything yet."

Erin snorted. "You can't stop there. Not once you've told us there's a secret! Blurt it out, girl. We're all friends."

Brianna opened her mouth, then shut it abruptly. "I don't know..."

"Erin's right," said Petra, "you can't leave us hanging. What's happened?"

"I've been accepted for Trinity!"

The other two stared at her.

"Trinity?" asked Petra cautiously. "Do you mean overseas? Is that in England?"

Brianna nodded with enthusiasm. "Ireland. Trinity College, Dublin, no less," she added with a note of pride.

"You've been accepted for Trinity College? What, as a student?" Erin asked.

Brianna nodded again, barely suppressing an enormous grin. "They've accepted me as a postgraduate student."

"You mean, you're leaving here and going to Ireland?"

"I start at the beginning of next term. I'm so excited; I can barely keep a lid on it. I'd hoped to get in, but I didn't really expect to be successful when I sent my application."

Erin stared at her in disbelief.

Eventually, Petra asked what they'd both been thinking. "But what about Fergal? What does he think of this? And Wolf? I thought you were all coupled up?"

"Fergal's all for it," Brianna assured them. "I think he's quite proud of me." She saw the disapproval on her friends' faces. "He and I always had a very loose arrangement. He knew I'd move on when I was ready. In the meantime, he gave me a place to stay, and yes, it was fun while it lasted. We both knew it wasn't permanent. I'll miss Wolf, but he's Fergal's dog."

Petra and Erin looked at each other.

"We're just surprised," Erin said. "You seemed so great together as a couple."

For the first time, she saw a flicker of regret pass across Brianna's face.

"Fergal was never meant to be mine," she told them. "He's a lovely man, but we've both got our roads to follow."

Erin wondered if she imagined the soft sigh that edged that statement.

Brianna wouldn't be drawn any further, so after drinking to her good health and congratulating her, the women eventually concentrated on Sam who had just woken up.

It was several hours later when Erin prepared for bed.

The care of Sam was so all-consuming, she hadn't had much time to consider what she'd learned at lunch.

Dreams. Erin absently rubbed the ring as she remembered Petra's comments. There had been dreams. If Petra hadn't reminded her, she probably wouldn't have thought of them again. But they *had* seemed real.

In the turmoil of the last three months, so much had happened that anything irrelevant had vanished from her consciousness. Erin supposed she was operating in survivor mode—that, coupled with 'mum' brain, was it any wonder things slipped from her mind? From now on, Sam was her focus and all that was going to matter to her.

She read for a while before turning off the light. The nights were difficult. However hard she tried, Erin couldn't ignore the vacant place beside her on the bed nor the nightmare reality of the manner of Luke's death.

CHAPTER
EIGHTY THREE

SOMETIME LATER, SOMEWHERE BETWEEN awake and asleep, Erin felt a faint tickle, almost like a hair brushing her temple. She might have waved a hand to swipe it away. The tickle grew stronger, turning into a twisting swirl that drew her into its orbit.

She must have slept, because when she woke it was broad daylight. Disoriented, she looked for Sam before realising she was in a dream.

She was following a pair of women who made their way towards a long, low house.

An older man sat on a bench in the sunshine by the front door, plucking chords on a harp. A small boy, with a shock of curly hair, squatted beside him, playing in the gravel.

As Erin watched, a dark-haired woman stepped through the door with a basket of wet washing.

The women Erin was following stopped to have words with her, then passed a leather pouch to the dark woman.

Erin frowned, trying to interpret what was happening before it occurred to her that a payment had changed hands.

As if to settle the point, the dark woman pointed to a track leading up the hill. A small carved signpost read Uaimh Naomh Ciarnat.

Erin followed her guides as they climbed the hill, turned a sharp corner at the top and descended the steep slope to the bay.

They made their way around the foot of the cliff, following a well-worn path that led to an enormous cave. It was well above the tide line and the floor was dry. On a stone shelf to one side stood flints and tapers. The women lit one each and walked deeper into the cave.

Some way in, a metal grille barred the way. A small hatch was the only entrance to be seen. One of the women opened it and from her basket took a couple of loaves of bread which she passed through. Erin thought she heard a faint murmur from within.

The women fell to their knees, crossed themselves and began to pray. One crawled closer to the grille on her knees, clutched the metal bars, shut her eyes, put her cheek to the frame and wept as she prayed.

Erin had never witnessed such devotional intensity.

From the darkness, she heard a soft female voice. The person immured in there came nearer towards the light and the desperate woman. Although Erin couldn't understand the words she spoke, it was apparent she was offering comfort and advice. Erin went closer.

With a leap of recognition, she realised she knew the woman on the far side of the bars. She was no longer a girl. There was maturity to her and something more—her face was serene and her voice warm and kind. The soft candlelight lit the fair skin of her face with an unworldly sheen. Backlit as she was by a row of tapers, she resembled a medieval icon with a halo around her.

A holy woman! It was apparent the anchorite in the cave was venerated by those who made the pilgrimage to visit her.

She spoke for some time to the kneeling woman, who eventually bowed her head, dried her eyes and prostrated herself in the sand.

In the way of dreams, without distinct transition, Erin found herself outside the cottage again. A memory tugged at her. She'd seen this place before.

The dark-haired woman was now working in the vegetable garden, and the man stood beside her leaning on a spade. The child played beside them, this time with a stick he'd turned into a sword. He shouted some challenge to a vagrant thistle before striking its head off. The man smiled and said something to him. He grinned.

Erin gasped. It was like seeing a photo of a much younger Fergal. The broad smile, the confident pose, the essential sweetness in the way he interacted with his carer.

For a brief second, Erin thought she understood. There was a pattern, forming a story with no beginning and no end. In it, people travelled a road on their short life's journey. When they left, others took their place. But the way itself went on forever and Erin, Luke, Sam and everyone were part of that continuum.

A wail from the other room woke her. She clutched the sheets to her, shocked from the dream, and turned to look at the clock: 6.30 am. She'd overslept, and Sam was hungry.

It was a flurry of activity as she grabbed her dressing gown, picked up her son, changed him and, returning to the bedroom, settled him into the crook of her arm to feed him.

She smiled as he sucked, admiring his determination, the way his fingers curled in satisfaction against her breast.

She tried to recapture the dream. The details were fading fast, but the feeling of peace and quiet joy she'd felt from the cloistered woman mingled with the present warm pleasure of nursing her son.

She could remember nothing more. The dream melted away, brushed to insignificance by the weight of her child in her arms.

She reached up to brush a strand of hair from her face and heard the soft plink of something fall on the ground. It took her a moment to identify the sound.

The fourth finger of her right hand was bare. She'd noticed the ring had been getting loose over the last days. It had been careless of her not to remove it before she lost it.

In the process of transferring Sam from one breast to the other, she bent to retrieve the ring and placed it on the bedside table. She must remember to return it to Brianna before she left for Ireland.

ACKNOWLEDGEMENTS

Being a writer is an odd, solitary occupation. For weeks, an author covers blank pages with a pastiche of words dredged from their own imagination and experience. In time, with some coaxing, polishing and revision, a novel is born, and then the days of solitude are over. It only takes one person to write a manuscript, but it takes a team to 'make' a book, and I have been particularly fortunate in those who have worked with me on my novels.

Firstly, I owe an inestimable debt to Kelly Pettitt for her frank but constructive criticism during the various revisions of the original draft and for her meticulously detailed notes. She is also responsible for the cover artwork, the photograph of me inside the back cover, the design and format of the layout.

Sue Reidy has helped me with all my books. I rely on her clear-sighted reviews to point out deficits and inconsistencies in the manuscript. Authors, of course, are always too close to their own work to be truly objective, and I couldn't have a more intelligent reader to provide advice, guidance and encouragement during the revision process.

Finally, my deepest thanks to Adrienne Charlton for editing and proofreading the final manuscript. Adrienne has become an integral part of the publication process of any novel I write. As always, her attention to detail and accuracy are a critical part of the quality control process.

My gratitude, as ever, to my long-suffering husband Cavan, who supports and encourages me in a thousand ways. His quiet tolerance of authorial angst, his willingness to keep me supplied with coffee, and his amused acceptance that his wife, for lengthy stretches, resides in a different century, are the foundations on which I have been able to build my career as a writer.

Finally, my thanks to Reilly for spending the long hours with me and wagging encouragement; Pascal who lay on my lap as I typed on the keyboard; and Bandit, on whose broad back I cantered away from the frustrations inherent in the creative process.

ABOUT BLOOD NEVER LIES

A couple of years ago, my husband and I participated in the National Geographic Genographic Project and sent off our DNA for analysis. I've 'gifted' our results to Erin and Luke for this novel. My results, like Erin's, were straightforward. My ancestors clearly were not much given to wanderlust. It was my husband's results that intrigued me—what a mixture! As Fergal notes, "There'll be a story there, that's for sure." And so, a novel was born.

It seemed to me the most likely source of Scandinavian DNA was the Vikings, and who is not fascinated by them? They were one of the great exploring peoples of our planet. They settled westwards in Britain, Ireland, Iceland, Greenland and North America. Eastwards they travelled down the mighty European rivers as far as Byzantium. They sailed the Mediterranean Sea. Between the tenth and fourteenth centuries, they formed the famous Varangian Guard who served as personal bodyguards to Byzantine emperors. Historically, contact between indigenous peoples and explorers resulted in atrocities, and Norsemen were known and feared wherever they went.

That DNA test also provided the second theme for Blood Never Lies, namely how DNA forms and affects us all. For many years, when discussing identity, the argument raged between 'nature', as in inherited individuality, and 'nurture', those characteristics formed by upbringing, education and experience. Our new understanding of how DNA works shows that a simple binary approach was inadequate and inaccurate.

Most recently, a good deal of research has been done on epigenetics, which is defined by Oxford Languages as 'the study of changes in organisms caused by modifications of gene expression rather than alteration of the genetic code itself'. In other words, external modifications to DNA can turn genes 'on' or 'off'. On an individual basis, the different combinations of genes switched on or off are what makes each one of us unique.

More surprisingly, strong evidence exists that some of these changes, under certain stressful conditions, can get passed down multiple generations.

The third strand of the novel was a bit of self-indulgence. I play the Irish harp myself, and introducing a bard and his daughter as principal characters in Blood Never Lies allowed me to insert both harp music and the instrument into the plot of the novel.

I am a novelist, of course, not a scientist, historian or musician, so I hope readers will understand I have taken the above plot strands and woven them into fiction for your entertainment.

I hope you enjoy the story.

All novels are available in various formats from Amazon.com.

Paperback editions can be purchased within New Zealand from Paper Plus, Unity Books and other reputable book stores and suppliers. Alternatively, they can be ordered from Penelope's website - www.penelopehaines.com, and you can visit Penelope on Facebook - @penelopehainesbooks.

CPSIA information can be obtained
at www.ICGtesting.com
Printed in the USA
BVHW041029160423
662432BV00017B/290